About the Authors

Sheryl Lister has enjoyed reading and writing for as long as she can remember. When she's not reading, writing, or playing chauffeur, she can be found on a date with her husband or in the kitchen creating appetisers and bite-sized desserts. She holds a BS in Occupational Therapy and a post-professional MS in Occupational Therapy from San Jose State University. She resides in California, is a wife, mother of three, and works as a pediatric occupational therapist.

Barbara Wallace can't remember when she wasn't dreaming up love stories in her head, so writing romances for Mills & Boon is a dream come true. Happily married to her own Prince Charming, she lives in New England with a house full of empty-nest animals. Readers can catch up with Barbara through her newsletter. Sign up at barbarawallace.com

Kandy Shepherd swapped a fast-paced career as a magazine editor for a life writing romance. She lives on a small farm in the Blue Mountains near Sydney, Australia, with her husband, daughter, and a menagerie of animal friends. Kandy believes in love at first sight and real-life romance – they worked for her! Kandy loves to hear from her readers. Visit her website at kandyshepherd.com

Tuxedos and Tinsel

SHERYL LISTER

BARBARA WALLACE

KANDY SHEPHERD

MILLS & BOON

First Published in Great Britain 2025
by Mills & Boon, an imprint of HarperCollins*Publishers* Ltd
1 London Bridge Street, London, SE1 9GF

www.harpercollins.co.uk

HarperCollins*Publishers*
Macken House, 39/40 Mayor Street Upper,
Dublin 1, D01 C9W8, Ireland

ISBN: 978-0-263-41918-4

MIX
Paper | Supporting responsible forestry
FSC™ C007454

This book contains FSC™ certified paper and other controlled sources to ensure responsible forest management.

For more information visit: www.harpercollins.co.uk/green

Printed and Bound in the UK using 100% Renewable Electricity
at CPI Group (UK) Ltd, Croydon, CR0 4YY

BE MINE FOR CHRISTMAS

SHERYL LISTER

To my in-laws, Bobby and Petrina Lister, for keeping the magic of love alive for more than fifty years.

Chapter 1

Maya Brooks rolled her eyes as the woman on the phone went on and on. "Yes, Mrs. Harper. I know I told you the shop would be closed the last three weeks in December, but my plans have changed and I'll be able to provide the desserts for your party if you haven't found someone else."

"That would be lovely," Mrs. Harper gushed. "I've searched high and low for a suitable replacement but couldn't find anything close to your spectacular chocolate torte."

"I appreciate the endorsement. Let me make sure I've got everything you asked for." Maya finalized the menu details and date. "I can deliver your order two hours before the party. Will that work?"

"That's perfect, dear. I'm sorry your vacation plans were canceled."

"So am I," she murmured. "Thank you, again, and

I'll call you a few days before to confirm your order." She ended the call and dropped her head in her hands.

December had always been Maya's favorite month and she typically had her shop, Maya's Sweet Spot, decorated for Christmas the weekend following Thanksgiving. This year, instead of pulling out her decorations and shopping for more as soon as the calendar changed to November, she would be spending the time returning the few remaining wedding gifts from people who obviously missed the memo that her Christmas wedding had been called off.

"Hey, Maya."

Her head came up at the sound of her best friend and business partner Rhonda Davis's voice. With Rhonda's five-ten height, slender curves and a face that could stop traffic, Maya often teased her, saying Rhonda would be better suited as a high-fashion model instead of managing a bakery. "Hey, girl. How was your vacation?"

"It was great to spend time with my family, especially my grandmother, since I haven't seen her in a year. She's going to spend the entire month with my parents and go back home after Thanksgiving." She claimed the chair across from Maya's desk. "How did it go with your family?"

Maya shrugged. "Fine, I guess…if you don't count all the 'poor baby' and 'you'll find someone else' comments."

"That sucks. I'm sorry."

"Why? You weren't the one who decided two months before our wedding that you changed your mind and wanted to take your life in a different direction." Maya's ex-fiancé, Stephen Jacobs, had been a no-show at their engagement party—one that had been postponed twice because of his busy schedule. When she finally caught up with him the next day, his only words were "You should be glad I changed my mind before the wedding." No apology and no offer to pay half of the many cancellation costs. Nothing. She got angry all over again thinking about it.

"Ouch!"

She was instantly contrite. "I'm sorry for snapping at you, Rhonda. It's not your fault Stephen was a jerk. And, before you say anything," Maya said, raising her palms in mock surrender, "I know, I know, you tried to warn me that something wasn't right. Too bad I didn't listen."

Rhonda chuckled. "Next time."

"Please. There isn't going to be a next time."

"Humph. What you need is to indulge in a little holiday cheer with a fine, sexy man to get over Stephen. You know, giving thanks for some good toe-curling sex…a little mistletoe action… Trust me, there's no better way to jump-start the holiday season. It'll work wonders," she added with a smug smile.

Maya groaned. "I don't even want to know. Thanks, but no, thanks. I'll pass."

"Okay, but I'm telling you… Anyway, what happened to the decorations? You usually have everything pulled out by now. Didn't we just flip the calendar to November? I expected to see twenty sales papers on your desk. I even brought my walking shoes because I knew you were going to drag me shopping."

"I'm not really feeling the holiday spirit this year."

Rhonda stood, rounded the desk and pulled Maya out of her chair. "Come on, girl. You can't let that idiot ruin your favorite time of year. When we're done, Maya's Sweet Spot is going to be the best-decorated shop *anywhere*."

She smiled, unable to resist her friend's enthusiasm. "Oh, all right. But now that I'm going to stay open, I have twice the orders to take care of. It's a good thing, too. With the way all these stores are closing, I need to do everything I can to stay above water." Ever since the grocery store on the lot adjacent to her shop closed a year ago, the other businesses in the strip mall had shut down, one at a time, until only a handful of small shops remained, including hers.

"Speaking of that, I just saw the owner of the clothing boutique next door and she told me she received a letter from some real estate developer offering to buy her out. Apparently, they want to rezone this block for residential use."

"*What?* No, no, no. They can't do that."

"Wanna bet?" Rhonda wagged a finger. "See, I told you something was up. There's no way four stores are going to be closing at the same time. And then there was that guy."

"What guy?"

"Remember the guy in the suit I saw snooping around last month?"

"Yeah," Maya answered absently, still trying to wrap her mind around what Rhonda said. She had chosen this LA location because of its high visibility and constant foot traffic from several office buildings and a nearby residential area. After two years, she was finally turning a decent profit and had just paid her parents back the money they had lent her to start her business. Now someone was trying to steal her dream. Rhonda's voice pulled her back into the conversation.

"I knew he was up to no good—taking measurements and snapping pictures. Did you get a letter?"

She frowned. "No. I went through all the mail on my desk this morning and I didn't see anything."

"Maybe it's on my desk." Rhonda crossed the room and sat at the desk facing Maya's. She riffled through a stack of envelopes and held up one. "This may be it. The return address says EJJ Developers."

Maya came to stand behind Rhonda and read the letter. Dread settled in her belly. She didn't care how much money they offered, she wasn't selling.

"What are you going to do?" Rhonda asked.

"Nothing. I'm not selling."

"It says here that he'll meet with you at your convenience to discuss the offer, and there's a phone number."

"Fine. I'll call and tell him not to waste his time."

"You think it's going to be that easy?"

Maya released a deep sigh. "No, but my answer won't change. You know how long we searched for the perfect location. I'm not about to just hand over the keys."

"I hear you, Maya, but this is big business. They make a living running over the little guy."

"Well, they need to prepare for the fight of their lives, because this 'little guy' refuses to be run over." She hadn't gotten this far in her thirty years of life by rolling over and didn't plan to start now.

Rhonda stood and embraced her. "Girl, we've been fighting together a long time. You know I've got your back."

"I know." Maya and Rhonda had been best friends since ninth grade and had been there for each other through thick and thin. "If we're going to decorate, we need to get going. I have a lot to do this week and I have to prepare for Mr. Capshaw's party on Saturday."

"Saturday? He usually has his annual company holiday party the second week of December. Why is he having it a month early?"

"Apparently, he's combining it with some business venture he's celebrating. He's having cocktails, appetizers and desserts." She hesitated. "This year it's at the Bonaventure."

"Are you going to be okay delivering? I can do it for you."

Maya nodded. "I can't avoid going places just because they remind me of Stephen."

"True, but you were planning to have your wedding reception there. Really, I can take care of it. I may not set the table as elegantly as you do, but I promise it'll be nice," Rhonda added wryly.

Maya chuckled. "Thanks. I can handle it." She had to. Her business depended on it.

"Okay, if you're sure. I just thought of something. Doesn't the hotel have their own catering staff?"

"They do, and I asked about that. Mr. Capshaw said he'd taken care of it."

"I guess it pays to have some clout."

"It does and I'm glad. He's one of my best customers. Let's get started. I have a feeling it's going to be a long week."

Three months ago, Maya's world was perfect. Now not only had her heart been broken, but she also stood to lose her business. She could *not* let that happen.

Ian Jeffries sat alone at a corner table in the ballroom nursing a drink. He would rather be spending his Saturday evening at home watching college football, but his father asked if he and his brother, Chris, could represent their family's real estate development company at David Capshaw's holiday party. As the man was one of the investors in their latest development project, Ian couldn't very well say no. He scanned the ballroom again in search of his brother, who, so far, hadn't made an appearance. Ian planned to stay only an hour, but it was now going on two hours and he felt his frustration mounting. Lifting the glass, he took a small sip and set it on the table before pulling out his phone to check the game scores again.

"What's up, little brother?"

Ian set the phone on the table. "About damn time you showed up."

Chris laughed and lowered his body in the chair next to Ian. "It can't be that bad."

He snorted. "I hate these things. You could've just come alone, since you enjoy all this *socializing*."

"If you had spent more time talking to people instead of being holed up in your room drawing when we were growing up, your people skills would be better."

"Ha-ha, funny. My people skills are just fine. And if I hadn't been doing all that drawing, we wouldn't be here now." Ian's architectural skills and keen business sense had helped to move their family company from a small real estate business to a full-service firm—owning their own equipment, taking care of all construction from breaking ground to the final walk-through and having dependable contractors. He had done some of the smaller jobs alone but up to now had worked with one of the more experienced architects on bigger projects. It had taken close to a year to convince his father to let him design this latest project solo—one of the company's largest undertakings to date. This would be his first major project and he had no intention of messing it up, hence the reason he was sitting in this hotel ballroom.

"True, that," Chris said. "I don't know how you do it, but you can get the devil to buy air-conditioning."

"It's those *people skills*," Ian said sarcastically.

"Damn, somebody's in a foul mood. Lighten up. It's the holiday season. You know…being thankful…the season to be jolly."

"I'm not in a foul mood," he grumbled, glancing down at his watch again. "I'd just rather be somewhere else."

"Hot date?"

"No."

"Maybe that's your problem. When was the last time you had a little release? You know how you get when you haven't gotten any in a while."

"None of your business. And I don't know what you're talking about."

"We're in a room full of beautiful women. I'm sure at least one of them wouldn't mind putting you out of your misery."

Ian frowned and tried to remember his last liaison. He mentally counted and realized it had been almost six months. He had been so busy working to get this latest project off the ground that he'd put his social life on hold. And he needed some distance from women. His scowl deepened as he recalled how the woman he thought loved him only wanted to use him. He shook off the memories. Maybe he did need a little female company to take the edge off. He surveyed the room. As his brother pointed out, the ballroom was full of beautiful women, a few of whom were staring his way with sultry smiles. Yet none of them held his attention.

"It is the start of the holiday season—a perfect time to wind down. Or…you can always settle down with one woman. There's nothing better than going home to the love of my life."

"No, thanks. I like a little variety." Marriage wasn't on his radar for the foreseeable future. He was only thirty-two, so what was the big rush? Besides, he had already tried the relationship thing and it had almost ruined his family's company and him in the process. Ian had promised himself that it wouldn't happen again.

"That's only because you haven't found that one special woman."

"Because she doesn't exist," Ian countered. He smiled at a woman staring at him as she moved her body on the dance floor.

"How do you know? You're not looking."

"You're right," he answered, still checking out the women in the room. "Anyway, what took you so long to get here?"

Chris leaned back in his chair and smiled. "My beautiful wife and I have decided to start a family. I'm doing my part to make it happen and…let's just say I lost track of time."

"Congratulations. Shellie is going to make a terrific mom."

"Yes, she is. And because this will be our first Christmas together since we got married, I'm leaving her a little gift every day for the month of December. I'm going to get a kick out of watching her open each one."

"I'm sure she'll love that." Ian continued to scan the room until his gaze landed on a woman standing at a dessert table. Unlike other women in the room who were decked out in gowns and jewels, she wore a simple white long-sleeved blouse and black skirt that caressed the sweet curve of her hips and ended just below the knee, robbing him of a complete view of her shapely legs. Her hair was piled on top of her head in some kind of bun.

"Now, that's one gift I wouldn't mind opening," he murmured. Ian couldn't take his eyes off her. She leaned forward to reach for something, and her skirt pulled tighter across her apple-round bottom. His breath caught and his groin tightened. Yeah, he'd been on lockdown way too long. After several minutes, she hadn't moved. He stared curiously. Was she having that much difficulty choosing a dessert? Another minute passed and he stood. "I'll be back."

"Where are you going?" Chris asked.

"I think I'll check out the desserts."

Chris followed Ian's gaze to the table and chuckled. "The desserts *on* the table or the one standing in *front* of the table? I guess the drought will be over soon." He lifted his glass in a mock toast. "Here's to hoping she'll improve your disposition. Can't have you ruining the holidays, Scrooge."

"Shut up, Chris," Ian said as he walked away. When he got closer to the table, he finally caught a glimpse of her face. The woman had an understated beauty—a girl-next-door kind of look—that piqued his interest. His gaze was drawn to her mouth as she bit on her gloss-slicked lips and he imagined nibbling on their lush fullness.

Ian stood next to her for a full minute, inhaling her intoxicating fragrance, and she never noticed him. "Is it that hard to decide on a dessert?"

She startled slightly and whipped her head in his direction. "I'm sorry. Did you say something?" Her dark eyes mirrored confusion.

He smiled. "I asked if you were having a difficult

time choosing a dessert. You've been standing here for a while." He surveyed the vast assortment covering the table—individually proportioned cheesecakes, tortes, truffles, mousses and more. "Although I can see why you'd be having a hard time. Everything looks exquisite." Ian had had a sweet tooth for as long as he could remember, and chocolate was his favorite…food and women. And the brown-sugar beauty standing next to him topped his favorites list at the moment.

"No. I was just making sure everything was laid out the way I want."

His brow lifted. "You're working? You made these?"

"Yes. What do you think?"

"It looks amazing. What do you suggest?"

"Depends on what you like."

A slow grin spread across his lips. "Chocolate. Rich, decadent, sinful…" His gaze traveled slowly down her body and back up to her face. He leaned close to her ear and whispered, "Chocolate." He heard her sharp intake of breath.

"Um… I…you can try the chocolate raspberry truffle bars, chocolate torte with a ganache, triple chocolate mocha truffles or the black-and-white pudding parfait." She pointed to each one with a trembling finger.

"What's the black-and-white pudding parfait?"

"It's chocolate pudding topped with white-chocolate whipped cream."

"Hmm, I may have to try that one later." He could think of a few ways to eat that pudding and none of them involved using a spoon.

"And there's always the chocolate fountain for dipping."

"Yes, there is." Another image flashed in his mind.

"I think for now I'll take one of these triple chocolate mocha truffles and a dance."

"Dance?"

He nodded slowly and bit into the truffle. "This is amazing."

"I can't dance with you."

"Why not?"

"I'm supposed to be working."

He grasped her hand and gently led her out to the dance floor. "Everything on that table is perfect. I'm sure one dance won't get you into trouble." Ian pulled her into his arms and started moving to the slow tune playing. Feeling her soft curves pressed against his and being engulfed in her scent robbed him of all rational thought. The only thing on his mind was finding out how that chocolate would taste on her skin.

Chapter 2

The moment the sexy stranger wrapped his arms around her, sensations Maya never experienced coursed through her body. Her nerves were already on overload from his verbal play at the table. She tried to pull away, but he tightened his arms around her and held her closer to his hard body. She resisted for a short moment, then brought her arms up around his neck and melted into his embrace.

At length he said, "My apologies. I should have introduced myself first. I'm Ian Jeffries, and you are?"

She lifted her head. "Maya. Maya Brooks."

Staring at her with an intensity that heated her insides, he said, "It's a pleasure to meet you, Maya."

"Nice to meet you, too." Pulling away from his magnetic gaze, she turned her head and closed her eyes. His deep voice, handsome face and seductive smile had turned her knees to jelly and impaired her ability to think and talk. Her inner voice screamed that she should get far away from Ian as fast as she could. A man like him could make a woman sell her soul for just one kiss. And why did he have to smell so good?

It had been a long time since she was in a man's arms, so ignoring that pesky voice, Maya settled more comfortably in his arms as the music continued to play. It was only a dance… Although the calendar said it was the beginning of November, the room had been transformed to a winter wonderland, exactly as she imagined it would have been for her wedding reception. Tonight, she could pretend. The heat of his hand sliding sensually down her back penetrated the cotton blouse as if it were on her bare skin, and she bit back a moan. She had dated Stephen for a year and couldn't remember him ever being able to set her body on fire with just a simple pass of his hand.

Maya lifted her eyes to meet his at the same time he turned his head. Their mouths were so close she could feel the heat of his breath. He leaned forward and she tilted her chin. Suddenly, she remembered they were standing in the middle of a ballroom and she was supposed to be working. She stumbled backward and Ian pulled her flush against his body. An involuntary moan slipped from her lips.

"Careful," Ian said with a chuckle.

"I… I have to get back to work." She stepped out of his arms, made a beeline toward the exit and hastily glanced around the room to see if Mr. Capshaw had noticed. She spotted him standing with a small group of men, laughing heartily, and breathed a sigh of relief. As soon as Maya pushed through the door, a tug on her hand stopped her.

"Maya, wait."

"Ian, I need to get back to my job," she said without turning around.

"How much longer do you have to work?"

Truthfully, there wasn't anything else she needed to do. The hotel staff would take care of replenishing the desserts as needed, but Maya prided herself on offering the best services to her clients and often stayed around for a while to ensure that there were no problems. Tonight, however, she was torn between fleeing the hotel as fast as she could and dancing the night away with the fine man still idly rubbing his thumb in small circles in her palm. "An hour or so," she said breathlessly.

Ian turned her to face him. "Do you have to work tomorrow?"

"No," she answered hesitantly. Her shop was closed on Sundays.

A slow grin made its way across Ian's face. "I'll wait for you." He kissed her and, instead of going back into the ballroom, sauntered off down the hallway.

Maya slumped against the wall and took in several deep breaths to calm her pounding heart. No denying she was attracted to Ian, but after the mess she had gone through with her ex, she shouldn't be entertaining thoughts of even talking to a man. Pushing off the wall, she made her way to the kitchen and made arrangements to pick up her containers.

"Oh, there you are," the executive chef called in his heavily accented English, coming toward her, a wide grin plastered on his face.

Her brow lifted a fraction at the stark change in his demeanor. When she first arrived, he had been curt and none too happy that she had been contracted to provide the desserts instead of his staff. She curbed the urge to glance behind her to see if he was talking to someone else.

"My dear, these desserts are simply divine. I must say my favorite is the black-and-white pudding parfait. It's a chocolate lover's dream! Would you mind if I kept your contact information…for a few special occasions?" he added, lowering his voice to a whisper.

"I left my cards in my car."

"No worries." He rushed over to a table, came back and pushed a small card and pen in her hand.

The mention of chocolate conjured up an image of her and Ian at the dessert table—his nearness, piercing midnight eyes, smooth-as-honey voice—and a rush of heat spread through her body. The man had a way with words. Still thinking about Ian, she absently scribbled her address on the card and handed it back. "Thank you so much for your kind words. It means a lot coming from you."

"No, thank *you*, Maya. Are you sure I can't lure you away to come work for me?"

Maya chuckled. "I'm flattered, but I enjoy working for myself."

He shrugged. "Can't blame a guy for trying."

"Is there anything else you need me to take care of?"

"No. My staff will take care of everything."

"I'll drop by on Monday morning to pick up my containers." They engaged in polite conversation for a few minutes, and then Maya left. The chef's staff had everything under control and this would be the perfect time to slip out before Ian noticed she was gone. Something about the way he held and kissed her told her this man was dangerous to her psyche and she didn't want to risk another encounter with him. But the perfectionist in Maya wouldn't let her leave without checking the table one last time.

* * *

Ian walked directly to the hotel's registration desk. Holding Maya in his arms had set off a raging desire within him that only she could satisfy. He didn't know how he would accomplish it, but he had to convince her to spend the night with him.

"May I help you, sir?" the smiling clerk asked.

"Yes. I'd like to book a room for the night."

She clicked a few keys on her computer. "There are no standard rooms available, but I do have a one-bedroom suite. It has a living area with a sleeper sofa, wet bar—"

He removed a credit card from his wallet and placed it on the counter. "Even better." He planned for them to use every square inch of that suite. Ian signed the paper, put the card back into his wallet and accepted the room key.

"Enjoy your stay, Mr. Jeffries."

"I plan to. Thank you." He stopped at the gift shop first and then went up to his room to deposit the bag. Ian took a quick peek at his watch. He had forty minutes to come up with a way to persuade Maya to go along with his proposal. As soon as he entered the ballroom, Mr. Capshaw called out to him.

"Ian, there you are."

"How are you, Mr. Capshaw? Nice party."

He laughed heartily. "I can't think of a better way to start the holiday season, and we have a lot to celebrate this year." Capshaw's slightly slurred voice indicated that the man had probably reached his limit two drinks ago.

"Yes, we do," Ian agreed.

"Grab your brother and meet me at my table where the other investors are sitting."

Ian walked back to where Chris sat talking on the phone. He tapped Chris on the shoulder.

"Okay, I'll be home soon," Chris was saying. He hung up and glanced up at Ian with a grin. "Where's the woman you were dancing with? You must be losing your touch."

"I haven't lost anything. She's working."

"Working?"

"Yeah. She made the desserts. Man, you have to try the triple-chocolate mocha truffles."

"She works for the hotel?"

He shrugged. "I assume so. Mr. Capshaw wants us to meet him over at the table with the investors."

"Good. We can talk to them for a few minutes, and then be out of here."

"Actually, I'm going to stay awhile longer."

"I thought you were anxious to leave," Chris said, rising to his feet. "Your change in plans wouldn't have anything to do with the woman who just entered, would they?"

"Maybe." Ian followed his brother's gaze and saw Maya heading toward the dessert table with another hotel employee. Their eyes locked for a brief moment before she turned away to focus on whatever the other woman was saying. A bump on his shoulder drew him out of his thoughts.

"Mr. Capshaw is waiting," Chris reminded Ian.

Giving Maya one last look, Ian followed his brother over to where the investors had gathered on the other side of the room. After a round of handshakes, Mr. Capshaw proposed a toast to the partnership.

One of the men asked, "Are we on schedule for the groundbreaking?"

Chris cut a quick look at Ian before answering. "We've run into a small hiccup, but—"

"What kind of hiccup?" Mr. Capshaw asked.

"One of the business owners doesn't want to sell. Someone from our office plans to meet with the owner this week, and I'm sure contract negotiations will follow."

"That's good to hear," Mr. Capshaw said, raising his glass.

Ian and Chris excused themselves minutes later. Once in the hallway, Ian said, "I thought all the owners accepted the offers."

Chris scrubbed a hand across his forehead. "I thought so, too. But Sam told me yesterday that there's one owner who called and said she had no intentions of selling."

"Great. This is my first major project since that mess a year ago. It took forever to convince Dad to give me another shot, and I don't need this."

"It's not the same, Ian. No one is deliberately trying to sabotage you."

"The result will be the same. Now what?"

"Sam is going to talk to the owner this week, increase the offer and hope she'll come around. I can't see her turning down an amount significantly over what the building is worth."

"Let's hope not. That would ruin my holiday for sure."

"Two years in a row…oh, hell no! You were such a grouch last year you could give Scrooge a run for his money. If Sam can't make any headway with her, we might need you to step away from your drafting table and work your magic."

"I'll do whatever it takes. Keep me posted." Ian

checked the time again. “I’m going back in. I don’t want to miss Maya.”

“Maya?” Chris asked with a laugh. “I guess it didn’t take long for her to get your attention, which is odd.”

“Why?”

“You never react to women this way, especially when it’s someone you’re only looking to have a one-night stand with. Which makes me wonder about this particular woman.”

Ian frowned. “I don’t follow.”

“I always told you that when the love bug bit you, you were going to go down *hard*. Looks like it’s your turn, little brother. See you around.”

Ian muttered a curse, telling Chris exactly what he could do with that statement, pivoted on his heel and walked away.

Chris’s laughter echoed through the hall behind Ian.

He pushed through the ballroom doors, immediately sought out Maya and spotted her at the far end near the other exit. He strode purposely across the room, ignoring two women who tried to detain him. “Maya,” he called when he was in earshot.

She turned, seemingly surprised to see him. “Ian. I thought you’d left.”

His brow lifted. “Why? I told you I’d wait. Are you off work yet?”

“I…” She nodded.

“Good.” Ian led her to the dance floor and gathered her in his arms. “I want to dance with you again.” He held her close and swayed to the ballad the band played, loving the way she fit in his arms. “Maya.”

“Hmm.”

“Are you in a rush to leave?”

“Well…um, no.”

"Would you join me for a drink? Just to talk."

"Okay."

He smiled, took her hand and led her out off the dance floor. He stopped to grab another truffle first, then led her out to the bar. It took a moment, but he spotted a table at the far side and hurried over before someone else could claim it. The waitress came to take their order.

"A glass of Chardonnay, please," Maya said.

"I'll have a cognac." Ian never drank his first one. After the woman left, he focused on Maya. "So, are you some kind of chef?"

Maya smiled. "I'm a pastry chef."

"How long have you been a pastry chef?"

"Professionally, six years. But I've been fascinated with baking and chocolate for as long as I can remember."

"If everything else tastes as good as that truffle, I'd say you've perfected the art. I'm looking forward to sampling a few more of your delicious treats," he said. The waitress came back with their drinks. "Thanks." Ian lifted his glass. "To great conversation."

She touched her glass to his and took a sip of her wine.

"I've never met a pastry chef. Seems like it would be hard work to come up with all those different desserts."

"Not really. Many of them are well-known recipes and others are those that I've tweaked to make them my own. What about you?"

"I like to draw, so I became an architect."

"That has to be fascinating."

He chuckled. "It has its moments."

"Did you grow up in LA?"

"Born and bred."

They both laughed. They spent the remainder of the evening swapping childhood stories.

Maya glanced down at her watch. "Wow. I didn't realize it was so late."

Ian took a peek at his. Over two hours had passed. "Neither did I." He paid the bill, then escorted her out to the lobby.

"Thank you for the drink, Ian. I had a great time."

"So did I. I'm not ready for it to end."

"Neither am I," she said softly.

"Spend the night with me, Maya."

Her gaze flew to his. "What?"

He stared intently into her eyes and repeated the question. "Just one night to explore whatever it is that's happening between us."

Maya shook her head. "Ian, I don't… I can't…we don't even know each other."

"We will by morning," he said, capturing her mouth in an urgent kiss. Ian lifted his head. "One night," he implored. His eyes were riveted to the rapid beating of the pulse in her neck and he knew she was just as affected. "Tell me you don't feel this attraction, and I'll walk away now."

"You know I do." She stared up at him for several charged seconds, then nodded.

Ian released the breath he had been holding. "I promise you won't be disappointed."

Maya shook her head again. "No promises, Ian. I don't want anything beyond tonight."

"Then we're in agreement. The only promise I'll make is a night of pleasure you won't ever forget." He lowered his head and nibbled on her lush bottom lip. When her lips parted, he slid his tongue inside and kissed her slowly, provocatively, giving her a taste of what he planned to do to her. Her body trembled and she moaned. Ian was as hard as a steel beam and he needed to get her upstairs now.

Chris's words rushed back to Ian. *I always told you that when the love bug bit you, you were going to go down hard.* She definitely fascinated Ian, but he'd only known Maya for a few hours, so it wasn't love. However, one thing about Chris's statement was true—Ian had never reacted so strongly toward a woman.

Chapter 3

What are you doing agreeing to a one-night stand? Maya's inner voice screamed. Too bad she didn't have an answer. She had never done something so bold in all her life. Her mind and body were at odds but, somehow, clearly her body had gained the upper hand. She felt like she was in one of those old cartoons with the angel on one shoulder and the devil on the other. The sensible side of her said women did not sleep with a man they just met, that she should date for a while and then see. But there was a side of Maya begging to get out that argued, *Sensible and practical is overrated. Isn't that what you did with Stephen? And look where that got you?* This was so unlike her. She hadn't even asked where they were going. For all she knew, he could be a serial killer. Okay, she didn't believe that last part, but still. She glanced around the hotel lobby. At least there would be dozens of witnesses. Then again, last-minute reservations were expensive.

"Maya?"

She blinked and realized Ian was talking. "I'm sorry. What did you say?"

"I said I hope you don't mind that I reserved a room here."

"No. Wait. When did you reserve a room?" Maya's first thought was relief, then curiosity.

Ian grinned sheepishly. "Right after I left you earlier. Are you having second thoughts?"

"Um…no." Actually, she was flattered. Stephen had never taken the initiative to even make dinner reservations.

He squeezed her hand and smiled. "I'm glad. Can you excuse me? I need to speak to the concierge for a minute."

"Okay." She watched him confidently stroll across the lobby. The man certainly knew how to command a room. She put him close to six feet tall—wearing a pale gray suit she knew had never touched the rack—clean shaven, closed-cropped black hair, smooth coffee-with-cream skin and eyes. Several women did double takes as he passed. In fact, one woman stopped, turned and stared with her mouth hanging open. Maya chuckled.

"Ready?" Ian asked when he returned.

She took his extended hand and walked with him to the elevators. The reflective glass elevators rose swiftly, making the city lights pass by in a blur. Maya continued to have mixed emotions about what she was getting ready to do while they rode the elevator up to their floor. As much as she tried to deny it, Stephen's deception had been a major blow to her self-esteem and some part of her wanted…no, needed to feel desirable again. And Ian made her feel that way. Tonight, she decided, would be all about her. Tomorrow she could go back to her old, practical self. The elevator came to a halt on the thirtieth floor and she allowed him to guide her down the hall. He stopped at a door, unlocked it and stepped back to let her enter. Her gaze swept over the room and she realized he had booked a suite. Maya jumped slightly when Ian came up behind her and placed his hands on her shoulders. He turned her to face him and she tried to hide her embarrassment.

"Nervous?" Ian asked.

She nodded. "A little." That wasn't exactly the truth. She was *a lot* nervous.

Ian angled his head and stared intently at her. He obviously sensed it, because he pulled her into his embrace and said, "Maya, I want you, but if you're having second thoughts we don't have to do anything."

She knew he wanted her, felt the solid ridge of his erection pressed against her belly and read the desire in his eyes. She also saw honesty reflected in his face and it had a calming effect on her nerves. "I want you, too."

"Good. I want to kiss you again."

"That's all?"

He chuckled low and dark. "Sweetheart, kissing you is just the start of what I want to do to you…what I'm *going* to do to you." Ian lifted her hand and placed a lingering kiss on the back, turned her palm up and circled his tongue over the pulse point on her wrist.

Her breath hitched. Electricity shot from her arm straight to her core and she felt a rush of moisture between her thighs.

"I hope you don't have anywhere to be tomorrow," he murmured, still teasing the pulse point. "I plan to touch, taste and explore every delectable inch of your gorgeous body. When I'm done, neither of us will be able to move."

Maya's eyes widened when his statement filtered through her haze of desire. What had she gotten herself into? Before she formed a reply to his heated promise, he slanted his mouth over hers in a kiss that was hot, hard and literally made her weak. He tasted of chocolate and cognac. The heady combination sent her senses spiraling out of control and she gripped the lapels of his suit coat to keep from sliding to the floor. Desire unlike anything she had ever felt raced through her body and she trembled as his tongue made sweeping, swirling motions inside her mouth. He brought his hands up to frame her face, holding her in place and delving deeper. When he finally lifted his head, Maya was breathing like she had run a marathon.

"Mmm," Ian said.

"What are you doing to me?" she asked, still trying to catch her breath.

A wicked gleam leaped into his eyes. "Tasting you."

Oh. My. God!

He leaned forward again, but was interrupted by a knock on the door. "Ah, right on time." He stepped around her and went to open the door.

She tilted her head, puzzled. A hotel employee entered pushing a cart with two covered domes. Ian tipped the man and closed the door behind him. "Did you order dinner?"

A smile played around the corners of Ian's mouth and he shook his head. "It's a little dessert." He lifted the covers to reveal a bowl of strawberries, a bowl of melted chocolate and two servings of the black-and-white pudding parfait.

Maya laughed. "Is that from Mr. Capshaw's party?"

"I told you chocolate is my favorite."

"Well, go ahead." He shrugged out of his jacket, loosened and removed the tie and then tossed them on the sofa. Next, he went to work on his shirt. Keeping his eyes trained on her, he undid the buttons, one by one, until it hung open. Her mouth ran dry when he discarded it, leaving him in trousers that hung low on a trim waist. Lean muscular arms, defined chest with a light dusting of hair and washboard abs. *Chiseled chocolate!* She was so busy gawking she didn't realize he had moved until he stood in front of her, and had undone the first button on her blouse.

"Will you trust me tonight, Maya?" Ian asked, his fingers lightly tracing the tops of her breasts above her bra.

There was something about the way this man touched her. "Trust you?"

"Yes. Will you trust me to give you pleasure? If you don't like something, you can stop me at any time." He bent and replaced his fingers with his tongue.

Maya could hardly talk. "Ye…yes." For one night it would be about her and she wanted everything he had to give.

He continued unbuttoning her blouse. "Nice. Sexy."

She glanced down at her black lace-edged bra. Thank goodness she'd had the presence of mind to wear matching underwear.

He helped her out of the top and carefully laid it across the corner of the chair, then reached behind her to lower the zipper on her skirt. Ian squatted down. "Step out."

She did as he asked, along with the sensible two-inch pumps she always wore when working.

"I've been wanting to touch these beautiful legs all night," he said, skimming his hands along her calves, up her thighs, and dragging her panties down and off. He came to his feet.

Maya started shaking again. "I… I thought you were going to have dessert."

Ian picked up one of the parfaits, snaked an arm around her waist and walked her backward to the large table. "I am." He dipped his finger in the whipped cream, smeared it across her lips and proceeded to lick it off. He groaned. "Absolutely delicious." He dug out another portion, this time a mixture of the cream and the pudding, and made a path from her neck to the top of her breasts.

The sensation of the cool dessert followed by the scorching heat of his tongue sent shivers down her spine, and all she could do was brace herself against the table and moan. "Ian," she whispered.

"Do you like that?"

"Yes."

"What about this?" Ian unclasped and removed her bra. He smeared the pudding across her breasts, then made sweeping circles around her breast until he reached her nipple. He took the hardened bud into his mouth and sucked, repeating the action with the other breast. "You taste so good, so sweet."

Her eyes slid closed and Maya managed a strangled moan. She couldn't even begin to respond to his question. Never had a man done to her the things Ian was doing now, or made her feel so alive.

"I take that as a yes. Well, let's see how you like this."

She felt a warm sensation and looked down to see him drizzling the warm melted chocolate in a path from her chest to her belly and disappearing between her legs. He picked up a hulled strawberry, dipped it in the chocolate pooled in her belly button and, holding her gaze, brought it to his lips. The sight turned her on even more.

"Mmm. The strawberry is good, the chocolate better, but neither compares to the delectable flavor of your skin." He picked up another berry, dipped it and smeared the chocolate across her lips.

Maya snaked her tongue out and licked the chocolate from his finger, then drew the strawberry into her mouth, chewing slowly. Emboldened by his play, she took some of the chocolate, rubbed it across the muscular planes of his chest and licked it clean. "Mmm, yes. It's *very* good." She smiled, delighting in his sharp intake of breath and the tremor in his body from her touch.

Ian lifted her and laid her down on the table. "You missed a spot," he said, sucking gently on her bottom lip.

The table was cold beneath Maya's back, a stark contrast to Ian's hot mouth and hands. He left her mouth, trailed his hands down the front of her body and followed with his mouth. She gasped when she felt the warm liquid on her left inner thigh, then her right one, moving higher and coming close to her already wet center. She writhed and moaned at the exquisite sensation, and her thighs quivered in anticipation. Her hips shot up off the table when he settled between her spread legs, his tongue sweeping across her core in one long stroke.

He groaned. "Damn, baby. Every inch of this sexy body is pure sweetness."

Ian slid one finger inside her, then another, playing her like a finely tuned instrument, while his tongue tapped out its own seductive beat against her clit. The twin assaults were so erotic she didn't last a minute. Maya screamed his name, exploding into a thousand pieces as an orgasm tore through her. She shuddered uncontrollably, her breaths coming in short gasps.

"We're only getting started. There's much more and it gets better," Ian said, rising to his feet. He brought his fingers to his mouth and sucked them clean. "Pure sweetness."

Although she was spent, the carnal sight sent Maya's passions rising again. And how much better could it get? she wondered, still trying to catch her breath.

The rapturous expression on Maya's face combined with the sensual picture she made lying on the table almost made Ian come right then and there. He quickly shed his pants and briefs and searched his pockets for the condoms he had bought. He tore one off, sheathed himself and came back to where she still lay on the table. He pulled her to a sitting position, needing to kiss her again. Without breaking the seal of their mouths, Ian shifted their bodies, stood between her legs and pulled her hips to the edge of the table. He guided himself slowly, inch by incredible inch, inside her. They both groaned. He pulled back and thrust again in a fine, circling motion, loving the way her tight walls clutched him.

Ian lowered Maya back to the table and lifted her legs onto his shoulders, wanting and needing to go deeper. Her passionate cries aroused him further and he increased the pace. He grasped her ankles, spread her thighs wider and thrust harder into her, her breasts moving in tandem. Their breathing grew ragged and sweat broke out on his body as she arched up to meet him stroke for stroke. It felt so good being inside her. He could feel his orgasm building and knew he wouldn't last much longer. Ian drove into her until she cried out wildly, her inner walls contracting around him. Pleasure ripped through him with an intensity that almost blew his head off and he yelled her name. Maya's muscles clenched his throbbing shaft as his body continued to shudder violently. He gently lowered her legs, withdrew and braced his trembling arms on the table.

Several moments later, when he could finally move, Ian swept her into his arms and carried her to the bathroom. They were both sticky from all the chocolate. He started the water and adjusted the temperature. "Go ahead."

"Thanks." She stepped into the shower stall and closed the door behind her.

The water cascading down her body sent heat flowing to his groin and Ian left before he was tempted to join her. But he lost the battle two minutes later and came back. She startled slightly when he came up behind her. "I couldn't stay away," he murmured close to her ear, and stepped into the spray.

Maya turned, circled her arms around his neck, smiled and came up on tiptoes to kiss him. "I'm glad."

That was all it took to snap his control. Ian backed her against the tile wall and pinned her arms above her head as he kissed and caressed his way down her body.

"Ian," she moaned.

"I'm right here." He stepped out of the shower just long enough to don the condom he had wisely placed on the sink. After he turned Maya around, he placed her hands on the wall and then ran his hands down her back and over her hips. He tilted her forward and entered her from behind. She was so tight, so hot. Too far gone, Ian tightened his grip on her waist and set a strong, driving rhythm that made the shower door vibrate. Their moans and cries bounced off the walls as he pounded in and out of her.

"Ian!" Maya convulsed with a loud wail.

Moments later he threw his head back and exploded in a rush of pleasure that forced a raw expletive from his throat and nearly dropped him to his knees. His head fell forward limply. Ian trailed his fingers down her slick spine, then turned her to face him. He stroked a finger down her cheek and placed a soft kiss on her lips. Their eyes locked and he felt a jolt in his midsection. But he pushed it aside, reminding himself that this was just for one night.

Chapter 4

Maya woke up the next morning alone in bed. Glancing over at the clock on the nightstand, she noted it was after ten. She couldn't remember the last time she'd slept past eight, but then again she had not gotten much sleep last night. She listened for sounds of water running in the bathroom but heard nothing. She frowned, strained her ears, listening for movement elsewhere in the suite. Again nothing. Had Ian already left? A wave of disappointment washed over her. Sure, they had agreed on the one night, but she would never have thought he'd leave without so much as a goodbye. However, it was probably a good thing. It would save them both that awkward morning-after moment.

Dragging herself to a sitting position, she groaned softly. Every inch of her body was sore. She padded across the floor to the bathroom to wash her face and brush her teeth with one of the travel kits the hotel had provided. Maya stared at her reflection in the mirror—hair was a tangled mess, lips still kiss swollen and body covered with marks from their passionate encounters. She felt her cheeks warm with the recollection of what had occurred between her and Ian. The man possessed an unbelievable amount of stamina. After the second time in the shower, they slept for a few hours before he woke her in the wee hours of the morning for a third round. She'd had more pleasure in one night with Ian than in one year with Stephen.

Uncomfortable walking around naked, she wrapped herself in a towel and went in search of her clothes. "Ian," she gasped. "You scared me. I thought you left." He was sitting on the edge of the bed when she came out of the bathroom.

"I would never leave without saying goodbye, especially since I'm not ready to say goodbye." Ian rose to his feet and came toward her. He slid his arms around her waist at the same time his head descended, capturing her mouth in a slow, drugging kiss. "Good morning."

Maya's head was still spinning from the kiss and it took a moment for his words to register. "What are you talking about?"

He led her over to the bed and sat next to her. Taking her hand, he said, "Maya, I know we agreed to one night, but I'd like to amend our agreement."

As much as she wanted to see him again, she wasn't sure it would be a good idea. On the other hand… "What kind of amendment?"

"I want to propose that we continue to see each other."

"For how long?"

He shrugged. "For as long as we enjoy each other's company."

She contemplated his offer. An affair with no definitive end could prove to be dangerous. Hell, an affair of any length with this man would be dangerous. She could see herself easily falling for him and didn't want to risk her heart again. But the woman he had unleashed last night wanted more. "Maybe we can see each other until the holidays are over." Hopefully, being with Ian would help ease the sting of her failed engagement.

"What if we still want to see each other when the holidays are over?"

"We won't."

His brow lifted slightly. "What if we do? How about we agree to an affair through the holidays and then reassess our options?"

Certain she would be able to walk away after Christmas, Maya nodded. That would be roughly two months—not enough time to get emotionally attached. "Okay."

"Great! I say we celebrate with breakfast after we shower."

She recalled what had happened the last time they showered together. She was positive the guests in rooms on either side had heard them last night. "Um…you can go first."

He chuckled. "Lucky for you I don't have any more condoms. Otherwise I think I might have to persuade you to take another shower with me."

He rimmed her lips with his tongue and thrust inside when she parted them, forcing her to remember what they had shared. Yeah, it was a good thing he didn't have more. She needed some recovery time.

"More of that chocolate wouldn't be a bad idea, either. Chocolate...your kisses... I can't think of a better combination." Ian kissed her once more and stood. "I'll be out in a few minutes."

She stared at his slender, muscular frame and tight round butt in nothing but those gray boxer briefs and sighed. The man looked scrumptious coming *and* going, and she was sorely tempted to go downstairs for more condoms. That was when she knew she had a problem. The longer she sat, the more she began to rethink extending their affair until she was in a full-blown panic. She wanted him too much, and something told her it wouldn't be easy to walk away from Ian. She couldn't take a chance with her heart again.

Maya hurried through the suite, threw on her clothes and tried to do something with her hair. She had to get out before he finished showering. Dressed, she surveyed the suite for anything she might have missed. Satisfied, she glanced in the direction of the bedroom when she heard the water shut off. She felt bad about the way she was leaving but knew if he touched her, she would never be able to resist. She tipped over, opened the door and closed it quietly behind her. She touched her palm to the door and whispered, "I'm sorry."

Maya hurried down the hall to the elevator and didn't relax until she was in her car and pulling out of the lot. As soon as she got home to her two-bedroom condo, she collapsed on her bed. Sadness engulfed her and she tried to convince herself that she had made the right decision. She dug out her cell phone and turned it on. It immediately chimed, indicating missed messages. Rhonda had sent two texts and called three times between last night and this morning, each message more frantic than the previous one. Before she could listen to the last message, her house phone rang. In an age when most people used their cell phones for everything, Maya's mother insisted that she keep a landline. *You never know when the power will go out. That cell phone won't do nothing for you if you can't charge it,* she always said.

"Girl, where have you been?" Rhonda said as soon as Maya answered. "I've been trying to call you since last night. Are you trying to give me a heart attack? I even called the hotel last night looking for you. I didn't know whether you were safe or lying somewhere in a hospital."

Maya rolled her eyes. "Rhonda, are you finished?"

"I guess. You could've let somebody know you were safe," she muttered. "Are you okay?"

"Yeah. Fine."

"Where were you?"

She was somewhat embarrassed by the fact that she had engaged in a sex-a-thon with a man she had just met and wasn't sure she wanted to share those details.

"Maya, did something happen?"

Sighing heavily, she said, "Yeah. A whole lot happened."

"That doesn't sound good. Did you have a problem with the hotel or Mr. Capshaw? Or did you have a hard time being at the hotel?" she added sympathetically.

"No. That wasn't it. I… I…"

"You what?" Rhonda asked when Maya trailed off.

"I met a man at Mr. Capshaw's party and spent the night at the hotel with him," Maya finally blurted.

There was silence for a full five seconds before Rhonda screamed into the phone. "*Oh, my God!* I don't believe it. You did *what*?"

"I'm not repeating it. You're the one who suggested it. Happy now?"

She giggled. "Are you?"

"It was the most erotic night of my life," she confessed.

Rhonda screamed again. "I'll be over in thirty minutes to hear the details."

Maya heard a loud click and shook her head. She really wanted a long soak in the tub but opted for a shower instead, knowing her friend would be ringing the doorbell in exactly thirty minutes or less. She was just putting her hair into a ponytail when she heard the door. Her hair had gotten wet last night and Maya would have to wash it and flatiron it sometime today.

"Hey, girl," she said, opening the door to Rhonda.

"Hey." She handed Maya a cup and followed her to the living room. "I stopped and got you a decaf mocha. Although, by the looks of you, you could use a shot or two of caffeine," she added slyly. Taking a seat on the sofa, she said, "Okay, spill it. And don't leave anything out."

"Can't I get a chance to enjoy my coffee first?" Maya chuckled at the death glare Rhonda shot her. She dropped down on the sofa and told her how Ian had come over to the dessert table, his verbal play and the dance. "The way he held me… Stephen never made me feel like that the entire year we dated."

Rhonda snorted. "Don't get me started on that jerk. Anyway, how did you get from the dance floor to the bedroom?"

"He came right out and asked me to spend the night. I knew we were attracted to each other, but I never expected him to be so bold."

"Well, don't leave me in suspense." She leaned forward. "How was it?"

"It was all that and *more*!" They both screamed and

giggled like teenagers. "Girl, he had servings of the black-and-white parfait, a bowl of the melted chocolate from the fountain and strawberries sent up to the room and…"

Rhonda screamed again. "What does he look like?"

"His name is Ian and he's about six feet, fine as all get-out, slender muscular build, rich milk-chocolate skin—chiseled chocolate."

Rhonda fanned herself and fell back against the sofa. "Whew. I'm getting warm just hearing about it. Sounds like a night to remember."

Maya smiled. "It was."

"So, are you going to see him again?"

She dropped her head. "It was only supposed to be one night, but he wants us to continue seeing each other. I agreed, but I just got out of one bad relationship. Stephen broke my heart and I don't want to feel that pain again. Ian is charming and I can see myself falling for him. I can't let that happen."

"What are you going to do?"

"I've already done it. I sort of sneaked out while he was in the shower and he doesn't have my phone number," Maya said sheepishly.

Rhonda threw up her hands. "What am I going to do with you? You didn't even give the man a chance."

Maya dropped her head in her hands and groaned. "I know, I know. I feel so bad, especially since I agreed to amend our one-night stand."

"Well, at least you can say you've had your toes curled once in your life."

That she could. But already she was beginning to have regrets about tipping out on Ian. After Rhonda left, Maya spent time going over her schedule, washing her hair and finally having that long soak in the tub.

She was at the shop bright and early Monday morning getting her baked goods ready for the day. She didn't usually have a lot left over, but whatever she had was donated to a local shelter. Halfway through the morning, she left Rhonda to man the store while she went to pick up her containers from the hotel.

The moment she stepped into the Bonaventure Hotel lobby, memories of her night with Ian rose swiftly in her mind. She tried to push them aside to no avail. Wanting to get in and out as soon as possible, Maya quickened her steps. On her way out, she was still chuckling at the chef's pitiful expression at her refusal to work for him. But he did agree to pass her name along to a few people who might want desserts for an intimate gathering and tried to coerce her into giving him the recipe for her black-and-white parfait. The mention of the dessert brought on more heated memories. Her nipples puckered beneath her blouse, and the space between her legs throbbed with the same rhythm Ian had started Saturday night. What she wouldn't give for just one more night.

Wednesday afternoon, Ian sat hunched over his drafting table staring at a blank page. He was supposed to be working on a design for a new senior living complex, but his concentration was at an all-time low. It had been three days since Maya sneaked out of the hotel room, and he couldn't stop thinking about her. When he had emerged from the shower and found her gone, he was angry and more than a little disappointed. Why had she left? He thought they were on the same page, but apparently she'd had second thoughts. Usually, he had no problems moving on from a woman, but Maya wasn't like other women. Something about her had piqued more than a passing interest, and he didn't want to stop and analyze the reasons why. He should probably just let it go and move on. But he couldn't.

An hour later, he gave up all pretense of working. Ian stood, stretched and walked out to his secretary's desk. "Ms. Smith, I'm going to be out of the office for a couple of hours. If something comes up, you can reach me on my cell."

"No problem, Mr. Jeffries."

He was going to the Bonaventure to find Maya. In his car, he cranked up the air-conditioning. Winter was a month away, yet the temperatures still hovered near eighty. On the drive, he thought about what he would say to her. Other than asking why she left, he didn't have a clue. He did know that he was going to have a hard time not dragging her up to a room and continuing what they had started on Saturday. And if he got his hands on some more of that chocolate, all bets were off. For the past three nights, he'd had visions of all the things they had done with those desserts and woke up with a hard-on each morning. That last go-around they had changed positions at least three times and ended up half off the bed. Ian always enjoyed being adventurous in the bedroom, but no other woman had inspired him to use food during foreplay. And he suspected no other woman would. The memory of their kisses came back to him. As much as he enjoyed those truffles, they didn't compare with the sweet taste of her mouth.

Ian parked in the registration area and entered the lobby. "Excuse me, I'm looking for Maya Brooks. She's a pastry chef," he said to the concierge.

The woman frowned. "I don't think we have an employee by that name, but maybe she's new. I'll call the executive chef. He'll be able to help you."

"Thanks." He could have sworn she said she worked at the hotel.

"If you'll follow me, sir."

He followed her to the entrance of an expensive steak house located on the thirty-fifth floor, where a man wearing a chef's jacket waited.

He introduced himself. "Hello. I understand you're looking for one of my employees."

"Yes," Ian said. "Maya Brooks. She provided the desserts for a party here on Saturday night."

"I'm sorry. Maya doesn't work for the hotel. She was contracted directly by the client."

Ian did his best to hide his shock and, yes, panic.

The man folded his arms across his chest and frowned slightly. "Why are you looking for her?"

"I attended the party Saturday and enjoyed several of the desserts." *Enjoyed* probably wasn't the most accurate word, but it was appropriate for the conversation. "I'm planning a small gathering and wanted to see if Ms. Brooks was available," he lied.

"Hmm. What was your favorite?"

"The black-and-white pudding parfait."

The chef's features relaxed. "Mine, too. Isn't it exquisite?"

"It was absolutely unforgettable." *In more ways than one.*

"Well, she did ask me to pass on her information to prospective clients. Wait here and I'll get it."

"Thank you." Ian breathed a sigh of relief. He was one step closer to finding Maya. The chef returned moments later and handed Ian a piece of paper. Ian thanked the man again and hurried off with a huge grin on his face. Back in his car, he programmed the address into his GPS and was surprised to find it was in a residential area. Did she work out of her home? He drummed his fingers on the steering wheel, debating whether to go directly to her house or wait until tonight. Now. He couldn't wait. It was already after four and that made it close to evening, he reasoned. Besides, after getting through the downtown traffic, it would be evening when he arrived. He called his secretary to tell her he would not be returning and then, starting the engine, eased out of the lot and onto the road.

It took him over an hour to get to Maya's place and, luckily, someone was exiting the gate as he reached the entry to her condominium complex. He parked in an uncovered spot, circled back to her unit and rang the bell, hoping she was home. His head came up when the door opened.

"Ian! What are you… How did you… What are you doing here?" Maya asked, surprise clearly evident in her voice.

He drank in the sight of her and let his gaze wander over her luscious body in a fitted T-shirt and skimpy shorts, and standing barefoot. Every detail of their night together came rushing back, and his body reacted in kind. She wasn't out of his system. Not by a long shot.

Chapter 5

Maya couldn't believe Ian was standing at her door. How had he gotten her address?

"You left without saying goodbye."

"I—"

Ian moved closer until their bodies were touching. "Invite me in, Maya," he whispered against her lips. When she nodded, he backed her into the house and shut the door behind him, pulling her into his arms and slanting his mouth over hers.

Heat shot to her core and she moaned in his mouth. Their tongues tangled and danced and she felt herself losing control. Maya broke off the kiss.

He eased back and rested his forehead against hers. "Why did you leave?"

"How did you get my address?"

He smiled. "The chef. He said you told him to pass along your information to interested clients," Ian clarified.

She remembered being distracted and thinking about Ian. Had she written down her home address instead of the one to her shop?

"You didn't answer my question."

Maya exhaled deeply. "I don't know. I just started thinking and…" She turned and walked over to the sofa and sat.

He followed, lowered himself next to her and took her hand. "Talk to me, Maya. I thought we were in agreement. Did I do something, say something?"

"No, no. It's nothing like that."

"Then what is it?"

She closed her eyes briefly to gather her thoughts. "Ian, two months ago I was engaged and had planned to get married next month."

He tried to hide his shock.

"That all changed when my ex decided he wanted to take his life in a different direction, namely one with a woman whose father could give him better access to the corporate ladder he was determined to climb," she added wryly. "I know I agreed to something casual, but I really don't know if I can do that right now."

Ian's jaw tightened. "I'm sorry, Maya. I don't know what to say."

"I'm sorry, too."

"I still want to see you."

"I want to see you, too, but…"

"I can't even imagine how much he hurt you, but you're a beautiful woman, too beautiful to lock yourself away. Can we just keep with our agreement and see where it goes?"

She needed to stop looking into those eyes that threatened to suck her in. And he *really* needed to stop touching her. There was no way she could stick to her decision with his hands on her. "Ian, I…ohhh." Now he was playing dirty, bringing his lips into the action. He wrapped an arm around her shoulder and trailed kisses along the curve of her jaw and neck.

"We'll have so much fun together," he said, still kissing his way to her chest.

Maya's eyes slid closed and she breathed a sigh of surrender. She reached up, brought Ian's face to hers, and gave him a slow and sultry kiss.

"What are you doing tonight?" Ian asked when they came up for air.

"I don't have anything planned. Why?"

"I'd like to take you out to dinner. And before you say no, you skipped out on brunch, so you kind of owe me," he added with a sly grin.

A surge of guilt rose and Maya felt her face flush. "I know. I feel really bad about that."

Ian did his best to look sad, but the smile playing around the corners of his mouth ruined it. "Left me all alone and starving."

She burst out laughing. "Yeah, right. You look like you haven't eaten in days."

His smile faded and his eyes lit with desire. "Actually, I haven't. I've been craving something decadent and I only know one place to get it," he murmured, sliding his hand up her thigh.

The air surrounding them changed from playful to sizzling in a nanosecond. She didn't know who moved first, but they nearly tore each other's clothes off. Within a minute, they were both naked and she was straddling him on the couch. He palmed her face while his mouth plundered hers. She squirmed, trying to get closer, and he grasped her waist, lifted her and drove into her with one deep stroke, filling her completely. Maya cried out at the sweet invasion.

Ian muttered a curse and pulled out. "Wait…wait a minute." He reached for his discarded pants, found his wallet and dug out a condom.

She had totally forgotten about protection. Thank goodness one of them was thinking.

He sheathed himself and brought her down on him again. "Ride me, baby."

Holding on to his broad shoulders, she raised her body and eased back down, once, twice and a third time. She shivered and moaned when Ian captured a nipple between his lips and tugged gently.

"Ah, yes. The brown-sugar sweetness I've been wanting," Ian groaned.

Although Maya was on top, Ian dictated the pace, firmly holding her hips and moving with deep steady strokes. He thrust upward with every one of her downward strokes. She rode him faster and faster and he matched her pace, their moans filling the room. Ian locked his mouth on hers, reached between their bodies and teased her using his thumb, increasing the sensations. Sparks shot up her spine and she jerked her mouth free of his and screamed as an orgasm hit. Before she could recover, Ian bucked wildly beneath her.

"Maya!"

Their bodies shook and shuddered while they fought to catch their breaths. Maya collapsed against his chest and rested her head on his shoulder. *Reason number ten why I need to stay away from this man.*

At length, Ian asked, "Is it just me, or is it hot in here?"

She laughed softly. "Only in LA will you find eighty-degree temperatures in November." She rose and went to turn on the air conditioner. "I'll be right back. There's a bathroom right down that hall you can use," she added, gesturing in that direction.

Maya closed the door to her bedroom and lightly banged her head against it. "What are you doing, Maya Nicole Brooks?" As much as she enjoyed sex with Ian, she had to find a way to keep her emotions from coming into play. She had never been good at separating the two, but this time she would. Her heart depended on it.

Ian watched Maya's naked body until she was out of sight. His passions stirred to life. He flopped back against the sofa and closed his eyes. The air conditioner did nothing to cool him off. The more time he spent inside her body, the more he wanted. And he shouldn't want her this much. Sighing deeply, he came to his feet and went to wash up. When he came back, Maya still hadn't returned. He dressed and then surveyed the room. Upon his arrival, Ian had been so focused on Maya he hadn't taken more than a cursory glance around her place. Cream-colored walls and carpets—standard rental colors—but the blues and greens she had added gave the room a tropical feel. He noticed a stack of large boxes on the other side of the room. Was she moving?

"I'm ready."

He turned at the sound of Maya's voice. She now wore an off-the-shoulder pink top, a long skirt and short-heeled sandals. "Why did you change? I rather liked the first outfit."

"Ha-ha. That outfit does not leave the house."

"Yeah. You have a point." For some reason, he didn't want any other man seeing her in such revealing attire. "I like your place. Makes me think of a tropical island."

Maya angled her head and crossed her arms. "Most men wouldn't notice things like that."

"I'm an architect, remember? I notice things most men wouldn't," he added pointedly. He gestured toward the boxes. "Are you moving?"

"No. Those are my Christmas decorations."

"There are seven boxes over there. Are you decorating the entire complex?"

Maya laughed. "Of course not. But I *love* Christmas. I collect angel ornaments, so two of the boxes are just for them. My Christmas music playlist is ready with 'Silent Night' by The Temptations at the top." She shrugged. "It's my favorite time of the year and I get a little out of control."

He shook his head. "I'd say so."

She placed her hands on her hips. "Don't tell me you're a Scrooge."

Ian chuckled. "No, but I don't typically decorate. I live alone and can't see spending all that money on decorations no one will see."

"Do you live in a house, condo or apartment?"

"House. Why?"

"Then lots of people will see your decorations when they drive by. You don't have an excuse. When I buy a house, I plan to go all out—lights, snow…"

"Like those pimped-out houses featured on TV?" A huge grin blossomed on her beautiful face and she nodded. Ian couldn't help getting caught up in her excitement. "That I'd like to see. And where would you get snow from?"

"I'd love to drive up to Big Bear and bring some back, but, depending on the weather, it would probably melt within a few hours, so I'll have to settle for the fake stuff in the stores. You said you're an architect. Are there any notable buildings with your signature on them?"

Ian smiled. "Not yet, but soon hopefully. I have designed a few smaller buildings."

"Your house?"

"No, but I did do my brother's. He wanted it as a gift for his wife."

"That's so sweet. Maybe I'll get you to design my house one day."

"Maybe. So, where would you like to go for dinner?"

Maya shrugged. "Doesn't matter. What do you have a taste for?"

Ian lifted his brow a fraction. He threw his head back and roared at her embarrassed expression when she realized what she'd asked.

"Um…there's a Mexican restaurant not far. We can go there. Let me get my purse. I'll be right back," she mumbled, and exited like the room was on fire.

Still chuckling, he wondered if she knew just how close she had come to being on the menu tonight. *Looks like it might be a great holiday after all.*

Thursday morning, Rhonda breezed into the kitchen, snagged a still-warm cinnamon roll and came over to the stove, where Maya stood. "You're never smiling at six thirty in the morning. What gives?"

Maya looked up from the raspberry sauce she was stirring. "Morning, Rhonda. As I recall, you're the one who's not a morning person. And what's wrong with smiling?"

Rhonda eyed Maya. "Nothing, but we have a meeting with that man from the developer's company this afternoon and you were pretty upset yesterday when we closed. So what happened between then and now? Did they pull the offer?"

"I wish," she said with a roll of her eyes. "Ian stopped by my house last night."

"*Ian?* How did he get your address?"

"Apparently, when I gave the chef at the Bonaventure my contact information—smart me had left my cards in the car—I wrote down my home address. I told him he was free to share it with prospective clients. I'll have to go back and give him the shop's address."

Rhonda sighed wistfully. "A determined man. I wish stuff like that would happen to me. So?"

"Against my better judgment, I agreed to our original agreement. The man does not play fair," she said, recalling the way she had ridden him last night on her couch.

"That look on you face tells me, fair or not, he plays well."

"Yeah, he does. But I need to get my mind off Ian and on the meeting this afternoon. I'm not looking forward to it, because I know it won't be the end."

Later, after closing, Maya sat in her office thinking about her meeting with the man from EJJ Developers. Just as she predicted, he was not happy when she wouldn't entertain the offer for her property. The price he quoted was above the building's market value and more than she had paid, but none of that mattered. Saving her business did. And as much as she wished she could wave a magic wand and make this all go away, Maya knew she hadn't heard the last of the developer. Her cell chimed. Picking it up from the desk, she read a text message from Ian: I want to see you tonight. Her first thought was to reply with a resounding yes, but the rational part of her warned against letting him get too close. After several minutes of inner debate, she typed back: Can't. Need to work late to prepare for a party. It was partly true. She did have to provide desserts for a client tomorrow. The cell chimed again.

Ian: R u free Saturday night?

Maya: Yes.

Ian: Good. Can't wait to kiss you again. I'll bring the melted chocolate. I just need you to provide that brown sugar sweetness I can't get enough of.

Her pulse jumped. Warm chocolate, more of his expert kisses and extraordinary bedroom skills... She was in so much trouble.

Chapter 6

"This woman is driving me crazy!" Chris stormed into Ian's office, closing the door forcefully.

Ian turned from his drafting table. "Shellie finally realized that she could do better?"

Chris snorted. "Of course not. My wife knows there is no other man for her. I'm talking about the woman who's holding up the condo project."

"She still won't sell?" he asked incredulously.

"No. We offered more than the fair market value and she won't budge. It's been two weeks since Sam went to her shop. He's called twice and she basically told him not to bother calling again."

Ian blew out a long breath. "I need this deal to go through. What are we going to do?"

Chris propped a hip against the table and folded his arms. "Dad is going to try to schedule a meeting with her for the first or second week of December. Since today is Thursday and Thanksgiving is next week, he thought it would be better to hold off."

"It must be serious if Dad's going to hold the meeting."

"He doesn't want to mess around with this. Apparently, word got back to him that a couple of the investors from Capshaw's party are getting antsy. Hopefully, she'll come around. I don't want this to mess up the holidays. You should plan on coming. We might need you."

Ian nodded. "I'll do whatever it takes to get this done. Just tell me when."

"Good." Chris angled his head and studied the design on the table. "Is that for the office complex?"

"Yeah. I want to have two or three designs ready, based on what the client requested. I'm ready to take on more projects, but Dad still seems reluctant. The other three architects will be doing the same and I want mine to stand out."

"Well, judging from these, I'd say you've pretty much got the deal locked up. And don't worry about Dad. He knows how good you are at your job. Oh, before I forget, Shellie said you're invited for dinner tonight."

Ian smiled. "As much as I love my sister-in-law's cooking, I'll have to take a rain check. Maya and I are hanging out tonight."

Chris's brow knit in confusion. "Maya?"

"Yep. The woman from the party."

"You're still seeing her? I thought it was supposed to be a one-nighter. It's been two weeks."

Yeah. Two weeks of the best sex of Ian's life. Visions of their lovemaking last Saturday popped into his head. "We agreed to a short-term affair just until the end of the year."

"And you're sure you'll be able to walk away after that time?"

He shrugged. "Why wouldn't I? I'm not looking for anything long-term and neither is she." Somewhere in the back of his mind, a nagging voice told him walking away might not be as easy as he thought, but he immediately dismissed it. Ian glanced down at his watch, stood, shut down his laptop and rolled up the papers. "I need to get going."

"For a casual affair, you sure are eager to see her. And on a weeknight," Chris said with a smile. "You've never acted this way with other women."

"How do you know?" Ian asked, making sure to lock up his files. He was taking his designs home to work on them…if his evening with Maya ended early.

"Remember, I've been around since you were born. So I know you pretty well." Chris followed Ian out of the office and waited while he locked the door. "Sounds to me like things are not as casual as you'd like to believe." He clapped Ian on the shoulder. "Have fun and don't forget what I told you at the party." He strolled off down the hall to his office without waiting for a reply.

He ignored Chris's reference to being bitten by the love bug. Ian had no intention of being bitten by anything. But no matter what he tried to tell himself, he enjoyed being with her. His anticipation mounted the closer he got to Maya's place. And by the time he rang her doorbell, his heart was racing with excitement. She greeted him with a smile that made his heart leap.

"Hi, Ian. Come on in."

The greeting was barely off her tongue before he lifted her in his arms, kicked the door closed and kissed her with a hunger that stunned him and gave him pause. He eased back and lowered her to the floor.

"Now, *that's* a greeting," Maya said, taking his hand and leading him to the living room. "It was your turn to pick the place for dinner, so what did you decide?"

"Actually, I was thinking we could stay in tonight—pick up something to eat and take it back to my place." Where in the hell had that come from? Ian had never invited a woman he was casually dating to his house, and he tried to figure out a way to rescind the offer.

Maya's eyes lit up and she smiled brightly. "That's a great idea. I don't really feel like going to a restaurant. But I wish you would've told me earlier so I could make dessert."

Her smile and enthusiasm, along with the mention of her desserts, killed any notion he had of reneging. "Don't worry about it. We can always get dessert later, if you want."

She waved him off. "Wait a minute while I check the kitchen. I usually keep a little something, just in case. Can I get you something to drink?"

"Just some water please."

"Okay." She started to the kitchen, then turned back. "And I know you like chocolate."

As soon as she was out of sight, Ian scrubbed a hand down his face and groaned. What was he thinking?

"I'm ready."

He spun around at the sound of Maya's voice. His gaze strayed to the small gift bag in her hand. "You made a dessert already?" he asked, taking a bottle of water from her outstretched hand. He unscrewed the cap and took a huge gulp.

She shook her head. "No. I had some chocolate-chip cookie dough in the freezer. They'll only take about fifteen minutes. But, if you don't mind, I can pop them in the oven at your place."

Ian nearly choked on the water going down his throat. He coughed and tried to catch his breath. *Cook? At his place?* Granted, he had a state-of-the-art kitchen, but he had never allowed any woman, including his ex, at his stove. That implied an intimacy he purposely avoided.

"Are you okay?" Maya asked with concern.

He nodded. "Fine, fine. Just swallowed wrong." He composed himself and took a small sip of water.

"You sure?"

"Yeah."

"So, about the cookies…here or your place?"

He stared at her for a lengthy minute. "We can do them at my place." He'd already invited her over and it would seem rude to have her bake them here. Or at least that was what he told himself.

They agreed upon and ordered from an Italian restaurant. On the drive to Ian's house, Maya sat quietly thinking about the invitation to his house. Frankly, she was a little surprised, given the nature of their relationship. Most men didn't invite women into their homes unless… She quickly struck the thought from her mind. No. They agreed. Just through the holidays. A hand on her thigh interrupted her thoughts.

"You okay?"

"Yes. Why?"

"You're quiet. You mentioned not wanting to go out. Is anything wrong?"

"No. Just some work stuff. Nothing I can't handle." She hadn't heard anything from the real estate company since she'd declined their last offer almost two weeks ago, but knew they weren't going to back off. The thought of losing her dream weighed heavily on her mind. Not wanting to dwell on that prospect, she asked Ian, "What about your job—do things slow down for you over the holidays?"

"Sometimes, but this year we're hoping to get a project off the ground soon," Ian answered, turning into a cul-de-sac.

Maya's complex was located in a nice neighborhood, but Ian's home was in one of the more expensive areas—immaculate lawns, large stately houses with balconies, two-and three-car garages. He pulled into the third driveway. "Wow, this is fabulous."

"Thanks." He got out, retrieved their food from the backseat and then came around to her side.

She stared at the large two-story structure as they headed up the walkway. The house was impressive, even in the dark. He unlocked the door, stepped back for her to enter and touched a light switch. "Very nice," she said, glancing around the large foyer and into the living room to the right—polished wooden floors, dual staircase, and elegant and expensive furniture.

"Come on back to the kitchen," Ian said.

"This kitchen is amazing. I'd love to have one this size for all the baking I do."

He chuckled. "Do you want to bake the cookies now or later?"

"Now is fine. Can you preheat the oven to three hundred and fifty degrees?"

He placed the bags on the kitchen table, set the oven, and got plates and silverware. "Would you like a glass of wine?" Ian pulled out a small cookie sheet and handed it to her.

"Sure." She arranged the cookies on the sheet and slid the tray into the oven.

He retrieved and opened a bottle of pinot grigio from

a small wine cellar containing half a dozen bottles, seated her at the table and took the chair across from her.

They ate in silence for a few minutes and then Maya asked, "What made you go into architecture? I remember you telling me you loved to draw, but was there something else?"

"When I was eight, one of my neighbors' houses burned down. I was fascinated with the rebuild. Every day, when I came home from school, I would get as close as I could and watch. I wondered how they knew where to place each piece of wood, how they knew which room was which and the sizes…everything." He smiled as if remembering. "The architect happened to be there one of those afternoons and he, surprisingly and patiently, answered the million and one questions I had, showed me blueprints. Even gave me his card."

"That is so cool."

"Yeah. After that, I was always in my room working on some great masterpiece. Told my parents I was going to design the biggest building in Los Angeles."

Maya laughed. "And have you?"

"Not yet, but I'm working on it."

The timer on the oven went off and Maya removed the cookies, put them on a plate to cool and came back to the table to finish her dinner.

"Do you want something else?" Ian asked when they were done.

"No, thank you. This was some of the best seafood Alfredo I've ever had."

He stood, topped off their glasses of wine and picked up the plate of cookies. "Let's take this into the family room."

She followed him and settled onto the buttery-soft black leather sofa. She surveyed the room. Two matching recliners flanked the sofa and a large flat-screen TV was mounted on the wall above the fireplace in front of them. A bar with three stools occupied the other side of the room.

"I was trying to let my food digest before trying one of the cookies, but I can't wait," Ian said, reaching for one. He bit into it and groaned. "This is so good. I could eat all of these in one sitting."

She smiled, secretly thrilled about his praise for her desserts. She laughed as he devoured four of the twelve she had baked in a matter of minutes.

"Okay. I need to stop." He picked up a remote and pressed a button, and music floated through the room. "Come dance with me." He stood and pulled Maya to her feet.

She recognized the distinctive sound of Kem's voice immediately. She wrapped her arms around Ian's neck and leaned her head against his shoulder. They swayed slowly as Kem sang "Human Touch."

"I know you told me last weekend how many hours a day you spend baking, but how do you come up with your recipes?"

"Some of them are family recipes. Others are twists on familiar recipes or me just mixing ingredients together and experimenting."

"Obviously, you're doing something right. I haven't tasted one bad thing."

"Thank you." Ian was the first man she had dated who seemed genuinely interested in her career. He was making it hard to keep her guard up. Relaxing and dancing with him in this intimate environment didn't help, either.

"I don't think I ever asked and it wasn't on the card

the chef gave me, but do you have a name for your business?"

"You haven't and yes I do… Maya's Sweet Spot."

Ian stopped dancing. "It's a perfect name."

She lifted her head and met his eyes.

"I can think of several sweet spots on your body, starting here," he murmured, nibbling on her neck.

Her breath caught.

"And here."

The feel of his warm mouth skating across her chest woke every nerve in her body and she moaned softly. Maya knew she should slow things down, say something… anything. She needed to keep her barriers.

"Oh, and I can't forget about here," he said, slanting his mouth over hers in a passionate and intoxicating kiss. Caressing her face, he said, "In fact, I'd like to reacquaint myself with every sweet spot on your body. And search out a few more."

The desire burning in his eyes and seductive proposal tempted her beyond reason. He swept her into his arms and reclaimed her mouth. Each stroke of his tongue weakened her resolve until she could do nothing except yield to the pleasure. Her body wanted this. She only hoped her heart didn't follow.

Chapter 7

Dressed in a T-shirt and shorts, Ian padded barefoot downstairs Saturday morning to his kitchen, pressed the button on his single-serve coffeemaker brewing system and went out to retrieve the newspaper. Thanksgiving was still five days away, yet one of his neighbors had his lawn filled with boxes, strings of lights, large bows and a host of other Christmas decorations. The sight made him think of Maya. By the time he came back to the kitchen, his coffee was ready. He added sugar, sat at the bar and took a sip.

Her enthusiasm about Christmas brought a smile to his face, as did remembering their time in his home two nights ago. The more time he spent with her, the more he wanted to be with her. He was even contemplating shopping for Christmas decorations and a tree. Maybe she would help him decorate. His smile faded and he lowered the cup to the counter. What the hell was he thinking making plans as if they were a real couple? They weren't. He'd never had a problem separating the physical from the emotional, but this time he was fighting hard to maintain his distance. He shook his head, opened the paper and lifted the cup again. His phone rang. He set the cup down, reached across the bar for the phone and checked the display.

"Morning, Mom," he said after connecting.

"Good morning. Are you busy?"

Ian paused. "Ah, no," he answered slowly. Any time his mother started the conversation with that question meant trouble.

"Oh, good. I'm getting a head count for Thanksgiving dinner and wanted to know if you might be bringing a lady friend. Chris mentioned you were seeing someone."

He planned to strangle his brother on sight. Chris, of all people, knew the details of Ian and Maya's relationship, one that did *not* include family dinners.

"Is she a nice girl?" his mother asked excitedly.

"No, wait, yes, but she's not—" He searched his mind for the right words to explain his relationship with Maya. It wasn't like he could tell his mother the truth—that he and Maya were only having a sexual relationship. Yet he felt the stirrings of something more. No. He didn't want anything more. Wouldn't put his heart out there again. Then why couldn't he stop wanting her?

"Ian!"

His mother's annoyed voice snapped him out of his inner debate. "I'm sorry. What did you say?"

She sighed impatiently. "I asked whether you were bringing your lady friend."

"No. It's not that kind of relationship. So who's coming?" he asked, hoping to distract her from further questions.

She rattled off a list of relatives and close friends. "Then what kind of relationship is it?"

Ian smothered a groan. "We're just friends and I'm sure she'll be spending the day with her family. I have to get going, Mom. There are a few drawings I need to go over."

"You're not getting any younger, Ian, and don't you see how happy your brother is?"

He pinched the bridge of his nose. "Mom, Shellie is a great woman and she's perfect for Chris. I'm sure the perfect woman will come along sometime in the distant future. I just want to keep my focus on all the things going on at the office for now."

"Well, that's progress. Last time you said it would never happen. How are you coming with that big project?"

Did I just say that? "So far, so good, except there's one business owner who doesn't want to sell. Hopefully, she'll come around soon."

"Your father mentioned he's planning to bring you in for the meeting in a couple of weeks. Well, if anyone can change her mind it's you."

"Thanks, Mom."

"I'll see you next week, baby. Love you."

"Love you, too, Mom."

Ian disconnected, got his coffee and headed for the room he had set up as an office. He took a seat at his drafting table, picked up the drawing he had started of the senior living complex and added more details. Nowadays designs could be done almost exclusively on the computer, but he still preferred to draw his by hand first. Minutes later, his mind went back to Maya. He tried to push the thoughts aside and focus on his task but gave up after several minutes. He buried his head in his hands. She was getting to him.

He went to his bedroom for socks and tennis shoes, then headed for his small home gym. He hoped the physical exertion would curb his desire for Maya. After an hour, the only thing exhausted was his body. Thoughts of Maya continued to dominate the space in his mind, but he was determined to ignore them. Ian toyed with going out for a swim in the pool, but nixed the idea, since the temperatures had dropped by a good fifteen degrees over the last two days.

He spent the remainder of the day working in his office, stopping only to eat. As he lay in bed that night, memories of making love to Maya and her lingering presence in his room surfaced and filled him with a longing he was helpless to fight. Ian decided that tomorrow—distance be damned—he had to see her.

Sunday afternoon, the moment Maya opened the door and smiled at him, sensations he couldn't describe swirled in the pit of his stomach. He had called her earlier and asked if he could come over.

"Hey," Maya said. "Come on in. Let me get my purse and list, and then we can go."

He followed her inside and closed the door behind him. "List? Exactly how much stuff do you plan to buy? You said you only needed a few items." He had agreed to go shopping with her, which was a testament to how badly he wanted to see her. Ian only shopped out of necessity.

"I do, but I always make a list so I don't forget anything," she called over her shoulder.

What had he gotten himself into? She came back a moment later and he led her out to his car. Once en route, he asked, "Why are you shopping for Christmas decorations so early?"

"Actually, this is late for me."

His eyes left the road briefly to glance at her incredulously.

She laughed. "I put up my decorations the day after Thanksgiving. December tends to be really busy with all the holiday parties, and if I don't do it now, I may not get around to it. Hopefully, I can find everything in one store."

Ian felt his eyes widen. "Do you typically find what you're looking for in one spot?"

"Nope. Most times I end up at six or seven places."

He swallowed hard and tried to keep the panic out of his voice. "You don't plan on going to that many stores today, do you?"

"Of course not. I know most men would rather endure a root canal than go shopping, so I won't torture you. Whatever I don't find today, I'll get tomorrow after I'm done baking."

Thank goodness! "Okay. You mentioned being busier next month. Have you booked many events?" They only had a month left, and for some reason, knowing he might not see her much didn't sit well with him.

"Yes. I have something every week through New Year's. I also have two clients this week for Thanksgiving."

"You're working on Thanksgiving?"

"No. They'll pick up the day before."

"Do you make the desserts for your family, too?"

"Thankfully, no. My mother, aunt and grandmother take care of it. Every year, I have a hard time not jumping in to help. But one look from my grandmother sends me running. What about you? Do you have family here?"

"Yes. We all get together at my parents' house. My mother and several aunts put out a feast. The guys are responsible for the cleanup." He parked in the Cost Plus World Market lot, got out and came around to her side. They walked hand in hand to the store entrance.

"That's a great idea," she said, continuing the conversation. "I think I'll mention it to my mom. She'll *love* it." Maya chuckled. "My dad, on the other hand, probably won't."

"My dad and uncles weren't too keen on the idea, either…until the women threatened to go on strike. Brought them right around." They both laughed. "Wow, there's a lot of stuff in here." Ian glanced around and saw everything from china and flatware to soaps and pillows. He hadn't a clue as to how she would be able to find what she needed…or how long he would have to be in the store. Maya picked up a small basket and moved through the store like a woman with a purpose and seemed to know exactly where she was going. She selected two silver baskets, a set of silver candles and blue candleholders. As they walked toward the back, he noted a wall of wines and a variety of coffees, teas and food.

"Since we're here, you should get some stuff to decorate your house," Maya said.

Ian turned to face her. "I don't know."

"Oh, come on. Don't be such a party pooper," she teased. "You can't tell me being in this store hasn't put you into the holiday spirit."

"Are you coming to help me decorate?" He couldn't tell who was more surprised as the words left his mouth.

"Um…sure, if you want me to."

They stood in awkward silence for a few moments. “There are a couple of angel ornaments over there.” He gestured and quickly walked over to an ornament display and picked up a set of two gold glitter angels with a gem head.

She joined him and smiled. “I bought similar ones last year. I have a glass one and a set of three silver-plated ones. Among several others.”

He shook his head and continued to follow her around as she shopped. Before he knew it, they had gone back for a cart and filled it with decorations for his house. By the time they returned to her house, Ian was more confused than ever about his feelings.

“You can just put those bags by the fireplace with the boxes,” Maya said, entering her condo.

He placed the bags where she indicated and came back to help remove her jacket.

She took it from him and draped it over the back of a chair. “Do you want something to drink?”

“No. The only thing I want is to kiss you.” Ian gathered her in his arms and stared into her eyes, trying to understand why he wanted her so much. He lowered his head and touched his mouth to hers, then captured her lower lip and sucked gently. Her lips parted and his tongue found hers. He kissed her slowly, deeply, feeding from the sweetness within. She moved closer to him and molded her body against his. He shuddered. Suddenly, an emotion unlike anything he had ever experienced spread throughout his chest. He broke off the kiss. “I’d better get going. I have some work to finish for a meeting tomorrow morning.”

Maya stared up at him, seemingly confused. “Okay.”

He donned his jacket, took her hand and walked to the door. “I’ll talk to you later.” Unable to resist, he kissed her once more and slipped out the door. In his car, Ian leaned back against the headrest and closed his eyes. His heart thumped hard in his chest and beads of perspiration dotted his forehead. *What is going on?* The feelings coursing through his body scared the hell out of him. He glanced down at his hands, which were trembling. Taking a deep breath, Ian willed himself calm. It was nothing, he assured himself. Just getting caught up in the holiday spirit brought on from shopping. He'd be back to normal in a couple of hours.

Except he wasn't back to normal hours later. In fact, four days later, his emotions were still running high. Because of her schedule, he and Maya had been playing phone tag all week and had merely exchanged a few texts. Normally, when it came to women, that old adage "out of sight, out of mind" worked perfectly for him. This time, his feelings for her were steadily intensifying despite the lack of communication.

During Thanksgiving dinner, Ian couldn't help noticing the heated looks, subtle touches and secret smiles that passed between his brother and sister-in-law. Chris seemed…content. He glanced around the dining room table and saw the same contentment reflected in the faces of his parents, aunts and uncles, and two of his cousins who were married. For the first time, Ian felt a twinge of jealousy. He toyed with the food on his plate, his appetite rapidly waning, and was more than happy when dinner ended.

"You all right, Ian?" Chris asked when they were alone in the kitchen.

"Yeah, why?"

"You're quieter than usual and you didn't have seconds."

Ian shrugged. "I wanted to save room for dessert."

"That's never stopped you before."

"I just have a lot on my mind with work, that's all."

Chris scrutinized Ian for a lengthy minute. "I see. So, how's Maya?"

"I guess she's fine. I haven't talked to her since Sunday."

"And you're miserable as hell," he said with a chuckle.

"Why would I be miserable? I keep telling you it's not that kind of relationship."

"If you say so. I'm going to get dessert. You coming?"

"In a minute, after I empty the trash."

Chris nodded and left the kitchen.

Ian stared after Chris until the door closed. He braced his hands on the counter and bowed his head. His brother was spot-on, but he had no intention of saying so. Releasing a deep breath, he grabbed up the trash bag. Maya was coming over to help him decorate on Sunday, which gave him three days to get his head back on straight.

Sunday afternoon, Maya parked in Ian's driveway and shut off the engine. Before she made it up the walkway, the door swung open and Ian stood there barefoot, wearing jeans and a T-shirt that molded to his magnificent physique. He unleashed a smile that warmed her all over.

"Hey. Come in." He kissed her and closed the door. "What's in the bag?"

She held up the bag. "I made truffles for a bridal shower. I thought you might like some, so I made a few extra."

He placed his hand on his chest. "A woman after my own heart."

His heart. Was she really after his heart? Although his words were teasing, a tiny part of her wished she did have his heart. She went still.

"Maya?"

She shook her head to clear the errant thought and extended the bag. "So," she said brightly, "are you ready to decorate?"

Ian took the bag, still staring at her curiously. "Yeah. Let me run upstairs and get my shoes and a sweatshirt first. Make yourself comfortable. I'll be right back."

"Okay." As soon as he was gone, Maya covered her mouth in disbelief and paced the floor. Maybe helping Ian decorate was a bad idea. They were behaving like a real couple—the shopping, hand-holding, laughter, decorating—and it was getting to her. All week she'd been wrestling with her growing feelings and she had no idea how to make them stop.

"All right, let's get these lights up outside."

She whirled around at the sound of Ian's voice. "I don't remember you buying any lights."

"I picked them up this week," he said, leading her out to the garage. He pressed a wall switch and two of the three garage doors lifted. "I figured I might as well add the lights, since you talked me into getting those lighted lawn structures."

She helped him carry everything out to the front and waited while he went back for a ladder. Over the next three hours, they strung the lights, arranged and rearranged the lighted lawn decorations. It was near dusk when they finished.

"I think we're done," Ian said. "Be right back." He jogged to the garage, plugged in the lights and jogged back.

"*Wow!* It's beautiful." Maya took in the sight of all

the twinkling white icicle lights bordering the first and second levels, and the single white lights framing the large picture window.

Ian joined her at the curb and slung an arm around her shoulder. “It does look good, huh?” He turned her face toward his and tilted her chin. “Thank you,” he whispered just before taking her mouth in a long, drugging kiss. “Your lips are cold. Let’s get you inside and warm you up.”

Maya shivered from his kiss as much as from the cold. She followed him inside to the kitchen and slid onto a barstool.

“I made chicken soup and thought we could have that and turkey sandwiches.”

“You made soup? From scratch?”

He chuckled. “Yes, but I took a couple of shortcuts. I used store-bought chicken stock, and sautéed the vegetables to give it that simmered-all-day flavor.”

“I’ll have to remember that the next time I make chicken soup.” She laughed and hopped down from the stool. “I need to wash my hands.”

“I’ll have everything ready in a few minutes.” He directed her to the kitchen table when she returned and it wasn’t long before he brought bowls of soup and plates with the sandwiches over.

“Mmm, this smells delicious.”

Ian took the seat at the head of the table. “Hopefully, you’ll say the same thing about the taste.”

Maya spooned up a portion, blew on it for a few seconds to cool it, then put it in her mouth. “This is really good.”

“Thanks.” They ate in silence for a while. “I have one more decorating project I’d like you to help me with before you leave.”

"What's that?"

"My tree."

"Wow, you're really going all out," she said with a smile.

Ian reached for her free hand and stared intently at her. "You inspired me."

The tender look in his eyes rendered her mute momentarily, but she quickly recovered and gently pulled her hand from his. "Aw, I'm glad. That's what friends are for," she added to lighten the mood. They completed the meal while conversing. After cleaning up, he led her into the formal living room, where a live tree at least eight feet tall stood. Boxes of ornaments had been neatly stacked beside it.

Ian rubbed his hands together. "Shall we?" He handed her one box and opened another.

As they hung ornament after ornament, once again, the intimate atmosphere caused an inner turmoil and made her wish for something beyond their original agreement.

"Here, I saved the last one for you."

Maya opened the box and found a beautiful angel tree topper—angelic brown face, silver gown, lace bodice adorned with pearls and shimmering sequins, and cascading organza ribbon.

"I know how much you love angels."

She was in deep, deep trouble. With his help, she climbed the ladder, placed the angel in her spot, climbed down and waited while he lit the tree. "It's lovely."

"I couldn't agree more," he whispered.

Maya turned to find his gaze locked on her.

"One last touch." He produced a small cellophane package from behind his back and held it up.

"Is that…?"

"Yep. Gotta have a little mistletoe." Ian lowered his head. "Maya," he murmured against her lips, "will you help me christen my tree?"

Her mind screamed *no!* But her body answered with a resounding yes. He undressed them both and drew her down to the carpet in front of the tree. When he kissed her again, she locked her arms around his neck and forgot about everything except the pleasure he was giving her.

Chapter 8

A week later, Maya put the final touches on the chocolate torte and packed it, along with a strawberry cheesecake and the individual three-layer red velvet cake slices the host wanted for each of her dinner guests. She stifled a yawn brought on by another night of restless sleep. She hadn't slept well since the night she and Ian made love in front of his Christmas tree. Everything about that night was different. Their lovemaking was no less intense, but the way he touched and kissed her felt different. And when their eyes locked…she knew she had fallen in love with him. Maya braced her hands on the table in front of her. How could she have allowed her emotions to get involved? She had lain awake every night asking herself the same question and wondering how to keep him from finding out.

"Hey, girl. You just about ready?" Rhonda asked, breezing into the room.

"I just need to add the rest of these cake slices."

"I know there's an extra piece, right?"

"Yes, Rhonda. You only asked about it ten times," Maya said with a laugh, closing the container. "Help me load this in my car and you can get your cake."

"Gladly." Rhonda picked up one storage container and Maya grabbed the other. "Are we still on for dinner tomorrow night or do you and Ian have another hot Saturday night planned?" she asked with a giggle.

"Yes, we're still on. We have that meeting with EJJ Development on Monday and I want to be prepared." She couldn't afford a distraction right now, and Ian was definitely a huge one. She and Rhonda were going to work on a strategy over dinner tomorrow night.

"I don't know how we're going to fight this, Maya," she said with a deep sigh, placing the container in the back of Maya's SUV.

"I don't know, either. But I *do* know that I'm not going to lie down and let them run roughshod all over me." She was trying to remain positive but knew she faced an uphill battle.

"I hear you. Anyway, how are things with Ian?"

"Okay, I guess," Maya said nonchalantly. But Rhonda could read her like a book.

Rhonda studied Maya, then brought her hands to her mouth. "Oh, my God. You've fallen for him, haven't you?"

She dropped her head and heaved a deep sigh. "I don't know what I'm going to do. This wasn't supposed to happen."

"Does he know?"

Her head snapped up. "Of course not. What we have will be over at the end of the month. He doesn't want anything past that and neither do I."

"Are you sure? I know you were hurt before, but—"

"No *buts*. This was nothing more than a holiday fling, and that's all it will be."

"What about him? Are you certain he doesn't want more?"

Her mind went back to their last encounter. No, she wasn't sure, but she didn't want to take a chance. "It doesn't matter." Maya closed the hutch. "I'd better get going. I'll see you in the morning."

"Okay. I'll lock up…after I get my cake, that is."

She chuckled and the two women embraced. "Bye, crazy woman."

"Bye, and you need to think twice about shutting Ian down cold. From what you've told me, he sounds like a nice guy."

"Whatever," she mumbled, rolling her eyes and getting into the car. Yeah, he was a nice guy, and so much more than what she had been expecting when she met him a month ago.

Ian called on Sunday and wanted to come over. She knew there would be no way to hide her feelings, so she let it go to voice mail. By the next morning, Maya still had no clue how to deal with her feelings. Every moment they had spent together played over and over in her mind, particularly the last time. Something had changed between them—from the possessive way he'd held her to the way he'd tenderly washed her body when they had showered—and the shift was palpable. *Stop thinking about him! You have more important things to focus on...like saving your business.*

Forcing her mind back to the task in front of her, she filled gift-box molds with melted chocolate and placed them on a shelf in the walk-in freezer. The boxes would be decorated with FDA-approved, food-grade edible luster dust and pearls, and filled with chocolate truffles for wedding shower gifts. Next, she made dough for cinnamon rolls. The shop would open in two hours, and the rolls were her bestselling product in the morning.

"So, I'm wondering, will the dough still rise if you keep beating it like that?" Rhonda's amused voice asked from the doorway.

Maya's hands froze. She glanced down and realized that she had been brutally attacking the dough. She began again, this time kneading the dough with a little less force.

"Are you worried about the meeting this afternoon or Ian?"

"A little of both, I guess."

"Ian is easy. See where the relationship goes." Rhonda came and placed her arm around Maya's shoulder. "I wish I could assure you we're going to come out winners this afternoon, but I'm worried, too. Last night, I did a little more research on eminent domain and I don't think they have a case."

"Maybe, but if the city sees a way to make big money, they won't care." She placed the dough in a bowl to rise and washed her hands. "I don't want to talk about it anymore. Four o'clock will be here soon enough."

"You're right. I would offer to help you bake, but..." She laughed. "How about I put the truffles in the chocolate boxes and package them? You'd think I had learned something after all these years of hanging around you, but hey...we all have our talents."

"Yeah, well," Maya said with a shrug. "I'll take any help I can get. Thanks."

The women worked steadily until opening time.

After the morning rush, Maya took a quick breather before prepping for her next event. She was so focused it took her a moment to realize her cell was ringing. She wiped her hands on a towel and hurried across the kitchen to catch it.

"Hey, baby," Ian said when she answered. "How's your day going?"

"Hey. Busy. Really busy." She hadn't looked at the display before answering.

"More catering jobs?"

"Yeah. I have two this week."

"Any chance we can get together later today? There's something I want to talk to you about."

Her heart rate kicked up. "It sounds important. What is it?"

"I don't want to say over the phone and yes, it's very important."

She glanced over at the wall clock. "It's eleven now. I may be able to meet you for a few minutes around two, unless something comes up. I have to get back for an appointment at four. Can I call you around one to let you know for sure?"

"That's fine. I have to go out to check on a work site, but I'll have my cell."

"Okay." She disconnected and tapped the phone against her chin. What was so important that he couldn't tell her over the phone? Was he ending their affair? The timer on the oven went off, drawing her out of her thoughts. "I'll find out soon enough."

Ian leaned back in his chair and rotated it toward the window. There was so much he wanted to say to Maya and he had to do it face-to-face. Somewhere along the way his feelings changed and she had slowly eased into his heart. He sensed it when they went shopping, but he knew for sure after they made love on his living room floor in front of the tree. It was the first one he had put up in the three years he'd lived in the house. He didn't want their affair to end. He wanted to talk to her about something more long-term. He checked his watch. Landon, one of the other architects, would be at Ian's office any minute to accompany Ian to the construction site of an office complex. He rose to his feet and walked over to retrieve his jacket just as a knock sounded.

"Perfect timing," he said, opening the door. "Chris. I thought you were Landon."

"You have a minute?"

"Not really. What's up?"

"I wanted to talk to you about the meeting this afternoon."

"Can it wait?"

"No."

Ian glanced around Chris's shoulder when Landon appeared in the door. "Well, it'll have to, big brother. Gotta go."

"Ian, wait. I think you should—"

He waved his brother off. "Whatever it is, I'll be ready for it. Be back later."

Out at the work site, he and Landon met with the construction foreman, walked through the building and compared the structure to the blueprints. Ian kept checking his watch, anxious to see Maya.

"Looks like we're on schedule. Excuse me a moment," he said when his cell rang. Ian walked a few steps away, checked the display and smiled upon seeing

Maya's name. "Hey, sweetheart. Where are we meeting?"

"I'm sorry, Ian, but I won't be able to meet you. My shipment was mistakenly left off the truck and I have to go to UPS to pick it up. I need it for tomorrow. Can we talk tomorrow?"

He ran a hand over his head and muttered a curse. "What about tonight? I can come to your house later."

"I have an appointment at four."

"I know. I have a late meeting at work, too. I can come by afterward. Six thirty?"

"All right. I have to go."

"I'll see you later."

"Ian?"

Ian spun around at the sound of Landon's voice.

"I think we might have a problem."

He stifled a groan. This was all he needed today.

By the time they made it back, Ian had five minutes to get cleaned up for the meeting with the lone holdout. He hurried to his office and used his private bathroom to change.

Chris met him on the way to the conference room. "Ian, there's something you should know before going in the meeting."

"You always say that," he joked. "I promise to be on my best behavior and bring out all the charm needed to get this deal done." He reached for the doorknob and Chris placed a staying hand on his arm. "Man, would you relax?" Ian said with a chuckle. "Now come on. We're already late." He opened the door and froze. His smile faded and his eyes widened when he saw the two women seated at the table. *No, no, no.* His stomach dropped. "Maya?" he whispered.

She slowly came to her feet. "Ian?"

Ian turned back and met his brother's grim expression.

"Sorry, bro."

He turned back to Maya. Her expression went from shock to anger in a flash.

Ian's father cleared his throat. "Ah, Ms. Brooks, I see you've already met my youngest son, Ian. With him is my oldest son, Christopher. If you all take your seats we can get started."

Maya's angry gaze never left Ian's. "There's no need. Hell will freeze over before I sell you my shop," she gritted out. She snatched up her papers and purse and stormed past Ian out the still-open door.

Ian rushed after her. "Maya, wait." He reached out and caught her arm.

She snatched out of his grasp. "Don't touch me!"

"Maya, I'm sorry. I—"

"This is just another building to you, but it's *my life.* I will lose *everything.* You conspire to force me out of my business and the best you can do is *I'm sorry*? Are you sorry enough to drop this whole thing and let me keep my shop?"

His jaw tightened, but he remained silent.

"That's what I thought."

"Maya. I didn't know."

"And next you're going to tell me you knew nothing about this deal," she said sarcastically.

"Yes. Wait, no." Ian scrubbed an agitated hand down his face, took a deep breath and started again. "Yes, I knew about the deal. No, I didn't know your shop was the holdout."

"This whole relationship was one big lie." Maya chuckled mirthlessly. "So that was the important news.

At least now I know why you wanted to talk to me so bad." She turned and started down the hallway again.

The tears standing in her eyes were killing him. He stepped in front of her, blocking her path. "No, baby. That's not what I wanted to tell you. You have to believe me, Maya. I *didn't* know and nothing about our relationship has been a lie." He cradled her face between his palms. "I wanted to tell you, I love you. I love you, Maya."

She said nothing for several charged seconds, and for a brief moment her gaze softened before going cold again. "Nice try."

"I'm very serious. I do love you," he reiterated. Ian blew out another long breath. "I know you're really angry right now and I'm worried about you. Let me drive you home."

"I don't need anything from you, least of all your concern," she snapped. "Just stay away from me." She stepped around him and rushed down the hall.

This time he let her go. He stared after her, feeling like his heart was breaking. Ian let the wall take his weight, closed his eyes and banged his head softly against it. How could this happen?

"Mr. Jeffries?"

Ian opened his eyes and straightened from the wall. It was the woman who had sat next to Maya. She had smooth honey-brown skin, was tall, slender and moved with the grace of a model striding down a runway.

She extended her hand. "I'm Rhonda Davis, Maya's best friend and business partner."

"Call me Ian," he said, taking the proffered hand. "I'm sorry we have to meet under these circumstances." He pulled a business card from his pocket and handed it to her. "Can you please let me know that Maya made it home safe? I'm concerned about her. I'd call myself, but right now I'm the last person she wants to talk to."

She studied him for a moment. "You've fallen in love with Maya, haven't you?"

"Yes. I just realized that I love her more than anything."

She hesitated, then took the card. "I'll see what I can do." She turned and walked away.

He stood in the hallway a moment longer before going back to the conference room.

"Looks like your relationship with Ms. Brooks is going to work in our favor," his father said as soon as Ian entered. "Your brother tells me you've been seeing her a few weeks."

"Yes."

"Good, good. Keep wooing her. Do whatever it takes to get this deal closed."

Ian shook his head. "I can't do that, Dad. I won't hurt her like that."

His father sat up in his chair. "What do you mean, you can't do it?" he gritted out. "You're going to let some woman you just met come between you and your obligation to this company? We've offered her almost twice what that shop is worth, so I don't understand her problem."

"Dad," Chris jumped in, "you know that's not fair."

Ian braced his hands on the desk. "Dad, you know as well as I do how hard it would be to start over if she has to move."

"This is about business. We can't afford to disappoint our investors. They've put up a lot of money and expect results."

"So has Maya," he countered. "Even with the amount we offered, she may not be able to recover her losses. Put yourself in her shoes. How would you feel if someone asked you to uproot your life?"

His father sighed heavily. "Ian, I understand what you're saying, but I don't see any way out for Ms. Brooks." He stood and walked to the door. "I'm sorry, son."

When the door closed behind his father, Ian slammed his hand on the table, spun around and let out a frustrated groan. "Why didn't you tell me, Chris?"

"I tried to tell you earlier, but you wouldn't listen. And before you jump down my throat, I only found out this morning when Sam dropped the file off in my office. I take it she's pretty mad."

"And hurt. She thinks I orchestrated the whole relationship to get her shop." He paced the room. "I love her, Chris. I can't make her lose her shop. It'll destroy her." He stopped, braced his hands on the table again and bowed his head. "I feel like this is a repeat of last time."

"This is nothing like last time, Ian. Laura tried to steal blueprints for her brother's company so they could win a bid. The only blueprint stolen this time was the one to your heart." He chuckled. "I guess I was right about that love bug biting you in the butt, huh?"

Ian angled his head and smiled faintly. "Guess so. But it doesn't matter now. If I close this deal I'll lose her for sure. If I help her keep it, I can kiss my career goodbye. Dad will have me stuck drawing closets for the rest of my life."

Chis placed a hand on Ian's shoulder. "You're one of the smartest people I know. If anybody can come up with a solution, it's you. I'll see you later."

He nodded. "Tell Shellie hello." Alone, Ian sank

into the closest chair and buried his head in his hands. Money notwithstanding, relocating meant that Maya couldn't take orders and would likely lose most of her clientele, and like she'd said, it could potentially destroy her business. He couldn't see any way out of this mess and didn't know what he was going to do. The only thing he knew for sure was that he couldn't…*wouldn't* let the woman he loved lose her livelihood.

Chapter 9

Maya dropped down on the sofa in her condo and swiped at the tears that hadn't stopped since she left the office complex. "There's no way I can survive a move, not in this economy. All my clients…"

Rhonda sat next to her and offered a box of tissues. "Are you going to be okay?"

She snatched out two tissues. "I'm about to lose my business and the man I foolishly fell in love with set me up. I'm just *great*."

"Sarcasm doesn't look good on you."

"I'm sorry," she said, leaning her head back against the couch. "It's not your fault that I keep finding losers." She let out a frustrated groan. "I can't believe he set me up like that. Everything, from the first night until now, was nothing more than an elaborate plan to get me to sell my building."

"For what it's worth, I don't think Ian knew it was your building. He seemed genuinely surprised."

"Yeah, right."

"No, seriously, Maya. His face registered the same shock as yours when he walked into that conference room. And he cares about you."

Maya glared at Rhonda. "Just whose side are you on? You're supposed to be *my* best friend."

Rhonda sighed. "You know I'm on your side, but the man is worried about you. He even wanted to make sure you got home okay."

She rolled her eyes. "It's all an act."

"You don't believe that any more than I do. I saw the way he looked at you. And he told me he loves you."

"I don't know what to believe right now." His declaration of love still resonated with her, but she wasn't sure if she could trust his words.

"On another note, you were right. He is definitely chiseled chocolate. His brother is just as fine. Do you know if he's single?"

She skewered Rhonda with a look.

"Okay, okay. Now's not the time. What are you going to do about Ian?"

"Nothing. We're done."

"Come on, Maya. Don't judge him too harshly. Like I said, I think he really cares about you. At the very least, give him a chance to explain." She shrugged. "You never know, he might be willing to help you."

"I don't want to talk about it anymore," she mumbled.

Rhonda gave Maya's hand an assuring squeeze and stood. "Things will work out. I'm going home. Call me if you need me."

Maya slowly came to her feet. "I'll be fine." She saw her friend to the door, then trudged down the hall to her bedroom. She should have stuck to her decision after that first night. Now, not only was everything she'd worked so hard to build in jeopardy, but she had also gotten her heart broken…again.

She moved around her shop the next morning in a haze. Sleepless nights and 4:00 a.m. days didn't go well together. She had ruined one batch of dough already, which put her behind schedule, and she tried to focus so as not to mess up the batch currently in front of her. After getting the cinnamon rolls in the oven, she made the custard for the fruit tarts and cupcakes for an elementary school class party that would be picked up later that morning.

"Morning, Ms. Brooks."

Maya stifled a groan. She had forgotten that the part-time culinary student she'd hired started today. "Hi, Phoebe." Twenty-two years old and barely five feet, Phoebe possessed a lively personality and enthusiasm for baking that had won Maya over immediately. Before Maya could say anything else, the young woman pulled a chef's jacket, hair net and toque from a tote bag. Maybe this was a good thing.

"What do you want me to do? I'm so excited about working with you. You make the most amazing chocolates."

She smiled. "Follow me." She put Phoebe to work and went out front to start filling the display cases. By the time she opened at seven, Maya was so impressed by the young woman that she considered hiring her permanently. That is, if she still had a place for her to work. Shaking off that negative thought, she put a smile on her face and greeted the first customers.

"Girl, it's busy in here today," Rhonda whispered two hours later as she passed Maya on the way to the register.

Maya was grateful for her customers and enjoyed

every moment of the sweat and tears she poured into Maya's Sweet Spot. The thought of it all going away caused a deep pain in her soul and she had to force down the emotions that threatened to rise again.

"Maya."

She whirled around. "What are you doing here?" she whispered. Ian stood on the other side of the counter wearing a navy suit, looking as good as he had the night they first met. Her traitorous body reacted to his nearness almost immediately.

"I had to make sure you were okay."

Maya wanted nothing more than to jump over the counter and into his arms. Determined not to let him see how much he affected her, she said, "I'm fine."

"That makes one of us," he murmured before glancing around the shop. "I see your decorating skills extend beyond your home. It's very festive and warm. I like the angel on the counter."

Ian moved closer to the counter and she instinctively moved back. Even with the display case between them, she could still feel his heat.

"I need to talk to you."

"I'm really busy."

"Baby, I just need five minutes. There are only three people in here right now and I'm sure Ms. Davis can handle things. Please," he added when she hesitated.

She peeked over her shoulder and found Rhonda viewing the exchange with mild amusement. "We can talk in my office." She led him back to her office, closed the door and waited for him to speak.

He came and placed his hands on her shoulders. "I know you think I engineered some kind of plan to seduce you into selling your building, but I didn't. I would never knowingly try to destroy your career. And, sweetheart, nothing about what we shared was fake. It's the most real thing in my life. I don't want what we have to end, Maya. I meant what I said yesterday and I'm going to keep saying it until you believe me. I love you. I love you more than anything and I promise I won't let you lose your dream, even if I have to build you another shop myself." He placed a small gift bag that she hadn't noticed he was carrying on her desk. "I know you have to get back to work. I'll see you later." He brushed his lips across hers and exited, closing the door softly behind him.

She wrapped her arms around her midsection and took several deep breaths to slow her heart rate. Even though she was still hurt, Ian had a way of getting to her. Turning slightly, Maya lifted the bag and took out a wrapped box. She carefully removed the paper and opened the plain brown box. Her breath caught. Inside was a carved wooden box with Maya's Sweet Spot engraved on the front. The moment she lifted the lid, her favorite Christmas song, "Silent Night"—not the typical windup music box version, but the version by The Temptations—began to play. She couldn't stop the tears from falling. He remembered. How was she going to let him go?

By the end of the week, Maya was beyond exhausted. She placed her purse and tote on the coffee table and collapsed on the sofa to open the package that had been left for her at the complex office. She hadn't ordered anything and didn't see a return address. She pulled out the attached note card and read: *An angel for my angel. Something to add to your collection.* Puzzled, she tore off the gift wrap and opened the box. "Oh, my," she whispered in awe. She couldn't believe it. Ian had sent her a Swarovski crystal angel ornament. She carefully removed it and placed it on her tree. The crystal caught the light and burst into a kaleidoscope of color. It was absolutely beautiful. She went back to the note. *His angel*. Her heart leaped. She hadn't seen or spoken to Ian since he walked out of her shop three days ago with his words of love and a promise to help her. Maya's gaze strayed back to the ornament again. She still wanted him…and loved him with every fiber of her being. She prayed the rest would work itself out.

Chapter 10

For the remainder of the week Ian divided his time between keeping up with his workload and researching a workable solution to the condo project. He searched websites for similar projects, trying to come up with something that would satisfy all parties, but he was unsuccessful. He also hadn't made any headway with Maya. She hadn't returned any of his calls since he walked out of her shop. He wanted to talk to her, touch her and hold her in his arms. He missed kissing her and yes, making love with her. As a result, he was frustrated, horny and miserable.

Ian leaned against the door frame of his living room staring at the Christmas tree and thinking about Maya's shop. It was small, but very functional and she had maximized her space. With her warm personality, she had created an inviting space. The architect in him could already visualize ways to expand the area to include a few tables and maybe a coffee and tea bar that would encourage customers to sit and enjoy her delectable pastries. She was also correct about it being located in the perfect spot. The combination of residential homes and commercial buildings, along with accessibility to the main highway, gave her a built-in clientele. It was one of the deciding factors when they chose that spot to house the condo project. Ensuring that the project went through would go a long way in boosting Ian's career. But advancing his career at the expense of hers was something he could not do. When he saw her that first night, the only thing on his mind had been the sex. He never planned on wanting her so completely. Never imagined falling in love. But he had. And he knew she loved him, too. He couldn't lose her.

Pushing off the wall, he headed to his home office. He was in for another long night, but Christmas was two weeks away and he was determined to spend it with Maya. Three hours later, still no closer to an answer, he stumbled from his office and fell across his bed fully clothed.

When he arrived at work the next morning, Ian needed a double shot of caffeine to get his mind working. He deposited his laptop bag and blueprints on his desk and headed directly down the hall to the coffee room. Fifteen minutes and one cup later, the haze around his brain began to clear. While he was searching the internet, an article caught his attention. He clicked on the link and started reading. His eyes moved rapidly across the screen. A smile curved his mouth and he hit the intercom.

"Yes, Mr. Brooks," his assistant answered.

"Ms. Smith, can you please set up an emergency meeting with all the investors on the Sutton Park condo project for Monday morning at eleven. Include my dad and Chris. When you're done, I need your help."

"I'll be in as soon as everything is set."

"Thank you." He hit the off button and rolled up his sleeves. He had a lot of work ahead of him but was confident he could pull it off.

Chris cornered Ian when he entered the conference room Monday morning. "What's going on?"

"Take a seat and you'll find out in a minute."

Chris eyed him skeptically, but Ian merely smiled and gestured for Chris to take a seat. He took a quick glance at the wall clock and called the meeting to order. "Good morning, ladies and gentlemen. Thank you for agreeing to meet on such short notice. I know you are all anxious to know why I called the meeting, so let's get started."

He waited a moment for his secretary to pass out the information packets, then turned on the projector. "There has been some concern about the one holdout on the Sutton Park project, and I believe I've come up with a way that will satisfy both parties. Your vision for this property is one of elegance and comfort. I'd like to add *convenience*. How many times have you forgotten something at the store and had to drive miles to get it?" Several people nodded. "What about going to the dry cleaner's?" He nodded at his secretary, who passed around plates holding a mini cinnamon roll and truffle. Ian smiled at the expressions of delight on each person's face as they all bit into the tasty treats. "And what if you were able to get these pastries and desserts every day?"

"Why, this truffle tastes like the ones I get from Maya's Sweet Spot," Mr. Capshaw said. "Ms. Brooks makes the best desserts around."

"I'm glad you feel that way, Mr. Capshaw. I'm not sure you knew this, but Maya's Sweet Spot was our holdout."

Mr. Capshaw's eyes widened.

Now that he had their attention, Ian flipped through the screens showing the redesigned property that included a minimarket, a dry cleaner's and a bakery. "Just think what it would mean to have Maya's breakfast goodies available within minutes of waking up." He continued citing the advantages, and by the time he finished, the group voted unanimously in favor of the new design.

Ian had scaled one hurdle, but the most important one was yet to come. The text he had been waiting for came an hour later. He walked down the hall to his father's office. "Dad, I need to leave for the rest of the afternoon."

"I'm proud of you, son. I wasn't sure you could pull it off, but you were brilliant. Going to celebrate?" he asked with a chuckle.

"Not quite. I have a more personal matter."

His father's brow lifted. "This wouldn't have anything to do with Ms. Brooks, would it?"

Ian grinned. "Yes, it would. And if I'm lucky, Mom just might get that second daughter she's been campaigning for," he added with a wink. He sauntered out, leaving his dad with his mouth hanging open.

Maya kept checking her phone all weekend hoping Ian would call. She loved him and missed him. But by Monday, she had given up all hope that the relationship could be salvaged. She had not heard anything from his company, either, and resigned herself to the fact that she would, most likely, end up having to rebuild her business again somewhere else. There was no way she could win the fight. And with economic times being the way they were, she would be lucky to survive the upheaval. Maya locked the shop and went home. She parked in her spot, started up the walkway and stopped short.

"What in the world?" She approached the mounds of white covering the grass in front of her door. Not believing her eyes, she bent and touched it just to be sure. "Snow."

"You said the only thing missing from Christmas was snow. I took a chance that it wouldn't melt before you got home in this sixty-degree weather."

She turned to face Ian. "I can't believe… How did you…"

Ian slowly walked toward her. "I had it brought down from the mountains. I'd bring you the mountain if I could."

"I love you," she blurted.

He stopped. "What did you say?"

Her heart raced with excitement and she felt like screaming it to the heavens. "I love you."

He closed the remaining distance, hauled her into his arms and crushed his mouth against hers. She didn't care that they were standing on the sidewalk, only that he was here.

"Can we go inside?"

"Yes, of course."

Ian followed her a few steps, then stopped. "I need to get something out of my car. I'll be right back."

She watched him jog back down the path and smiled. He came back holding two tubes. "What's in there?"

"Let's go in and I'll show you."

They entered and he unrolled the papers from the first tube and placed it on the coffee table. She realized immediately that it was an architectural blueprint. She took a seat on the sofa and leaned forward to study the drawing. There were several rooms with one word written in each one. She scooted closer. “What is this? Why do all the rooms have my name in them?”

He lowered himself to one knee next to her. “Because this is the blueprint to my heart, and you own every room inside it.”

Her heart stopped for a second before starting up again.

He withdrew a small box from his pocket and opened it. The princess-cut center stone was surrounded by round accent diamonds with elaborate vintage sculpting along the sides and front. “Marry me, Maya. I love you and I will honor, protect and cherish you all the days of my life. And I’ll do my best to turn your every dream into reality.”

She was off the couch and in his arms as soon as the words were off his tongue. “Yes, yes, yes!” She lifted his face and kissed him with a passion that left them both gasping for air.

Still trying to catch his breath, Ian said, “I have one more thing to show you.”

Maya eased back onto the sofa and waited while he opened the second tube. More blueprints. These were far more complicated than the first set.

“This is the condo project.”

“Oh,” she said dejectedly, the joy of the previous moment now waning.

Ian chuckled. “You don’t have to sound so sad, sweetheart. I promise you’ll like it.” He pointed to a section. “I redesigned the project to add corporate space.”

Her heart rate kicked up again. “What does that mean?”

"It means that Maya's Sweet Spot will not be relocated. I presented this to the investors earlier and they approved it. There will also be a minimarket and a dry cleaner's."

She brought her hands to her mouth and tried to process what he was saying.

"I also took the liberty of redesigning the shop, to expand it a little and give you room to add a few tables and maybe a coffee or tea bar, so people can sit and enjoy their treats. You may have to close a few days to get it done, but—"

She launched herself at him again and held him tight. "I don't know what to say. Thank you, thank you."

"I love you so much, baby. Whatever you want, I'll get it if it's in my power."

Tears streamed down her face. She caressed his face and held his gaze intently. "I just want you, Ian Jeffries. I love you." And he owned every room in her heart, too.

Epilogue

Two years later

Maya took a slow tour around her newly designed shop. "I can't believe it," she whispered over and over.

"Girl, your hubby did his *thing* with this shop!" Rhonda said, coming to stand next to her.

"Yes, he did." Ian had designed the space to include a dozen or so tables and the coffee and tea bar, and made sure she had Wi-Fi for those patrons who wanted to enjoy their pastries while working. Her kitchen had also been enlarged with an additional oven and more counter work space. Maya had never thought she could be this happy.

"Do you know how many orders we've gotten for Christmas?" Rhonda had been working overtime to create brochures and postcards for every resident in the six-hundred-unit property.

"I can imagine. I'm glad I hired Phoebe full-time."

"With all these orders, you may have to hire some part-time help for the holidays." Rhonda nudged Maya. "Your sexy husband is coming in the door. Girl, the way he's looking at you, I hope he doesn't burn the place down before we have the grand opening. I'm going in the back to help Phoebe. Hi, Ian. Bye, Ian."

Maya chuckled and watched Rhonda disappear around the corner.

"Does this meet with your approval, Mrs. Jeffries?"

She spun around at the sound of Ian's voice and smiled. "It more than meets my approval, Mr. Jeffries. It's incredible," she said, spreading her arms and gesturing around the shop. "I don't know how to thank you."

Ian closed the distance between them and pulled her into his embrace. He placed a tender kiss on her lips. "I know the perfect way to thank me."

She looped her arms around his neck and gave him a sultry smile. "Is that right?"

He nodded and a wolfish gleam lit his eyes. Bending close to her ear, he whispered, "Bring home two cups of the black-and-white parfait and I'll show you."

She remembered every vivid detail of their first night together, and just like then, heat thrummed through her. "That sounds like an offer I can't refuse."

"I love you, Maya Jeffries. You were and still are the best Christmas gift I ever received. I can't wait to have you under my tree again."

"Neither can I." She pulled his head down and kissed him with all the love she felt flowing through her heart. Of all the gifts he had given her, his love was the sweetest one.

* * * * *

HER CONVENIENT CHRISTMAS DATE

BARBARA WALLACE

To all the square pegs in the world.
May we love our edges.

CHAPTER ONE

THE BAR WAS one of those pop-up, themed locations that were trendy at the moment. Holiday Cheer was the name and its existence had temporarily transformed the mezzanine of the Regis Hotel into a garish, yet strangely enticing Christmas wonderland. The walls were made entirely of poinsettia blossoms, while strings of holiday lights crisscrossed the air like tiny multicolored stars.

In the middle of the cheer, at a bar framed by Christmas trees, Susan Collier was having a deep, meaningful conversation with her cocktail glass.

"So what if I don't have a date? It's not like I have the plague. Plenty of women go to weddings without a plus-one."

Her cocktail, the sympathetic ear that it was, didn't disagree.

Too bad Ginger and Courtney weren't as sympathetic. The two catty little trolls from marketing enjoyed a good laugh about her while powdering their noses. So good, in fact, they didn't realize Susan was in the stall listening to every word.

"Is it any wonder?" one of them had said. "She's got a perpetual stick up her bum. I don't know why Maria invited her to the wedding in the first place."

"I should fire them both for insubordination," Susan muttered. The cocktail offered itself up in mute solidarity. Lifting the glass, she polished off the contents in one swallow.

"You're drinking those pretty quickly. Sure you don't want to slow down?" the bartender asked when she signaled for another.

"Didn't realize there was a speed limit." She tapped the rim of her empty glass with her index finger. "Keep 'em coming. And, if you're worried about me toddling off and driving, don't. I used a car service." Because that was what women without dates did. They car serviced.

"Aren't you afraid they'll miss you upstairs?"

Susan snorted. Did he mean the wedding to which she'd received an obligatory invitation just because her office was next to the bride's? The one for which she had stuffed herself into shapeware and a vintage dress with the hopes it would make her Kardashianesque rear end look its best? Doubtful.

"Just make the drink," she told him.

"All right. But don't say I didn't warn you," the man replied.

Warning taken. Whatever the warning was.

She didn't know why she'd bothered attending this wedding in the first place. If Maria Borromeo hadn't been one of the few people who was moderately friendly toward her, Susan would have canceled when her brother Linus backed out of being her date. No one would have cared then any more than they would care if she spent the entire reception sucking back gin cocktails in the bar.

She knew her reputation. *Shrewsan*, they called her

when they didn't think she was listening. It was no secret she was the least popular Collier at Collier's Soap. Her brothers—half brothers, that is—inherited all the positive Collier traits. Things like the Collier charm and lanky athletic good looks. She, on the other hand, didn't get the Collier anything. Nor did she get any of the good Quinn characteristics either, as her mother used to love pointing out. Except perhaps a passing resemblance to a great-aunt Ruth, the dumpy one.

The bartender returned with another red cocktail with an extra cherry this time. Susan forgave him for his earlier question. He was a good guy, Mr. Bartender. She liked how his red flannel shirt and neat white beard matched the Christmas decor.

"What do you call this thing anyway?" she asked him when he set the drink down. The cocktail list had been full of cute holiday-themed names that she hadn't bothered to read, zeroing in on the first one that listed gin instead.

"A Christmas Wish," he replied. "Guaranteed to make your wishes come true."

Susan barked out a laugh. "You mean if I drink enough of these I'll meet Prince Charming?"

"Is that what you want?"

"Hardly." Clearly he wasn't as good a listener as her cocktail friend. Cinderella Complexes were for the Gingers and Courtneys of the world. She was rich and successful in her own right, and her half brothers weren't wicked. "I'm not waiting for some man to rush in and rescue me from my miserable existence."

Although every once in a while…

She stared deep into the contents of the glass where tiny bubbles rose from the bottom. Every once in a while she wished there was someone who really understood her. Her brothers…they loved her, but great as they were, they didn't really "get" her. They didn't understand what it was like to be the perpetual square peg in a round hole, always pretending she fit.

How lovely it would be to share her life with someone who saw the truth. With whom she could fit without having to pretend. Who thought her beautiful and special, warts and all.

She was getting maudlin. And the room was spinning. Maybe the bartender was right and she'd had enough. Why else would she be wishing for things that weren't ever going to happen?

"Hey, mate, do me a favor and get me a glass of soda water, will you?"

A tall, perfectly carved physical specimen of a man approached the bar, his face dripping wet. From the red stain on his shirt collar, Susan guessed he'd been the recipient of a Christmas Wish square in the face.

"Word of advice," he said to the bartender, his words coated in a Yorkshire accent. "Before you agree to be in a wedding, make sure you haven't hooked up with anyone on the guest list."

"Ran into a bitter ex-girlfriend, did you?"

"Two. And they compared notes." He grabbed a stack of cocktail napkins and began wiping the liquid from his face.

"Must have been *some* notes," she muttered.

He looked in her direction for the first time. "You're not going to lob your drink at me too, are you?"

"Why would I do that?"

"I dunno. Female solidarity or something. You're

here for Hank and Maria's wedding, right? For all I know, they're your friends too."

"That would require me to have friends." Had she said that out loud?

He arched his brow in a mixture of half surprise, half curiosity. Oh, well, too late to take the comment back now. Besides, it was the truth. She didn't have friends. She had family, she had colleagues and she had acquaintances, but friends? That would involve allowing people closer than arm's length, an impossible task when you were a square peg. It was hard enough trying to pretend your edges didn't matter.

"Sounds like I'm not the only one who got burned tonight. Weddings aren't the fun people make them out to be, are they? Unless you're the bride and groom, that is, and even then… Thanks, mate."

The bartender had returned with the soda water along with a white cloth napkin. "No problem. I don't suppose I can get an autograph when you finish? I'm a huge fan. That stop you made against Germany a few years ago? I've never seen anything like it."

"Thanks. Definitely a finer moment than this one."

Ah. Susan recognized him now. This was the infamous Lewis Matolo. Maria mentioned her fiancé knew the former footballer. She'd been in a downright tizzy over his attendance at the wedding. Matolo, or "Champagne Lewis" as the tabloids called him, came with a reputation. Then again, if your nickname involved alcohol, that was probably a given. He'd gotten the moniker after they snapped his picture leaving a London nightclub, shirtless, with a woman under each arm and an open bottle of Cristal in each hand. From what Susan had read, it wasn't an unusual occurrence.

She watched as he dipped a corner into the glass and began dabbing at a red spot on the front of his shirt. Sadly, he didn't succeed in doing anything more than turning the spot into a damp pink stain.

"You're going to need detergent," Susan told him. "Otherwise, all you're doing is making it worse."

He looked up through his long lashes. "Are you sure?"

"I own a soap company. Trust me." Scented soaps and moisturizers hardly made her an expert. More like she tended to dribble food down her front. But being a soap mogul sounded better.

"You own a… Oh, you're Maria's boss. Hank mentioned you."

Oh, good. That made two of them whose reputations preceded them. "Susan Collier, at your service," she said, saluting him with her glass.

He nodded, apparently assuming it wasn't necessary to offer a name in return. "So what's got you holed up avoiding the good times in the ballroom, Susan Collier? Shouldn't you be upstairs dancing with your date?"

"I didn't come with a date."

"Sorry."

Not him too. Why was everyone suddenly sorry for her dating status all of a sudden? "For your information, I could get a date if I wanted one. I chose not to. A woman is not defined by her dating record."

She tried to punctuate her statement with a wave of her arm only to come dangerously close to needing her own damp cloth. To make amends for her clumsiness, she took a healthy sip. These drinks were delicious.

"Again, okay. I only meant sorry for presuming.

Didn't mean to touch a nerve." Hands up in appeasement, he backed a few inches away.

From his place a few feet down the bar, the bartender chuckled. "Maybe you should quit while you're ahead, mate."

"No kidding. Tonight's definitely not my night," he said as he strained to look down at his shirt. "You're right. Made it worse, didn't I?"

"Told you," Susan replied. "It's the grenadine. Stuff's impossible to get out. Tastes good though."

"I'll take your word for it. Damn. Now I'm going to smell like a fruit bowl for the rest of the night."

"I hate to ask, but what did you do to earn a cocktail to the face in the first place?"

A better question would have been what didn't he do? Lewis tossed the napkin on the bar. He'd been drowning in the karma from a decade of bad decisions for the past nine months. "Nothing," he lied. "One minute we were talking, the next I had a maraschino cherry in my hair."

"Just like that?"

"Yeah, just like that."

She knew he was lying. It was evident from the look she shot him over the rim of her glass.

"You're leaving something out," she said. "I can tell by the way you're not saying anything."

"What?"

"You heard me." She was swaying on her bar stool, the way someone did when the room was starting to spin. Hopefully the bartender was paying attention. "People don't toss perfectly good drinks for no reason," she said. "*Especially* good drinks. So what did you do?"

It was none of her business, Lewis wanted to say,

except the glint in her eye made him bite his tongue. Even drunk, she had an astuteness about her.

What the heck. She'd hear anyway. "I might have asked them for their names."

"You forgot who they were? Both of them? After you slept with them?"

He didn't say he was proud of it. In fact, he was horrified. "They were from my playing days," he replied.

"Oh, why didn't you say so? They were from his playing days," she announced to the bartender. "That totally makes it all right."

"I didn't say it was right. Just that's why I forgot them." He was lucky he remembered his playing days at all.

"I completely understand. It must have been hard keeping all those groupies straight."

Yes, it was, because there had been a lot of groupies and a lot of alcohol and they were all a giant blur of bad behavior. Lewis kept his mouth shut, however, because it was no excuse. Besides, the woman was drunk and he knew from experience that alcohol and arguing didn't mix. "Are you always this sarcastic to people you just met?" he asked.

"Meh. Depends on how easy a target."

"You're saying I'm easy."

She eyed him through her lashes. "You tell me, Champagne."

How he hated that name. If he never heard the nickname again, it wouldn't be soon enough. The irony of the situation—if that was the right word—was that he didn't remember the picture being taken.

"I'm beginning to see why you don't have friends."

His companion's lower lip started to tremble.

Terrific. On top of everything, he'd gone and hurt her feelings. Why not stomp on a puppy for an encore? "You're not going to cry, are you?"

She responded with a sniff. "Don't be silly. I don't cry."

She was doing a darn good impression of tearing up. Lewis handed her one of the cocktail napkins from his pile. "Here, dry your eyes."

"I told you. I'm not going to cry."

"Then wipe your nontears with it before they make your mascara run," he said. "And, I'm sorry. The comment was uncalled for."

"Yes, it was. It's also true."

"I'm sure it's…"

"I'm in a bar getting drunk by myself and no one from upstairs has noticed I'm missing."

"I'm sure someone has noticed," Lewis replied. Granted, she wasn't the kind of girl he'd look for, but she was hardly forgettable. Her black dress was sexy in a naughty-secretary way—prim but tight enough to show she had curves. She had black curly hair that she'd pulled into a high ponytail—to match the dress he presumed. It worked together to give her a no-nonsense vibe. If there was such a thing as a no-nonsense sex kitten, she was it.

"If it helps, no one's looking for me either," he said.

"Of course they aren't," she said, dabbing her eyes. "You insulted two women."

"And here I'd gone five whole minutes without thinking of my stupidity." Good to know her tears didn't dull the bite of her tongue.

"Now you know why no one's looking for me, except my friend here." She waved her half-empty martini glass, the red liquid sloshing against the sides. "Unless you want your reputation to get worse, you might want to slide down a few stools."

"Trust me, my reputation can't get much worse, luv." A drink in the face was nothing when everyone in the UK thought you were washed up. Maybe not everyone, he corrected, but the people who counted. Like the people at BBC Sport who thought Pete "White Noise" Brockton made a good commentator.

"More likely, you're going to mess up your reputation sitting with me," he told her.

"Whatever. Here's to our rotten reputations. Oh, no!" The liquid had splashed over the rim when she'd waved her drink. Running down the stem, it dripped onto the napkin he'd tossed down earlier. "And she'd been such a good friend."

Her lip was wobbling again. Reaching into her space, he took the glass from her hand before she could take another sip.

"Hey! What are you doing?"

"I think you've had enough." Personified drinks were never a good sign. From out of the corner of his eye, he saw the bartender hold up four fingers.

"Why does everyone keep saying that?" She went to grab the drink only to pitch forward. Fortunately, her hand grabbed the bar rail, keeping her from falling completely.

Without missing a beat, she continued. "It's Christmastime. A girl should get as many wishes as she wants."

"Christmas Wishes," the bartender supplied when Lewis frowned. "It's the name of the drink."

"Well, you're going to wish you didn't have this last

wish tomorrow morning. Why don't we switch to water for a little while? Get you hydrated."

"I don't need water. I'm fine."

"Trust me." Lewis set the drink on the bar as far down as he could reach. If she wanted it, she was going to have to stand up and walk around him. "You're an expert on soap? I'm an expert on getting drunk. You need water."

"Fine. I'll have the water." The way she huffed and rolled her eyes like a teenager proved his point. Lewis had a feeling she wouldn't be caught dead making such an expression sober.

"Thank you. Bartender?"

Giving a nod, the bearded man poured two large glasses, minus ice. "Room temperature will go down a little easier," he said.

Good man. Lewis took the fuller of the two glasses and handed it to Susan. "Here, drink up. Then I'll call a car to take us home. You'll have to pick up your car in the morning."

"Don't have one," she said in between swallows. "Took a car service."

"Even better."

"Wait a second. You're taking me home?" She looked up at him through her lashes.

Wow. Her eyes were really pretty. He wasn't sure if it was the sheen from the tears or the bar lighting but the hazel color had a copper center that looked lit from within. They were almost hypnotic.

"I'm making sure you get home safely," he told her. While he imagined she could handle herself, Lewis didn't like the idea of sending her home alone—car service or not. "We'll share a ride and I'll have the driver drop you off first."

"Oh." Her gaze dropped to her glass. "That's very nice of you."

There was no missing the disappointment in her voice. He didn't stop to think, but after going on about no one liking her, his dropping her off was probably a kick in the teeth. When she sobered up, she'd be really embarrassed.

"Bad form to leave a woman alone when she's been drinking," he said. "Or, to take advantage of her." Not that he would have taken her home, but he might as well take the sting out of his rejection.

It worked. A tiny blush bloomed in her cheeks. "You're a very decent person," she said. "Even if you did forget those women's names."

Lewis couldn't remember the last time he was called decent. "Thank you. If you get a chance, spread the word. I'm in need of an image makeover." A big one. Otherwise, he'd be stuck as "Champagne Lewis" for the rest of his life. Or worse, he'd fade into obscurity.

"You and me both," she replied.

"Amen to that, sister." Helping himself to the other water, he clinked the bottom of his glass against hers. "Amen to that."

CHAPTER TWO

IF THERE WERE two things Susan detested, they were headaches and people bothering her when she wanted to be left alone. Saturday morning brought both: a blinding headache and a phone ringing loudly right next to her ear.

Lifting her head from the sofa—where she'd collapsed facedown after stumbling from the bathroom—she glared at the caller ID, planning on killing the person.

Just her luck, it was her brother Thomas. One of two people in the UK she couldn't kill. He was also the only person whose call she had to take. As CEO of Collier's, he was technically her boss.

That didn't mean she had to be pleasant though. "Do you know what time it is?" she growled.

"Happy Saturday to you, as well. It's ten o'clock in the morning."

Really? She pulled the phone from her ear to check. When she'd lain down, it was just before seven that day. "Sorry. Thought it was earlier."

It suddenly dawned on her why Thomas could be calling. "Rosalind didn't have the baby, did she?" She pushed herself upright, ignoring how the blood rush made the room—and her stomach—sway.

"Not yet. The doctor thinks she'll go right on her due date, same as she did with Maddie. And you sound like dirt."

She felt like dirt. No longer having to worry about being alert, she slid down into the cushions. "Maria's wedding was last night. I overdosed on sloe gin."

"Sounds like a good time."

"Not as good as you'd think." And ending with her nearly falling on her face when she tripped going up her front steps—right after she'd insisted she was perfectly able to navigate the walk on her own. She could just imagine the look that had crossed Lewis Matolo's face when he caught her by the waist. A combination of smugness and disgust, no doubt. At least he was gentleman enough not to say anything out loud.

"Is there a reason you're calling?" she asked. "Because otherwise, I would like to go back to dying."

"Actually, there are two reasons, if you can stave off your demise for ten minutes."

"I'll try, but I'm not making any promises. What do you need?"

"The first thing isn't a need, it's an invitation. Rosalind and I were talking last night. About how fantastical the last eighteen months have been. Between her accident and last Christmas…"

Fantastical was a good word for it. Eighteen months earlier, Rosalind had disappeared after her car plunged off a bridge in Scotland. She had reappeared last Christmas hundreds of miles away with amnesia of all things. Rediscovering their relationship had been a challenge. Susan liked to think she helped the cause by sharing some hard truths Thomas hadn't been willing to tell his returning bride.

Of course she was the only one who thought so at the time, but the three of them had put the issue behind them.

"We thought, with the baby arriving soon, it would be the perfect time to reestablish ourselves as a family," Thomas continued.

"What do you mean?"

"We've decided to renew our vows on Christmas Eve. Nothing huge. Just family and a few close friends."

"That sounds…lovely." Susan hated the tiny knot of jealousy that twisted in her midsection. Her brother had fought hard for his life and family; a proper sister wouldn't envy his happiness.

Especially when his voice hummed with a bashful excitement. "Maddie's going to be the maid of honor," he said. "She'll be heartbroken if her favorite aunt isn't there."

"I'd be heartbroken if I missed seeing her," Susan replied, the knot easing slightly. The prospect of seeing her young niece dressed like a princess was too charming to resist.

"So you'll be there?"

"Of course." It wasn't like she had Christmas Eve plans.

"Great. I'll let Rosalind know. The other reason I called…" On the other end of the line, Susan heard the clink of a teacup. "I'm going to need you and Linus to host the Collier party again this year. I promised Rosalind I would take time off when the baby was born so we could bond as a family."

Susan groaned. Not again. Collier's had been holding

a company Christmas party for its employees ever since the days of Queen Victoria. What was once a show of largesse toward the workers had morphed into a fancy cocktail party hosted by the CEO. Last year, Thomas had begged off because of Rosalind's amnesia, leaving her and Linus to play the benevolent owners.

"Can't Linus host by himself?" Everyone loved Linus.

"I'd prefer both of you to be there. Especially since Linus has been…"

"Unreliable?" She thought of how he'd left her in the lurch last night.

"Distracted," Thomas replied. There was a pause, during which she imagined him studying his cup of tea while he thought of the right words. "Look, I know the party's not your favorite event…"

"Try least favorite," Susan corrected. The whole affair was an exercise in awkwardness for everyone involved. Smiling and making small talk with people like Ginger and Courtney. It'd be like the wedding times ten. "I was actually thinking of staying home this year…"

"You can't. You're a Collier. It wouldn't look right."

"I doubt people will care—they're more interested in the free booze."

"Susan…"

"Fine." She noticed he hadn't corrected her. "I'll host the party."

"Thank you."

"Is there anything else or can I go back to dying now?" Her head was demanding coffee and aspirin before it could handle any more conversation.

"Die away," her brother replied.

They said their goodbyes, and Susan tossed her

phone on the cushion next to her. Five minutes, she thought as her eyes fluttered closed and her body fell sideways. Five minutes and she'd head to the kitchen for caffeine.

The phone rang again, the shrillness next to her ear making her wince. She fumbled for it without opening her eyes. "What did you forget?"

"Nothing that I know of," said an unfamiliar voice. Deep and with a strong northern twang, it caused tingles to trip up her spine. "I was calling to see how your head felt this morning."

How did this stranger know she had a killer hangover? "Who is this?" Susan pushed herself into a seated position—again.

"Lewis Matolo. The bloke who brought you home, remember?"

Remember? She was hoping to forget. Nearly bursting into tears, tripping over her own two feet. She'd worked hard her entire adult life to project an image of togetherness and control to the outside world…and Lewis Matolo had seen none of that.

She also remembered him being incredibly attractive. If you were into the cocky, athletic sort.

"How did you get my number?"

"I texted Hank and Maria and asked them."

"You bothered them on their honeymoon." Her heart actually fluttered at the idea. Why on earth would he go to that much trouble to track her down? Surely, not simply to check on her well-being.

"Don't worry. They were killing time at Heathrow waiting for their boarding call. I'm glad to see you made it to your apartment safely. No tripping up the stairs?"

Thankfully, he couldn't see how warm her face was.

"I told you, the sidewalk was slippery from the cold weather," she said.

"Uh-huh." It was clear from the amusement in his voice that he hadn't bought the excuse then and he still wasn't buying it now. Susan blushed a little deeper.

"Since you didn't fall and break your neck," he continued, "how would you feel about lunch?"

"Lunch? With you?" A dumb question, she knew, but he'd caught her off guard. She needed a reality check before her heart fluttered again. Why would someone like him be asking her out?

"No, with Prince William. I have a…business proposition to run by you."

How stupid of her. Of course he would be calling about business. Doing her best to hold back a sigh, she said, "New business ideas are my brother Thomas's bailiwick. You're better off calling him directly. I don't get involved in that end."

"You misunderstand. This isn't about Collier's. It's about… Let me just say I think I have an idea that might benefit us both."

Beneficial to her but didn't involve Collier's? He had her attention. "Go on?"

"I don't suppose you've read Lorianne's blog today?"

Lorianne Around London was the UK's most popular gossip website. A treasure trove of royal, political and celebrity gossip, the blog was influential and widely read, even by those who claimed they didn't. "The only thing I've seen today is the inside of my eyelids. Why?"

"You might want to check it out on your way to the restaurant," Lewis replied. "There's a "Blind Item" you might find interesting. Now, are we on for lunch?"

Susan ran a hand through her curls. Her hair was

a stiff mess from being retro-styled and she still had a splitting headache. Without checking a mirror, she knew she looked like a plump, raccoon-eyed nightmare. Hardly suitable for public viewing.

On the other hand, Lewis's offer intrigued her foggy brain. A business venture that benefitted her, didn't involve Collier's and was somehow connected to a "Blind Item" in *Lorianne Around London*? How could she resist?

"Where and when?" she asked.

The Christmas tree next to the fountain was decorated with pairs of miniature shoes. At night, it was lit with hundreds of rainbow-colored lights, but at midday all you could see were mini sneakers and stilettos. It was supposed to be making an artistic and social commentary, but damn if Lewis could figure it out. Walk a mile in another's shoes, maybe? Guess he wasn't sophisticated enough because he preferred the lights.

Still frowning, he turned his attention back to the restaurant. It was ten minutes past their agreed-upon time. Susan didn't strike him as the kind of person who ran late. He'd done a little digging on her when he'd texted Hank and Maria. If anything, Susan was the kind of person who arrived early and grew annoyed when you didn't too. She hadn't been joking last night when she said she wasn't very well liked at her company. In fact, Maria had used a very specific word to describe her, and for a second Lewis wondered if his plan was a good idea.

He caught the eye of a waiter who immediately approached the table. "Can I get another sparkling water?" he asked.

The young man nodded. "Of course. Right away."

As the man walked away, Lewis noticed a handful of diners looking in his direction. The Mayfair restaurant was too posh a location for autograph seekers. The people who dined here were supposed to be nonchalant about dining with celebrities. That didn't mean they weren't above sneaking a peek when one was in their midst, however.

When he was a kid, places like this were a foreign country. They were for people who lived on the other side of the city, who drove nice cars and whose kids always had new clothes. They definitely weren't for nobodies who bounced from foster home to foster home. Sometimes he pinched himself that he was really able to walk into a restaurant like this one and order whatever he wanted. Sometimes he masked his anxiety with extreme cockiness.

Sometimes—most times, in the past—he'd drunk to keep from feeling exposed.

It's all right; you belong here.

For how long though? Celebrity was a fleeting thing. Washed-up athletes were a dime a dozen. If he couldn't get a broadcast job, what would he do? Football was the only world he knew. The sport defined him. Made him matter. Made him *somebody.*

It's your reputation, Lewis. That's how his agent had put it after telling him he'd lost the BBC commentator job. *People are afraid you're going to pull one of your antics again. No one wants to risk waking up to see their studio analyst double-fisting bottles of Cristal on the front page.*

In other words, he needed to prove to the world he had shed his Champagne Lewis persona for good. He'd been trying to deliver that message for the past nine months, but karma kept tripping him up. Like last night. He was surprised that the drink-tossing incident hadn't made it onto Lorianne's blog. The woman had spies everywhere.

Reading today's item, however, made him realize a few things. First, that he was damn lucky, and second, that if he wanted the world to know he was a changed man, he needed to do more than simply give up drinking and stay home. He needed to give the public proof, something splashy, that would convey the message for him.

The idea as to how had hit him like a jolt this morning. It was crazy, but it was worth a shot.

Now he needed his proposed partner in crime to appear.

He was about to turn his awareness back to the window when a flash of blue caught his attention. Finally. Susan Collier cut through the dining room, her peacock blue jacket popping amid the room's gold-and-green garlands. She wore a pair of oversize sunglasses covering her face and moved like a person who didn't have a moment to spare. Quite a different appearance from the soft, hazy woman who'd tripped her way up her front stairs the night before.

"Sorry I'm late. We got stuck in traffic."

Lewis saw it for the excuse it was. He also always seemed to have problems with the traffic on days he was hungover. "No problem. I've been sitting hear enjoying the view. It's beginning to look a lot like Christmas."

"It should. They started decorating the day after Halloween."

She looked down at the bench he sat on. Although

the alcove table could accommodate up to six people, it had been set for intimacy. This meant the only seating was the velvet bench that curved along the wall. She had no choice but to slide to the middle so they could sit side by side. “Interesting choice of table,” she remarked.

“I like sitting by the window.” He moved over to make room. Not too much room though. He wanted to sit next to her. That was the point.

“Don’t suppose you read Lorianne’s site,” he said when she’d settled in—her sunglasses remaining in place.

“You mean ‘Blind Item’ number five? How could I resist? You had me intrigued.” Reaching into her shoulder bag, she pulled out a neatly folded piece of paper. It was a printout of Lorianne’s blog.

> This A-plus bad-boy former athlete with the fancy name was seen playing the gentleman for a member of one of London’s most established families last night. He walked the lady to the door and didn’t stay the night. Fluke? Or has he washed his hands of his wild ways?

She folded the paper in half again. “Those are some of the lamest clues I’ve ever seen. ‘Fancy name’ for Champagne Lewis? ‘Washed his hands’ for Collier’s Soap? Was this your doing?”

“I wish. Our driver must have given her the tip. Lorianne’s known for her network. He must have texted her after he dropped us off and Lorianne shoved it in her column.” That was the beauty of the internet. In the old days, the public would have had to wait another twenty-four hours for the news item to go public.

"Interesting, don't you think?" he asked.

"How so?" Susan replied.

"Good afternoon. Glad you could join us." It was their waiter, returning with Lewis's sparkling water. "Can I get you anything? A cocktail perhaps?"

"The lady will have a Bloody Mary." Lewis ignored the way Susan's head spun around to stare at him.

"A glass of water will be fine," she told the waiter, in a no-nonsense tone.

"And the Bloody Mary."

The poor young man looked from Lewis to Susan and back, clearly unsure who he should listen to. "She'll have water and a Bloody Mary," Lewis told him. He leaned in so he could lower his voice. "Hair of the dog, Trust me."

"And if I don't?"

"You'll be nursing that headache of yours all day." A drink wouldn't ease the pain of her throbbing head necessarily, but in his experience, it helped more often than not. "I'm the expert, remember?"

"Fine." She told the waiter to bring her both. "If alcohol is such a cure-all, why aren't you having any?" she asked once the waiter had gone.

"Simple. I'm not hungover. Plus, I don't drink. Anymore," he added when she opened her mouth.

"You don't? Since when?"

Since he'd woken up with one too many hangovers and realized what a mess he'd made of his career, that's when. "Been nearly nine months now."

"Oh. I didn't realize."

"Few people do." And those who did, didn't believe it would stick. "I decided last spring it was time to get my act together. Turn over a new leaf, as it were."

"How's the new leaf working out for you?"

"There's been a few bumps." Like last night. "Turns out being sober is only half the battle. Dealing with the mess you left behind…"

"I'm guessing last night was a bump."

"For both of us, wouldn't you say?" He took a sip of water. "Are you going to wear those glasses throughout lunch?" It was impossible to gauge her expression when it was hidden by those big black lenses. "Feel like I'm having lunch with a Russian spy." Or a woman embarrassed to be with him.

Although her lips pulled into a smirk, she removed the glasses. "Satisfied?" she asked.

Her excess from the night before revealed itself in a pair of dark circles that washed the color from her face. Her eyes' warm copper center was still visible though. Lewis had wondered if he'd imagined the unusual color. He hadn't. He hadn't imagined the intelligence in her eyes either.

"So…" She dropped her gaze, blocking his view once more. "You said you had a business proposition for me."

"Yes." Apparently they were going to get right down to business. Lewis could deal with that. "Now that I've retired, I'm hoping to get into broadcasting but no one wants to give me so much as a meeting. They're all afraid to take a risk."

"No offense, but can you blame them?"

"Maybe once upon a time, but I'm not the same guy I was nine months ago. I've grown up, and if they gave me a shot, they would see that I know my stuff. I'd be damned good."

He shifted in his seat so he could look her straight on. "It's maddening. They won't even meet with me. It's as though the world has slotted me into a role and now I'm stuck in it for life. Whether it fits or not."

"Everyone thinks they know you," she said in soft voice. She was folding and unfolding her glasses with great thoughtfulness.

"Precisely." The rush of someone understanding made Lewis want to grab her hands and squeeze them. "Telling them isn't enough. They need tangible evidence that I am not the same person. That's where you come in." Taking a chance, he reached over and laid his hand on her forearm.

In a flash, her hands stilled. Lewis felt the muscles in her arm tense. Slowly—very slowly—her gaze rose to meet his. "How so?"

Before he could answer, their waiter returned. As the man placed her drinks on the table, his eyes flickered to Susan's arm, which she quickly pulled away. Lewis tried not to smile. "Are you ready to order?" the waiter asked.

So eager had he been to discuss business, neither of them had had a chance to look at the menu. "Not—"

"I'll have the egg-and-avocado sandwich," Susan announced. "Is that all right? Or do you need to change my order?"

Man, but she had a bite to her. And here he'd thought last night's sharpness was from the alcohol. "Sounds perfect. In fact, I'll have the same. You're very decisive, for a woman who didn't have time to study the menu," he said once the waiter had moved on."

"I read the item at the top of the page and decided it sounded good. I'm not much for hemming and hawing when there's a decision to be made."

"You don't like to waste your time."

"Not if I can help it." She swished her celery-stalk garnish around in the glass and took a crisp bite off its end. "Bringing me back to my question. What are you looking for from me?"

Lewis placed his hands on the table. He thought about covering her arm again, but that might look too forward. This was where actions and word choice mattered. "You might think I'm crazy, but I got the idea from Lorianne's site. Until now, I've been staying out of the public eye, hoping people would realize I'd given up the party life, but it hasn't been working. People only believe what they see."

"Or think they see," she added.

She caught on quick. "Precisely. This morning, I read Lorianne's 'Blind Item,' and I realized I had things backward. Instead of being out of the public eye, I need to do the opposite. I need to be seen as much as possible, only, in the way I *want* to be seen."

"In other words, you want to create a new tabloid persona. Makes sense. Although I'm not sure where I come in."

"Well…" This was where the proposition got tricky. "I was hoping you'd be my partner in crime," he said. "Nothing says *changed man* like a relationship with someone completely against type. A woman who is the total opposite of all the other women I've ever dated. You."

Susan stared at him, drink hovering just below her lower lip. "Are you trying to get another drink tossed in your face?"

"Wait." She'd set her drink down and was gathering her things. "Hear me out."

"I already heard you. You spent your sporting career

dating beautiful women. Now, to prove you've changed, you want to date someone who isn't beautiful and that someone is me."

"That's not what I meant at all."

"Really?" She cocked her head. "What did I miss?"

"Yes, I dated a lot of beautiful women, but..." He threw up his hands in case the noise she'd made was the precursor to a drink toss. "They were just good-time girls."

"The kind of girls whose name you forget."

"Right. I mean, no. You should never, ever forget a lover's name." He could almost hear the thin ice cracking beneath him with each sentence. So much for making sure his words mattered.

"You're smart," he rushed on. "You own a respected business. Doesn't Collier's Soap have the queen's blessing?"

"We have a Royal Warrant, yes."

"See? You're someone society takes seriously. No one would expect to see you involved with a party boy like me. So if you *were* involved..."

"They would assume you must not be the empty-headed wild man anymore."

Forgetting about overstepping, he clasped her hand in his. "That's it exactly."

Her fingers were cold and damp from her glass. Lewis pressed his hands tight to warm them. "And it's not as though you're unattractive," he added.

She didn't smile. So much for humor. He was mucking this up big-time. "Look, you're smart. You're cute." Cute wasn't the right word, he realized. She radiated too much class and intelligence to be labeled merely cute. Sophisticated? Maybe. Different?

Yeah, different. Unique.

"Bottom line is, I need your help, if I'm to have any chance of getting a network job," he said. "Lorianne has already marked us as a potential couple. It would take a while to find another woman as qualified." Not to mention one whose company he enjoyed as much as he did Susan's, surprisingly.

"Why is being a broadcaster so important?" she asked. "Surely there are other jobs out there?"

"Because I think I'd be good at it. No, I know I'd be good at it," he told her. There was more though. "Besides, football is the only thing I've ever known. I'm not ready to leave it behind."

The field and the fans had been the only real home he'd ever had. Without them, all he'd have would be a handful of hazy memories of the glory days. He wasn't ready to be kicked to the curb, unwanted, again. To go back to being nobody.

He blinked. Susan was frowning at him from over her drink.

"Were you even listening?" she asked.

"Sorry. I drifted off for a moment."

"Obviously." She took a long sip of her drink, which, Lewis noticed, was about a third gone. "You said on the phone this proposition would be mutually beneficial. You explained what you would get out of this 'arrangement,' but what's in it for me?"

"Simple," he replied. "You get seen with me."

Thank goodness she'd swallowed before he spoke or she would have spit tomato juice all over the table. "You're joking. That's your idea of mutually beneficial?"

He leaned back against the bench, his arms stretched out along the back. "You disagree?"

Talk about ego. Like he was such a prize.

She took in his chiseled features—far more prominent in the light of day—and the way his cashmere sweater pulled across his equally chiseled torso.

Okay, he *was* a prize.

Still, did he think her so desperate she needed a fake boyfriend?

Aren't you? She ignored her own question.

"I think you have an extremely high opinion of your appeal." She paused to sip her drink. Much as she hated to admit it, the combination of tomato juice and vodka was easing her hangover. The tension in her shoulders and neck were lessening with each sip. "Why would I care whether I was seen in public with you?"

"To quote… 'my own brother didn't want to be my date.'"

"When did I say that?" It was true, but she couldn't see herself sharing the information.

"While we were waiting for the car."

Susan thought back. Much of the trip home was fuzzy. She vaguely remembered growing angry when they passed the ladies' room and going on a tirade about being single which may have morphed into a drunken pity party.

Oh, man, now she remembered. Stupid Christmas Wishes. "I was drunk. People say and do a lot of foolish things when they are under the influence, as I'm sure you would agree."

"In vino veritas."

He flashed a smirk as he reached for his water. "As

for the value of my appeal…? There are a lot of women in the UK who would tell you I've got plenty."

"Then why don't you ask one of them to be your fake girlfriend? Oh, wait, let me guess. Oh, right, they're all supermodels and party girls."

"You're not going to let that go, are you? I was trying to lighten the mood."

"Doesn't change the fact that you clearly need me more than I need you." Or the way it stung.

"You're right," he replied. "I do need you more than you need me."

Points for honesty. Sitting back, she waited to hear his expanded sales pitch.

"Believe it or not, you would get something tangible out of the relationship," he told her.

Beyond being able to rub the fake arrangement in Ginger's and Courtney's faces—which she had to admit, a part of her found appealing. "How so?"

"If my plan works, the two of us will be in the tabloids and gossip columns, a lot. Both our profiles will be raised."

"Why would I care about a higher profile?"

"You tell me, Ms. Collier."

He was appealing to her ego again. It wouldn't be only the Courtneys and Gingers of the world she'd be showing, it would be the world. The equivalent of a giant ad announcing her desirability. As if she were that lonely.

"What makes you think the tabloids, or anyone for that matter, would believe we were a real couple?" she asked. Simply out of curiosity.

"Are you kidding? Celebrities arrange public relationships all the time in order to sell an image. Remember that pop star who was dating the guy from the Brazilian team? Totally to keep people from knowing he was shagging his equipment manager."

"No way."

"It's the truth. I know the equipment manager."

Susan remembered seeing the singer on the cover of several magazines at the hair salon talking about finally finding love. She'd been a nobody newcomer before the relationship.

A thought suddenly occurred to her. "You're not…?"

"No."

Not that it mattered. She still wasn't going to say yes to this silly idea.

"Granted you and I wouldn't become an international sensation, but, if we do this right, we will get mentioned in the papers. We only need to be together a few months. Long enough for people to believe we are the real deal."

"Even though we aren't."

"Right. But the only people who will know are you and me. Everyone else will think you won me over with your brilliant mind and razor-sharp wit."

"And, if I say yes—not that I am—how long would we need to play act?"

"Just over a month. At least through the holidays."

Meaning he would be her "boyfriend" at the Collier's Christmas Party. Wouldn't that be interesting? To be part of a couple for once instead of standing around watching everyone else? Even if it was only pretend.

Despite his offered upsides, the idea struck her wrong. Did she really want to spend weeks with a disinterested man just so she could stick it to a few petty witches? Seemed like she should be better than that.

Then there was the obvious.

"Wouldn't it be easier to simply date a different category of women instead of subterfuge?"

He looked at her for a second, as though weighing his words, his sensual lips drawn in a frown. "If I were looking to get into a long-term relationship, maybe, but…"

"You don't have to go on. I get your point." He was looking to repair an image, not actually change his tastes.

"I'm not asking you to decide this very moment," he said. "Let's have some lunch, and you think the idea over. Let me know later on."

"Thank you." She doubted food would change her mind, but she'd rather not ruin the mood until after she'd eaten.

In the meantime, she was curious if she still looked like death now that her headache had eased. When the waiter arrived with their food, she excused herself and went to the ladies' room.

Whoever decorated the restaurant had the foresight to install ambient lighting as opposed to fluorescent in the sitting room so women checking the mirror would feel good about their appearance. Unfortunately, all the ambient lighting in the world couldn't brighten her washed-out complexion. She'd tried to hide the damage with powder and concealer, but the dark circles stubbornly remained. Searching into her bag, she pulled out a compact and touched up her blush. No sense bothering with lipstick since it would only wear off again when she ate. Then she combed her hands through her curls and stepped back.

Her shoulders slumped. She looked like she felt.

Tired, and hungover. The jacket was too boxy for her short frame, making her look like a squashed blueberry. People probably thought she was Lewis's agent or business manager. Certainly not a potential girlfriend. Correction, fake girlfriend.

What made Lewis think the idea would work? No way, people wouldn't believe they were an item.

Behind her, the door opened and two university-age girls slipped in. Susan immediately envied their long hair which they wore in messy topknots. Envied their cropped sweaters and leggings too. No one would mistake them for a sports agent.

All her life, she had wondered what it would be like to *fit*. To feel accepted by someone. Anyone. She had a lot to offer, if people would only look.

Don't be so dramatic, her mother would say. *People don't look if there's nothing to look at.*

Belinda was full of those little bon mots.

Lewis Matolo was offering people something to look at.

Would it be so horrible if the world saw her as someone different? Just for a little while?

Rummaging through her bag, she located a hair tie and forced her curls into a messy bun. Then, she shed her jacket. The black turtleneck wasn't stylish, but at least the world could see she had a waist.

The world. Susan chewed her lower lip. Was she really that crazy?

Lewis was biting into his egg sandwich when she returned. She tossed her bag on the bench and slid in next to him. "You've got a deal."

CHAPTER THREE

"ARE YOU SURE?"

"Positive," Susan replied. "You don't have to keep asking."

But Lewis felt like he did. They were on their second cup of tea. An entire meal had gone by and he was having trouble processing the fact that she'd agreed to play his girlfriend. "I'm surprised, is all," he said. Flummoxed was a better word. "You didn't look very enthusiastic when I pitched the idea." Which was why, when she'd come back from the washroom and announced she was all in, he'd been floored.

"I'll admit, the plan sounds insane, but it's only for a short time, right? Not like you're proposing marriage or anything."

"Dating only, I promise." Marriage was one of those concepts that made his insides squeeze, along with commitment and emotions. As it was, this arrangement would be the longest relationship he'd ever had. Then again, so would anything longer than a three-day weekend.

Her smile seemed to tighten for a second. "Right," she said, setting her teacup down. "How does this work?

Do we draw up contracts? Write out conditions? What does one do in a fake relationship?"

Fortunately, Lewis had given the matter some thought on the off chance she'd agree. "Obviously, the goal is to be seen together in as many different settings as possible. Like a real couple."

"And we do this until the tabloids notice?" she asked while pouring the last of her tea. "I know you're considered a tabloid magnet, but that doesn't seem terribly efficient."

"You're right, it's not. That's why I'm going to have my agent leak a few discreet comments. We're also going to have to attend one or two social events where there's press. Actually, I've drawn up a few notes laying out how I think this plan should proceed."

He reached into his back pocket and pulled out a folded piece of paper. Moving his teacup aside, he smoothed it flat. "We want everyone to see us, but at the same time we want to look subtle—like this is the real deal—so I've come up with a progression of steps."

Susan's arm pressed against his as she leaned in to get a better view. "Date at a public venue. Attend a society event. Be seen doing coupley Christmas things?" She turned to look at him. "Coupley Christmas things?"

"You know, Christmas shopping or walking in Kew Gardens. Whatever it is women drag their boyfriends to do during the holidays."

"I see. Clearly, you've given this a lot of thought."

"Did you think I would invite you to lunch without some kind of plan in mind?" Lewis replied. He wasn't stupid. If Susan had said yes, he knew a woman like her would expect details. "You're going to have to start giving me a little more credit."

Then again, could he blame her? The whole point behind this charade was to prove he had more to offer than being a drunken party boy.

"Considering I didn't know fake girlfriends really existed until ninety minutes ago, you'll have to cut me some slack. I do have one question," she said, tapping her cup. "How can we be sure people—the tabloids—will believe us?"

It was a reasonable question. The honest answer was they couldn't. Not entirely. "I get the impression that as long as the story gets attention, they—the papers—won't dig too deep," he told her. "However, you bring up a point I hadn't thought about. Lorianne has spies everywhere—it's how she gets her scoops—so we'll need to make sure we act like a couple whenever we're together, even when we think no one's paying attention."

"Is that why we're having lunch in a cozy corner booth? Again, I'm impressed."

Lewis was flattered. It wasn't often that the woman he was with complimented his intelligence. Other skills usually took priority. "Thank you," he said. "Oh, and another thing…we need to keep this arrangement between us. No one but you, me and my agent, Michael, will know. Will that be a problem?"

She shook her head. "I'd already assumed the arrangement would be need-to-know. If it were a problem, I wouldn't have agreed in the first place."

Good. They were on the same page.

"What are you doing?"

She'd taken a pen out of her bag and was making notes on the paper. Lewis watched her write the words *Christmas Party* with a date. "My brother Thomas has informed me that I'm cohosting the corporate Christmas party again this year. I think it's only fair that my 'boyfriend' attend with me."

"Corporate Christmas party, huh?"

"For employees and other people we do business with. The ad agency, banks, etc."

He had to admit he'd wondered if she'd insist on some type of work-related couple appearance after her speech last night. "This wouldn't be to show up those ladies from the bathroom, would it?"

Her shrug was enough of an answer.

Whatever. It was fine with him if she wanted to put a few people in their place. "I'll mark my calendar. While we're scheduling, do you need me to play arm candy for any other events? New Year's Eve? Christmas Day?"

"As it so happens..." She suddenly stopped and shook her head. "Never mind. The Christmas party will be enough."

"Are you sure?" She was holding back.

"Yes, I'm sure. Now please stop asking that question." Clicking her pen, she wrote the word *Agreed* at the top of the page along with her name and the date. When finished, she held out the pen. "Since you didn't answer my question about a contract, I hope this will do."

"Seeing as how I would have settled for a handshake...?" He added his signature below hers. It was official: one image makeover in a half dozen assorted steps. Whether it would work was anyone's guess.

"I now pronounce us a couple," he announced.

For better or for worse.

What had she gotten herself into? "When you said we were going to watch a basketball game, I thought you meant at a pub," Susan said. Some quaint place with brick walls and a fireplace. "Not surrounded by twenty thousand spectators at London's O2 arena."

She was decidedly overdressed in a pencil skirt and heels. For some insane reason she'd decided to dress daringly. Her way of showing the world she was worthy of Lewis's attention. Now she felt stupid.

"I didn't know London even had a basketball team," she said as they walked up the ramp.

"There's an entire league," Lewis answered, "but they don't play here. This is a special event. Two American teams."

That explained the crowds. It didn't explain why he'd chosen a basketball game for their first date though, so she asked.

"Why else? To send a message. I wanted people to see that I'm more than a footballer. I appreciate all sports."

"Thus broadening your appeal as a broadcaster. Clever."

"Thank you."

They stepped out of the ramp into the brightly lit arena filled with people. Susan had been to the O2 before, for concerts, but this was the first time she'd seen it prepped for a sports event. Below them, American basketball players were warming up on the shiny parquet floor. "Our seats are down there," Lewis said in her ear as he pointed toward the court. His hand molded to the small of her back as he guided her down the steep steps.

They were really doing this. Pretending they were a couple. Her legs began to shake and from more than just navigating the steep stairs in stilettos. She gripped the railing.

"What's wrong?"

She didn't realize she'd stopped moving until Lewis spoke. He looked at her, his brown eyes narrowed in concern. "Sorry. I— It just dawned on me that we're on a date."

"You're only figuring that out now?"

"You know what I mean."

"Not really," he replied.

Until this moment, their arrangement had been conceptual. She hadn't thought about the fact that in order to be taken for a real couple, they would have to behave like a real couple. Which made this evening a date complete with all the touching and other date-like behavior. Lewis was going to have to pretend he was attracted to her. Did he really think they could pull this off?

They were blocking the stairs. That was one way to attract attention. "Never mind," she said. "It doesn't matter."

"If you say so."

Their seats were in the middle of the row, close to the front, but high enough they could see the entire court. They also had a clear view of the giant electronic screen that hung over center court. It was like having a one-hundred-inch television in your living room.

She looked around at the people milling about. "I doubt anyone will notice us in this crowd," she commented.

"Oh, they'll notice us," Lewis replied. He leaned closer, his nose practically nuzzling the outer shell of her ear. "My agent has arranged for us to be outed after the third quarter."

Outed? This time she had to lean into him. "What do you mean?"

"You'll see," he replied with a grin. "Just keep your eye on the scoreboard."

She stared at the screen, which at the moment was playing an advertisement for a Christmas concert. "I don't like surprises," she told him.

"You're going to have to get used to them if you're planning to hang around with me."

Why? Was he that spontaneous?

Check that. They were talking about a man who had once jumped naked off a boat into the Thames.

Susan looked at the man folded into the seat beside her. His eyes were shining as he watched the action below. He looked back and forth, taking in everything that was going on. "You're not going to do something outrageous are you?" she asked.

"Yeah. I've got the words *I love Susan Collier* painted on my chest. I'm planning to tear off me shirt so everyone can read them."

She rolled her eyes. "Very funny."

"You're the one who asked the silly question." Before she could respond, he reached over and patted her knee, his large hand warm and firm in its touch. "Relax. This is about changing my image, remember? Plus, I'm sober," he added. "I'm far less outrageous without the alcohol."

Ironic, then, that they should meet because of her drunkenness.

"What made you stop drinking?"

It was a question she had wanted to ask. He looked so at peace with the decision, she was curious. She wasn't surprised when he shrugged as though the decision was no big deal. "Forgot one too many names. Jumped into one too many fountains."

"I would think one fountain would be too many." She gasped when he held up three fingers. "You're kidding."

"We can go for four if you're feeling adventurous. Seriously though," he said, the smile leaving his eyes, "when my career ended, so did the party. When you're on top of the world, being a wild man makes you cool. When you're out of the spotlight, you're just a washed-up drunk. I decided I'd rather try to climb back to the top and maybe remember it this time."

As offhand as he tried to sound, there was no mistaking the regret in his voice. Susan took a good look at the man to whom she'd bound herself for the upcoming weeks. If you looked past the chiseled features, you could see the signs of a life lived hard. She spied tiny scars on his chin and cheekbones and the bump of a broken nose.

"Do you miss playing?" she asked.

"Only every bloomin' day." He pointed to the court where the American players were shooting basketballs at the basket. "See that player there? Number twenty-three? He's the best basketball player in the world."

"Okay." He looked like all the other players to Susan.

"Everyone in this building is here to see him," Lewis told her. "Sure, they care about the other players too, but him…he's the reason they came."

"Because he's the best."

"Exactly. I can't begin to describe what it's like. Being on the pitch, knowing everyone is pinning their game hopes on you and your ability. Feeling the love of thousands. There's no high like it. And when you're in the middle of playing, it's like there's nothing else in the world. There's you, and the ball and the match."

His faraway gaze was so beautiful, it made Susan's throat catch.

"You were really good, weren't you?" she said, embarrassed that she didn't know.

"I was the best. When I was at the top of my game, no one could beat me." She believed him. The arrogance had too much certainty behind it to be false.

"How did you start playing?" She turned in her seat so she could look at him while he spoke. The expressions on his profile were far more interesting than anything going on below.

"Just started," he said with a shrug. "Neighborhood kids played in the street—I asked if I could play. No one else wanted to tend goal, so they let me."

"Let me guess. Soon as they saw you play they made you permanent."

A grin slid across his face. "Pretty much. After that, I played for whatever team I could until I was signed by Manchester for their academy team."

"Your parents must have been proud." Remembering the way her father used to beam every time Thomas or Linus achieved one of their many achievements, she could only imagine how his family had felt when their son joined the Premier League Under 16 program.

"Doubt they knew. I lived with foster families until I was old enough to live in digs at the academy. Never met my dad, and Mum couldn't get off the drugs. The smack pulled her back every time."

Dear Lord.

"I'm sorry."

"Don't be. I don't even remember the woman at this point. She's more of a blur than anything. What about your parents?"

"My dad died a few years ago and my mother…" Her mother wasn't a topic the family liked to talk about. "My mom is an actress. Belinda Quinn."

"That name sounds familiar."

"She played the sexy neighbor on *The Confidents*."

"Was that the show where some poor guy inherited a ton of money from somebody and they moved to a swanky neighborhood?" His bare-bones description was about as deep as the show. "I used to watch old episodes when I was a kid. Your mom was a looker."

"She was *something*," Susan replied. "Except into being a mother. My dad's fault she got saddled with an albatross of a daughter."

"She didn't actually say that, did she?"

Susan put on a haughty voice. "Damn near ruined her figure, I did, and her career. Not to mention the whole messy business of kids demanding attention all the time. After all, what about *her* needs?" She picked at the lint on her sweater. "My mother has what they call histrionic, narcissistic personality disorder. A fancy way of saying she's a self-centered lunatic," she said when he frowned. "Psychology's a bit of a hobby for me. I've done a lot of reading." A desperate attempt to understand why her mother didn't want her. "Anyway, when she and my father divorced, she relinquished custody. We've shared maybe a dozen words since."

"How old were you when she left?" Lewis asked.

"Eight. I came home from school and she'd gone. Last words she said to me were 'Not now, Susan, I've got a headache.'"

"So both our mothers took a flyer. Lucky us, we have something in common." Their eyes met and a beat of understanding passed between them.

Lewis cleared his throat. “Enough childhood talk. We’re here to enjoy a basketball game, right?” With that, he began explaining the action on the court.

The evening passed quickly. Watching the game, with its fast pace and athleticism, was a lot more fun than Susan expected. For someone who claimed to know only a little about the game, Lewis had a very keen grip on the strategy. She imagined he would sound marvelous explaining football too. No wonder he wanted to be a commentator.

By the third quarter, they were both on their feet cheering for three-point shots.

“Exciting, isn’t it?” Lewis remarked after two players came crashing together under the basketball net. “Gets the blood pumping.” He popped a piece of her popcorn into his mouth with a grin. “Clock ticking. Everyone rushing at the same fast pace in organized chaos. It’s fantastic.”

Susan took in the glow on his face. The first two times they met, he’d been clean-shaven. Tonight, a five-o’clock shadow covered his cheeks, turning his classic-looking features dark and dangerous. Add the adrenaline shining in his eyes and the result was breathtaking. He was clearly in his element.

“You’d be amazing on television,” she told him.

Her slip earned her a blush, enhancing what was already camera perfect. “Thanks,” he said. “Nice to know someone thinks so. If only the networks were as enthusiastic.”

If there was anything “*Shrewsan*” understood, it was being publicly judged without cause. Everyone was so certain they knew how she ticked. Without giving it a second thought, she squeezed his fingers. "We'll just have to do our best to make sure you get a shot."

On the floor, a buzzer rang announcing the end of the third quarter. While the players gathered around their respective benches, she and Lewis settled back into their seats. "I thought you said something was supposed to happen during the last quarter," she said. "Your agent didn't forget, did he?"

"Michael? No way. He's got a publicist on staff who knows her stuff. Bailed me out of public embarrassment more than once, she has."

"If something's going to happen, it's going to have to happen soon. According to the clock, there's only twelve minutes left in the game." She pointed to the center screen which was playing a highlight from a few minutes earlier.

When the highlight ended, an electronic Santa Claus came bouncing across the screen. He stopped, pointed upward and the words Mistletoe Camera scrolled by. The image fizzled away and suddenly, there was a view of the crowd. People cheered and waved as the camera zoomed in tighter and tighter until it focused on an unsuspecting couple. The pair laughed and shared a kiss.

"Mistletoe Camera?" She'd never heard of such an idea.

"An American thing," Lewis told her. "Big hit over there from what I hear. The promoters thought the gimmick might be fun to do here, as well. Crowd seems to be enjoying it."

The camera moved on, this time to a pair of middle-aged men who were clearly not together. Oblivious, they faced away from one another until the cheering crowd forced them to look up. As soon as they realized, they too broke out in laughter. The camera remained on them until they shared a bro hug.

"So it appears," she remarked. "Nothing says romance like thousands of people watching you kiss. Wait a second…?" How did Lewis know what the promoters had planned?

Her question was cut off by the crowd suddenly roaring louder than ever. She looked up at the screen to see why and her stomach dropped.

The Mistletoe Cam was pointed at *them*.

CHAPTER FOUR

"YOU..." THERE WAS a smile on her face, but Lewis could see the muscles twitching in her jaw. She was gritting her teeth.

"Wasn't me, luv. It was my agent." He murmured the words in her ear so that on camera it looked like they were sharing a secret.

While he was speaking, he slipped an arm around her shoulder. He knew as soon as Michael mentioned the promotion that Susan would hate the idea, which was why he'd kept the plans a secret. He didn't want to risk her looking annoyed for three periods. Or worse, walking out on him.

"You said yourself, nothing says you're in a relationship like kissing in front of ten thousand people."

"I was being sarcastic. I didn't mean we should follow suit."

"Why not? You've got to admit, it's a great idea. At least the crowd thinks so." The egging on had gotten louder when he put his arm around her. Lewis leaned in closer. They had a limited window before the camera moved to another couple. "They're getting restless. Better give them what they want."

Her eyes widened. "You...you don't mind?"

Why would he mind? It was just a kiss. And she was an attractive woman. He'd been watching her smile and laugh all night long. When she relaxed, her softness came out. There was real vulnerability beneath the armor. The kind that made you want to treat her special. She really was adorable and begging to be cuddled.

"I'm game if you are," he replied. "What do you say? Ready to tell the world we're together?"

"Um..." She licked her lips, making them shiny and enticing. "Okay."

Good answer since he planned on kissing her anyway. Cupping her cheek with his free hand, he bent in for what he meant to be a gentle kiss. The crowd responded with applause. Emboldened by their enthusiasm, he let the kiss linger. Susan tasted delicious. Salt, artificial butter and something indefinable that had him tempted to lick his way past her lips.

When he finally did end the kiss, she looked up at him with what he swore was wonder in her darkened eyes. The look caused something primal to click deep inside him, and for a crazy second he thought about finding some dark corner where he could demonstrate how he really kissed a woman.

If they were in a real relationship, he would. In a heartbeat.

But they weren't. The kiss was simply a hook to sell a story, and what he thought was wonder in her eyes was probably nothing more than the arena lights reflecting in their greenness.

"What do you think?" he asked, leaning back in his seat. He'd keep his arm around her shoulders for now. "Believable?"

* * *

For the rest of the game, Susan tried her best not to look as stunned as she felt. If that was Lewis's idea of a casual first kiss, what did he do when he gave his full effort? It was all she could do not to crawl into his lap and beg for more.

She *should* be angry that he kept the plan a secret. If she had known his plan involved the two of them putting on a public display, she would have…

What? Refused? Then she would have missed out on the most amazing kiss of her life. God bless the Mistletoe Cam, she decided. Were kisses like this what she could expect over the next few weeks? Well then, Merry Christmas to her.

Over her lifetime, Susan had grown accustomed to walking in on whispered conversations. It started at age five when her mother would end telephone conversations abruptly upon Susan entering the room. At the office, she could count on finding at least one or two employees with their heads together, usually complaining or gossiping. Whenever they saw her, they would break up and pretend they had been talking about work.

Today there seemed to be more heads together than usual, starting with a small group by the reception desk. Every single one of them had turned to look at her when she stepped through the front door. That could only mean one thing: There was a mention of last night in the paper.

Last night. She fought a smile as she walked toward her office. Fake or not, she had had a terrific time.

When she concentrated, she could still feel Lewis's kiss. Of course, later that night he'd dropped her off at her apartment with nothing but a friendly hug, but she wouldn't dwell on that.

Upon reaching her office, she found Linus sitting on the edge of her desk. It was an annoying habit he had, that of refusing to use a chair. When he saw her, he pointed at her with a rolled-up newspaper. "If it isn't my sister, the cover girl."

"What are you getting on about? And get off my desk. You're messing up my piles." She hung her wool coat on the back of her door before shooing him off her work with a wave of her hand.

"I gather you haven't seen this morning's edition of the *Looking Glass*." He unfurled the newspaper. "I lied about the cover. Turns out you're more page-five material."

Grabbing the tabloid from Linus, she quickly flipped to the page. There, under the headline Merry Kiss-Mas was a photo of her and Lewis.

Wildman Champagne Lewis Matolo Looks Tamed As He Cozies With A Mystery Lady, read the subhead.

The corners of her mouth twitched upward. The photographer had caught the moment just before they kissed. Her face was lifted to his, and they were looking at one another as if each were the only person in the room. There was a second photo too, which, from their excited expressions, looked like it was taken in the fourth quarter when they were cheering for a last-minute rally.

This explained all the odd looks. She gave in and let her smile bloom. Lewis had to be thrilled.

"You little minx. Why didn't you tell us you were seeing someone?"

She cast her brother a look over the top of the paper. “Minx? Seriously?”

“First word that came to mind, and you didn’t answer my question. When did you start dating Lewis Matolo?”

“We...” Linus’s question reminded her they hadn’t worked out a proper backstory. Since she was alone, she was going to have to go with the obvious and fill Lewis in later. “We met at Maria’s wedding. He went to school with her new husband. We shared a couple drinks in the bar and hit it off.”

“A couple? Thomas said you were hung over when he spoke to you the next morning.”

“Thomas has a big mouth, and what business is it of yours anyway?” Tucking the paper under her arm, she cast him another look as she made her way to her chair.

Much to her consternation, Linus followed, and perched himself on the edge of the desk again. “Is this where I say none?”

“Unless you’d like me to say it for you.” Folding her arms, she sat back and waited for him to get to the point. Because there was a point; Linus always had a point. She just wished he’d hurry up because she wanted to call Lewis.

“Here’s the thing,” he said finally. “Normally, I’d agree with you, but in this case...”

“What do you mean, in this case?”

“Do you know who Lewis Matolo is? I mean really know?”

Of course she knew, and she knew exactly what Linus was driving at, as well. “Get to your point.” Might as well hear him say it out loud.

Her brother tapped a knuckle against his lip, a habit he had when thinking. “How do I put this...”

"He's a drunken arse." Thomas Collier's pronouncement entered the office two seconds before he did. The chairman of Collier's Soap strode into her office wearing his standard severe black suit. Dark and handsome, he was night to Linus's day.

Add Lewis to the mix and you would have one heck of a gorgeous trio, thought Susan. With her as the plump wrong note.

"Why don't you say it a little louder, Thomas? There might be a few people at the reception desk who didn't hear you," she snapped. "And he's not a drunken anything. Anymore. He stopped drinking."

"You just said you shared a couple drinks at the wedding," Linus said.

Oh, brother. She didn't realize they were going to analyze every single word. "*I* drank. *He* had water," she replied. "Not that what I do is any of your concern. In case you didn't notice, I'm a grown woman. I'm not required to explain my actions to you."

"Unless your actions blow back and bite Collier's," Thomas replied. "Do you have any idea the kinds of stunts this guy has pulled? Bar fights, drunken howlers."

"Stop it. I've read the headlines, same as you."

"Then you know he's a degenerate. Even his teammates got tired of his antics. He bounced around to every team in the league because the other players hated dealing with him."

"Again, he *was* a degenerate. All of that happened when he was drinking." The ferocity of her defense surprised her, but she didn't like Thomas's tone. Her brothers didn't know Lewis. They didn't see the vulnerability in his eyes when he talked about his childhood. "There's a lot more to him than the headlines would lead you to believe." Her eyes glanced down at the newspaper and their photograph. "A lot more.

"Besides," she added, "I would think you'd be glad for the potential publicity. It is the Christmas season after all."

"Oh, sure," Thomas replied, "I'm thrilled to death. Nothing says Merry Christmas like having the company name tied to scandal."

"Oh, for crying out loud. There isn't going to be a scandal." Her big brother could be such a stubborn jerk. Once he got a notion in his head, he wouldn't shake it. "I would think you of all people would be open to the idea that people change."

That shut him up. They wouldn't be having a Christmas Eve vow renewal if Thomas and his wife hadn't learned to change. "Or do you think you and Rosalind have the monopoly on personal growth?"

"Don't be ridiculous. Of course, we don't," Thomas replied. "But..."

She finished the sentence for him. "Are you saying your relationship problems wouldn't have made headlines?"

"No, they would not have because neither of us was headline fodder." Implying that her "boyfriend" was and therefore their relationship would be in the press. It was all she could do not to tell him that was the point. In fact, if things went according to plan, the two of them would be all over the paper.

Her brother looked at her with the cool intensity he usually reserved for business meetings. "Two years," he said. "Two years, it took for me to get this company stable again after Dad ran it into the ground. Doing so very nearly cost me my marriage. The last thing I want is for it to be dragged down now by a scandal."

"For the last time, there won't be a scandal." The only way that could happen was if news of their fake relationship leaked out, and she and Lewis weren't planning to talk.

"We just want you to keep your wits about you." As he so often did, Linus moved in as the voice of reason and distraction. "Guys like Lewis Matolo know how to play women to get what they want."

"You don't know anything," she told him. "You've never even met Lewis." And, so what if he was using her? Lewis had never been anything but honest regarding his intentions.

"I don't have to. Trust me, I know. We're cut from a similar cloth."

No, they weren't. The defense sprang to her lips despite her having zero evidence beyond a couple conversations, one of which centered around him using her to get what he wanted.

Linus leaned forward so his face was level with hers. "Look," he said. "We're not trying to be jerks here. We're simply looking out for our baby sister. We just don't want to see you get involved with something that might come back to haunt you."

Because God forbid her relationship have some kind of future.

That, she realized, was what really hurt. Not Thomas's worries about gossip, but their automatic assumption that her relationship was doomed. Was it so unbelievable to them that a man like Lewis could be attracted to her?

Granted it was a business arrangement but her brothers didn't know that. You'd think they would have a higher opinion of her choices.

But then why should they venture off script, right?

"I don't really care what you want," she snapped. Or what they thought of her either. "It's my life and who I date is my business. Now, if you don't mind, it's the end of the month. I have a whole bunch of work to do and you're sitting on my reports." Plus she needed to call Lewis so they could discuss their next step.

"Do what you want," Thomas said as Linus rose to his feet. "But you better be right about his being a different person. First negative article I see with the name Collier attached and I'll have your boyfriend's head on a platter." The toughness would have worked better if Linus hadn't snorted.

"He means his legal team will," her middle brother said. "Still, be careful, okay? Players are called players for a reason."

"Are we done with the lecture?" Susan asked. She really wanted to talk with Lewis now. Hoping they'd take the hint, she reached for her desk phone. It worked. They shut the door and left her in peace. Although Thomas did manage one last stern look through the glass wall.

Susan immediately picked up the paper to study the pictures again. Just who did they think they were, poking their noses in her love life? And Thomas calling Lewis a degenerate. Wait until the Collier's Christmas Party. She and Lewis would show everyone exactly how wrong their opinion was.

Even if they had to pretend to do so.

Has Champagne Lewis given up his wild ways? The former goaltender was seen canoodling with a brunette mystery woman at the O2 arena last night.

Sources say this isn't the first time the couple has been seen together. The two were spotted at Esprit last weekend enjoying a romantic Sunday brunch.

Lewis slapped the tabloid on the table with a grin. "Not bad," he said. "Not bad at all." There were two things the press loved: a good celebrity romance and a good redemption story. He should have thought of this plan months ago.

His eyes dropped to the photograph of him and Susan. Thankfully she wasn't too annoyed about the "Mistletoe Cam" incident. Yes, keeping it a surprise was a dirty trick, but it also kept her reactions natural. The way her eyes widened in surprise, the way her lips parted. You couldn't fake those kinds of things.

She wasn't the only one caught by surprise though. The original plan was to share a quick peck on the cheek. Lewis hadn't counted on her mouth looking so alluring, nor had he anticipated how good her kiss would taste. Licking his lips, he swore he could still taste her sweetness.

Kisses didn't usually linger with him. In his mind, women were more or less interchangeable. Warm bodies that kept him from noticing he was alone. He wondered if the fact that this was his first sober kiss in a long time was the reason he found it so memorable. He'd been tempted to test the theory by kissing her again at the end of the night. But then, when they reached her doorstep and Susan looked up at him with those marvelous green-and-brown eyes…he'd backed away. Susan wasn't interchangeable. She deserved more respect than to be kissed simply for the sake of kissing.

But damn, he'd wanted to kiss her again. Wanted to so badly.

On the kitchen counter, his phone began buzzing an SOS signal, the vibration pattern he'd assigned Susan. He answered and hit Speaker while at the same time opening his refrigerator. "What can I do for you, Miss Collier?" he asked as he scanned the contents.

"Did your teammates really dislike you?"

"That's an odd way of starting a conversation," he replied. It appeared his housekeeper had done some grocery shopping for him. There was a fresh gallon of orange juice next to the milk.

"Did they?"

"I never spent enough time with them to know one way or another. Hung to myself mostly. Unless there was a party." He paused to take a swig of juice. "What's this about?"

"I'm sorry. Something my brother mentioned. He said you bounced from team to team because no one liked you."

"More like management disliked paying my heavy contract fees." Although he wasn't surprised to hear his bad-boy reputation had fueled different stories. Once again, his partying ways left their mark. "I take it your brother saw the paper."

"He did. He called you a degenerate."

"I've heard worse."

The pause on the other end of the line made him uneasy. "He's worried about scandal," Susan said. "I hadn't considered how this might affect the company.

Collier's has only recently gotten back on solid footing. If people discover…"

"They won't. I promise. I'm going to be on my best behavior." He had too much to lose.

"I know you will," she replied.

Her faith surprised him. She was the first person he'd met who really believed he'd changed. "I don't want to put you in a bad spot. If you want to back out, I'll understand."

"I don't want to back out—I gave my word and I intend to keep it. Besides… I had a good time last night."

Lewis smiled at the shyness in her voice. "We're famous you know," he said.

"Everyone in my office is whispering and giving me looks. They probably don't think I've been kissed before."

"You have been, right?"

"Yes. Although never quite so publicly."

"You're not still sore about my keeping the Mistletoe Camera thing a secret, are you?"

The soft sigh on the other end of the line sounded playfully exasperated. "I've recovered. But I want a promise that next time I'll get a little advance warning."

The memory of her glazed eyes popped into his head. "No worries there. I doubt there'll be a Mistletoe Cam at our next outing." Meaning he wouldn't have an excuse—that is, a reason—to kiss her.

"I suppose there wouldn't be, unless we were attending another basketball game. That's…good."

Was the clipped tone in her voice disappointment or relief? "I think so," he said. "I mean, it being a good thing. Can't go heavy on the PDA if I'm supposed to be changing my ways, right?"

"Right. Absolutely." He still couldn't tell. There was noise in the background. Maybe she was guarding her end of the conversation.

His ego took a little kick. A *little* disappointment would have been nice. It'd been a pretty decent kiss in his book. Heck, women were known to pull off their tops just to get his *attention*.

Those were women who wanted him though. Susan was with him as quid pro quo. She didn't really want him...

"Lewis?"

He shook his head. How long had he been staring into the neck of the orange juice bottle? "Did you say something?"

"I asked about the next step. Now that people know we're...that is, you know..."

"A couple," Lewis supplied. The word felt oddly normal.

"Exactly. What do we do now?"

Good question. According to his list, step two was to be seen at a few more formal events. Fundraisers with the proper people to establish his new social circle.

And he knew exactly the event. "How do you feel about the Kew Gardens?"

"In general? They're lovely. What does that have to do with us?"

"We're going to make our first official appearance there," Lewis told her. "This Saturday night. I hope you have a formal cocktail dress in your closet."

"I think I can rustle one up," she replied.

He had no doubt. "In the meantime, I'll talk to Michael about keeping up the momentum."

There was a pause on Susan's end of the line. He

imagined her pretty pink lips drawing into a frown. "What does that mean?"

"Keeping us in the public eye, luv, of course," he said. "If all goes right, it'll be a fun week."

The next few days were unlike anything Susan had ever experienced. It was like she'd changed identities overnight.

"What's he like?" became a common question.

Along with "Is he as wild as they say?"

The photo from the basketball game—with help from Lewis's agent, no doubt—had set off a domino trail of publicity. A couple of local radio personalities had seen the story and it had become fodder for one of the morning talk show segments. That, of course, had led to more articles.

One, rehashing Lewis's past romantic rendezvous, she found uncomfortable to read. Another focused on her, with the article playing up the fact that she had ties not only to Collier's Soap, but to former sex kitten Belinda Quinn.

Thankfully, as she told Lewis, her mother was filming some island reality show in the middle of nowhere and was unreachable, saving them from having to deal with *that* particular crazy.

Susan felt like a rock star.

The best part? Courtney and Ginger were practically apoplectic with jealousy. Was it petty and childish of her to take pleasure in their envy? Yes, but she was enjoying it regardless.

The two women spent the first couple of days after the "Kiss-mas" article appeared whispering behind her back. Mostly disbelief that Susan was the woman Lewis had chosen to date.

Like he would have dated either one of you, Susan longed to say.

All right, given they were both gorgeous, Lewis probably would have dated them, but she bet he wouldn't have remembered their names. Lewis would always remember hers.

And Lewis had kissed her. It might have only been for the cameras, but it was still a kiss—something Courtney and Ginger couldn't claim.

It wasn't until Day Three that their whispers became more pointed. And louder.

"A friend of mine used to tend bar at Narcissus and he said his credit card was always getting turned down for lack of funds."

Susan was walking back to her office when she heard the comment. Glancing at the cubicle of her admin, Freema, she spied Ginger and Courtney hovering by the doorway. There was no doubt about whose credit card they meant.

"Ginger," she called over to them. The blonde's spine straightened the second she heard her name. "Shouldn't you be working on our upcoming media buys? You, too, Courtney?"

Two wide-eyed, gaping expressions greeted her. At least they had the good sense to be embarrassed over getting caught. "We, um…were just chatting," Courtney finally managed to spit out.

"Well, I suggest you save your chatting for your lunch hour and let Freema do her job. And…" Because she could, she took a couple steps closer for dramatic effect. “I’ll remind you—once—that my personal life is none of your concern. Do I make myself clear?”

Ginger’s red cheeks said it all. “Yes.”

“Good. Because I don’t want to have this talk again.” Folding her arms, she stood and maintained steady eye contact until the two women moved away. As she was leaving, she swore she heard the word *Shrewsan* muttered under one of their breaths. Lunchtime would be quite the gossip session, she imagined.

Let them complain. She was a rock star.

A giant illuminated tunnel greeted the car as they pulled through the main gate at Kew Gardens a few nights later. As they passed beneath, Lewis heard Susan gasp. “Oh, my! This is amazing.” Leaning forward in her seat, she looked upward. “It looks like something out of that sci-fi TV show where they enter the wormhole.”

“It does at that,” Lewis agreed. Hundreds of overhead lights twinkled all around them like stars. “You know what this means, don’t you?”

She looked across the seat at him, the lights reflecting in her eyes. “What?”

“If the car starts shaking uncontrollably, abandon ship.”

“Not in this dress I’m not.”

If it were another woman, he would have started pretending to hit turbulence and saying *she’s breaking up* in his best Scottish accent. She would have laughed and thought him rakishly charming, even if she were too young to get the reference.

Tonight however, he had a difficult enough time making any lame jokes. He was wound tighter than a drum. For Susan, this was just another event, but for him, it would be the first time he'd attended a black-tie event with the intention of staying and mingling. No signing autographs and blowing off early with a bootlegged bottle of whatever he could grab.

Susan's diamond earrings sparkled as she angled her head to look upward again. "I think they strung Christmas lights over the entire driveway," she said. "It looks absolutely magical."

It certainly did. Lewis had never been to Kew Gardens—nature walks weren't really his thing—but the Christmas lights were famous. "The flyer that came with the tickets did say we would be treated to a fantastical holiday light show. Guess they weren't kidding."

"What charity are we supporting anyway? I never thought to ask. Be embarrassing if I couldn't remember the names of my boyfriend's causes."

Lewis tensed. No one had ever referred to him by that word before. It unsettled him. More nerves, he decided. Susan was only joking.

"You shouldn't have too much trouble remembering," he told her. "It's for the Sports Trust for Children."

"Isn't that one of the prince's charities? You don't believe in doing things small scale do you?"

"Wish I could tell you this was part of some grand strategy, but the truth is, I've been donating to the Sports Trust for years. Usually I give the tickets to this event away though."

"Why?"

"I'm not much for brie and crackers," he replied.

"No, I mean why the Sports Trust? In case someone asks," she said.

"Do people ask those sorts of questions?" Seeing

how everyone in the room was a supporter, he would assume they didn't care.

"Never hurts to be prepared. What if I run into a reporter or some person on the board of directors? They might wonder why you all of a sudden decided to start attending boring cocktail parties. If we're smart, we'll have our stories straight. I don't want to scramble the way I had to with Thomas and Linus."

"You handled that situation well enough." Admirably actually. "But I see your point. In this case, you can tell people the truth. Football kept me off the streets. In fact, if it weren't for sports, God knows where I'd be." He wouldn't be attending charity cocktail parties, that's for sure. More likely he'd be working some dead-end job and trying to stay out of trouble. "Sports gives kids a way to escape and be kids, if only for a few hours. If my money can help a kid out of trouble then that's a good thing, right?"

"A very good thing," she replied.

He wasn't sure why, but her smile made him feel like he'd aced a test. It mattered that she knew he was capable of sincerity.

In keeping with the season, the Victorian greenhouse hosting the event was illuminated with soft pink-and-blue spotlights, giving the building a purple glow. Lewis directed their driver to pull into the valet line to let them out.

"I haven't been here since my grandfather took us as children," Susan said as they stepped onto the sidewalk.

"Puts you one up on me," Lewis replied. "I've never been."

He looked around at the rolling lawns. They looked lush and manicured, despite it being winter. The building itself was an astounding stretch of glass and metal, its doorway guarded by a set of robed statues. "Lot fancier than I expected," he said.

"I always assumed my memory of this place was distorted by childhood, but maybe not. If I remember correctly, this particular building was filled with all sorts of rare plants."

They followed the other guests up the granite steps to the entrance where they were welcomed by a pair of giant poinsettia towers and a whoosh of warm, moist air. It was like stepping into a giant tropical forest. Plants of every shape and size surrounded them.

"Smells like spring," Susan said.

Indeed. There was definitely a hint of fresh dirt to the air. A sharp contrast to the cold night air.

The coat check was in the corner, marked by a pair of ferns decorated with tiny Christmas ornaments. If he hadn't been looking for it, he might never have found it. He turned to Susan intending to help her with her coat only to find she'd already slipped the garment from her shoulders. His breath caught at the sight of her. She'd been waiting on her steps when he picked her up, so this was the first time he'd had a chance to see what she was wearing and the sight took his breath away. At the wedding, she'd gone for a retro look: black, white and tight. Tonight she had a more graceful look. Her pale pink dress had a gathered bodice and long flowy skirt. While the dress didn't hug her curves the way the dress at the wedding had, the outfit fit tightly enough to let people know she had a shape while the V-neck showed off her ample cleavage. He liked that her breasts were soft and natural looking too. He'd seen enough enhancements in his life to actually find them boring.

In fact, he liked how everything about her looked soft and natural, right down to her hair which she let curl around her shoulders.

"You look great," he said.

Her skin turned the color of her dress. "Thanks. I don't go to a lot of formal events so I wasn't sure if this would work. I was afraid this might be too…" She paused as a woman in a sequined minidress and with mile-long legs sauntered by. "Dowdy."

"Nonsense. It suits you." Shoot. That sounded like he was saying dowdy suited her. "I mean, not everyone is the sequined-mini type."

"I'm certainly not, that's for sure," she said before adding in a lower voice, "Think I'd catch a cold baring that much skin."

"Skin is overrated. Seriously." She was giving him a look of disbelief. "I'm not saying I don't appreciate a miniskirt as much as the next guy, but there's something to be said about maintaining a little mystery, know what I mean?" He handed over their coats and waited for his claim ticket.

"Really? I always got the impression men wanted to get down to business as quickly as possible."

"Obviously, you've been hanging around the wrong type of man."

She blushed again. This time the color went past the V and the effect hit him square in the gut. He meant what he said. It was much more fun wondering how much of her very white skin was capable of blushing than seeing it from the start.

He reached out and twirled one of her curls around his index finger. "Trust me, luv. You look as good as anyone here. More so, even, because you've got class."

"And you are a very smooth talker, Mr. Matolo," she replied with a smile. "If things don't work out in the broadcast world, you can always get a job selling used cars. Come on, we've got mingling to do."

Lewis watched as she started along the leafy walkway. She didn't believe him, but it was true. She projected a level of class that came from years of breeding. Even when drunk at the wedding, she'd held herself with refinement. Lewis could barely muster it when he was sober. Sure, he had looks and charm, but at his core he was the little street kid being kicked from home to home. The one whom, if he hadn't been able to block a ball, wouldn't have been looked at twice by the people in Susan's world. The one who didn't belong…

"Are you coming?" Susan asked.

"One minute. Thought I'd enjoy the view a moment, first."

Score blush number three, although she tried to cover it with an exasperated eye roll. "Now you're just trying to get a rise out of me. If you really want a view, come check this out."

It was a Christmas jungle. In addition to the tropical plants, strategically placed Christmas trees dotted the walkway intersections. Each was decorated with a different color of the rainbow. Red. Orange. Yellow. Green. Blue. Violet. Only they weren't covered with traditional ornaments. Instead, silk butterflies and flowers mixed with the lights.

It wasn't the Christmas display that captured his attention, however. It was the dozens of men and women clustered around the display. All dripping with money and status. A couple close to them turned in his direction, their gaze subtly looking them up and down. Judging. Whispering.

Suddenly he was that little boy again, waiting to be told he didn't belong.

"I need a drink," he said. He headed to the bar.

CHAPTER FIVE

DID HE SAY he was getting a drink? Susan hurried after him, wishing her legs were longer so she could keep up. Amazing how the man could cut through a crowd like butter.

She finally caught up with him—nearly collided with him, actually—when he stopped cold about a foot from the bar. "What are you doing?"

"I—I..." He washed a hand across his lips. "Something stupid."

Exactly what she'd feared. The question was why? After all his talk about reforming his image, why would he risk sabotaging himself right as his plan was taking off?

There were too many people around to have this conversation. Lewis's arrival had most of the room starstruck. She could see people all around them sneaking glances.

Grabbing his hand, she moved past the bar and down the back pathway where she spied a water display in the far corner. The splashing water from the falls discouraged most people from standing too close. They would have privacy there.

There was only one other couple lingering by the water's edge. The pair shot them a look upon arrival, with the woman, not surprisingly, looking a bit incredulously at Susan. Ignoring them, Susan pulled Lewis off the walkway and into the foliage. There was only a small spot of bare ground, but if they stood close together, they wouldn't trample anything. "What are you doing, Lewis?" she hissed, just loud enough to be heard over the water. "I thought you were a 'changed man.' Pretty sure making a beeline for the bar isn't one of the sobriety rules. And don't try to tell me you meant to grab a glass of water, because I saw the look on your face."

It was like a mask had dropped over his features. The muscles by his jaw began to twitch.

He wore a different expression now. Eyes lowered, his brow drawn together. "I know. It was stupid. I wasn't thinking."

Something had flipped his switch. "People don't just fall off the wagon without some kind of trigger. What happened?"

He shook his head. "It doesn't matter."

"Yes, it does matter," she told him. "I didn't agree to this little charade only to have you muck it up and embarrass us both."

Plus, not that she'd say so out loud, his sudden change in demeanor worried her. He was supposed to be this sexy, confident "reformed" playboy. The man she saw a moment ago had looked vulnerable and dare she say, insecure. Insecurity was *her* albatross. Men with perfect faces and perfect lips didn't experience self-doubt.

"You don't have to worry," Lewis told her. "It was a momentary blip. Nothing more."

"I believe you." After all, he'd stopped himself before

even getting to the bar. "Still, I'd feel better if I knew what set the blip off."

"Silly really," he said, looking downward. "I've faced down some of the world's toughest players with thousands of people watching without flinching, but put me in a room full of tuxedo-wearing strangers and I'm a bundle of nerves." Susan's breath caught as he moved his hand toward her shoulder, only to fiddle with a frond hanging behind her. "I'm sure that sounds ludicrous to someone like you."

"What do you mean *someone like me*?" The branch he was playing with was brushing against her curls, causing little ripples of awareness.

"This is your world. Sophisticated. Highbrow. You belong in it."

Hardly, but this wasn't the time to argue. At least about that. "Excuse me, Mr. Celebrity Millionaire. This is your world too."

"You know," he said, "I tell myself that very thing all the time. That I belong."

"But?" She could hear the doubt in his voice.

"But then I look at these people and I can hear them thinking *What is he doing here?* It's like they know where I came from."

"So what if they do?" she asked. "You have nothing to be ashamed of. Heck, half of this room is probably wondering how they can wrangle an introduction. More than half, likely."

"For now."

Susan frowned. "I don't understand."

"You said it yourself. I'm a celebrity. The more distance between me and my playing days, however, the less it'll matter. Until eventually I'll be just some bloke who was once a somebody and they'll wonder..." He shook his head. "Never mind."

"Tell me. Please." If whatever was on his mind was distressing enough that he would consider drinking, she wanted to help.

He answered so softly, she almost didn't hear. "And they'll wonder why they ever wanted me around in the first place. Silly, huh?"

A piece of her heart broke for him. "No," she told him. Illogical perhaps, but far from silly. He wasn't talking about reality; he was talking about a feeling that dwelled deep down inside a person. A feeling logic couldn't always touch.

"The Collier men are all very tall," she told him. "Very tall, very handsome and very charismatic, like my father. My mother is very beautiful. Like stop-traffic beautiful."

He was looking at her with dark, fathomless eyes. "I'm not following."

"When I was seven or eight—right before my mother took off—my parents threw a party. I wore this fancy party dress and my father told me how pretty I looked. I asked if I was as pretty as Mommy. And when he replied, *Absolutely*, my mother replied, *Don't lie to the girl, Preston*. That was the moment I knew that I wasn't like the rest of them. No matter how hard I tried, I would always be the odd one out."

Now it was she who felt judged as Lewis's gaze bore down on her. She'd meant the example as a sign of solidarity. Instead, she'd revealed that she was the Ugly Duckling of her family. He must think her daft. Why did she share anything?

His deep brown eyes moved closer. "Thank you.

Knowing you understand means a lot." He ran the back of his hand down her cheek. "More than you could know."

A shiver worked its way through Susan's body. Odd, since she'd suddenly grown very warm. Between the greenhouse temperature and the warmth emanating from Lewis's body, the air around her had grown thick. It was making her light-headed.

"Everything all right?" Lewis asked.

"Can we sit down somewhere?"

"Of course. Come with me." He tucked a curl behind her ear.

Since the other couple had departed—escaping the awkwardness of standing near a couple whispering in the bushes no doubt—Susan assumed they would head back to the walkway. Instead, Lewis took her hand and together they picked their way toward the waterfall.

"You were looking a little pink," he said, as he guided her to a seat on a nearby rock. The air was noticeably cooler by the water.

"We're going to get in trouble for being off the walkway."

"We won't stay long. Besides, the gardeners or whatever walk through here, don't they? That's why there are paths."

Susan shook her head. "You're funny. One minute you're telling me you worry about fitting in and the next you're flouting the rules. One would think you're self-sabotaging."

"Psychoanalyzing again, are we?"

"I told you, psychology's my thing." Fat lot of good it ever did her though. Being able to psychoanalyze everyone but herself.

"Bit of an odd hobby, isn't it?" Lewis asked.

"What can I say? I'm rubbish at arts and crafts. I got into it when I was a teenager. My attempt to understand my mother better."

He touched her knee, his hand bringing a steadying warmth. "Did you? Understand her better?"

"I learned a bunch of terms, all of which boiled down to her being a selfish piece of work who didn't want to share the spotlight with a child. They want so much attention, you know."

She tossed aside the last part with an overdramatic voice, but the sting never really left. When she was younger she blamed her looks, thinking if she was taller or thinner or elegant like the Collier boys, then her mother might have wanted her around. As she grew older, however, she realized her mother wouldn't have wanted the competition. The sad truth was her mother just plain didn't want her.

"At least you knew how she felt," Lewis said. "My mum cried holy hell when they took me away, but not so much that she couldn't get her act together."

"Just like Belinda," she said. "Guess that makes us two odd peas in a pod."

"Guess so," Lewis replied with a smile.

She slipped her hand over his, and their fingers entwined. With the connection came a strange, full kind of feeling. Kinship, Susan realized. For the first time she felt understood. It was a heady, seductive feeling.

Ironic that she would set out to comfort him and end up being the one comforted.

"I'm not the only one who's an enigma," he continued.

"What do you mean?"

"Well, for one thing, I keep looking for this unlikable shrew part of you, and I can't see it. I mean, you've got sharp edges, but who hasn't, right?"

He couldn't have said a nicer thing if he tried. "Thank you."

"Just calling it like I see it. And what I see looks pretty nice. Very nice, in fact." His smile sobered as his gaze dropped to her lips. Susan's pulse quickened, remembering the last time he'd looked at her mouth.

Instead of leaning in like she thought he would, however, Lewis suddenly released her hand and rose to his feet.

"We should get back on the path before we get in trouble," he said. "Won't do either of our reputations any good if we get tossed out on our ears. I can see the headline now. Stay Off the Grass, Lewis!"

"I'm sure they'd come up with something punnier than that." Although an example escaped her. She was too busy hiding her disappointment behind smoothing her dress. Her embarrassment too, for thinking he'd been about to kiss her. Talk about foolish. There were no cameras, no giant screen. Why would he want to kiss her if there was nothing to gain?

They snuck out of the plants the way they'd come, emerging to the backs of several other partygoers who were standing on the path.

"And here we thought we were being so sneaky. I bet half the party saw us." She looked over at Lewis who was smoothing the front of his jacket. He looked as crisp and elegant as before.

"If they did, no one would say anything," he said. "My guess? They didn't care."

"Or they were too polite to make a scene with photographers about." She and Lewis might have joked about negative headlines, but in reality, the sponsors of the event wouldn't want the bad press.

"Either way, we lucked out then, didn't we? Come on, I'll buy you a glass of champagne before we mingle. I don't suppose you know anyone here?"

Other than one or two faces she recognized from Collier's functions, not really. Since attending solo wasn't much fun, she only went to charity events when Linus needed an emergency date, which wasn't often. She didn't want to tell him that though, because it would reveal how pathetic her social life was. This faux romance was the most social activity she'd had in who knows how long.

"Excuse me, Mr. Matolo?"

They'd managed to go no more than a handful of steps before they were stopped by a pair of official-looking gentlemen. The younger of the two reminded Susan of a thinner, nerdier version of the Duke of Sussex with red hair and a neatly trimmed goatee. The other resembled an owl. Rotund with tortoiseshell glasses and an extremely receding hairline.

It was the younger one who addressed them. "I'm Christopher Redmayne, from the Sports Trust for Children and this is Graham Montclark."

She felt Lewis's body stiffen from six inches away. "As in Montclark Communications?" he asked. Montclark was Britain's largest private media corporation. "I believe I've read your name atop a scoreboard or two."

The balding man didn't return Lewis's smile. "I'm sure you have. The company sponsors several sporting venues."

"The two of us have been waiting for you to step away from the water display," Redmayne said.

So much for escaping comment. "I'm sorry about that," she said. "I—"

"Susan was feeling a bit light-headed. I thought the air might be cooler by the water." Lewis clasped her hand and squeezed. "Didn't want her keeling over or anything. I hope that wasn't a problem?"

"No, of course not," Redmayne replied. If it was a problem, Lewis's explanation coupled with the fear of a guest fainting kept him from saying so. "Are you feeling better, Ms…?"

"Collier, and yes. Thank you. Lewis knew exactly what I needed. In fact, he was just about to get me something cold to drink."

"Good. Good," Redmayne replied. "A cold drink is always a good idea."

Interestingly though, the two men didn't make a move to step aside or leave. They remained planted in the middle of the path, apparently intent on having a conversation.

"Collier," Montclark said. "Any relation to Thomas?"

"My brother."

The businessman nodded. "Good man. Miraculous story, that business with his wife."

"Yes. The whole family was shocked when she returned. In a good way of course. We like to think of it as a true Christmas miracle."

"Graham is one of our advisors. I was telling him how generous you've been to our organization," Redmayne said. "Your support is very appreciated. It's always a surprise, to see who is willing to step up and help."

"You do good work," Lewis replied. "Why wouldn't I support you?"

"That's nice to hear." At that moment, a server walked by carrying a tray of champagne. Holding up a hand, Redmayne stopped the man from passing. "Could you get a glass of water for Ms. Collier?" he asked.

"Actually… Champagne will be fine." This conversation defined the term awkward. If it was going to continue, she would need more than water.

"I'll take the water, if you don't mind," Lewis said. You could tell both of the other men were struggling not to look surprised. "I'm a teetotaler these days."

Susan smiled at him with pride. The admission couldn't have been easy for him. Not in this environment where he already felt judged.

Redmayne recovered first, with the grace one expected from an experienced networker. "I should take a page from your book. Every holiday I swear I'm going to cut back on excesses and every year I'm filled with regret because my pants are too snug." The four of them shared an uncomfortable chuckle.

"Anyway," Redmayne continued, "I hate to talk business when the two of you are here to enjoy yourselves, but we're hosting a Christmas event for our young ambassadors on December eleventh. Heath Chilton was supposed to lead a sports clinic but we found out this morning that he's having a second knee surgery and won't be able to attend so…"

"You're wondering if Lewis would be able to step in!" In a voice suiting a loyal girlfriend, Susan finished the sentence for him. Actually she suspected Redmayne wanted to ask if Lewis could use his contacts to get a current player—hence the awkwardness—and she jumped in to get Lewis's name on the table first. From the look Redmayne shared with Montclark, it was a good thing she had. "I think that's a terrific idea. Lewis was just saying how he wanted to get more involved with the program. Weren't you?"

He picked up her train of thought immediately. "Yes, I was, and I'd be honored to step in."

Redmayne was scrambling for a polite way to escape the hole he was in. "That's very generous of you, but, um…" He looked at Montclark, who opened his mouth to finish.

Lewis cut them off. "In fact," he said, "I know what Heath charges for public appearances. If it would help the organization's bottom line, I would be glad to donate my time free of charge."

Well done. Susan smiled into her champagne. A light gleamed in Montclark's eyes. The idea of saving a sizable amount of money clearly appealed to him. "We're looking to inspire these kids. Can we count on you to show up, ready to perform?"

"Mr. Montclark, I always show up ready to play," Lewis told him. "You have my word."

The reassurance didn't seem to impress the businessman, but the organization had its back against the wall. That they'd approached Lewis for any kind of assistance this close to the event said they were desperate. Susan knew what the two men were thinking. A free-of-charge, former player was better than no player at all.

The waiter returned with Lewis's water. "Here's your water, Mr. Matolo," he said. Servers probably didn't usually address the guests by name but the young man's starstuck expression as well as the excited tremor in his voice explained the break in protocol.

"Thanks, mate. Appreciate it."

Tucking the tray under his arm, the young man prepared to leave only to pause. "I've watched every game you ever played in."

"Wow," Lewis replied. "What'd you do? Start watching when you were in diapers?"

Susan watched Montclark taking in the exchange, particularly the waiter's starstuck face. After a few minutes more of conversation—and a request for a selfie—the young man moved on and Montclark cleared his throat. "Very well," he said, "since you are willing to make a firm commitment and waive your appearance fee..."

"Anything to help the organization," Lewis replied.

"We appreciate you stepping up on such short notice. Redmayne will send your agent all the information." The three men shook on the arrangement.

"Remind me to tip that server extra," Susan said once Redmayne and Montclark had moved on to the buffet table. "His timing couldn't have been more perfect if we paid him." There was no doubt his enthusiasm was what had finally convinced Montclark.

"Should I tip you too?" Lewis asked.

"Beg your pardon?"

"For backing them into the corner in the first place. We both know they wanted to use my connections, not hire me. If you hadn't jumped in with the idea, it never would have come up."

"You wanted to rehab your image. What better way than to dazzle them with your newfound dedication to charity?"

"Not to mention impressing Graham Montclark."

"Oh, do his stations carry the matches? I hadn't realized." Putting a hand to her chest, she blinked with false innocence.

Lewis chuckled, his accompanying smile devilishly crooked. "Well played, Ms. Collier. I knew I picked the right woman."

His words had the smoothness of raw honey dripping from a spoon. They ran through her, leaving a slow warmth.

He means the right woman for the arrangement.

She needed a dose of reality to counteract the sweetness. None of this was real. She'd be wise to keep that in mind before she did something incredibly stupid.

Like fall for the man.

CHAPTER SIX

LEWIS HAD DATED a lot of women in his adult life. Too many really. None of them, though, were like Susan. Granted, that was the point, but never had he thought that different would be so interesting.

They were on their way home, still in character, as it were. He had his arm slung across the back seat while Susan sat close to his side. Not overly close, and certainly not draped across his lap like a lot of his dates. Susan was far too classy for that kind of behavior.

Susan was a lot of things. She was smart and sophisticated, not to mention perceptive. When he had freaked out, she'd known exactly what to say.

An odd experience, it was, being understood. When she touched his hand, the warmth shot straight through him, the sensation simultaneously comforting and terrifying.

He wasn't used to sharing pieces of himself. Better to maintain distance, he always said. It made leaving easier. With Susan, however—and maybe it was because they were so alike—with Susan, sharing felt normal.

The car turned a corner. In spite of the late hour, there were plenty of lights on. Some of the windows already had candles and in one or two, he spied Christmas trees. “Early birds,” he murmured.

“Who are early birds?” Susan asked. When she turned to look at him, he caught a whiff of vanilla shampoo. Reminded him of cookies.

“The trees,” he replied. “Some people already have theirs up. They’re early birds.”

“Probably the same people who start playing Christmas music the day after Halloween and have their shopping done a month early.”

“I’m going to go out on a limb and guess that you aren’t one of those people.”

“Definitely not.” Even in the dark he could see her eyes widen in horror. Whether she realized it or not, her little protest had shifted her closer to him. Her shoulder brushed against the edge of his coat. “No shopping until December first. That’s my rule.”

Lewis looked at his watch. “Good news then. You can start officially start shopping. It’s after midnight.”

“Huzzah! I’ll fire up my computer as soon as I get home.”

“That’s the Christmas spirit.” Unable to help himself, he wrapped his arm around her shoulder and squeezed, pulling her body into the crook of his arm as he did so. He liked that she was huggable. When you pulled her close, her body was warm and comfortable. The kind of body built for cuddling.

He’d never been one for cuddling before.

“I don’t know what I would have done without you tonight,” he said. “You were brilliant.”

Despite the shadows, he could feel she was blushing. “I told you before, you played as big a part in convincing Montclark as I did. If you really want to thank someone, thank the waiter."

"Man's timing *was* impeccable." It was Susan, though, who made him feel confident. "I don't think I would have made it through the entire party if you hadn't been there to talk me off the ledge."

"Don't be silly. You righted yourself all on your own," she said.

Perhaps, but her gentle reassurance was what had kept him righted from that moment on. "The stories you shared…"

Her gaze fell away. "Who knew sharing my childhood angst would be so powerful?"

"Don't sell yourself short." They both knew the real meaning behind her story. She'd peeled back a layer of herself to let him know he wasn't alone. That she, in her own way, understood how it felt to be on the outside looking in.

For as long as he could remember, he'd been left of center. Separate and alone, even when surrounded by people. Oh, he put on a good face, but in the end that's all it was, a face. Even when he was part of a team, he never truly felt a sense of solidarity. Why bother when you were only going to move on?

But tonight, he didn't feel alone. He and Susan were a team. The idea was headier than anything he ever felt. It took his breath away, and at the same time, scared him. He didn't do close. He did self-preservation.

Regardless, she deserved to know just how much her honesty meant to him. "All that stuff I told you tonight…" He chose his words carefully in case the driver was listening. "I've never told anyone before."

Her breath caught, and a second later her head came to rest on his shoulder. “Me neither,” she said.

“Your apartment is right ahead, miss,” the driver said.

His announcement was a switch, ending the moment. Almost immediately, the two of them straightened, with Susan shifting one way and Lewis the other. The gap that formed was imperceptible, but Lewis’s side grew cooler nevertheless.

He busied himself with watching the traffic while Susan fiddled with her bag and the driver parallel parked.

“Tonight was fun.”

At the sound of Susan’s voice, he turned his head. “I’m glad you enjoyed yourself.”

“I did. Between this and the basketball game, you’ve set the bar pretty high. Makes me wonder what you’ll come up with next.”

“You’ll have to wait and see.”

The driver opened the door, and they stepped onto the sidewalk.

“Should I wait?” the driver asked.

“I… No. I’ll be right back,” he replied. “I have an early morning tomorrow.”

Ignoring what looked like a flash of disappointment flaring in Susan’s eyes, Lewis guided her up the walkway to the red door marking the entrance to her apartment building. “If you give me your keys, I’ll open the door for you.”

“I think I can handle a key,” she replied before reaching into her bag and pulling out a large key ring. “It’s hardly complicated.”

“Yes, but the driver is watching. Since we don’t know

if he'll try to sell us out, I should make a point of unlocking and walking you in the door."

"Absolutely. We've got to keep up appearances, don't we? However, the front door has a keypad. The lock is for my apartment door."

There it was again, that distance, and he couldn't figure out why. Nothing he had said seemed inappropriate. "All right then, why don't you give me the key code."

"Fine," she said with a sigh.

As he punched in the numbers, Lewis fought the urge to turn around and check on the driver who might or might not be paying attention.

No sooner had he opened the door, than Susan started over the threshold.

"Wait." He grabbed her wrist to keep her from disappearing. "I need to kiss you goodnight. The driver might be watching. We want to give him something he can peddle to Lorianne or another columnist."

"Right," she replied. "We want to give the right impression."

Lewis couldn't tell if the sarcasm in her voice was meant to be humorous or not. With the shadows obscuring her expression, it was impossible to tell. It didn't matter though. Appearances needed to be maintained. Slipping his arm around her waist, he closed the space between them and kissed her. Just as he had at the game, he only intended a brief, chaste peck. The moment his lips touched hers, however, any thought of chaste flew out the window.

Her mouth was made for kissing. Their lips slanted together like links in a chain, Susan's mouth yielding without urging. Her head fell back and her body arched against him. Lewis's body, still humming with awareness from earlier, reacted immediately. Pulling her close, he pressed his hips to hers, delivering a deep, soulful kiss while his free hand tangled in her curls.

Susan's eyes were glazed when they finally broke apart, or so he told himself. Again, he couldn't see her expression, but since *he* was dazed, he hoped she was, as well. From one kiss. His body was on full alert now, wanting nothing more than to take her upstairs and continue.

Fortunately common sense had maintained a tenuous grip, and he was able to step back. "Continuing" wasn't part of their deal.

Taking a breath, he stepped backward again, down to the step below. "Well, that should give the driver some gossip to peddle," he said.

Hopefully his grin didn't look as shaky as it felt.

"I think it's time we slept together."

Susan tripped over a crack in the sidewalk and nearly dropped her coffee. It was three weeks into their "relationship," and they were spending the weekend afternoon Christmas shopping. Until now, they'd stuck to highly visible social events where their status as a couple was documented by official photographers and social reporters. Lewis felt the timing was such that they should embark on Step Three of his plan, or what he called "doing coupley things." His agent said he would tip off the tabloids that the two of them would be spending the day on Regent Street on the off chance they wanted to snag a photo of the budding romance.

At the moment, the only thing they'd snag would be a shot of her staring at him bug-eyed.

"Not literally, obviously," Lewis said catching her elbow.

No, of course not. Susan focused on adjusting her jacket so he wouldn't see her disappointment. Sleeping together didn't involve an audience, and Lewis didn't initiate any displays of affection unless someone was watching.

How could he turn his emotions on and off like that? All gentle touches and intimate glances in public only to back away the moment they were alone. They'd even taken to stepping inside the doorway of her building to say goodbye so he wouldn't have to kiss her goodnight.

Clearly she'd been a little too enthusiastic in her response the other night. Honestly, what did he expect though after essentially telling her she was special on the drive home?

Then again, maybe the admission had been for show too. They hadn't been alone.

Recovering herself, she made a show of taking a sip of coffee. "What would be the point of pretending we're sleeping together?" she asked. Besides frustrating her.

"Because people expect to see a real relationship move forward. It's the twenty-first century. People in serious relationships sleep together."

"I know that." She may not have had a serious love affair in her lifetime, but she had dated people for more than a few months. "I mean, what would be the overall goal? We'd get a blind item saying you spent the night or a pic in the *Looking Glass* of us heading out to breakfast?"

"You got a better idea?"

"Not really, but…"

She'd been thinking about this a lot the past few

days. There was a hole in Lewis's plan. "Blind items aren't read by everyone. There's no guarantee your message is going to reach the people you need to influence. Same with attending a few social events." The more she thought, the more she wondered if their plan was a waste of time.

Or maybe it was that the phoniness of it all was beginning to chafe. Tipping off photographers, pretending for witnesses. Every gimmick was a reminder that she wasn't good enough to be a real girlfriend.

It wouldn't be so bad if he weren't so damn amazing when they were together. Like today when he'd shown up on her doorstep bearing coffee for their shopping adventure. He even tucked in her scarf under the guise of keeping her warm while they walked. All for the benefit of anyone who might be watching.

Why wasn't she worthy of such treatment in private? Susan sighed. When she agreed to play along, it was so people like Courtney and Ginger would stop calling her pathetic. Now she wondered if she was merely proving them right.

"Earth to Susan…" A leather glove waved in her face. "You there?"

"Sorry," she replied. "You were saying?"

"I was saying you're right. We need to make a bigger splash. I'll talk to Michael about scoring a profile article in one of the weekly mags. How do you feel about becoming a cover model?"

Awkward. "Who on earth would want to read an article about me?"

"I would. You're a fascinating woman." His smile made her stomach tumble. There he went again, making her feel special. "But I'm thinking about a profile about both of us. One of those 'How Love Saved Me' articles. What do you think?"

Terrific. So not only did he want to take their fake romance to the next fake level, he wanted to give an interview about how much he fake loved her. The idea gave her heartburn. "I think I need to check your coffee," she said.

"Nothing but Italian roast, I swear. Here, do you want to test it?" He held out the cup.

Susan pushed it back. "I'll take your word for it."

"The more I think about it," Lewis continued, "the more I can't believe I didn't think of the idea sooner. A feature article would convince people a lot faster and it would give Collier's some good publicity, as well."

"I didn't realize you were in a rush," she said.

"I'm not looking to dawdle—the season will be starting soon enough."

"You're going to have to hustle if you want to be featured before the holidays," she said. "Even weekly magazines have a lead time. Too close to the holidays, and you'll have to keep up the ruse through January. We only mapped out an agreement through the holidays, so unless you want to extend things…"

"I'll call Michael first thing on Monday morning," he said. "I don't want to tie you up longer than necessary."

What he really meant was tie him up. The sooner he established himself as a reliable potential commentator, the sooner he could go about finding a woman who was more his type. She swallowed the bad taste that suddenly filled her mouth.

No sense dwelling on the inevitable. They had nearly a month to go before they parted company. Today was about "being coupley."

"Is there a game plan for this shopping expedition or are we just going to parade up and down the street letting people stare at us?" she asked.

"Up to you. I'm more of an online shopper myself."

"How personal."

"How convenient," Lewis replied. "One click and you're done."

Susan wondered if she was part of his "one click." They'd decided they weren't spending Christmas together. Did fake couples bother to exchange gifts if they weren't being watched?

Stop whining. You knew what you were getting into.

"As much as I enjoy people staring, I think we should do something. Do you feel up to tackling a toy store? My niece Maddie wants Bugnoculars."

"Bug-what?"

The way he scrunched up his face in confusion was adorable. "Binoculars that let you look at bugs close up," she explained. Her niece had become a budding entomologist. "Actually, she wants two pairs. One for her and one for her stuffed pet, Bigsby. Oh, and a kitten too, but I was informed she's already put in an order for the animal with Santa."

"Hope for her sake, he comes through."

"Last year she asked for a visit from her dead mother, and got her wish. A 'gray tiger kitten with a red bow' shouldn't be too difficult, considering."

Naturally her sister-in-law's reappearance at Christmastime was merely coincidence, but Maddie believed it was all Santa. Susan saw no sense bursting her bubble. In a few years the little girl would learn the truth about Santa and that part of her innocence would die forever. "How old were you when you stopped believing in Santa?" she asked.

"Six," Lewis replied. "I told one of the other kids at the foster home that Santa was bringing me a race car set, and he let me know the score."

Six years old. It saddened her, thinking of how disappointed he must have been.

"Wouldn't you know, *his* mom got her act together for the holidays and showed up with the exact set I wanted. I got to watch him and his brother play with the thing all day."

She didn't dare ask about Lewis's mother, suspecting she knew the answer. "Didn't they let you join them?"

"Nah. Wasn't part of the family," he said, eyes looking off in the distance. In that moment, his profile looked so forlornly beautiful it made her throat clutch. She squeezed her coffee cup to keep from pulling him into a hug. Lewis shook his head. "I was too young." Maybe she was projecting, but his offhand comment came out flat. "What about you," he asked. "When did you figure it out?"

"Fourth grade." She remembered well. "My classmates told me. Turned out I was the only one who was still a believer. The whole class got quite a laugh." The memory of her embarrassment swirled in her stomach. "Oh, well," she said. "Whatever. It was a long time ago. I've recovered."

"My resilient little pea?"

His what? Right, they were two odd peas in a pod. Was it strange that whenever they shared sad childhood tales, she ended up feeling warm from the inside out?

She decided to change the subject before things became too maudlin. "Hamleys is only a block away. Ready to tackle the crowds?"

Breaching the gap between them, Lewis took her arm and tucked it in the crook of his own. "Crowds are what we want, luv. Remember?"

Good thing too because it was the opening weekend of Santa's grotto. As a result, the toy store was filled with children dressed in their Christmas finery waiting to go upstairs for their chance to speak with the man himself while their parents snapped a photo for the annual Christmas card. If ever there would be a place where they'd be noticed, this was it. Most of the kids would be too young to recognize Lewis, but their parents weren't. Susan saw a number of heads turn in their direction as they walked in.

"I think the science toys are on the second floor," Susan told him.

She made it halfway to the staircase before she realized Lewis wasn't following. Figuring someone must have stopped him for an autograph or photo, she turned and scanned the crowd. It wasn't difficult to find his tall form in the crowd and she soon spied him by the animatronic display. The store was famous for its fantastical panoramas. This year, the wall was a winter resort with animals of all sorts enjoying the great outdoors. Teddy bears rode a ski lift. A pair of rabbits were ice skating on a pond. There was even a cutout of a lodge where a sloth lay stretched in a hammock by a roaring fire.

Lewis was mesmerized. His eyes were wide and shining and he had an almost slack-jawed look of wonder about him. Maddie wore a similar look when Susan had brought her last year. Lewis's expression caused warmth to spread through her chest. He looked beautiful when his guard slipped. She wanted to wrap her arms around him and soak him up.

Suddenly it hit her. He was viewing the display with a child's eye for good reason. "You've never been in here at Christmastime, have you?" she asked.

"Never been in here period," he replied. "No reason to."

And probably too far away when he was a child. How much childhood had he lost moving from home to home? While she was the odd person out in her family, she at least had one. Her heart ached picturing the little boy watching his foster siblings play with the toy he wished for. It wasn't just the toy that caused the pain; it was being shut out.

Without giving it a second thought, she wrapped her arms around his biceps and rested a head on his shoulder. Her way of saying he wasn't frozen out anymore. The shifting of muscles beneath her cheek told her Lewis had looked down in surprise, but he didn't say a word.

"Pretty amazing, isn't it?" she remarked. "It must take them months to plan everything out. All the little details."

Lewis chuckled. "There's a red squirrel dancing in one of the trees. I had a teammate who danced like that. Hector Menendez. Called it his booty dance. I should send him a video to show him how awkward he looked." He took out his phone.

Susan was watching another set of rabbits, this pair chasing one another around a tree trunk. "My grandfather used to bring us here when we were little."

"Same one who took you to the Kew Gardens?"

Susan nodded. “He took us a lot of places. The company museum was his favorite—always a good time.”

“Didn’t like learning about soap?”

“Thomas and Linus liked it. I was four years old. I just wanted ice cream. Come to think of it, there are days when I’d still rather eat ice cream than be at Collier’s. For that matter, I’d take ice cream over anything.”

“Anything?” Lewis asked. Actually he purred, making her insides flip. “I can think of a few things I might like better.”

There must be someone nearby watching because he had his nose dangerously close to her temple. Very well. She’d play along. “Is that so? Like what?”

“Sugar cookies, for starters.”

Susan nearly snorted. That was so not what she expected. But then, this was a show, not a seduction. Why shouldn’t he give a nonsensical answer? “Cookies over ice cream? Close call, but I don’t think so.”

“That’s your opinion. Lately I’ve been finding the aroma very tempting. Has anyone ever told you that you have gorgeous hair?”

The non sequitur threw her, along with a brush across the top of her head that felt a lot like a kiss.

For the crowd.

“I’ve gotten a few compliments,” she replied.

In reality, her hair was a source of vanity for her. She had the Collier black hair, one of the few family traits—maybe the only family trait—from that side of the family that had been passed down to her.

“Good. Glad to hear it didn’t go unnoticed.”

Like the rest of her, she almost said. Instead, she whispered, “Thank you,” and, closing her eyes, rested her cheek a little more firmly against his woolen coat.

"Did you know your hair smells like sugar cookies?" Lewis whispered back.

Susan's eyes flew open. Pulling back, she looked at him expecting a grin. He was dead serious though. If anything, his eyes were slightly hooded. "Your shampoo," he said. "Reminds me of sugar cookies."

He just said he preferred sugar cookies. Was he trying to say…

The sound of her phone interrupted her thoughts before they could become coherent. Pulling her phone from her bag, she saw her brother Linus's face on the caller ID.

"Might want to head to the hospital," he said when she answered. "Baby number two has arrived."

CHAPTER SEVEN

"THE BABY'S HERE! The baby's here!" Susan's niece nearly lifted off the ground, propelling herself into her aunt's arms. A wispy little live wire she was, bouncing up and down on her toes even as she hugged Susan's midsection. "I'm a big sister," she announced in a loud, proud voice.

"And everyone in the hospital knows," Susan replied. "You need to keep your voice down though, so you won't wake the babies in the nursery."

Lewis watched the moment unfold from a few feet away. They stood outside one of the birthing suites in the maternity ward having hurried over as soon as Linus had called. He noticed Susan wore a giant smile as she admonished the girl, a clear indication she didn't really mind the boisterous greeting. She pressed one hand to her niece's back, while the other gently smoothed her bobbed brown hair. Even if she hadn't told him how much she adored Maddie, he'd have known from the tender expression on her face.

She knelt down so she was eye level with the girl. "Do you have a brother or a sister?"

"Brother. His name is No-Well."

"That would be Noel." A man joined them. Judging from his lanky frame, Lewis assumed it was one of Susan's brothers. Linus, the middle one, most likely. He looked too laid-back to be a new father. "She read the name card on the bassinet and thinks he's named after the Christmas song," he said. "Noel Christopher Collier."

"Got a bit of a Christmas theme going there, don't they?" The remark was out of his mouth before he could catch it.

Susan didn't seem to mind. In fact, she laughed. "My brother and his wife have a thing about Christmas. They think some kind of Christmas magic brought them back together."

Whatever floats their boat. Someone needed to believe in Christmas miracles.

He listened while Susan peppered her brother with questions about the baby's weight and other pertinent details.

"When did she go into labor?" she asked.

"Middle of the night, from what Thomas said. I'm not too clear on the details. Maddie was with the housekeeper when I picked her up."

"You weren't home," Maddie said. "We called you."

"I'm sorry, sweetheart. I didn't hear the phone. I was out Christmas shopping."

"With a friend," Linus noted. He'd finally acknowledged Lewis's presence. A pair of extremely intelligent blue eyes looked him up and down. "Hello."

There was definitely scrutiny in the greeting. As well as a good dose of protectiveness. Lewis's eyes darted to Susan who blushed and looked away. Lewis couldn't blame the man. If he had a sister and thought she was dating someone like him, he'd scrutinize the guy too.

"Lewis Matolo," he said, extending his hand. "Pleased to meet you."

"Linus Collier. Likewise." If he was insincere, the man's smile didn't show it. "Sorry to interrupt your shopping date."

"No problem. We can shop anytime. It's not every day someone has a baby."

"I'm Maddie." The little girl had her hand out, mimicking her uncle. When Lewis accepted, she yanked his arm up and down with enthusiasm. Had she been an adult, he would have popped an elbow.

"Hello, Maddie," he said. "Congratulations on your baby brother."

"I'm getting a kitten too. Santa's bringing him," she replied before tilting her head and switching gears in the way only children could. "Are you Aunt Susan's boyfriend? Uncle Linus says you are."

Lewis's cheeks grew warm. He wasn't expecting the third degree from a six-year-old. "I…um…" From his place behind his niece, Susan's brother was waiting for his response.

Susan stepped in before he could answer. "Lewis is a very good friend," she said. "He was helping me pick out your Christmas present."

"Really?" Maddie's eyes widened. "What did you get?"

"We can't tell you that," Lewis replied. "It would spoil the surprise."

"Aunt Susan says surprises are overrated."

"Yes, I know. She told me how she felt about them when we went to a basketball game recently." Susan ducked her head to hide her pinking cheeks. Lewis waited until she glanced at him through her lashes and then he grinned.

The exchange didn't escape her brother who scrutinized them both. "I'm sure Aunt Susan meant unpleasant surprises," Linus said. "Not good surprises like presents."

"Absolutely," Susan answered. "Some surprises are definitely worth waiting for. Like Christmas presents. So you're just going to have to wait, little munchkin."

"Okay." Maddie's disappointed expression didn't look very permanent. In fact, the frown disappeared about a second after it appeared, in correlation with the suite's door opening up.

"Daddy!" the little girl bounced away from Susan and toward the dark-haired man who'd stepped into the corridor. He immediately scooped her up in his arms.

Thomas Collier, Lewis presumed. His shirt and slacks were wrinkled, and he had the shadowed cheeks of a man who'd been up for hours. "You made it!" He flashed a grin in Susan's direction. "Linus said he was having trouble finding you."

"I didn't hear the phone," Susan said. "I was out shopping."

"With a friend," Linus added.

"So I see." Thomas turned his attention to Lewis. "Hello."

"Congratulations," Lewis replied. There was no welcoming handshake as the man had his hands full with his daughter, but part of Lewis wondered if there would have been one anyway. Clearly, Thomas was the more serious of the two. His gaze, laser-like in its focus, had a hint of wariness.

"Thank you," he replied. "Kid was an impatient little

guy—Rosie barely got settled before he decided to appear. Fifteen minutes later and he might have popped out in the lift." The second half was directed at Linus and Susan.

"Sounds like a Collier," Linus said. "Susan was born in the back seat."

"Only because Belinda thought a back seat delivery would make for better drama," Susan replied. Her face was beet red, the poor thing.

Not knowing what else to do, Lewis wrapped an arm around her waist. "If you're going to make an entrance, might as well make it memorable, right, luv?" He pecked her on the cheek.

Out of the corner of his eye, he saw both Collier brothers raised their eyebrows.

"Daddy, can I see Mummy now?" Maddie asked.

"Sure, sweetheart. Everyone can."

One by one, the family stepped inside the pastel-colored room where a beautiful and tired-looking brunette lay in bed. A few feet away, in a clear plastic bassinet, a tiny bundle lay swaddled in a soft yellow blanket.

"Noel Christopher Collier." Pride filled Thomas's whisper.

"He looks like Dad," Linus said. "Only with a little more hair."

"You're a jerk," Susan said. "He's beautiful. Really, really beautiful."

"All Rosalind's doing. She's the one who did the work." The adoration in Thomas's voice was palpable.

Lewis stood by the door and watched the scene evolve. So much love and pride in one small room. Susan had told him on the way over that the Collier legacy meant everything to her older brother. It was evident. You could feel the sense of family in the air. How could Susan not see it? That she was part of the circle.

He wasn't. He was the outsider. The unexpected, unwanted guest being politely tolerated.

His eyes sought Susan. She was frowning at him from across the bassinet. "Why are you standing by the door?" she asked.

"Coffee. Thought I'd pop down and get us some." It was the first excuse that came to mind. He needed space to clear his head. A cafeteria run fit the bill.

Coward that he was, he slipped out the door without waiting for her reply.

"Hold on! I'll go with you." Linus's voice called out.

Great. Instead of an escape, he was going to get an escort. The sandy-haired man caught up with him just as the elevator door opened.

"I figured you might need some help carrying everything," he said with a grin. "Both Maddie and Rosalind put in an order for milk and cookies. We might as well buy a half dozen. Susan never met a cookie she didn't like either."

Something about the joke grated on his nerves. "So what? Lots of people like cookies."

"True, but Susan's love of cookies is legendary. We've been teasing her about it since we were kids."

"I'm sure she loved that," Lewis muttered. Already self-conscious because she didn't look like her mother or brothers, her being teased about her eating habits must have stung. Now he understood why she thought she didn't fit in.

"Did you say something?" Linus asked.

"Talking to myself," Lewis replied. Wasn't his place to pick a fight with Susan's brother.

Linus however, wasn't ready to let it go. He moved so he was in front of Lewis, his back to the elevator buttons. Arms folded across his chest, he gave Lewis another long, studious look. "You're annoyed, aren't you?"

"No," Lewis lied. "Just don't think you should be singling her out when everyone has a sweet tooth."

"Huh," Linus said.

"What's that supposed to mean?"

"Nothing," the man replied. "It's nice to know you're protective of Susan's feelings."

Lewis felt his shoulders tightening. "Shouldn't I be? Seems to me, a lot of people should care about Susan's feelings."

"Perhaps, but not all of them are known to go through women like water."

"No. Some of them are related."

Linus's eyebrows shot up and for a second, Lewis worried he'd pushed his luck too far. Then he saw what looked like a gleam of respect.

"Are we going to see you at the gathering at Christmas?" her brother asked, changing the topic.

"Your company party? Absolutely. I promised Susan I'd be there with bells on."

"No, I meant the wedding on Christmas Eve. Well, vow renewal, second wedding. Whatever you want to call it."

Lewis thought back to the day they'd signed their agreement and the way Susan had hedged when he mentioned the holidays. She clearly didn't want him at a family event.

"The holidays haven't really come up yet," he replied. "We're taking things one day at a time."

"Oh," Linus said. Awkwardness filled the small space. "Well, perhaps we'll see you there," he replied.

"Maybe." Probably not. Weddings were for family, not fake boyfriends.

Why the thought made his stomach hurt, he didn't know.

"Your friend Lewis seems much more low-key than I expected," Thomas remarked shortly after Linus and Lewis left the room. Susan had hoped new fatherhood would distract him, but no such luck.

"What did you expect?" she asked. "That he'd show up..." She was about to say shirtless and carrying a bottle of Cristal, but a quick look at Maddie reminded her that wasn't appropriate. "...ready to go crazy? I told you, he's not that person anymore."

"Relax. I wasn't trying to criticize the guy."

No, only lobbing a passive-aggressive comment in his direction. "Lewis is a lot...more...than people give him credit for," she told him. "He's smart, he's gentle, he's considerate..."

"Handsome."

Her sister-in-law lay in bed, her eyes half-closed, with Maddie curled up by her side. Exhausted from the excitement, the little girl was nearly asleep but Rosalind had clearly been listening.

Rosalind stroked her daughter's hair. "He's very handsome," she repeated. "The tabloids don't do him justice."

"No, they don't," Susan agreed. There were times when she would look at him quickly and the sheer perfection of his profile made her breath catch.

"I still can't believe my sister is going out with Champagne Lewis," Thomas said.

"Why?" Because she wasn't a supermodel? Because she was a pathetic shrew? "Is it really such a big stretch?"

"You've got to admit, you two are different."

"Not as much as you'd think," she replied. Maybe on the outside, but on this inside they were two odd peas in a pod. The thought made her smile. "Anyway, it doesn't matter. We're not…"

Her brother, who'd been staring at his newborn son, turned his head. "Not what?"

"Running off and getting married anytime soon."

She almost said they weren't really dating. But it was a secret and if she told Thomas the truth, he'd use it to justify thinking Lewis was still some kind of "bad boy." Which he wasn't. He was everything she said and more.

And she was going to hold on to the illusion for as long as she could.

"For goodness' sake, stop interrogating the woman," Rosalind said in a sleepy voice. "Her love life is none of our business. We don't need to butt in."

"If you remember, she had no problem butting into ours," Thomas said.

Susan winced. She *knew* he still held a grudge over her interference last winter.

"That was different," Rosalind said. "We had our collective heads in the clouds. We wouldn't have had Noel if she hadn't said anything. Now be quiet so I can get some sleep."

"Thank you," Susan replied. Her brother looked down at his feet.

"You're welcome," Rosalind said. "Besides, we already know he's special or you wouldn't have brought him to the hospital."

We already know he's special or you wouldn't have brought him to the hospital.

Her sister-in-law's words stuck in Susan's head the entire way home.

When Lewis and Linus had returned from the cafeteria, she noticed a distinct change in her faux boyfriend's manner. He seemed distant.

"Thank you for coming to the hospital with me," she said. "I know it wasn't quite the fun day you had planned."

"You're welcome. I just hope I wasn't in the way."

"Hardly. I was more worried my brothers would pin you down and interrogate you. They didn't, did they?"

"No."

"Linus didn't say anything stupid when the two of you went to get coffee?"

"No."

The distance was driving her insane. Reaching across the seat, she brushed her fingers across the back of his hand. "What's wrong?"

"Nothing. Seriously," he added as though sensing she was about to press. "It… I'm not used to being included in family events is all."

And he felt out of place. The pieces suddenly came together. "I'm glad you were there," she told him.

"Were you?"

"Yes. Very much. I'm glad my brothers got to see firsthand how good a man you are."

"Now you're reaching." He gave a soft laugh.

"All right, maybe a little. But I think Linus will come around. Thomas...he might be a harder sell. He has a highly overdeveloped sense of responsibility. I used to tell him he had *monomania*, which is a fancy way of saying he's hyperfocused on the business. Comes from listening to our grandfather drone on about the family legacy during his formative years."

"You're playing armchair psychologist again."

"Force of habit." Understanding what made people tick made dealing with them easier. If she could link a reason to an action, then it took away some of the sting. Sometimes, anyway. "Plus, I've spent a lot of time observing my brothers."

"Are you sure you studied the whole picture?" he asked.

"After more than two and a half decades, I'd better have. What makes you ask?"

He shrugged. "No reason. Just that I didn't get the impression either man was acting out of responsibility. Doesn't really matter, though, does it? What they think? After all..."

After all, it wasn't as though he would be a long-term part of her life.

"I'm curious," Lewis said suddenly. Turning sideways, he rested an elbow against the back of the seat. Grateful to have him in her orbit, Susan shifted as well so that they sat face-to-face, their knees touching. "What would your psychology books say about me?"

"You want me to psychoanalyze you?"

"Haven't you already?"

"Maybe." She looked at her lap. "I might have kicked around a few concepts." They only served to depress her.

"Like what?" he asked.

"Why do you care?"

"Color me curious. You sound so certain about your brothers. Makes me curious what you think of me."

Was it really curiosity or was he trying to send her a message? Reminding her not to get too attached.

"What if I don't want to share?"

"Then I'll presume the worst." Lewis's grin was overly wide. "And I'll pester you until you give up the info."

"Fine." He *would* pester her too. "Keep in mind this is completely nonscientific, but if I had to make a hypothesis, I would say children who grew up in foster homes are prone to anxiety, commitment issues, low self-esteem and often have a resulting fear of abandonment."

Lewis didn't answer and the shadows made it impossible to read his expression completely. Susan's stomach sank. "It's only a theory," she said, turning to face the front once more.

"Low self-esteem? Seriously?" she heard him say. "Do I seem like I have low self-esteem to you?'

"I wouldn't say low," Susan replied. Although, he *had* been worried about being accepted at the fundraiser.

"No offense, luv, but I think you might want to rethink your theory. Excepting for the other night—which was an extraordinary circumstance—my self-esteem and anxiety are just fine."

"And fear of commitment? Am I wrong about that one?" She probably shouldn't ask with the driver present, but she couldn't help herself.

"Depends. Is fear the same as disinterest?"

"No." Fear was better. Fear implied there might be a chance.

"Good to know," he said, nodding.

So much for an answer. On the other hand, did she really need one? The warning was clear. There was a warning hidden in his question—*don't get too attached or think long-term.*

Fine. Then she would take what she could for as long as she could get it.

They moved on to other topics. Thanks to Noel's arrival, they never finished their Christmas shopping and now Susan had to buy a baby gift in addition to the other items on her list.

"Why don't we go tomorrow?" Lewis said, for the driver's benefit, Susan suspected. "I know a great restaurant in Soho. We can grab brunch and then hit Regent Street again. What do you think?"

"Sure." She noticed he was pulling out his wallet to pay. Did that mean he intended to stay? Her heart skipped a beat.

"So, what's the plan?" she asked once they'd stepped outside. The car's taillights disappeared into the traffic.

"Tonight? We grab some takeout, watch a movie and I sleep on your sofa."

A right proper sleepover. All aboveboard and completely phony. But she was tired of phony. She was a woman, dammit. She wanted to be held and kissed like a woman.

The moonless night left his face bathed in shadows, making it impossible to read his expression. His eyes appeared dark and hooded. The warmth from his body floated around her, enveloping her with his scent. One she couldn't label and that was uniquely him.

Take what you can, a voice whispered in her ear.

"You...you don't have to sleep on the sofa."

Lewis stepped back. "I'm not sure that's a good idea."

"Oh." Rejection cut through her. Hugging her midsection, she struggled to keep the disappointment from her voice.

"It's not that I wouldn't want to sleep with you," he said. "In fact..."

"Don't," Susan said. She so didn't want to have this conversation. "The last thing I need to hear is a lot of phony flattery and excuses. You made it very clear that you weren't interested in me in that way. It was stupid of me to think you might change your mind."

Beyond stupid. She wanted to go inside, pull the covers over her head and pretend the last five minutes had never happened.

"Susan..."

"It's been a really long day, Lewis," she said, cutting him off again. "Why don't we say good-night. We can wake up superearly and pretend we spent the night together, okay?"

"Susan..."

"Good night, Lewis. I'm sorry you have to..."

He kissed her.

He closed the distance between them and he kissed her. Like an animal springing on its prey, his mouth covered Susan's before she could make a sound. Her eyes fluttered shut as she melted into him. Wow, could this man kiss. This wasn't gentle or sweet like the other kisses though. This kiss was primal. The kind of kiss that claimed a person. Clutching his shoulders, Susan met him need for need until neither of them could breathe. They broke apart, their breaths loud and ragged in the night air.

"Still think I don't want to sleep with you?" Lewis asked between gasps.

If he didn't, he was a damn good liar. Her body, from head to toe, believed him. "Then why?" Why did she feel like he was still about to reject her?

Lewis's hands were tangled in her curls, combing them away from her face over and over. "A woman like you is made for serious relationships," he said. "The kind a man dates when he's thinking about things like homes and kids. If I..." He smiled. "If I were the kind of guy who thought of such things, I'd tether you to my side for eternity."

"But...?" Susan asked. There was definitely a but coming whether she wanted to hear it or not.

Lewis's hand slid from her hair to cup her cheek momentarily. "But I'm not that kind of guy."

"I know." He'd made his views on commitment quite clear in the taxi.

Take what you can, the voice reminded.

"What if I said I didn't care?" she asked. "What if I'm okay with here and now?"

She reached down and entwined her fingers with his. "Houses and kids are nice dreams, but sometimes a woman just wants to feel wanted."

Her heart was in her throat when she finished. Talk about laying it all on the table. It was up to Lewis now. If he rejected her, so be it. At least she'd know.

Lewis's hand was cupping her cheek again. The whites of his eyes were brilliant in the dark as he searched her face. "Are you sure?"

Could he not see the certainty on her face? Releasing his hand, Susan slid her palms upward along the padded front of his jacket until she reached the point where the zipper stopped. He was layers of darkness. Navy jacket, black sweater. With a deep breath to steel her nerves, she slipped her gloved hand under his jacket. "What do you think?" she asked.

What felt like the longest beat of her life passed. Susan kept her eyes locked with his; the knot of nerves in her chest twisted.

There was the rustle of nylon and suddenly, Lewis's hands were at the front of her wool coat. One by one, he undid the buttons, his eyes never leaving hers, until her coat hung open.

"I think," he said, playing with the hem of her sweater, "that we should go inside."

"This is new," Lewis said later, wrapped together with her in a cocoon of blankets, in Susan's king-size bed. Her cheek was resting over his heart and the taste of her kisses was still on his lips.

"What's new?"

"Staying awake." He buried his nose in her curls, inhaling the vanilla scent of her shampoo. "Usually I fall asleep." Or start planning his escape. Pulling a woman close to savor in the afterglow wasn't his style.

And yet, here he was, with Susan curled against his body, drawing lazy circles on his torso.

"You romantic devil."

"Never said I wasn't a player, luv."

For some reason he was determined to hammer that shameful point home tonight. He immediately regretted the statement when Susan's hand stilled. There was no reason to be harsh. She knew this was a temporary arrangement.

"Did you know that you're the first woman I've slept with stone-cold sober?"

"Seriously?" She lifted her head. Even in the dark, he could see her surprise. "You mean you haven't…?"

"Nope. Been too busy keeping my head down, proving I'm a good boy."

"Oh, you were good…"

"I know," he replied. Her laugh vibrated through him, and he pulled her close. Could you feel someone rolling their eyes? "You weren't so bad yourself, you know."

"Glad I didn't disappoint."

"Definitely not." Being with her was…well, it was amazing. He'd mapped every inch of her soft curves with his hands, and then went back and did the same with his mouth. Something else he'd never felt the need to do: savor the experience.

All this newness made him uneasy. Different was turning out to be unnerving.

"You didn't tell me your brother and his wife were renewing their wedding vows."

Her hand stilled again.

"Linus told me. He seemed surprised I wasn't attending."

"I didn't think you'd want to go," she replied. "You can, of course. If you want."

Gee, with that kind of enthusiasm… "Don't worry about it. I only mentioned it so you wouldn't be caught off guard if Linus mentions we talked about it."

Honestly, he didn't know why he'd brought it up.

Maybe he was looking for further affirmation that she wasn't looking for more.

Or was he hoping for the opposite?

Listen to him. One night with the woman and he was psychoanalyzing too. It was a short-term arrangement. No need to turn the affair into anything deeper. Once they holidays ended, he and Susan would go their separate ways.

And he was fine with that.

Really.

Truly.

Wasn't he?

CHAPTER EIGHT

"I WANT TO TELL you a story. Once upon a time there was a boy who really, really loved sports. Every chance he got, he practiced. Good weather. Bad weather. He worked at becoming the best he could be. And you know what? It paid off. He became a superstar.

"But then you know what happened? He stopped working so hard. He started taking his skills for granted. He developed bad habits. He told himself, 'I'm a superstar. I don't need to practice that much.' For a while, he got away with it. Eventually though, his athletic skill started to slip. Suddenly, he wasn't the superstar anymore. He was just a guy with a lot of bad habits who'd forgotten what was really important."

Susan sat in a far row of the indoor facility listening to Lewis tell the youth ambassadors his story. He'd told her last night that he wanted to use the opportunity to teach the kids what happened when they lost sight of what mattered. It was impressive, how honest Lewis was being about his own failings. Heartbreaking too, when you realized how much his partying had cost him. Thank goodness he'd seen the light before the lifestyle killed him.

Otherwise, the world would be a bleaker place. Not

to mention her bed. She smiled recalling the last few nights. Since the night Noel was born, the two of them had been engaged in a full-fledged affair, and it was better than she could have imagined. The way Lewis touched her when they made love made her feel like the most beautiful woman in the world. It was going to be awfully hard going back to life without him after their fake love affair was over.

Something inside her cracked a little at the thought. They'd attend a few more events, the company party and then say goodbye. Unless, that is, they needed to continue the arrangement a little while longer.

How sad was that? Hoping Lewis's image didn't improve enough so she could keep him in her life a few weeks longer.

"He's doing a marvelous job. Goes to show people love a good redemption story. Even kids."

A man she didn't recognize sat down in the seat next to her.

"Michael Ryder," he said.

So this was the infamous Michael, Lewis's agent. He looked like a talent agent. His pinstriped suit was very expensive and his hair very styled. He also obviously had a penchant for cigars. The scent clung to his clothes. Trying not to wrinkle her nose, Susan shifted herself a little farther away.

"I have to admit," he said after they'd shaken hands, "that when Lewis first came up with this crazy scheme, I had my doubts. But it looks like it might have some value after all. He never would have scored an event like this without you."

On the field, the kids broke out in laughter over something Lewis had said. "He doesn't need me to help him secure speaking engagements," Susan replied. "He's perfectly capable of charming people on his own."

Ryder smirked. "Spoken like a true loyal girlfriend."

"Don't have to be a girlfriend to recognize his abilities."

"Wow. You're good. I can see why Lewis was so keen on partnering up with you."

"Is there something I can do for you, Mr. Ryder?" Susan decided she didn't like the man. He was too keen on reminding her she wasn't Lewis's real girlfriend.

"I came by to tell you that *Personal Magazine* is interested in doing a story about the two of you. A reporter's going to sit down with you both next week."

"Great. Lewis will be thrilled."

"Yeah. They loved the whole love as the redeemer angle. They're bringing a photographer to get some shots of you both at Lewis's apartment. Readers love that homey behind-the-scenes stuff. You *have* been to his apartment, haven't you?" he asked in a low voice.

"Yes." Just the past night, as a matter of fact. Although his tone was so annoying she wouldn't have admitted if the answer was no.

"Good. Make sure you know where all the glassware and stuff is. We want to ensure you look at home. Know what I mean?"

"Why don't I leave some intimates on the bathroom floor to really hammer home the message?"

"Funny. Stick to leaving an extra toothbrush."

"Fine. I'll make sure to buy one tonight." She seriously did not like this man. "Unless there's something else you need to discuss, I'd like to continue watching Lewis."

Unfortunately though, it looked like she'd missed

the end of his talk. The kids were breaking into groups for some kind of skills training. While the volunteers played shepherd, Lewis walked to a nearby bench and stripped off his sweatshirt. Susan's eyes automatically sought out the strip of skin on his back that came exposed when his shirt pulled up. He had the most beautiful back. She loved watching the muscles play across his shoulders when he moved his arms. She loved running her hands over those shoulders too.

"Oh, man, you've got it bad."

Hadn't the agent moved on? Susan slid her gaze sideways. "I beg your pardon?" she asked.

"The look on your face. You look like you're worshipping the guy." Susan rolled her eyes. "Don't get me wrong," Ryder said. "If you look at him like that during the interview, there won't be a person alive who won't believe you're not madly in love. Problem will be getting him to look at you the same way. The Lewis I know has trouble remembering girls' names."

So did the Lewis she knew. "That was when he was drinking," Susan said. "He's not the same person now."

"Only, I'm not sure sobriety translates into acting skills. If he were really a one-woman man we wouldn't be doing this crap."

The man made a very good, albeit harsh, point. One that settled hard in the pit of her stomach.

"You needn't worry. Lewis knows how to put on a show when he has to."

"Good." The agent started to stand, only to sit back down. "Hey, do yourself a favor, will you? Don't get too sucked in by our boy."

"Don't worry," Susan replied. "I'm not stupid. I know exactly where I stand with Lewis."

Besides, his warning was too little, too late. She was already irreparably sucked in.

When Lewis was a kid and played his first game in net, he had been on top of the world. Sure, it was only a street game, but he remembered how it had felt like he'd won the World Cup. He'd succeeded and the neighborhood kids liked him. Over the years, he'd had many moments of victory, but as amazing as they were, none had the pureness of that first game.

Until today.

He lay prone on the turf, the smell of rubber backing tickling his nose. "That's it," he said. "I'm done."

Thirty-six kids faced off with him. Thirty-six kids beat him and scored. Lewis had to work harder than he'd ever worked to make sure each ball just missed his outstretched hands. By the tenth or eleventh goal, the kids knew he was letting them win, but they didn't care. If the laughter was any indication, they were having too much fun. So was Lewis.

Pushing himself to his knees, he blew the whistle around his neck. "All right. Fun as it's been, we've got to pack it up." A loud moan filled the facility, pumping him even higher. "What's with the booing? You're going to a Christmas party! With cake."

That got them moving to the sidelines quickly.

A girl, who looked to be around nine years old, approached him. "Mr. Matolo? Can I take a selfie with you?"

"Sure. Give it over and we'll take a proper one," he said. How much things had changed. When he was nine, he barely knew what a cell phone was let alone had one stashed in his equipment bag. And when he was playing, he'd been too arrogant to give fans the proper time.

He stayed on his knees so the two of them would be the same height. Of course, as soon as the others saw what was happening, more came running over with their phones to do the same. Not all though. Several of the kids looked over and went back to their bags. Lewis noticed a couple pulling out scraps of paper including one who tore off part of his lunch bag. Some things hadn't changed after all. There were still kids going without.

An idea came to him. Cupping his hands into a megaphone, he called into the stands. "Hey, Susie! Come here for a moment, and bring your phone." He smiled as she got up and started toward the stairs. Susan didn't know it, but she'd been his good luck charm. Knowing she was in the stands, believing in him, gave him the courage to tell his story. He loved the way she believed in him. Every time he looked in her direction, an empowering warmth spread through his insides. Different from the heat of attraction, it made him want to prove her trust wasn't misplaced.

"Mr. Matolo? Can I have your autograph?" It was the kid with the torn lunch bag bringing him back to the moment at hand.

"Hold on for one minute," Lewis told him. "I need to make a quick announcement."

He cupped his hands once again. "If anyone wants to take a picture, but doesn't have a camera, come get in line. My friend will take the pictures and have Mr. Redmayne send you a copy." Surely the director wouldn't mind doing a little extra to make sure the kids were happy.

While waiting for Susan, he signed paper scraps and

several of the kids' T-shirts. He was in the middle of writing on one kid's shoulder when he noticed a shadow fall across the crowd.

"I owe you an apology," Graham Montclark said. "I came by because Chris was a nervous wreck over hiring you. You never mentioned you were a motivational speaker when you made your offer the other night."

"I'm not," Lewis replied. "I simply told these kids the truth. If it stops one of them from making the same mistakes I made, all the better."

The other man digested his words. Lewis hoped they'd come out as sincerely as intended. A word from Graham Montclark would be the in he needed.

"Do you have any idea how many stairs there are between the stands and this playing field?" A slightly out-of-breath Susan came walking toward them. From her adorably flushed cheeks, he guessed she'd run the entire way. "Not to mention security guards. I almost had to cheat on you in order to gain access. Hello, Mr. Montclark. Nice to see you again."

"It's good to see you as well, Ms. Collier. I was just telling Lewis here that he should consider a career as a motivational speaker."

"He was inspiring, wasn't he?" The way she beamed in his direction made Lewis's insides turn end over end.

"While I appreciate the compliments, all I did was give the kids some straight talk and attention. Nothing special about that."

"Don't sell yourself short," Susan replied. "Perhaps you should consider doing events on the side."

"On the side of what?" Montclark asked. "You're retired aren't you?"

Bless her. Once again, she'd opened the door for him.

When they got home, he was going to kiss every ivory inch of her. “My agent has been talking with a few outlets about my being involved with the media side of the sport. In fact, I think one of the stations might be yours.”

“Is that so?” Montclark replied. “I hope they’re treating you right.”

They weren’t treating him at all. “They’re being fair.” To his surprise, he found he meant it. “After all, as you know, I come with some past baggage.”

“I don’t usually get involved in day-to-day operations myself, but if anyone gives you trouble, let me know. You’ve more than impressed me today.”

“Thank you. I appreciate the vote of confidence.” His eyes caught Susan’s. Unbelievable. Was it possible this whole crazy plan was actually going to work? Was he actually going to rebuild his reputation and return to the spotlight? If so, it was all because of the woman he’d picked for a partner. She really was his good luck charm.

His stomach immediately sank. What was he going to do when their arrangement ended?

Nothing. He didn’t know why he kept asking himself the question.

“Mr. Matolo, will you take our pictures now?” one of the children asked.

“Absolutely! We’ve wasted enough time.” He turned his attention back to the task at hand. “Miss Susan, snap away. We’ve got a Christmas party to attend.”

He could dwell on end dates another time.

Susan had to hand it to her brother. He didn’t do things halfway. Thus it was no surprise when she walked into the annual Collier’s holiday party to discover Christmas had arrived early. The ballroom was a winter wonderland of crystal and white like the ice castle in Maddie's favorite animated film. In fact, there was an ice castle. A giant sculpture in the middle of the room, around which were tables laden with hors d'oeuvres. Behind her, outside the ballroom, there was a staircase decked with white poinsettias. She hadn't gone upstairs yet, but she'd been told it led to a rooftop bar where people could sit around a fire pit and sip hot chocolate.

It was magnificent, and she was standing in the doorway alone.

Only for a moment. "Who takes home the castle?" Linus asked, joining her. Susan breathed a sigh of relief. As substitute host and hostess, she and Linus were expected to arrive early in order to greet all the guests. After his flakeout over Maria's wedding, she'd been worried he'd leave her to the wolves again. She looked him up and down. "You made it," she said.

"Thomas would have killed me if I hadn't, same as you," he replied. "I wasn't in the mood to court death this holiday."

"Good call." If Thomas hadn't killed him, she would have. "Let's hope next year he doesn't decide to have another baby so we can hand the job back to him."

"Sounds good to me." He looked around the room, then back to her. "Where's your boyfriend?"

"He had some business to take care of." That was exactly how Lewis put it too. Business to take care of. "He'll be here soon," she replied.

Her answer came out more defensively than she meant. Of course he would be there. He'd promised.

She adjusted the neckline of her dress again. The red-and-silver brocade was flashier than her usual style. Knee-length and classically draped in the front, it had a plunging back. The minute she saw it, visions of Lewis kissing her exposed back danced in her head. She couldn't wait for him to see her in it.

At the current moment, she'd settle for just seeing him come through the door. "Where's your date?" she asked Linus. "Or are you going solo again this year?"

Her brother shoved his hands in his pockets. "What do you think?" he asked.

Single then. If Lewis didn't show, then she'd at least have a dance partner.

Honestly, why was she worrying about Lewis? He'd promised. Maybe it was because the holidays were drawing closer. After this, Lewis had no obligations to her. She thought after Graham Montclark's comment the other day that he might discuss their future, and whether he thought they should continue their faux romance past New Year's. Instead, he'd said nothing. When they were together, it was easy to pretend they didn't have an arrangement; other times Susan felt like she was in a holding pattern. One ruled by nights of incredible wonder.

"You're making that face again," Linus said.

Susan frowned. "What face?"

"The one you've been making all week. Where your eyes glaze over and you get this dreamy smile. Somebody's in love." He nudged her with his shoulder.

"Stop being an ass," Susan replied as her cheeks warmed. "I'm not in love."

"Could have fooled me. Little Miss Dreamy Eyes."

Oh, brother. Please don't tell her she was going to be stuck listening to his stupid nicknames. Linus loved his stupid nicknames. "Lewis and I are enjoying each other's company, that is all," she told him.

"Uh-huh."

"We are. I'm not in love with Lewis Matolo."

Aren't you? After days of being ignored, the question slammed into her brain. How long was she going to pretend the man hadn't gotten under skin?

Easy, she answered back. For as long as it took. Fake it till you make it, as the saying went.

Since she was having the conversation in her head, however, Linus felt comfortable continuing. "He certainly seems to care about you. Nearly took my head off in the hospital elevator the day Noel was born."

"What? What did you do?" Besides mentioning the wedding. She *knew* something had happened that afternoon.

"Why are you assuming I did anything?"

"Because I've known you since birth," Susan told him. "You always do something."

Linus was insistent. "I swear I did nothing. At least not on purpose. All I said was that we needed to buy extra cookies because you love them so much. He suggested I stop picking on you."

Warmth seeped through her veins. She couldn't remember the last time someone had defended her honor.

"I'm not surprised. Lewis likes to look out for the underdog," she told her brother.

Linus gave her a look. "You're an underdog?"

"He was defending me against a comment you made. What do you think?"

"Either way, he's not what I expected," Linus said.

"I told you but you and Thomas refused to believe me. Thomas still doesn't believe me."

"Meh." Linus waved off her complaint. "You know

Thomas. Anything that could remotely impact the company gets him uptight."

Susan looked away. He would really hate if he knew the truth then.

"If it will make you feel better, I'll talk to him," Linus said. "Let him know Lewis passes my sniff test."

"Thank you. I'd appreciate that. And for the record... I hate when you make jokes about my sweet tooth."

Linus leaned back in surprise. "We've been making those jokes since we were kids."

"I know. Thanks to my mother." Belinda used to love to point out how calories weren't Susan's friend and never missed an opportunity to remind her with a subtle jab. "Might as well just say you think I'm fat."

"We don't think that." Linus continued to look shocked. "We just know you like cookies."

"Well, it feels like you think so. Especially since that's how Belinda meant it."

"Belinda was a piece of work. None of us should take anything she said seriously."

Easy for him to say; Linus and Thomas weren't her children. "Still, I would appreciate if you stopped making the joke. Especially around my... Lewis."

"No need to worry there," Linus said. "He didn't find the comment funny either. In fact, he pretty much said the same thing as you did. About you feeling like we were calling you fat."

Because Lewis understood her. Susan couldn't help her smile or the fullness in her heart. She'd always wondered what it would be like, having someone in her life who knew what she was thinking or feeling without her having to say a word. To be able to look across a crowd and know she wasn't alone.

"You're getting that dreamy look again," Linus said. "You really like this guy, don't you?"

"Yeah, I do." More than liked, to be honest.

"I can tell. How come you didn't invite him to Thomas's vow renewal then?"

The question caught her by surprise. "Because it's a family thing."

"Doesn't mean you can't include your boyfriend. You brought him to the hospital."

"That was different. He was with me when you called. The ceremony on Christmas Eve is going to be intimate."

"And gathered 'round Rosalind's hospital bed eating cookies and letting Maddie climb on him wasn't?" He frowned. "You're afraid we're going to give him a hard time, aren't you?"

"Wouldn't you?"

"Absolutely, but in the best-natured way possible. That's what big brothers do. Tell you what," he said. "If you're worried, the five of us can go out beforehand and bond with him properly."

Oh, yeah, she could see Lewis jumping at the opportunity to have a "bonding" dinner with the Collier clan. She could picture the scene now. The three of them eating curry and peppering Lewis with questions. Her temporary relationship was going to be short enough; she didn't need their curiosity ending the arrangement prematurely.

"That isn't necessary," she told him.

"Sure it is. You said yourself, we weren't being fair to him. This will be our way of letting him know we approve of his dating our sister and we welcome him to the family."

"Really, you don't have to," Susan said.

"Why are you fighting the idea. You just asked me to be nice. If the guy's going to be around for a while…"

"He's not."

Her brother's eyes narrowed. "What are you talking about? Don't tell me you two are on the outs already? Is that why he's not here tonight?"

"No, no. I told you, Lewis will be here."

"Then what gives? Why so certain you two will be done? You've got to have a little more faith than that, Susie."

"Maybe I would if I didn't have an exit date."

"I beg your pardon."

Susan sighed. If she'd known they were going to start suggesting family get-togethers, she would have told them the truth from the start. But since when did her brothers bond with anyone? Let alone someone connected with her? "We aren't really dating." Briefly she explained their arrangement.

"You're kidding," Linus said when she was finished. Susan was stunned by his stunned expression. Maybe she and Lewis had done a better job pretending than she thought. "Why would you do something like that?"

"I told you, Lewis needs…"

"I mean you. Champagne Lewis I get, but why would you get involved in something like this?"

She shrugged. "Maybe I wanted an image makeover too."

"Unbelievable. Thomas is going to have a cow, you know."

A big mad cow too, which was why she kept silent in the first place. But only if Thomas found out. Which didn't have to happen. "Then don't tell him," she said.

"The whole affair will be over before Thomas gets back from paternity leave. There's no reason for him to get involved."

"Except for the whole Collier's thing. You know how he is about the company reputation."

"All the more reason to not spoil his time with the new baby. There's no need to trigger him unnecessarily."

"True." Her brother let out a long, frustrated breath, a sign he was seriously considering the suggestion. "We'll have to talk about this later," he said. "People are starting to arrive."

And the last thing they needed was someone to overhear. "I'm going to go check my hair," she said. "The bun feels loose."

"I'm going to go make sure everything is in order, or whatever it is Thomas expects us to do." He headed toward the back of the room where the event coordinators were congregated.

"Oh, hey," he said, stopping and speaking over his shoulder. "About that other thing we were talking about. You know, the cookies?"

"Yeah?" The abrupt change of topic would throw her except it was Linus, and Linus was known for it.

"You're nowhere near being fat."

"I know," Susan replied. She was normal. And even if she wasn't, Lewis loved her body. Every porcelain inch, he said. That was all that mattered.

Smiling to herself, she turned and headed to the powder room. On the way, a flash of black caught her eye. It was Courtney minus her partner in crime. Ever since Susan had told them off at work, she and Ginger had limited their interaction to only the most necessary business. Tonight, the woman smirked like a cat as Susan passed her.

Susan was surprised to discover she didn't care.

Imagine that. All this fuss about paying them back tonight, and it no longer seemed to matter.

CHAPTER NINE

FOR THE NEXT forty-five minutes, Susan smiled and said hello to every person who stepped off the elevator. Most responded politely and kept going, way more interested in the free drinks and food than in talking with her. Thankfully. It wasn't until Maria and Hank arrived that she had to make any kind of real conversation.

"Welcome home," she greeted the newlyweds with a smile. "How was America?"

"Big. We had a marvelous time. Especially in Hawaii," Maria answered. "I hated to come back. Don't worry, though, I'll be in the office on Monday. I know you're eager to discuss a few things."

"Maria, honey, it's a Christmas party," Hank said, his voice gently admonishing. "There'll be plenty of time to talk work next week."

His bride blushed. They were still in the phase where bickering in public required restraint. "I know, but this is Susan. I'm sure she wants to bring me up to speed."

Did she do that? Did she spend time at parties working? Susan thought back to different functions. Damn. "Not tonight," she quickly replied. "It's Christmas. I don't know about you, but I have more important things to talk about."

"So we read." Maria's remark had all three of them turning a subtle pink.

"Where is Lewis?" Hank asked. "I was hoping to catch up with him. We didn't get to talk very long at the wedding."

Indeed, where was Lewis? Nearly an hour into the party and he still hadn't arrived.

"He…um…got tied up with business and is running late," she repeated for the umpteenth time. "I'm sure he'll be here any minute."

"See? I'm not the only one distracted by business," Maria said.

"Apparently not." But as Hank answered, he flashed a sympathetic look in Susan's direction. It was the look of someone who knew Lewis's past habits. He's not the same man, Susan wanted to holler. A hard sell seeing how it was at their wedding that Lewis had a pair of drinks tossed in his face.

Just then the elevator dinged. The doors slid open and there was Lewis looking like he'd stepped off a runway in a black velvet blazer. Susan's heart leaped to her throat at the sight of him.

So much for faking not being in love. It'd be easier pretending Lewis wasn't gorgeous or Collier's sold auto parts.

She broadened her smile. Her feelings—or rather, their repercussions—were an issue for another time.

"I am so sorry I'm late, luv. My meeting went far longer than I thought." The apology tumbled from Lewis's mouth as he slipped an arm around her waist. "You look delicious," he added, kissing her cheek. "Maybe it was a good thing I wasn't there when you were getting ready or we'd both be late."

"If you're trying to flatter me into forgiving your lateness, it's working," Susan told him.

"Good. I'll flatter you some more later. Welcome back from the honeymoon, you two," he said, turning to Hank and Maria with a smile.

This was one of those times when the relationship felt real. Although they were sleeping together so it was also real in that sense. Deeper was the better word. This was one of those times when the relationship felt deeper. There was a sparkle in his eyes that was easy to mistake as adoration. She needed to remember though, he was just playing a part. Tonight he was honoring his half of the agreement by playing the doting boyfriend.

"I can't believe you two met at our wedding," Maria was saying.

"I told her when you RSVP'd as single, that you wouldn't be going home that way," Hank remarked.

"Which I admit, had me worried. Especially after that thing with Diane and Trish."

Lewis looked up at the ceiling lights. "Diane and Trish! Those were their names! I am really sorry about that little scene. I met those girls during a dark time in my life."

"Well, I'd be more annoyed if I didn't know they're total gold diggers. Hey, I love them," she said to Susan's stunned expression, "but that doesn't mean I don't know what they're like. It's why I agreed to give Lewis your phone number. I figured if he was chasing after you, he wasn't the promiscuous man Hank had made him out to be. Although you should apologize to them," she added, turning to Lewis with a reproachful look.

"I agree," Susan said.

"So do I," Lewis replied. "Which is why I sent them

both apology letters explaining everything after the wedding."

"You did?" She smiled at him with pride. "Wait a second," she said. "I thought you just remembered their… You jerk."

Laughing, Lewis pretended to rub the shoulder she'd playfully slapped. "Hey, can't a guy joke around about his bad-boy past? I can't believe you didn't think I would apologize."

"You're right." She was properly chastised. "I should have realized you're too good a man not to own your mistakes."

"Well, I did lead you on, so I can't be too annoyed, can I?" He leaned over and kissed her temple, causing Hank to offer a mock groan.

"Oh, man," his friend said. "You are smitten with a capital *S*. Never thought I'd see the day. Must be a Christmas miracle. Say, the four of us need to go out after the holidays."

Susan tensed. "You mean, in January?" What was it with people suddenly inviting them places?

"Sure. Lewis can help me lie about my glory days before I left academy league."

"Left?" Lewis said. "You were dismissed because your foot couldn't find the ball. You sure you want to ruin whatever lies you told your bride?"

While the three of them laughed, Susan drifted away into thought. January was only a few weeks away. She and Lewis would be done. This marvelous fun-filled night out they were planning would never happen.

"Tuesday?"

Giving a blink, she realized Maria was talking to her. "I know you usually choose to eat at your desk but the wedding proofs will be in so I thought maybe you'd like to join us for once." Maria and several other women went out for lunch every Tuesday.

"Um…maybe," Susan replied.

Maria looked pleased. "Great."

"Hey, babe, I want to grab a drink before the lines at the bar are too long," Hank said. "We'll catch up with the two of you later."

She waited until the couple disappeared into the ballroom before turning to Lewis. "Did I agree to go to lunch and look at wedding photos?"

"Yes, why?"

"No reason. Other than I'm surprised she asked." In the past, when Maria made the offer to join the group for lunch, Susan assumed it was because she'd happened across them as they were headed out.

"Perhaps she's seeing you in a new light," Lewis replied. "Congratulations. Means both of us are getting the makeover we wanted."

"Maybe." Changing the subject, she asked, "How did your business meeting go?"

"I'll tell you all about it later. When we have a chance to talk," he replied.

"We can't talk here?"

"Nah," he said, shaking his head. "This is your night. I'm going to help you make the entire company jealous."

"That was never my goal," Susan said. "Not all of it anyway."

"What was your goal then? Because I seem to remember a woman telling me she wanted to show the whole lot of them."

"I did. I…do. At least that's part of it."

"What do you mean?" The way he looked at her, his

expression direct and focused, it felt like he was trying to read her mind. He played with a tendril of hair by her ear. “Is there another reason?”

How did she explain? “I’m not sure I can put it into words,” she told him.

“Try.”

“All right, but not here.” Looking around for a quiet area, she saw that the staircase was empty. It was too early for anyone to venture to the roof. Most of the partygoers were still busy milling about near the bar. “Come with me.”

“This is cozy,” he said when they stepped outside. “I like the way you think.”

“I didn’t want anyone listening,” she told him. She’d been right about the crowd. The rooftop was empty except for the bartender who was tucked away behind the Plexiglas wall of the bar, out of the cold.

The flames in the gas firepit flickered brightly. Susan led Lewis to one of the sofas making up the surrounding circle.

No sooner had they sat down than the bartender emerged from his shelter, carrying a plaid blanket.

“Welcome to the rooftop,” he greeted as he handed the blanket over to Lewis who promptly draped the material around them.

“Wouldn’t want you to get cold,” he murmured, his breath warm against her temple.

The shiver that followed was anything but cold.

“Can I get you something to drink?” the bartender asked. “The special tonight is peppermint hot chocolate. Guaranteed to warm you from the inside out.”

“Depends,” Susan mused. “Does it have a holiday name?”

The man looked confused. “Peppermint hot chocolate,” he said.

“Then I think we’re good,” Lewis replied. “We’ll create our own warmth.” He scooped Susan’s legs up over his lap. She gasped as the cold from his hand touched her leg, but then snuggled against his chest. Being in his arms was like being nestled in a wonderfully safe cocoon.

“Now,” he said. “Tell me this reason you can’t put into words.”

For a second, Susan had forgotten what they’d been talking about. “I hate this party,” she said, laying her head on his shoulder. “All parties really, but this one most of all. Usually I make up an excuse and stay home, but this year Thomas didn’t give me a choice.”

“Why do you avoid it?”

“Isn’t it obvious?” She was always alone, in a room where she felt like everyone was dreading having to talk with her. “Think of the wedding times ten.”

A frown formed on Lewis’s face. “It makes you feel like a pathetic loser?”

“Bingo. All these groups of people who know each other chatting away and there I am, with a stupid smile on my face, wondering if any of them will invite me to join them.”

“And you were too afraid to join them yourself.”

“Not scared.” Scared was the wrong word. “More like I could feel the barrier between me and them, if that makes sense. Like I could go over to them, but I would still be the outsider without anything to say. You saw Maria. The only thing she could talk to me about was work.” At least it was, before they had Lewis to talk about. “And she’s one of the friendliest.”

It was embarrassing, listening to herself complain like this. She didn't like revealing this side of herself. For some reason, however, it seemed to happen around Lewis. Whether because the way he looked at her when she spoke loosened her tongue or because she felt he understood, she didn't know.

Losing herself in the blue of the fire, she continued. "Normally, I don't care what they think. We're talking about coworkers and employees. I don't need to be their friend. Every once in a while though…well, that's why I stay home. Being in my apartment is a lot more comfortable than being a wallflower."

"You could simply hang with your family," he said.

"I try, but Thomas believes in mingling and Linus is friends with the entire company. I look like the sad baby sister tagging along." Just like when they were kids.

"So along with getting a little revenge on those bathroom chicks, you wanted me to be here to keep you from feeling alone. Is that what you're telling me?"

"Sort of." The words still weren't completely right. "Have you ever wanted to be that person who everyone noticed? I mean, noticed in a good way? The person the whole room wants to be? Never mind. Forget I asked that." Of course he knew.

"You want to be one of the cool kids," Lewis replied.

"When you put it like that, it sounds so childish." Maybe it was. High school was a long time ago.

She felt Lewis's thumb stroking her dress, right above her hip bone. A slow, steady massage. She focused on the tempo, back and forth, back and forth until the feelings jumbled inside her formed a coherent sentence. "Not cool. Special," she said finally. Lewis went to speak, but she stopped him with a shake of her head.

"My brothers, my mother, even my father when he was alive. People pay attention to them. Notice them. People care about what they think because their opinions matter. *They* matter. I want to matter too," she said in a soft voice.

Lewis stared at the woman curled into his side. How could she think she wasn't special? "Oh, luv," he whispered, brushing a wispy tendril from her face.

He knew what she meant. That feeling of being less than the rest of the room. Of waiting to be called out as a fraud and asked to leave. And while Susan was the last person who should feel that way, he knew all the reminding her in the world wouldn't make her believe him. The feeling came from deep inside where words couldn't reach. Only thoughts.

Still, it didn't hurt to tell her. "You don't need me on your arm to matter."

"Don't I though?" She shifted her position, her legs leaving his lap. It added space between them, and he didn't like it. "Do you know how many people have wanted to talk with me at work since we started dating? They look at me differently now. And Courtney and Ginger? They've practically twisted themselves into knots trying to get on my good side. Call me immature," she said, "but I like the attention. That's the reason I wanted you as my date for the party. This might be the one time I get to be the popular girl."

"I'd never call you immature," he told her. She began to pick at the plaid material of the blanket. "If wanting to be popular is a crime, then half the world would be guilty." Including him. Heck, his glass house was probably ten times the size of hers.

"You're wrong though," he told her. "You don't need the spotlight to matter."

Like he expected she would, she scoffed softly. "You can have all the adulation and popularity you want, but all you really need are a few people who care. One person even."

"Easy for you to say."

Was it? There was a lesson for him in those words, but now wasn't the time to pick them apart.

"You sell yourself too short. You matter to your family. I know you don't believe it, but you matter to your brothers. And Maddie…"

She smiled at the mention of her niece. "Maddie's my little angel."

Noel would be one soon enough as well, he suspected. She wasn't the horrible, unlikable shrew she painted herself out to be.

She was amazing really.

If someone had told him a few weeks ago, when they hashed out this arrangement, how much he would enjoy their time together, he wouldn't have believed them. Today wouldn't have happened. He wouldn't have achieved half the success if she hadn't been by his side.

An inexplicable fullness gripped him. Looking at her now, white lights twinkling about her, he'd never seen anything as lovely.

"You matter to me too," he said. The reverence in his voice didn't come close to capturing how he felt. "A lot. You matter to me a lot."

The look in her eye said she didn't believe him.

Very well. He would just have to show her the best way he knew possible. Pulling her close, he kissed her.

And kissed her again.

"Let's get out of here," he murmured against her mouth. There was more he wanted to tell her. Plus he hadn't been kidding about how delicious she looked. Between her chocolate-tinged kisses and her creamy bare back, she had him starving.

"I can't. I promised Thomas." Her argument would have been more persuasive if she weren't kissing him back in between sentences. Eventually, she pulled away, out of his mouth's reach. "Besides, at the very least I deserve a dance downstairs."

Lewis took a good look at her mussed hair and swollen lips. There was no hiding what they'd been up to, that was for sure.

Well, she'd wanted people to notice.

Linus was stepping onto the dais to speak when they entered the ballroom. As soon as he saw them, he motioned impatiently for Susan to join him. Lewis stepped back into the shadows and watched as she hurried to the front of the ballroom. At least a half-dozen heads turned in her direction.

And she thought no one noticed her.

When she reached the stage area, Linus whispered something in her ear. Judging from the way she turned crimson, he could guess the commentary.

"I promise I won't stand up here long," Linus said, "because I know you'd much rather eat and drink free food than listen to anyone named Collier drone on. But my sister Susan and I wanted to take a few minutes and say thank you. This has been a true comeback year for Collier's. Thanks to your efforts, the Collier name is poised to continue succeeding, not only for the upcoming year, but with luck, for another four hundred!"

When the polite laughter subsided, he raised his

glass. “Seriously, Collier’s would be nothing without our employees. So on behalf of Thomas, Susan and myself—along with all our executive staff—thank you, happy holidays and a very happy New Year. Now get out there on the dance floor and have a good time!”

The crowd applauded, and the deejay struck up a party song. Lewis waited until Susan stepped off the stage before sauntering toward her.

“Now can we go home?” He already knew the answer, but he wanted to see her skin blush again when he made the suggestion.

At the same time, Linus walked by. “Nice of you to join us,” he said, giving them both a look. “We’ll talk later, Susan.”

Lewis looked back at her with a frown. “Are you in trouble?”

“Nothing dire. Although you could have told me my bun was falling.”

“Is it? I hadn’t noticed.” His hands settled on her hips, fingers splaying outward. “Everything seems in place to me.” He paused. “Oh. Now that you say something, it does look a little disheveled.” Dipping his head, he whispered. “As if you were snogging on the rooftop.”

Score another blush. If he thought she’d agree, he’d drag her back to the rooftop for a repeat performance. Seeing as how they couldn’t, they’d have to find another way to fill the time. “Since we’re going to stay,” he said, “would you rather eat or dance?”

As if to help his argument along, the deejay began to play a Christmas love song. Susan’s arms looped around his neck. “Dance,” she said.

Good. Food was overrated.

They did eat eventually and mingle, as well. He

wished Susan could have seen herself from his vantage point. She was charming and funny as she moved from group to group. Not a shred of shrewishness or unlikability in sight. "For a wallflower, you are amazingly charismatic," he told her later, while they were dancing. It was the end of the night, and the deejay was playing the last slow dance of the evening, or rather the fifth last slow dance as Lewis had slipped him a few bills to keep the songs coming.

"If I was, it's because I had a star on my shoulder," Susan replied. She had her cheek against his lapel and her arms wrapped around his waist. They probably looked more like they were hugging than dancing. "You make me feel charismatic."

Nonsense. She was her own star. She didn't need him to be anything. Someday she'd realize that.

"People are leaving. I don't suppose Linus will release you from duty."

"Afraid not," she replied. "Even if I weren't in the doghouse, I'm stuck here until the last employee leaves. Turns out that's the tradition. Something Linus said I'd know if I hadn't skipped out all the time."

"Any way we can convince all the employees to leave now? Pull a fire alarm or something?" He was dying to get her home so he could peel off that dress and share his good news. In that order.

"I wish." Letting out a long sigh, Susan burrowed closer. "Why don't you just tell me your news now? You know you're dying to, and I'm dying to hear it."

"Won't be as fun though." Still, she was right about him being eager to tell her. "Let's sit down though." It was the kind of news best told face-to-face.

"Do you remember when Graham Montclark said he

would vouch for my character if necessary?" he asked once they'd settled in at a nearby cocktail table. Susan nodded. "Turns out, he went ahead and vouched anyway."

"I don't understand."

"I got a call this morning from his network asking me to come in for a meeting. They've decided to add a new face to their game-coverage team and they think I'm the right face."

Slowly, Susan's eyes widened as the meaning of his news settled over her. "Are you saying…?"

"It worked." Man, but it felt amazing to finally say the words out loud. "Our crazy plan worked!"

CHAPTER TEN

Susan let his news sink in. Lewis was going back to football. He would feel like he had a home again. "That's…" It was a good thing. It was what he wanted. Rising from her chair, she threw her arms around his neck. "I'm so happy for you," she whispered. Lewis was getting his dream.

Meaning hers was over. With his mission accomplished, there was no more reason for their arrangement. Stupid her, telling him the affair could end with their agreement. Had she really thought she could sleep with Lewis and escape unscathed?

"I couldn't have done it without you," he said. "You believed in me."

"No, it was all you. You're the one who did the work and actually changed. All I did was help get the word out."

And now he didn't need her. She blinked away the lump in her throat.

"Look at me. I'm so happy, I'm getting teary," she said wiping her eye. "We need to celebrate."

"That's kind of the reason I wanted to go home."

Her heart twisted at the words. Wouldn't be too many more times she'd hear him say them. Not now that he no longer needed her. "How about we settle for a toast in the meantime? Champagne for me, water for you. I'll go get it."

Immediately he reached for her arm. "You don't have to do that."

"I want to." She needed the moment to shake the thoughts from her head. "This is your celebration. You sit and let me wait on you."

Pushing her lips into a smile, she scurried to the bar, choosing the one outside the ballroom so she could duck into the powder room and wipe her nose. Someday she'd get through an event without having to hide in the bathroom at some point, but not tonight.

And, because the world really wanted to mock her, Ginger and Courtney were seated along with a few of the PAs at the table nearest the door to the restroom. Both of them shot a trademark smirk in her direction as she approached.

Whatever. She didn't have time for them.

That is, until she was almost through the door. That's when she heard Courtney.

"Fake," she said.

Susan stopped in her tracks. Stepping behind the door, she leaned her ear close to the crack to listen, the nerves in her stomach doing a tap dance.

It was probably nothing.

"…heard her clear as day," Courtney said. "She told Linus that the whole romance was a scam to get him some publicity."

"You mean they aren't an item?" someone asked. "What about those pictures of them kissing?"

"Totally for the camera," Courtney said.

Susan's stomach felt like it had been punched. No

wonder Courtney had smirked at her. She'd overheard everything. The witch had probably spent the whole party spreading the story to anyone who would listen.

What was she going to do? Lewis was going to kill her.

She found a different entrance and rushed back to the table. Lewis frowned upon seeing her. "Where's your champagne? Did they cut you off?"

The ballroom wasn't the proper place for this discussion. There were too many people still gathered at the tables nearby. If they hadn't heard the story, she didn't want them to overhear anything now.

"You know what?" she said. "Screw Linus. Let's go home and celebrate properly."

Under any other circumstance, the way Lewis's brown eyes lit up would have made her knees weak. "Are you sure?" he asked.

"Definitely." They'd talk when they got to her place.

As it turned out, Lewis gave the driver directions for his place. That was fine. They could talk there, as well. She chewed the inside of her mouth while he pressed the combination on his apartment lock. It would be fine, she realized. Courtney could spread the rumor all over the company if she wanted. She and Lewis could always debunk it. Who would they believe—a known company gossip or the two of them? And even if they didn't believe her and Lewis, it was only Collier's. Wasn't like anybody who worked there was going to alert the press.

Yeah, she would tell Lewis and it would be fine.

The first time she saw Lewis's apartment, she'd joked that it looked like a set for a bachelor-life reality show. Lots of chrome and retro-style furniture and a hot tub with a view to rival the London Eye. She thought that again as she dropped her wrap on the glass dining room table.

Lewis stepped up behind her, his large hands curling around her shoulders. "Finally," he murmured. "I've been waiting all night to get you back here."

Preoccupied or not, Susan's eyes still rolled back at the growl in his throat. "Lewis, there's something I need to…"

His lips found the curve of her neck and those were the last words she said on the subject. It could wait until morning, she thought as her head fell back against his shoulder. There was still plenty of time to nip the gossip in the bud.

It was snowing when Lewis woke up. Big slow-falling flakes like the kind in TV movies. They blanketed the trees and parked cars with white. He pulled a nylon jacket over his running shirt and grabbed a knit cap. Running in the snow had always been a favorite pastime, even as a kid. While his teammates complained and moaned about working out in unseasonable weather, he embraced it. There was something strangely invigorating about cutting through the snowflakes. Besides, he could always count on the snow to clear his muddled head.

This morning, his head was clear as a bell, but he had too much energy to sit still. Susan was still asleep, wrapped up in the covers. He smiled and for a second he considered waking her up instead of running. But there would be plenty of time later. It was going to take a lot more than a run to burn off his high.

Other than the Youth Ambassador Event, Lewis couldn't remember the last time he'd felt this good about life. All the pieces of his goals were coming together. He was back in sports where he belonged, back on a team. And maybe now that he was back on top, he could convince Susan to continue their arrangement a little while longer.

Being with her was as close to belonging as a man could get.

After a few laps around the park, he made a quick stop for scones and a copy of the *Looking Glass*. The vendor sold *Personal Magazine* as well so he grabbed a copy of that too since Susan and he were scheduled to do that interview with the magazine later in the week. He was half tempted to cancel since the article wasn't needed. On the other hand, he liked the idea of Susan gracing the pages of a national magazine. Letting the whole country see more of her uniqueness.

That reminded him, he'd have to find a place for a Christmas tree. When he was done "waking up" Susan, he would ask her what she wanted to do for decorations.

The bed was empty when he unlocked the door. Susan was in the bathroom. It was that last loop. He knew he should have cut it short. Oh, well. He'd give her a few moments of privacy, and then join her. The shower wasn't built for two for nothing.

As he kicked off his running shoes, he idly flipped through the paper where he'd dropped it on the kitchen island. It was the usual headlines. The prime minister was fighting with Parliament. One of the royal duchesses had made an appearance in an expensive designer coat. He turned to page six and froze when he saw the headline.

Scam-pagne Lewis? Fans Duped by Publicity Stunt.

What the…? This was not good. Not good at all. This was…

He ran a hand over his mouth. This was a disaster.

Quickly, he scanned the article. It detailed how he and Susan had conspired to improve his image and get publicity for Collier's at the same time, even implying that he was paying Susan and that he was the same drunken playboy he'd always been. Half of it wasn't true at all, and that mattered. Once a narrative was cast, it was near impossible to sway public opinion.

This was going to ruin everything. Goodbye new career, new reputation. Men like Montclark would want nothing to do with him now.

Snatching the paper in his fist, he stormed into the bedroom and thrust open the bathroom door. Susan was just stepping out of the shower. Upon his bursting in, she grabbed a towel.

"What the heck, Lewis," she snapped.

"We've got a problem." He held up the paper so she could see the headline.

A curse escaped her lips. Taking the paper, she continued reading as she padded past him into the bedroom. Lewis followed, reaching the bed in time to hear her swear again.

She'd turned pale. "I didn't think it would make the papers," she said in a low voice.

"What are you talking about? Did you know something like this might happen?"

"Not this." She ran a hand through her curls, sending droplets of water across the comforter. "This is my fault," she said. "I told Linus last night and Courtney overheard. I didn't know she was there but at the end of the night I heard her and Ginger telling others. I'm not sure how it got in the paper though. One of the servers or bartenders must have heard her."

"Dammit. Didn't we agree that we couldn't tell *anybody* for this exact reason?"

"I'm sorry."

Sorry wasn't going to change the fact his reputation was ruined. Again. "Why would you tell Linus in the first place?"

"I didn't set out to," she replied. "He was going on about some family-bonding trip and it came out. I didn't know Courtney was there."

"Well, she was," he snapped. "And now all of London knows."

"I'm sorry." Her eyes were wet with tears.

Blowing out a breath, Lewis got up and retrieved a bathrobe from his closet. He couldn't have this conversation with her wrapped in a towel. She looked too vulnerable. The rational part of him knew it was an accident. That she hadn't intentionally set out to ruin their plan, but he wasn't ready to listen yet. Not when everything he wanted was tumbling out of reach. "I need to go for a run," he said.

"But you already went."

He looked down at his damp running clothes. "Another one. I need to clear my head."

"Don't." Her hand landed on his arm. Lewis turned around. His robe was oversize, the sleeves hanging several inches below her fingers. It was worse than seeing her in the towel.

"It's only one article," she said.

"Right now. You saw how the first one spread." By tomorrow they would be dissecting it on the morning talk shows.

The shrill sound of a phone ringing cut through the tension. "Yours," he said.

She rummaged through her bag. “It’s Thomas.”

He’d heard about the article, no doubt. “You better take it.”

“He can wait until we’re done talking.”

“What more do we have to talk about? The damage is done.”

“Not necessarily. We just need to get out ahead of things. We’ll tell people it was a vindictive ex-girlfriend or someone with a grudge. If we do it right, we can spin this in our favor.”

“How, when it’s the truth? We aren’t a real couple.”

Her lower lip started to quiver. Lewis had to look away.

“We both said it that night in front of your apartment. A casual hookup that doesn’t mean anything. We aren’t some grand romance.”

Why would she want to be with him now anyway? His chance at redemption was done. If he was untouchable before, because of his reputation, surely, he was doubly so now that the papers branded him a fraud.

He couldn’t see bouncing back. Not this time. Might as well walk away from Susan too, and end everything in one cut.

“You should go talk to your brother,” he said walking away. “Fix what you can.”

“What were you thinking?” Thomas asked. With the baby sleeping in the bassinet a few feet away, he kept his voice a whisper. That didn’t hide his frustration however. “A phony romance?”

He paced back and forth in front of the ornate giant tree the decorators had installed in his living room as Susan watched his progress from the couch. “I knew something was odd from the start, but Linus convinced me that you were the real thing. I couldn't believe when he told me last night. And now this?"

He pointed to the paper that lay on the cushion next to her.

"That," Susan replied, "is not my fault. Gossip columnists have spies everywhere. All it takes for things to spiral out of control is for someone to overhear a single conversation."

"If I find out one of my employees leaked the information, they're going to be out the door."

Susan kept quiet. As satisfying as it would be to toss Courtney and Ginger under the bus, she wouldn't. If they were guilty, Thomas would find out easily enough and deal with the problem. Susan didn't need to add fuel to the fire without proof.

"What did you and Lewis think you were going to gain by doing this?" The question came from Rosalind who, until she spoke, had been sitting quietly next to the bassinet watching.

"A new reputation," Susan replied. Still pacing, Thomas let out a loud scoff. "He really is a different person," she said. "About as far from Champagne Lewis as you can get. Only no one would believe him. Everyone was waiting for him to slip up."

"So to prove he was reliable, he decided to lie to the press. Fabulous." Her brother rolled his eyes.

"It's called a contractual relationship and it's done all the time by actors and athletes. Especially if they need a socially acceptable partner or have a project to promote. I wouldn't be surprised if my mother's had one."

"Oh, by all means, let's copy your mother's bad example."

"Thomas," Rosalind admonished.

"It's all right," Susan told her. Belinda certainly wasn't the best role model. "My point is, this wasn't some nutty scheme Lewis dreamed up. There's precedence."

"Let us get this straight," said Rosalind calmly. "You're saying that Lewis needed to be seen with someone like you to look respectable?"

"Precisely. I'm the complete opposite of the women people picture him dating. The idea was that being seen with me would prove he was no longer the same man. And he's not." Didn't matter if he'd broken her heart a half hour ago. She would defend Lewis's character until the end.

"He needed an image makeover and this seemed like the best and most subtle way to do it," she said. "It almost worked too. Graham Montclark vouched for him to the network. They were talking about giving him a broadcast job."

Until this morning. Susan couldn't imagine Lewis's despair. To be so close to what you wanted only to have it taken away.

Actually she could imagine. She wanted to curl up and cry her broken heart out for a week. Only thing stopping her was maintaining a front for Thomas's inquisition.

Thing was, she couldn't blame her brother for being angry.

"All right." He sat down in a chair across from her. "I get what Lewis was trying to do. Why would you agree though? What could you possibly be getting? And don't say publicity for the company, because we both know that couldn't have been your main driver."

She shrugged. “Maybe I needed an image makeover too.”

“What?” Thomas and Rosalind spoke together.

“Come on, there’s no need to act all shocked,” she said. “We all know I’m the unloved elf of the Collier family.”

“The what?” Thomas asked.

“The one who doesn’t fit in and who everyone would rather just went away.”

“No one wants you to go away,” Thomas said. “You’re our sister.”

“Half sister,” she reminded him. “And please, I know I drive everyone crazy. People at the company only tolerate me *because* I’m your sister.”

“I don’t believe that,” Thomas said. “Linus told me last night that you were the belle of the ball.”

“Because I had Lewis with me. When I’m with Lewis I feel different. Likable.” Wanted.

“Is that why you agreed to the idea?” Rosalind asked.

She nodded. “Yes. Kind of.” Close enough anyway. “I wanted people to see me as more than I am. I thought if people think someone like Lewis could fall for me, they would see there’s something likable about me after all and I wouldn’t…”

“Wouldn’t what?” Thomas asked. For the first time since the conversation began, his voice was gentle. The kindness threatened to dislodge her withheld tears.

“Be the loser outsider anymore.”

“What are you talking about? You’re not an outsider.” Thomas said. “You’re my sister.”

“Half sister,” she corrected again.

“Whatever,” he replied. “It’s not your fault who your mother is.”

"A woman who took off and stuck you with me," Susan added.

He waved off the comment. "Linus and I always figured you dodged a bullet when that happened. You call yourself a loser outsider now. Imagine the damage if she'd stuck around and raised you. Imagine the kinds of issues you might have had to face."

Susan didn't know how to respond. He was right; she would have been worse off. The three of them sat quietly for a few minutes, listening to the baby's gentle sleeping noises.

Eventually, Thomas leaned forward, resting his forearms on his knees. "Linus told me last night he didn't believe you. About the relationship being fake. He said you two looked pretty into each other and he thinks you only said it because you wanted to get him off your back."

He'd whispered something similar to her when they were on the dais. *You don't look like you're faking to me.*

"That was wishful thinking on his part." On her part too. "We had to put on a show in order to make people think the relationship was the real deal."

"By loving it up on the roof?" Susan looked up from her lap. "He told me on the phone."

"I've got to say, that doesn't sound too fake to me," Rosalind said.

"It was nothing serious. We figured since we were going to spend the month together and were attracted to each other, we might as well enjoy ourselves. We weren't some great romance," she added, quoting Lewis.

"And how'd that arrangement work out for you?" Thomas asked.

Susan didn't answer. Couldn't answer really, without her voice cracking. She studied the wrinkles in last night's dress.

"I'm sorry," her brother said.

"Me too." But hey, for a few glorious weeks, she'd felt special. "I've got no one to blame but myself. The whole point was to go against type, so I knew going in he wasn't going to stick around. Caveat emptor or something like that."

A tear escaped. The first of the day. Swiping it away, she looked over at Thomas. "I never meant for Collier's to get stuck in the middle of this. I'll step away from the company."

"What? Why would you do that?" he asked. "No one is suggesting you step down from anything."

"But the bad publicity. You're going to need to do something."

"It won't be firing my sister. You're a Collier. The company is as much a part of your legacy as it is mine and Linus's. Was I the only one who listened to Grandfather when he brought us to the company museum?"

He crossed the room to sit next to her. "Bottom line is that family is what makes Collier's. We've survived four hundred years. We'll survive a few weeks of tabloid coverage. Might even help. We're getting a lot of free advertising."

Susan gave up trying to rein in the tears. Letting them escape, she hugged her brother tight. "Thank you." It was the first time she'd ever truly felt like a Collier.

"You're welcome. And you're not an unloved elf. Just an annoying one."

Annoying, she'd take.

"Now," Thomas stood up and smoothed the front of his sweater. "I'm going to call the office and see what kind of statement they're putting out before Rosalind and I go Christmas shopping."

As she watched her brother head upstairs to his office, Susan felt moderately better. At least things were okay with her family.

Family. She repeated the word to herself with a sense of shame. Lewis had tried to tell her that she mattered to her brothers, but she hadn't believed him. Turned out Lewis was right. Someday she'd have to thank him. If she ever saw him again.

Baby Noel was starting to fuss in his bassinet. Must be nearly feeding time.

"I'm sorry. I disrupted your morning," she said to Rosalind, rising to leave. "I'll get out of your way."

"Hold it right there, unloved elf." Wearing a very deliberate expression, her sister-in-law rose from her chair. "It's high time you got a dose of the truth."

CHAPTER ELEVEN

"Do you remember last Christmas when you read me the riot act?" Rosalind asked. "You told me I was as much to blame for my problems as Thomas?"

"Of course, I remember."

"You said things no one else was willing to say. Things that were uncomfortable for me to hear."

"Someone had to."

"You're right. Someone did," Rosalind said. "And if you hadn't, we might never have had our little Christmas miracle here." She paused to scoop up the baby and cradle him. "That is why I'm going to return the favor."

Susan's skin was starting to twitch again. "How so?"

"I'm going to tell you some truths," Rosalind said. "Starting with the fact that for someone who's so obsessed with psychology, you suck at self-awareness."

Susan felt as though she had been slapped. "Excuse me?"

"You heard me," Rosalind said. "Do you honestly believe you're some ugly little lump that no one likes? Give me a break. If that's the case then why were you invited to a half-dozen weddings this year?"

"I don't know. Maybe because I'm the boss?"

"Correction. My husband is the boss and Thomas wasn't invited to half as many."

He wasn't? Susan always assumed he didn't attend because he'd scaled back his business commitments since their reconciliation. "Probably because they know he's been preoccupied, and figured they'd invite the one most likely to attend."

"What about Linus? Did they figure he was too busy, as well?"

"I..." She couldn't answer that. Everyone loved Linus. "He's been distracted lately too."

"So these people knew Thomas and Linus wouldn't attend their weddings, but figured you would and that was why you got an invitation?" Rosalind folded her arms. "Do you hear yourself?"

"If you're going to put it like that, of course it's going to sound ludicrous," Susan said.

"How would you put it then?"

Susan opened her mouth only to shut it again. She wasn't sure. "Company social invitations don't mean anything. There could be any number of reasons why I drew the short straw."

"And what about last night? Linus said you mingled with the best of them."

She'd already told them the reason. Lewis had been by her side. "Mingling is easy when you're dating a celebrity. I've been a rock star all month. Everyone wanted to chat."

"Or maybe," Rosalind said, "it was that for once, you were willing to chat back."

Susan frowned. What did that mean?

"I've seen you at Collier's functions," her sister-in-law went on. "You tuck yourself in the corner and act all aloof. When someone comes up to talk to you, you're fine, but otherwise you pull yourself away. You're the one being antisocial, not them."

"That's not true."

Rosalind arched her brow. "Really?"

All right, maybe she did stand off to the side, but it was only as a matter of self-preservation. Pretend you're not hurting, and you won't.

"You would too if your coworkers thought you were a shrew."

"What?"

At the sight of her sister-in-law's shocked expression, Susan felt a twinge of satisfaction. "*Shrewsan.* That's my nickname at work."

"Who calls you that?"

"Everyone."

"Seriously."

"Well, almost everyone," Susan said, feeling defensive now. "Courtney and Ginger…" She paused. Come to think of it, they were the only two people she'd heard use the term. She only assumed the rest of the company did, as well.

Was it possible she was allowing the nasty opinion of two trolls to color her opinion?

No, because her problems had been going on far longer than that. School. University. She'd been separated from the world her entire life.

She offered her final argument, daring Rosalind to come up with a counterpoint. "If I'm so damn likable, then why isn't my phone ringing with invitations? Why am I stuck spending weekends alone?"

"Probably because people think you'll say no if asked." Rosalind adjusted the baby on her shoulder.

"I've heard you back out of plans with Linus. I'm sure you back out of others."

Like invitations to lunch.

"Look, I get it," her sister-in-law continued. "Thomas told me what your mother is like. But did you ever think that the reason people don't socialize with you is because you don't socialize with them?"

"Why should I?" Susan said. "They're only going to..."

"What?"

"Leave." She didn't need to listen to this. Not today. "I've got a headache," she said, starting for the door.

"How do you know?" Rosalind asked. "How do you know people will leave if you don't give them a chance to stay?"

Was that what she did? Susan sat on the edge of the sofa and thought hard about Rosalind's words. All this time she was protecting herself, was it possible she was being her own worst enemy?

"Lewis left," she whispered.

"He's just upset." Rosalind's voice softened, the way Thomas's had earlier. And like before, Susan felt the tears threatening.

"You're worth a lot more than a fake boyfriend or a casual hookup. You're pretty and you're smart, and if Lewis Matolo didn't appreciate that for anything beyond what you could do for him, then he's the one missing out."

Susan would listen to a lot of things, but disparaging remarks about Lewis weren't on the list. "Lewis is amazing. He's the most amazing man I've ever met. I don't think he even knows how amazing he is. I'm just not in his league."

Rosalind sat next to her. "Yes, you are. You're a Collier. You have four hundred years of legacy behind you. You can be in any league you want."

She didn't know what to say. For the third time in twenty-four hours, she was being told she mattered to the family.

All you really need are a few people who care. That was what Lewis had said. Looked like she had those people.

If only she could make Lewis care for her too. "I think I'm in love with him," she told Rosalind.

Her sister-in-law snaked her free arm around Susan's shoulders. "Then let's hope he smartens up and realizes what he had."

Susan didn't know if that was possible.

Rosalind's lecture stuck with her the rest of the day and into the evening. How appropriate that it would be her sister-in-law who delivered the tough love. Last year at this time, it'd been Susan reminding Rosalind of something similar. As she nursed her glass of wine, she found herself circling a familiar cliché: the pot calling the kettle black.

Looking across the street, she saw most of her neighbors had their Christmas trees lit. One apartment was throwing a party. Seeing the people laughing in the window, she wondered if it was true and her insecurities were her own worst enemy. She'd certainly been wrong about her family. All those years of feeling like a square peg, unwanted and unlike the rest, and it turned out her brothers didn't care what shape she came in.

Of course, that didn't change things with Lewis. All the tough love in the world wouldn't make him want her. She'd laid herself bare and he'd rejected her.

Did he? Or did you hold him at arm's length too?

From the very start, she'd been waiting for their affair to end. Pretending for both their sakes that their lovemaking didn't mean anything.

But it did. She loved him. What they shared had been real on her part. She'd never told him though. In fact, she'd pretended she didn't care. She hadn't even invited him to Christmas Eve for crying out loud. How was he supposed to know she cared unless she let him in?

Downing the rest of her wine in one swallow, she grabbed her phone. Lewis's number was on speed dial. Number one. She pressed the button before her courage ran out.

His voice mail answered.

"Hey, Lewis, it's me." She rushed the words as fast as she could. "I know I'm the last person you want to talk with right now, but I wanted to let you know I'm sorry for..."

No, that wasn't what she wanted to say.

"I wanted to let you know that you were the best fake boyfriend around and that I love...loved every minute we spent together. As far as I'm concerned, the relationship was real—very real—and I'm sorry that I ever said anything to Linus. If I could take it back, I would because you deserve nothing but the best. Oh, and Lewis..."

She stopped herself from disconnecting.

"If there's any chance you feel the same or *could* feel the same...please come to Thomas and Roseanne's vow renewal on Christmas Eve. Not because I need a date, but because I want to see you again and there's nothing I'd like better than to spend the holidays with you. You...you matter to me."

There, she thought with a sniff. No one could say she hadn't made the effort. The rest was up to Lewis.

There was only one thing to do when the going got tough, and that was turn off his phone and belly up to the bar. And, because he was a glutton for punishment, he picked the place where the whole debacle had started. The bar was as empty as it had been a month ago. Emptier. Because a particular brunette wasn't perched on a stool nearby.

"Hey, welcome back."

Just his luck. It was the same bartender.

"Are you here alone or is your girlfriend with you?"

"Haven't you read the papers?" Lewis replied. "She wasn't my girlfriend."

"Could have fooled me. You two looked crazy about each other."

"Goes to show, you can't always believe what you see. Lady was way out of my league."

"Huh."

"What?" Lewis asked. He couldn't believe he was discussing his love life with a bartender. On the other hand, he was in a bar so who else was going to talk with him? It beat staying home and wondering what he was going to do with his life. "If you have an opinion, you might as well go ahead and say it."

The bartender shrugged. "You didn't strike me as someone who hesitates about going after what you want, no matter how out of reach it seems."

"Once upon a time maybe." When reaching meant getting out of a lesser situation. "Unfortunately, just because you want something doesn't mean it'll last." Especially if you didn't belong in the same world. People walk away.

Unless you send them away. Like he had Susan. Why wouldn't he though? He was washed up. His chance at redemption had blown up in his face. Why would Susan want to stick around when she could do so much better?

"Here." The bartender set a bright red drink in front of him. "You look like you could use this."

"What is it?"

"A virgin Christmas Wish. On the house."

Lewis had to laugh. There was a joke in there.

He stared at the bubbles rising in the red depths. Susan. The bubbles reminded him of Susan. Oh, how he wished he could fix what he'd messed up.

If wishes were horses, beggars would ride. He remembered someone telling him that as a kid. His first foster mum maybe. The one who was like Susan. Because of course.

"Excuse me. Are you Lewis Matolo?"

Looking up from the glass, Lewis saw a man in a bellman's uniform. "I saw you walk in," the man said.

He was middle-aged, with salt-and-pepper hair and weathered brown skin. "My name is Darcus Alajua," he said. "You met my grandson David at the Youth Ambassador Event."

The man pulled a phone from his jacket pocket to show its wallpaper—a picture of Lewis and a young boy of around eight.

"I remember him," he said. "Speedy little thing. Good footwork."

"I wanted to thank you. Meeting you is all he's talked about for the past week."

"Wow, with Christmas right around the corner, that's a pretty big feat," the bartender remarked.

Lewis was surprised. He remembered praising David's skills a few times, but he hadn't given the boy any additional attention or singled him out in any way that would merit the boy being that impressed.

"I'm glad he enjoyed himself" he said.

"It's more than enjoyed," Darcus said. His eyes dropped to the screen for a moment and grew misty. "David came to live with me a year ago because his mother…my daughter…has some demons. He's been discouraged, feeling sorry for himself. Sports has been the one thing he's enjoyed."

"I know the feeling." He'd been in David's shoes once.

"I know and when you talked about how football saved you, how it helped pull you out of tough times, it lit a fire in him. He's excited about something again."

"I'm glad. You tell him not to give up, and to keep playing. Sports isn't about being a superstar. It's about belonging and being a part of a team and learning to work at what you love."

The older man smiled, the lines on his cheeks fading and his face turning youthful. "I can see why he enjoyed your talk."

"I enjoyed giving it. Being with the kids reminded me of why I fell in love with football to begin with. When you grow up like I did, you need that escape."

"Yes, you do," Darcus said. "That's why it means a lot to the kids when someone like you comes back home."

Comes back home. Was that what he'd done? "Can I see that photo again?" he asked Darcus.

This time he studied David's face. The kid was looking at him like he had hung the moon.

Who else had looked at him like that? Susan.

Lewis handed the phone back with a smile. All his life he'd needed—wanted—a place where he belonged.

He thought that place was football. But it wasn't. Athletic stardom had never come close to how he felt when working with those kids. The only thing that made him happier had been when he was holding Susan.

You don't need the spotlight. All you really need are a few people who care.

Susan's smile had felt more like home than any stadium or spotlight ever could. She'd believed in him. Understood him. He hadn't needed the spotlight to win her support.

And he'd sent her away. Since when did he not go after what he wanted? He was Champagne Lewis Matolo, for crying out loud!

He pulled out his wallet. "Do me a favor, will you?" he asked Darcus. He handed the man a hundred-dollar bill. "You take this and buy David the best football cleats and shin guards money can buy. Tell him his friend Lewis owes him for making him see something very important."

If the company Christmas party had taken place in a winter wonderland, then Thomas and Rosalind's vow renewal was being held in its more glamorous cousin. Her brother had spared no expense in making the Christmas Eve ceremony special, right down to the grand piano he'd had installed in the living room for the occasion.

"I may have gone a little crazy," Thomas admitted as he took Susan's coat along with the bags of Christmas gifts she'd brought for the next morning.

"Rosalind would have been happy renewing our vows in the middle of a field, but Maddie wanted to have a sparkly wedding."

Susan took in the myriad of lights and candles,

enough to rival the Kew Gardens display. The regular lighting had been turned off because the decorations provided more than enough illumination.

"Good thing you don't overindulge your daughter," she said.

"Hey, it's Christmas Eve. If you can't go crazy with decorations at the holidays, when can you?" He kissed her cheek. "Merry Christmas. You look lovely."

"Thanks." She'd splurged on an evening gown for the occasion. Silver with sequins. No more hiding herself in the corner. If she was to be a square peg, she was going to own her edges. "I'm afraid I don't feel very lovely though."

"No word from Lewis?"

"Afraid not. We had an interview with *Personal Magazine* scheduled for yesterday, but I got a call from his agent saying the interview was canceled."

No surprise there. For a short while she'd hoped they might go through with the interview to contradict the negative publicity, but apparently not. Like Lewis had pointed out, how did you contradict the truth?

The answer was, you don't. She had this pipe dream that Lewis would use the article to make their casual encounters into something more. But he hadn't.

The fallout from Scam-pagne Gate, as it was lovingly called in the press, was swift and loud. Radio stations all over the UK commented on the story all weekend, which in turn, led to the morning shows holding round-table discussions about celebrity ethics and England's search for gossip. Lewis was once again a bad boy while her reputation vacillated between coconspirator to besotted victim.

As for Collier's? The company was experiencing their best holiday season in years so either people didn't care that she was involved with Lewis or her being involved with Lewis had helped the company project a saucy, youthful edge. Either way, at least something good had come out of the scheme.

Thomas eyed her with concern. "Are you going to be okay?"

"I feel like a right idiot," she said. She'd fallen for a man when she'd known from the start he wasn't interested in a long-term relationship. "But, I'm not the first person to have had their heart broken. I'll survive." It killed her when she thought of how good she and Lewis could have been together, but she couldn't make him love her. As magical as the past few weeks had been, she deserved more. First and foremost, a man who loved her back.

"Yes, you will," Thomas replied. "Just remember, you're not alone. Your family will always stand by you."

She smiled. "I know." Now.

Perhaps more than one good thing had come out of the debacle.

Rosalind's dose of reality had been hard to hear, but it also gave her a lot to think about. It made Susan take a good look at her behavior over the years. She'd become such an expert at pretending she didn't care about being an outsider, that she failed to see all the times she'd been offered a place inside. She had brothers who cared about her. Sure they were all completely different, and she would never mesh completely with them in a million years. But as Thomas showed the day she and Lewis were outed, when the chips were down, they had her back.

"By the way," Thomas continued, "we found out how the paper got the story. Turns out one of the bartenders at the hotel has a cousin who writes for the *Looking Glass*. She overheard Courtney and Ginger talking at the bar and convinced them to tell her the entire story. She then turned the info over to her cousin."

"Lewis warned me there were spies everywhere. What are you going to do about Ginger and Courtney?"

"Since I don't handle personnel issues anymore, I told senior management that while I wasn't happy with their behavior, I would leave the final decision to them. And you."

"Me?"

"Last time I looked, you were the one who handled human resources," he said. "Plus, you were the victim. If anyone should weigh in with an opinion, it's you."

In other words, Courtney's and Ginger's fates lay in her hands. How circumstances had changed.

Over the week, she'd thought quite a bit about the gossipy twosome. She finally realized that their need to put her down said more about them than it did her. What their reason was for disliking her, Susan didn't know, but that didn't mean their opinion was correct either. In fact, a long talk over coffee with Maria proved their opinion was in the minority. Susan was simply so busy wrapping herself in protective distance that she hadn't noticed.

The question now was how bad a punishment did they deserve? "They didn't purposely leak the story," she said. "More like they were being petty and foolish." On the other hand, their pettiness had caused her and Lewis a lot of pain. Mostly Lewis. When it came to Susan, the story had only hastened the inevitable.

"Still, they did do damage. It's only by sheer luck Collier's didn't suffer some kind of backlash."

"You can say that again. Personally, I think we should fire them," Thomas said.

"Not me." Susan couldn't believe what she was about to suggest. "I'd rather suspend them for two weeks and give them a stern warning."

Her brother lifted his brows. "Seriously?"

"And I want them to know that I was the one who saved their catty little butts." She wasn't so magnanimous that she didn't want them to owe her.

"Excuse me, you two." Linus stepped into the entryway. "Do you plan to spend the entire evening talking in the entryway or do you plan to attend the party?"

"Merry Christmas to you too." She kissed him on the cheek.

He looked past her shoulder. "Are you here alone?"

"What do you think?"

"Just checking. I need a drinking companion. Come with me to the bar." He tucked her arm into his. "By the way," he said over his shoulder, "your wife wanted me to tell you the maid of honor is getting antsy. She's worried you'll take too long and prevent Santa Claus from coming."

"You know," Susan said as they stepped into the main living room, "Thomas insists that Maddie will be running Collier's someday. I'm beginning to think he's right."

When Thomas said only a few friends and family would be invited, he hadn't been joking. Only a handful of people, a dozen at most, were in the room. Most were gathered by the piano listening to the Christmas carols. Four stockings, fire-engine red, hung from the mantel, the newest one a miniature version of the other three. The magic of it all was like salt poured into her heart, but she forced a smile for her brother's sake. It was just a broken heart. She would survive.

Linus led her to the opposite side of the room where a portable bar had been staged. Susan's eyes nearly popped out of her head.

"You again!" she said. "Are you the only bartender in London this holiday season?" The bartender let out a hearty laugh. "I'm beginning to think so. I was drafted into service by my uncle Chris. He's over there by the guests." He pointed to a portly man with a white beard and red reindeer sweater.

"Well it's good to see you…?" She realized she'd never gotten his name.

"Nick," he replied. "Is your boyfriend with you?"

A little more salt burned her heart. "I'm afraid we aren't together anymore."

"That's too bad. You two made an adorable couple."

She'd thought so too. "Some things don't always work out," she said sadly.

"Or maybe they just take time," he replied. Evidently they taught positive thinking at bartending school. "Can I get you a house special?"

"What's it called this time? Nick likes to name his drinks," she told Linus.

"Yep, and in honor of tonight's special event, we're serving True Love cocktails."

"Fabulous," Linus replied, sounding slightly more enthusiastic than she felt.

"Trust me," Nick told them. "You won't regret the choice."

Their cocktails were barely in hand when the pianist played a loud fanfare. "If you could take your seats," he announced. "Our ceremony is about to begin."

Maddie appeared at the top of the spiral staircase, and as the pianist played a soft classical piece, she began picking her way down the stairs. When she reached the bottom, she scurried to the front of the room to hug her father. She looked adorable. Susan smiled, then looked at the empty seat beside her.

How she wished Lewis were here.

Rosalind was next, looking resplendent in a simple white silk dress. She positively beamed with happiness. No wonder Nick named the drink True Love.

Feeling a little nauseous, Susan took a large sip and watched the ceremony. The look of utter adoration in her brother's eyes made her heart ache. How wonderful must it be to be loved the way Thomas loved Rosalind.

Some day, she told herself. Some day she would have that. At the moment, her heart still wished it were Lewis, but after a week, it was time for her to accept that that wasn't going to happen. Instead, she'd be grateful for the time they'd had.

As she blinked away the dampness from her eyes, she felt someone settle into the empty seat beside her.

"I hope those are tears of joy."

Susan stopped breathing. She was almost afraid to turn her head. Was that really Lewis sitting beside her? "You… I…"

He put his fingers to his lips. "Shh. There's a wedding going on." A second later, his hand captured hers.

The rest of the ceremony passed in a fog as the only thing Susan could focus on was the man beside her. Did his being there mean he returned her feelings or was he simply fulfilling one last obligation? A tear slipped down her cheek.

"Hey, now," Lewis said as the rest of the group burst

into applause. “What’s this?” He reached across and fanned her cheek with his thumb, his fingers lingering on her jaw when he finished.

What was he doing, smiling at her like she was the most important person in the world? People were still applauding and congratulating the happy couple, but she needed to know. The moment was too surreal to believe. Or rather, too perfect to believe.

“Come with me,” she said. Slipping past the crowd, she led him to the vestibule where they could talk in private. There, partially hidden by a poinsettia tower, she turned to him and finally asked what she’d been dying to ask the entire ceremony. “Why are you here?”

“I got your invitation.”

A week ago. She’d left her message a week ago.

She tossed her drink in his face.

“What was that for?” Lewis wiped the True Love from his face.

“Why do you think?” It was an instant reaction and probably over the top, but dammit! “You left me hanging for an entire week!”

“Is everything okay?” she heard Thomas ask.

All five members of her family appeared in the doorway, prepared to stand by her. Even distracted by Lewis, the show of solidarity squeezed her heart.

“Thanks, but I’ve got this,” she told them. “Lewis was just about to explain what the hell he was thinking showing up here after being MIA for a week.”

“I was trying for a romantic gesture.”

“You call leaving me hanging romantic?”

“Don’t be daft. I wanted to call you back as soon as I got the message.”

Out of nowhere Nick joined the group, brandishing a cloth napkin. Lewis took the cloth and wiped the last of the liquid from his cheeks. "Okay, I *should* have called you back as soon as I got the message, but I was out of town on business. I decided it would be better if I waited until I saw you in person so I could say I love you properly. Clearly I made a mistake."

"Clearly you did… Wait." Did she hear him right? "What did you say?"

"I said I made a mistake."

"No, before that."

Lewis smiled. "I said I love you, Susan Collier."

Before she could say another word, he drew her into a kiss. He tasted like peppermint and True Love.

God bless silly cocktail names.

"I'm the biggest idiot on the planet," he whispered when they parted. He rested his forehead against hers, his eyes shut tight. "I was so afraid of… I spent my entire life certain the only reason anyone would want me was because of what I could do on the field. That if I weren't a star…if I weren't in the spotlight, that people wouldn't care. I wouldn't be good enough for anybody." Pulling back, he opened his eyes to reveal unshed tears. "Especially not for you."

"You are an idiot." Her lips were trembling so much, the words barely made it out. "I don't care what you do. I never did." The irony of his confession hit her and she started to laugh. "I thought *I* wasn't good enough for *you*."

"Oh, sweetheart, you are so far out of my league. I consider myself lucky that you would ever give me the time of day."

"We're both idiots," she said. Letting their insecurities keep them from happiness. "I love you, Lewis Matolo."

He brushed her cheek. "I love you too, Susan Collier."

They were the three most beautiful words she'd ever heard.

"My last grand gesture didn't go right, but maybe this one will," he said. "I know we both have a lot of issues to work out, and I can't promise what the future is going to hold for us. But I'd like to find out."

There was a gasp from the room as he dropped to one knee. "Therefore, in front of your friends and family, I'm asking if you'll…date me. For real."

"Yes," she replied, wiping the tears from her cheeks. "I would be honored to be your real girlfriend."

"Daddy, are we having another wedding?" Maddie called out.

"Maybe someday," Susan replied, her heart giving a leap at the smile her answer brought to Lewis's face. "Right now, I think I'll focus on having a very merry Christmas."

Lewis Matolo: How a Fake Relationship Brought Me Love

It doesn't take a genius to see that Champagne Lewis is happy with life. Once the king of London nightlife, he's content these days enjoying a cup of tea and babysitting his girlfriend's niece and nephew.

"I love kids," Matolo says. "They remind you of what's important."

It's that love of children that led the star of *Football Tonight* to establish the Matolo Children's Foundation, which aims to help underprivileged and foster children develop leadership skills through sports. His partner in the venture is his girlfriend, Susan Collier.

"To think," he says, "it all started with a fake relationship..."

Susan stopped reading and tucked her copy of *Personal Magazine* under her arm. "It's brilliant. I told you we could spin this into something positive."

"Yes, you did, and it only took twelve months," Lewis replied. He laughed when she gave him a playful smack.

Hard to believe a year had passed since that horrible night they'd met, which in retrospect had turned out to be the best night of her life. It'd given birth to the best twelve months she'd ever had. Both she and Lewis were making an effort to work through their insecurities. Taking Rosalind's advice, she'd begun trying to be less standoffish and to be open to people. As a result, they were heading to the Regis to help their friends Maria and Hank celebrate their wedding anniversary.

Meanwhile it turned out Lewis hadn't blown his shot after all. The network loved Lewis's new notoriety. The executives thought he brought an extra edge to the broadcast.

"It's too bad the article's going to be out of date soon," Lewis said. "I've already given the network my notice." He'd decided the joy he felt working with kids was far more rewarding than broadcasting.

"I'm sure the world will forgive you," Susan said. "It's not like you left to chase wine and women. You didn't, right?"

"No way, luv. I'm a one-woman man these days."

Susan smiled. The best part of the year had been making their journeys together. Lately they'd even started talking about merging those journeys into one shared life, and if the little square box she'd accidently found in Lewis's drawer was any indication, that merger was right around the corner. Two odd peas no longer unwanted and alone.

Just as they reached the hotel, the first snowflakes of the season began to fall. "Looks like the Christmas season has officially started," Susan remarked. "They'll be playing carols on the radio next."

"A little early Christmas isn't so bad," Lewis replied. "Means the pop-up bars will be setting up shop."

"That's true." Hard to hate those when it was a pop-up bar that brought them together. "Do you think the same bar is here this year? We could stop in and say hello to Nick."

"We could see."

They walked up the stairs to the mezzanine, expecting to find the temporary structure. Unfortunately, when they reached the top step, the space was empty. There was nothing but a pair of high-back chairs and a table with a small Christmas tree.

"Sorry, luv," said Lewis. "Looks like we're out of luck."

No, she wasn't. Her luck was only beginning.

"That's all right," she told him. "I've already got my Christmas wish."

* * * * *

GIFT-WRAPPED IN HER WEDDING DRESS

KANDY SHEPHERD

To all my Christmas magazine colleagues, in particular Helen, Adriana and Jane – the magic of the season lives on!

CHAPTER ONE

So he'd got on the wrong side of the media. Again. Dominic's words, twisted out of all recognition, were all over newspapers, television and social media.

Billionaire businessman Dominic Hunt refuses to sleep out with other CEOs in charity event for homeless.

Dominic slammed his fist on his desk so hard the pain juddered all the way up his arm. He hadn't *refused* to support the charity in their Christmas appeal, just refused the invitation to publicly bed down for the night in a cardboard box on the forecourt of the Sydney Opera House. His donation to the worthy cause had been significant—but anonymous. *Why wasn't that enough?*

He buried his head in his hands. For a harrowing time in his life there had been no choice for him but to sleep rough for real, a cardboard box his only bed. He couldn't go there again—not even for a charity stunt, no matter how worthy. There could be no explanation—he would not share the secrets of his past. *Ever.*

With a sick feeling of dread he continued to read on-screen the highlights of the recent flurry of negative press about him and his company, thoughtfully compiled in a report by his Director of Marketing.

Predictably, the reporters had then gone on to rehash his well-known aversion to Christmas. Again he'd been misquoted. It was true he loathed the whole idea of celebrating Christmas. But not for the reasons the media had so fancifully contrived. Not because he was a *Scrooge.* How he hated that label and the erroneous aspersions that he didn't ever give to charity. Despaired that he was included in a round-up of Australia's Multi-Million-Dollar Misers. *It couldn't be further from the truth.*

He strongly believed that giving money to worthy causes should be conducted in private—not for public acclaim. But this time he couldn't ignore the name-calling and innuendo. He was near to closing a game-changing deal on a joint venture with a family-owned American corporation run by a man with a strict moral code that included obvious displays of philanthropy.

Dominic could not be seen to be a Scrooge. He had to publicly prove that he was not a miser. But he did not want to reveal the extent of his charitable support because to do so would blow away the smokescreen he had carefully constructed over his past.

He'd been in a bind. Until his marketing director had suggested he would attract positive press if he opened his harbourside home for a lavish fund-raising event for charity. 'Get your name in the newspaper for the right reasons,' he had been advised.

Dominic hated the idea of his privacy being invaded but he had reluctantly agreed. He wanted the joint venture to happen. If a party was what it took, he was prepared to put his qualms aside and commit to it.

The party would be too big an event for it to be organised in-house. His marketing people had got outside companies involved. Trouble was the three so-called 'party planners' he'd been sent so far had been incompetent and he'd shown them the door within minutes of meeting. Now there was a fourth. He glanced down at the eye-catching card on the desk in front of him. Andrea Newman from a company called Party Queens—*No party too big or too small* the card boasted.

Party Queens. It was an interesting choice for a business name. Not nearly as stitched up as the other companies that had pitched for this business. But did it have the gravitas required? After all, this event could be the deciding factor in a deal that would extend his business interests internationally.

He glanced at his watch. This morning he was working from his home office. Ms Newman was due to meet with him right now, here at his house where the party was to take place. Despite the attention-grabbing name of the business, he had no reason to expect Party Planner Number Four to be any more impressive than the other three he'd sent packing. But he would give her twenty minutes—that was only fair and he made a point of always being fair.

On cue, the doorbell rang. Punctuality, at least, was a point in Andrea Newman's favour. He headed down the wide marble stairs to the front door.

His first impression of the woman who stood on his porch was that she was attractive, not in a conventionally pretty way but something rather more interesting—an angular face framed by a tangle of streaked blonde hair, a wide generous mouth, unusual green eyes. So attractive he found himself looking at her for a moment longer than was required to sum up a possible contractor. And the almost imperceptible curve of her mouth let him know she'd noticed.

'Good morning, Mr Hunt—Andie Newman from Party Queens,' she said. 'Thank you for the pass code that got me through the gate. Your security is formidable, like an eastern suburbs fortress.' Was that a hint of challenge underscoring her warm, husky voice? If so, he wasn't going to bite.

'The pass code expires after one use, Ms Newman,' he said, not attempting to hide a note of warning. The three party planners before her were never going to get a new pass code. But none of them had been remotely like her—in looks or manner.

She was tall and wore a boldly patterned skirt of some silky fine fabric that fell below her knees in uneven layers, topped by a snug-fitting rust-coloured jacket and high heeled shoes that laced all the way up her calf. A soft leather satchel was slung casually across her shoulder. She presented as smart but more unconventional than the corporate dark suits and rigid briefcases of the other three—whose ideas had been as pedestrian as their appearances.

'Andie,' she replied and started to say something else about his security system. But, as she did, a sudden gust of balmy spring breeze whipped up her skirt, revealing long slender legs and a tantalising hint of red underwear. Dominic tried to do the gentlemanly thing and look elsewhere—difficult when she was standing so near to him and her legs were so attention-worthy.

'Oh,' she gasped, and fought with the skirt to hold it down, but no sooner did she get the front of the skirt in place, the back whipped upwards and she had to twist around to hold it down. The back view of her legs was equally as impressive as the front. He balled his hands into fists by his sides so he did not give into the temptation to help her with the flyaway fabric.

She flushed high on elegant cheekbones, blonde hair tousled around her face, and laughed a husky, uninhibited laugh as she battled to preserve her modesty. The breeze died down as quickly as it had sprung up and her skirt floated back into place. Still, he noticed she continued to keep it in check with a hand on her thigh.

'That's made a wonderful first impression, hasn't it?' she said, looking up at him with a rueful smile. For a long moment their eyes connected and he was the first to look away. *She was beautiful.*

As she spoke, the breeze gave a final last sigh that ruffled her hair across her face. Dominic wasn't a fanciful man, but it seemed as though the wind was ushering her into his house.

'There are worse ways of making an impression,' he said gruffly. 'I'm interested to see what you follow up with.'

Andie wasn't sure what to reply. She stood at the threshold of Dominic Hunt's multi-million-dollar mansion and knew for the first time in her career she was in serious danger of losing the professional cool in which she took such pride.

Not because of the incident with the wind and her skirt. Or because she was awestruck by the magnificence of the house and the postcard-worthy panorama of Sydney Harbour that stretched out in front of it. No. It was the man who towered above her who was making her feel so inordinately flustered. Too tongue-tied to come back with a quick quip or clever retort.

'Th...thank you,' she managed to stutter as she pushed the breeze-swept hair back from across her face.

During her career as a stylist for both magazines and advertising agencies, and now as a party planner, she had acquired the reputation of being able to manage difficult people. Which was why her two partners in their fledgling business had voted for her to be the one to deal with Dominic Hunt. Party Queens desperately needed a high-profile booking like this to help them get established. Winning it was now on her shoulders.

She had come to his mansion forewarned that he could be a demanding client. The gossip was that he had been scathing to three other planners from other companies much bigger than theirs before giving them the boot. Then there was his wider reputation as a Scrooge—a man who did not share his multitude of money with others less fortunate. He was everything she did not admire in a person.

Despite that, she been blithely confident Dominic Hunt wouldn't be more than she could handle. Until he had answered that door. Her reaction to him had her stupefied.

She had seen the photos, watched the interviews of the billionaire businessman, had recognised he was good-looking in a dark, brooding way. But no amount of research had prepared her for the pulse-raising reality of this man—tall, broad-shouldered, powerful muscles apparent even in his sleek tailored grey suit. He wasn't pretty-boy handsome. Not with that strong jaw, the crooked nose that looked as though it had been broken by a viciously aimed punch, the full, sensual mouth with the faded white scar on the corner, the spiky black hair. And then there was the almost palpable emanation of power.

She had to call on every bit of her professional savvy to ignore the warm flush that rose up her neck and onto her cheeks, the way her heart thudded into unwilling awareness of Dominic Hunt, not as a client but as a man.

She could not allow that to happen. This job was too important to her and her friends in their new business. *Anyway, dark and brooding wasn't her type.* Her ideal man was sensitive and sunny-natured, like her first lost love, for whom she felt she would always grieve.

She extended her hand, willing it to stay steady, and forced a smile. 'Mr Hunt, let's start again. Andie Newman from Party Queens.'

His grip in return was firm and warm and he nodded acknowledgement of her greeting. If a mere handshake could send shivers of awareness through her, she could be in trouble here.

Keep it businesslike. She took a deep breath, tilted back her head to meet his gaze full-on. 'I believe I'm the fourth party planner you've seen and I don't want there to be a fifth. I should be the person to plan your event.'

If he was surprised at her boldness, it didn't show in his scrutiny; his grey eyes remained cool and assessing.

'You'd better come inside and convince me why that should be the case,' he said. Even his voice was attractive—deep and measured and utterly masculine.

'I welcome the opportunity,' she said in the most confident voice she could muster.

She followed him into the entrance hall of the restored nineteen-twenties house, all dark stained wood floors and cream marble. A grand central marble staircase with wrought-iron balustrades split into two sides to climb to the next floor. This wasn't the first grand home she'd been in during the course of her work but it was so impressive she had to suppress an impulse to gawk.

'Wow,' she said, looking around her, forgetting all about how disconcerted Dominic Hunt made her feel. 'The staircase. It's amazing. I can just see a choir there, with a chorister on each step greeting your guests with Christmas carols as they step into the house.' Her thoughts raced ahead of her. Choristers' robes in red and white? Each chorister holding a scrolled parchment printed with the words to the carol? What about the music? A string quartet? A harpsichord?

'What do you mean?' he said, breaking into her reverie.

Andie blinked to bring herself back to earth and turned to look up at him. She smiled. 'Sorry. I'm getting ahead of myself. It was just an idea. Of course I realise I still need to convince you I'm the right person for your job.'

'I meant about the Christmas carols.'

So he would be that kind of pernickety client, pressing her for details before they'd even decided on the bigger picture. Did she need to spell out the message of 'Deck the Halls with Boughs of Holly'?

She shook her head in a don't-worry-about-it way. 'It was just a top-of-mind thought. But a choir would be an amazing use of the staircase. Maybe a children's choir. Get your guests into the Christmas spirit straight away, without being too cheesy about it.'

'It isn't going to be a Christmas party.' He virtually spat the word *Christmas*.

'But a party in December? I thought—'

He frowned and she could see where his reputation came from as his thick brows drew together and his eyes darkened. 'Truth be told, I don't want a party here at all. But it's a necessary evil—necessary to my business, that is.'

'Really?' she said, struggling not to jump in and say the wrong thing. A client who didn't actually want a party? This she hadn't anticipated. Her certainty that she knew how to handle this situation—this man—started to seep away.

She gritted her teeth, forced her voice to sound as conciliatory as possible. 'I understood from your brief that you wanted a big event benefiting a charity in the weeks leading up to Christmas on a date that will give you maximum publicity.'

'All that,' he said. 'Except it's not to be a Christmas party. Just a party that happens to be held around that time.'

Difficult and demanding didn't begin to describe this. But had she been guilty of assuming December translated into Christmas? Had it actually stated that in the brief? She didn't think she'd misread it.

She drew in a calming breath. 'There seems to have been a misunderstanding and I apologise for that,' she said. 'I have the official briefing from your marketing department here.' She patted her satchel. 'But I'd rather hear your thoughts, your ideas for the event in your own words.

A successful party plan comes from the heart. Can we sit down and discuss this?'

He looked pointedly at his watch. Her heart sank to the level of the first lacing on her shoes. She did not want to be the fourth party planner he fired before she'd even started her pitch. 'I'll give you ten minutes,' he said.

He led her into a living room that ran across the entire front of the house and looked out to the blue waters of the harbour and its icons of the Sydney Harbour Bridge and the Opera House. Glass doors opened out to a large terrace. *A perfect summer party terrace.*

Immediately she recognised the work of one of Sydney's most fashionable high-end interior designers—a guy who only worked with budgets that started with six zeros after them. The room worked neutral tones and metallics in a nod to the art deco era of the original house. The result was masculine but very, very stylish.

What an awesome space for a party. But she forced thoughts of the party out of her head. She had ten minutes to win this business. Ten minutes to convince Dominic Hunt she was the one he needed.

CHAPTER TWO

DOMINIC SAT ANDIE NEWMAN down on the higher of the two sofas that faced each other over the marble coffee table—the sofa he usually chose to give himself the advantage. He had no need to impress her with his greater height and bulk—she was tall, but he was so much taller than her even as he sat on the lower seat. Besides, the way she positioned herself with shoulders back and spine straight made him think she wouldn't let herself be intimidated by him or by anyone else. *Think again.* The way she crossed and uncrossed those long legs revealed she was more nervous than she cared to let on.

He leaned back in his sofa, pulled out her business card from the inside breast pocket of his suit jacket and held it between finger and thumb. 'Tell me about Party Queens. This seems like a very new, shiny card.'

'Brand new. We've only been in business for three months.'

'We?'

'My two business partners, Eliza Dunne and Gemma Harper. We all worked on a magazine together before we started our own business.'

He narrowed his eyes. 'Now you're "party queens"?' He used his fingers to enclose the two words with quote marks. 'I don't see the connection.'

'We always were party queens—even when we were working on the magazine.' He quirked an eyebrow and she paused. He noticed she quirked an eyebrow too, in unconscious imitation of his action. 'Not in that way.' She tried to backtrack, then smiled. 'Well, maybe somewhat in that way. Between us we've certainly done our share of partying. But then you have to actually enjoy a party to organise one; don't you agree?'

'It's not something I've given thought to,' he said. Business-wise, it could be a point either for her or against her.

Parties had never been high on his agenda—even after his money had opened so many doors for him. Whether he'd been sleeping rough in an abandoned building project in the most dangerous part of Brisbane or hobnobbing with decision makers in Sydney, he'd felt he'd never quite fitted in. So he did the minimum socialising required for his business. 'You were a journalist?' he asked, more than a little intrigued by her.

She shook her head. 'My background is in interior design but when a glitch in the economy meant the company I worked for went bust, I ended up as an interiors editor on a lifestyle magazine. I put together shoots for interiors and products and I loved it. Eliza and Gemma worked on the same magazine, Gemma as the food editor and Eliza on the publishing side. Six months ago we were told out of the blue that the magazine was closing and we had all lost our jobs.'

'That must have been a shock,' he said.

When he'd first started selling real estate at the age of eighteen he'd lived in terror he'd lose his job. Underlying all his success was always still that fear—which was why he was so driven to keep his business growing and thriving. Without money, without a home, he could slide back into being Nick Hunt of 'no fixed abode' rather than Dominic Hunt of Vaucluse, one of the most exclusive addresses in Australia.

'It shouldn't have come as a shock,' she said. 'Magazines close all the time in publishing—it's an occupational hazard. But when it actually happened, when *again* one minute I had a job and the next I didn't, it was…soul-destroying.'

'I'm sorry,' he said.

She shrugged. 'I soon picked myself up.'

He narrowed his eyes. 'It's quite a jump from a magazine job to a party planning business.' Her lack of relevant experience could mean Party Planner Number Four would go the way of the other three. He was surprised at how disappointed that made him feel.

'It might seem that way, but hear me out,' she said, a determined glint in her eye. If one of the other planners had said that, he would have looked pointedly at his watch. This one, he was prepared to listen to—he was actually interested in her story.

'We had to clear our desks immediately and were marched out of the offices by security guards. Shell-shocked, we all retired to a café and thought about what we'd do. The magazine's deputy editor asked could we organise her sister's eighteenth birthday party. At first we said no, thinking she was joking. But then we thought about it. A big magazine shoot that involves themes and food and props is quite a production. We'd also sometimes organise magazine functions for advertisers. We realised that between us we knew a heck of a lot about planning parties.'

'As opposed to enjoying them,' he said.

'That's right,' she said with a smile that seemed reminiscent of past parties enjoyed. 'Between the three of us we had so many skills we could utilise.'

'Can you elaborate on that?'

She held up a slender index finger, her nails tipped with orange polish. 'One, I'm the ideas and visuals person—creative, great with themes and props and highly organised with follow-through.' A second finger went up.

'Two, Gemma trained as a chef and is an amazing food person—food is one of the most important aspects of a good party, whether cooking it yourself or knowing which chefs to engage.'

She had a little trouble getting the third finger to stay straight and swapped it to her pinkie. 'Then, three, Eliza has her head completely around finances and contracts and sales and is also quite the wine buff.'

'So you decided to go into business together?' Her entrepreneurial spirit appealed to him.

She shook her head so her large multi-hoop gold earrings clinked. 'Not then. Not yet. We agreed to do the eighteenth party while we looked for other jobs and freelanced for magazines and ad agencies.'

'How did it work out?' He thought about his eighteenth birthday. It had gone totally unmarked by any celebration—except his own jubilation that he was legally an adult and could never now be recalled to the hell his home had become. It had also marked the age he could be tried as an adult if he had skated too close to the law—though by that time his street-fighting days were behind him.

'There were a few glitches, of course, but overall it was a great success. The girl went to a posh private school and both girls and parents loved the girly shoe theme we organised. One eighteenth led to another and soon we had other parents clamouring for us to do their kids' parties.'

'Is there much money in parties for kids?' He didn't have to ask all these questions but he was curious. Curious about her as much as anything.

Her eyebrows rose. 'You're kidding, right? We're talking wealthy families on the eastern suburbs and north shore. We're talking one-upmanship.' He enjoyed the play of expressions across her face, the way she gesticulated with her hands as she spoke. 'Heck, we've done a four-year-old's party on a budget of thousands.'

'All that money for a four-year-old?' He didn't have anything to do with kids except through his anonymous charity work. Had given up on his dream he would ever have children of his own. In fact, he was totally out of touch with family life.

'You'd better believe it,' she said.

He was warming to Andie Newman—how could any red-blooded male not?—but he wanted to ensure she was experienced enough to make his event work. All eyes would be on it as up until now he'd been notoriously private. If he threw a party, it had better be a good party. Better than good.

'So when did you actually go into business?'

'We were asked to do more and more parties. Grown-up parties too. Thirtieths and fortieths, even a ninetieth. It snowballed. Yet we still saw it as a stopgap thing although people suggested we make it a full-time business.'

'A very high percentage of small businesses go bust in the first year,' he couldn't help but warn.

She pulled a face that told him she didn't take offence. 'We were very aware of that. Eliza is the profit and loss spreadsheet maven. But then a public relations company I worked freelance for asked us to do corporate parties and product launches. The work was rolling in. We began to think we should make it official and form our own company.'

'A brave move.' He'd made brave moves in his time—and most of them had paid off. He gave her credit for initiative.

She leaned forward towards him. This close he could appreciate how lovely her eyes were. He didn't think he had ever before met anyone with genuine green eyes. 'We've leased premises in the industrial area of Alexandria and we're firing. But I have to be honest with you—we haven't done anything with potentially such a profile as your party.

We want it. We need it. And because we want it to so much we'll pull out every stop to make it a success.'

Party Planner Number Four clocked up more credit for her honesty. He tapped the card on the edge of his hand. 'You've got the enthusiasm; do you have the expertise? Can you assure me you can do my job and do it superlatively well?'

Those remarkable green eyes were unblinking. 'Yes. Absolutely. Undoubtedly. There might only be three of us, but between us we have a zillion contacts in Sydney—chefs, decorators, florists, musicians, waiting staff. If we can't do it ourselves we can pull in the right people who can. And none of us is afraid of the hard work a party this size would entail. We would welcome the challenge.'

He realised she was now sitting on the edge of the sofa, her hands clasped together and her foot crossed over her ankle was jiggling. She really did want this job—wanted it badly.

Dominic hadn't got where he was without a fine-tuned instinct for people. Instincts honed first on the streets where trusting the wrong person could have been fatal and then in the cut-throat business of high-end real estate and property development. His antennae were telling him Andie Newman would be able to deliver—and that he would enjoy working with her.

Trouble was, while he thought she might be the right person for the job, he found her very attractive and would like to ask her out. And he couldn't do both. He *never* dated staff or suppliers. He'd made that mistake with his ex-wife—he would not make it again. Hire Andie Newman and he was more than halfway convinced he would get a good party planner. Not hire her and he could ask her on a date. But he needed this event to work—and for that the planning had to be in the best possible hands. He was torn.

'I like your enthusiasm,' he said. 'But I'd be taking

a risk by working with a company that is in many ways still…unproven.'

Her voice rose marginally—she probably didn't notice but to him it betrayed her anxiety to impress. 'We have a file overflowing with references from happy clients. But before you come to any decisions let's talk about what you're expecting from us. The worst thing that can happen is for a client to get an unhappy surprise because we've got the brief wrong.'

She pulled out a folder from her satchel. He liked that it echoed the design of her business card. That showed an attention to detail. The chaos of his early life had made him appreciate planning and order. He recognised his company logo on the printout page she took from the folder and quickly perused.

'So tell me,' she said, when she'd finished reading it. 'I'm puzzled. Despite this briefing document stating the party is to be "A high-profile Christmas event to attract favourable publicity for Dominic Hunt" you still insist it's not to reference Christmas in any way. Which is correct?'

Andie regretted the words almost as soon as they'd escaped from her mouth. She hadn't meant to confront Dominic Hunt or put him on the spot. Certainly she hadn't wanted to get him offside. But the briefing had been ambiguous and she felt she had to clarify it if she was to secure this job for Party Queens.

She needed their business to succeed—never again did she want to be at the mercy of the whims of a corporate employer. To have a job one day and then suddenly not the next day was too traumatising after that huge personal change of direction she'd had forced upon her five years ago. But she could have put her question with more subtlety.

He didn't reply. The silence that hung between them became more uncomfortable by the second. His face tightened with an emotion she couldn't read. Anger? Sorrow? Regret? Whatever it was, the effect was so powerful she had to force herself not to reach over and put her hand on his arm to comfort him, maybe even hug him. And that would be a mistake. Even more of a mistake than her ill-advised question had been.

She cringed that she had somehow prompted the unleashing of thoughts that were so obviously painful for him. Then braced herself to be booted out on to the same scrapheap as the three party planners who had preceded her.

Finally he spoke, as if the words were being dragged out of him. 'The brief was incorrect. Christmas has some… difficult memories attached to it for me. I don't celebrate the season. Please just leave it at that.' For a long moment his gaze held hers and she saw the anguish recede.

Andie realised she had been holding her breath and she let it out with a slow sigh of relief, amazed he hadn't shown her the door.

'Of…of course,' she murmured, almost gagging with gratitude that she was to be given a second chance. And she couldn't deny that she wanted that chance. Not just for the job but—she could not deny it—the opportunity to see more of this undoubtedly interesting man.

There was something deeper here, some private pain, that she did not understand. But it would be bad-mannered prying to ask any further questions.

She didn't know much about his personal life. Just that he was considered a catch—rich, handsome, successful. *Though not her type, of course.* He lived here alone, she understood, in this street in Vaucluse where house prices started in the double digit millions. Wasn't there a bitter divorce in his background—an aggrieved ex-wife, a public battle for ownership of the house? She'd have to look it up. If she were to win this job—and she understood that it was still a big *if*—she needed to get a grasp on how this man ticked.

'Okay, so that's sorted—no Christmas,' she said, aiming to sound briskly efficient without any nod to the anguish she had read at the back of his eyes. 'Now I know what you *don't* want for your party, let's talk about what you *do* want. I'd like to hear in your words what you expect from this party. Then I can give you my ideas based on your thoughts.'

The party proposals she had hoped to discuss had been based on Christmas; she would have to do some rapid thinking.

Dominic Hunt got up from the sofa and started to pace. He was so tall, his shoulders so broad, he dominated even the large, high-ceilinged room. Andie found herself wondering about his obviously once broken nose—who had thrown the first punch? She got up, not to pace alongside him but to be closer to his level. She did not feel intimidated by him but she could see how he could be intimidating.

'The other planners babbled on about how important it was to invite A-list and B-list celebrities to get publicity. I don't give a damn about celebrities and I can't see how that's the right kind of publicity.'

Andie paused, not sure what to say, only knowing she had to be careful not to *babble on.* 'I can organise the party, but the guest list is up to you and your people.'

He stopped his pacing, stepped closer. 'But do you agree with me?'

Was this a test question? Answer incorrectly and that scrapheap beckoned? As always, she could only be honest. 'I do agree with you. It's my understanding that this party is aimed at…at image repair.'

'You mean repair to my image as a miserly Scrooge who hoards all his money for himself?'

She swallowed a gasp at the bitterness of his words, then looked up at him to see not the anger she expected but a kind of manly bewilderment that surprised her.

'I mightn't have put it quite like that, but yes," she said. 'You do have that reputation and I understand you want to demonstrate it's not so. And yes, I think the presence of a whole lot of freeloading so-called celebrities who run the gamut from the A to the Z list and have nothing to do with the charities you want to be seen to be supporting might not help. But you *are* more likely to get coverage in the social pages if they attend.'

He frowned. 'Is there such a thing as a Z-list celebrity?'

She laughed. 'If there isn't, there should be. Maybe I made it up.'

'You did say you were creative,' he said. He smiled—the first real smile she'd seen from him. It transformed his face, like the sun coming out from behind a dark storm cloud, unleashing an unexpected charm. Her heartbeat tripped into double time like it had the first moment she'd seen him. Why? Why this inexplicable reaction to a man she should dislike for his meanness and greed?

She made a show of looking around her to disguise her consternation. Tamed the sudden shakiness in her voice into a businesslike tone. 'How many magazines or lifestyle programmes have featured this house?' she asked.

'None. They never will,' he said.

'Good,' she said. 'The house is both magnificent and unknown. I reckon even your neighbours would be willing to cough up a sizeable donation just to see inside.' In her mind's eye she could see the house transformed into a glittering party paradise. 'The era of the house is nineteen-twenties, right?'

'Yes,' he said. 'It was originally built for a wealthy wool merchant.'

She thought some more. 'Why not an extravagant

Great Gatsby twenties-style party with a silver and white theme—that gives a nod to the festive season—and a strictly curated guest list? Guests would have to dress in silver or white. Or both. Make it very exclusive, an invitation to be sought after. The phones of Sydney's social set would be set humming to see who got one or not.' Her eyes half shut as her mind bombarded her with images. 'Maybe a masked party. Yes. Amazing silver and white masks. Bejewelled and befeathered. Fabulous masks that could be auctioned off at some stage for your chosen charity.'

'Auctioned?'

Her eyes flew open and she had to orientate herself back into the reality of the empty room that she had just been envisioning filled with elegant partygoers. Sometimes when her creativity was firing she felt almost in a trance. Then it was her turn to frown. How could a Sydney billionaire be such a party innocent?

Even she, who didn't move in the circles of society that attended lavish fund-raising functions, knew about the auctions. The competitive bidding could probably be seen as the same kind of one-upmanship as the spending of thousands on a toddler's party. 'I believe it's usual to have a fund-raising auction at these occasions. Not just the masks, of course. Other donated items. Something really big to up the amount of dollars for your charity.' She paused. 'You're a property developer, aren't you?'

He nodded. 'Among other interests.'

'Maybe you could donate an apartment? There'd be some frenzied bidding for that from people hoping for a bargain. And you would look generous.'

His mouth turned down in an expression of distaste. 'I'm not sure that's in keeping with the image I want to… to reinvent.'

Privately she agreed with him—why couldn't people just donate without expecting a lavish party in return? But she kept her views to herself. Creating those lavish parties was her job now.

'That's up to you and your people. The guest list and the auction, I mean. But the party? That's my domain. Do you like the idea of the twenties theme to suit the house?' In her heart she still longed for the choristers on the staircase. Maybe it would have to be a jazz band on the steps. That could work. Not quite the same romanticism and spirit as Christmas, but it would be a spectacular way to greet guests.

'I like it,' he said slowly.

She forced herself not to panic, not to bombard him with a multitude of alternatives. 'If not that idea, I have lots of others. I would welcome the opportunity to present them to you.'

He glanced at his watch and she realised she had been there for much longer than the ten-minute pitch he'd allowed. Surely that was a good sign.

'I'll schedule in another meeting with you tomorrow afternoon,' he said.

'You mean a second interview?' she asked, fingers crossed behind her back.

'No. A brainstorming session. You've got the job, Ms Newman.'

It was only as, jubilant, she made her way to the door—conscious of his eyes on her back—that she wondered at the presence of a note of regret in Dominic Hunt's voice.

CHAPTER THREE

TRY AS SHE MIGHT, Andie couldn't get excited about the nineteen-twenties theme she had envisaged for Dominic Hunt's party. It would be lavish and glamorous and she would enjoy every moment of planning such a visually splendid event. Such a party would be a spangled feather in Party Queens' cap. But it seemed somehow *wrong.*

The feeling niggled at her. How could something so extravagant, so limited to those who could afford the substantial donation that would be the cost of entrance make Dominic Hunt look less miserly? Even if he offered an apartment for auction—and there was no such thing as a cheap apartment in Sydney—and raised a lot of money, wouldn't it be a wealthy person who benefited? Might he appear to be a Scrooge hanging out with other rich people who might or might not also be Scrooges? Somehow, it reeked of…well, there was no other word but hypocrisy.

It wasn't her place to be critical—the media-attention-grabbing party was his marketing people's idea. Her job was to plan the party and make it as memorable and spectacular as possible. But she resolved to bring up her reservations in the brainstorming meeting with him. *If she dared.*

She knew it would be a fine line to tread—she did not want to risk losing the job for Party Queens—but she felt she had to give her opinion. After that she would just keep her mouth shut and concentrate on making his event the most memorable on the December social calendar.

She dressed with care for the meeting, which was again at his Vaucluse mansion. *An outfit that posed no danger of showing off her underwear.* Slim white trousers, a white top, a string of outsize turquoise beads, silver sandals that strapped around her ankles. At the magazine she'd made friends with the fashion editor and still had access to sample sales and special deals. She felt her wardrobe could hold its own in whatever company she found herself in—even on millionaire row.

'I didn't risk wearing that skirt,' she blurted out to Dominic Hunt as he let her into the house. 'Even though there doesn't appear to be any wind about.'

Mentally she slammed her hand against her forehead. What a dumb top-of-mind remark to make to a client. But he still made her nervous. Try as she might, she couldn't shake that ever-present awareness of how attractive he was.

His eyes flickered momentarily to her legs. 'Shame,' he said in that deep, testosterone-edged voice that thrilled through her.

Was he flirting with her?

'It…it was a lovely skirt,' she said. 'Just…just rather badly behaved.' How much had he seen when her skirt had flown up over her thighs?

'I liked it very much,' he said.

'The prettiness of its fabric or my skirt's bad behaviour?'

She held his cool grey gaze for a second longer than she should.

'Both,' he said.

She took a deep breath and tilted her chin upward. 'I'll take that as a compliment,' she said with a smile she hoped radiated aplomb. 'Thank you, Mr Hunt.'

'Dominic,' he said.

'Dominic,' she repeated, liking the sound of his name on her lips. 'And thank you again for this opportunity to plan your party.' *Bring it back to business.*

In truth, she would have liked to tell him how good he looked in his superbly tailored dark suit and dark shirt but she knew her voice would come out all choked up. Because it wasn't the Italian elegance of his suit that she found herself admiring. It was the powerful, perfectly proportioned male body that inhabited it. And she didn't want to reveal even a hint of that. *He was a client.*

He nodded in acknowledgement of her words. 'Come through to the back,' he said. 'You can see how the rooms might work for the party.'

She followed him through where the grand staircase split—a choir really would be amazing ranged on the steps—over pristine marble floors to a high-ceilinged room so large their footsteps echoed as they walked into the centre of it. Furnished minimally in shades of white, it looked ready for a high-end photo shoot. Arched windows and a wall of folding doors opened through to an elegant art deco style swimming pool and then to a formal garden planted with palm trees and rows of budding blue agapanthus.

For a long moment Andie simply absorbed the splendour of the room. 'What a magnificent space,' she said finally. 'Was it originally a ballroom?'

'Yes. Apparently the wool merchant liked to entertain in grand style. But it wasn't suited for modern living, which is why I opened it up through to the terrace when I remodelled the house.'

'You did an awesome job,' she said. In her mind's eye she could see flappers in glittering dresses trimmed with feathers and fringing, and men in dapper suits doing the Charleston. Then had to blink, not sure if she was imagining what the room had once been or how she'd like it to be for Dominic's party.

'The people who work for me did an excellent job,' he said.

'As an interior designer I give them full marks,' she said. She had gone to university with Dominic's designer. She just might get in touch with him, seeking inside gossip into what made Dominic Hunt tick.

She looked around her. 'Where's the kitchen? Gemma will shoot me if I go back without reporting to her on the cooking facilities.'

'Through here.'

Andie followed him through to an adjoining vast state-of-the-art kitchen, gleaming in white marble and stainless steel. The style was sleek and modern but paid homage to the vintage of the house. She breathed out a sigh of relief and pleasure. A kitchen like this would make catering for hundreds of guests so much easier. Not that the food was her department. Gemma kept that under her control. 'It's a superb kitchen. Do you cook?'

Was Dominic the kind of guy who ate out every night and whose refrigerator contained only cartons of beer? Or the kind who excelled at cooking and liked to show off his skills to a breathlessly admiring female audience?

'I can look after myself,' he said shortly. 'That includes cooking.'

That figured. After yesterday's meeting she had done some research into Dominic Hunt—though there wasn't much information dating back further than a few years. Along with his comments about celebrating Christmas being a waste of space, he'd also been quoted as saying he would never marry again. From the media accounts, his marriage in his mid-twenties had been short, tumultuous and public, thanks to his ex-wife's penchant for spilling the details to the gossip columns.

'The kitchen and its position will be perfect for the caterers,' she said. 'Gemma will be delighted.'

'Good,' he said.

'You must love this house.' She could not help a wistful note from edging her voice. As an interior designer she knew only too well how much the remodelling would have cost. Never in a million years would she live in a house like this. He was only a few years older than her—thirty-two to her twenty-eight—yet it was as if they came from different planets.

He shrugged those impressively broad shoulders. 'It's a spectacular house. But it's just a house. I never get attached to places.'

Or people?

Her online research had showed him snapped by paparazzi with a number of long-legged beauties—but no woman more than once or twice. *What did it matter to her?*

She patted her satchel. *Back to business.* 'I've come prepared for brainstorming,' she said. 'Have you had any thoughts about the nineteen-twenties theme I suggested?'

'I've thought,' he said. He paused. 'I've thought about it a lot.'

His tone of voice didn't give her cause for confidence. 'You…like it? You don't like it? Because if you don't I have lots of other ideas that would work as well. I—'

He put up his right hand to halt her—large, well sculpted, with knuckles that looked as if they'd sustained scrapes over the years. His well-spoken accent and obvious wealth suggested injuries sustained from boxing or rugby at a private school; the tightly leashed power in those muscles, that strong jaw, gave thought to injuries sustained in something perhaps more visceral.

'It's a wonderful idea for a party,' he said. 'Perfect for this house. Kudos to you, Ms Party Queen.'

'Thank you.' She made a mock curtsy and was pleased when he smiled. *How handsome he was without that scowl.* 'However, is that a "but" I hear coming on?'

He pivoted on his heel so he faced out to the pool, gleaming blue and pristine in the afternoon sun of a late-spring day in mid-November. His back view was impressive, broad shoulders tapering to a tight, muscular rear end. Then he turned back to face her. 'It's more than one "but",' he said. 'The party, the guest list, the—'

'The pointlessness of it all?' she ventured.

He furrowed his brow. 'What makes you say that?'

She found herself twisting the turquoise beads on her necklace between her finger and thumb. Her business partners would be furious with her if she lost Party Queens this high-profile job because she said what she *wanted* to say rather than what she *should* say.

'This party is all about improving your image, right? To make a statement that you're not the…the Scrooge people think you are.'

The fierce scowl was back. 'I'd rather you didn't use the word Scrooge.'

'Okay,' she said immediately. But she would find it difficult to stop *thinking* it. 'I'll try again: that you're not a…a person lacking in the spirit of giving.'

'That doesn't sound much better.' She couldn't have imagined his scowl could have got any darker but it did. 'The party is meant to be a public display of something I would rather be kept private.'

'So…you give privately to charity?'

'Of course I do but it's not your or anyone else's business.'

Personally, she would be glad if he wasn't as tight-fisted as his reputation decreed. But this was about more than what she felt. She could not back down. 'If that's how you feel, tell me again why you're doing this.'

He paused. 'If I share with you the reason why I agreed to holding this party, it's not to leave this room.'

'Of course,' she said. A party planner had to be discreet. It was astounding what family secrets got aired in the planning of a party. She leaned closer, close enough to notice that he must be a twice-a-day-shave guy. *Lots of testosterone, all right.*

'I've got a big joint venture in the United States on the point of being signed. My potential business partner, Walter Burton, is the head of a family company and he is committed to public displays of philanthropy. It would go better with me if I was seen to be the same.'

Andie made a motion with her fingers of zipping her lips shut. 'I…I understand,' she said. Disappointment shafted through her. *So he really was a Scrooge.*

She'd found herself wanting Dominic to be someone better than he was reputed to be. But the party, while purporting to be a charity event, was simply a smart business ploy. More about greed than good-heartedness.

'Now you can see why it's so important,' he said.

Should she say what she thought? The scrapheap of discarded party planners beckoned again. She could imagine her silver-sandal-clad foot kicking feebly from the top of it and hoped it would be a soft landing.

She took a deep steadying breath. 'Cynical journalists might have a field-day with the hypocrisy of a Scrooge—*sorry!*—trying to turn over a new gilded leaf in such an obvious and staged way.'

To her surprise, something like relief relaxed the tense lines of his face. 'That's what I thought too.'

'You…you did?'

'I could see the whole thing backfiring and me no better off in terms of reputation. Possibly worse.'

If she didn't stop twisting her necklace it would break and scatter her beads all over the marble floor. 'So—help me out here. We're back to you not wanting a party?'

She'd talked him out of the big, glitzy event Party Queens really needed. Andie cringed at the prospect of the combined wrath of Gemma and Eliza when she went back to their headquarters with the contract that was sitting in her satchel waiting for his signature still unsigned.

'You know I don't.' *Thank heaven.* 'But maybe a different kind of event,' he said.

'Like…handing over a giant facsimile cheque to a charity?' Which would be doing her right out of a job.

'Where's the good PR in that?'

'In fact it could look even more cynical than the party.'

'Correct.'

He paced a few long strides away from her and then back. 'I'm good at turning one dollar into lots of dollars. That's my skill. Not planning parties. But surely I can get the kind of publicity my marketing department wants, impress my prospective business partner and actually help some less advantaged people along the way?'

She resisted the urge to high-five him. 'To tell you the truth, I couldn't sleep last night for thinking that exact same thing.' *Was it wise to have admitted that?*

'Me too,' he said. 'I tossed and turned all night.'

A sudden vision of him in a huge billionaire's bed, all tangled in the sheets wearing nothing but…well nothing but a billionaire's birthday suit, flashed through her mind and sizzled through her body. *Not my type. Not my type.* She had to repeat it like a mantra.

She willed her heartbeat to slow and hoped he took the flush on her cheekbones for enthusiasm. 'So we're singing from the same hymn sheet. Did you have any thoughts on solving your dilemma?'

'That's where you come in; you're the party expert.'

She hesitated. 'During my sleepless night, I did think of something. But you might not like it.'

'Try me,' he said, eyes narrowed.

'It's out of the ball park,' she warned.

'I'm all for that,' he said.

She flung up her hands in front of her face to act as a shield. 'It…it involves Christmas.'

He blanched under the smooth olive of his tan. 'I told you—'

His mouth set in a grim line, his hands balled into fists by his sides. Should she leave well enough alone? After all, he had said the festive season had difficult associations for him. 'What is it that you hate so much about Christmas?' she asked. She'd always been one to dive straight into the deep end.

'I don't *hate* Christmas.' He cursed under his breath. 'I'm misquoted once and the media repeat it over and over.'

'But—'

He put up his hand to halt her. 'I don't have to justify anything to you. But let me give you three good reasons why I don't choose to celebrate Christmas and all the razzmatazz that goes with it.'

'Fire away,' she said, thinking it wasn't appropriate for her to counter with three things she adored about the festive season. This wasn't a debate. It was a business brainstorming.

'First—the weather is all wrong,' he said. 'It's hot when it should be cold. A *proper* Christmas is a northern hemisphere Christmas—snow, not sand.'

Not true, she thought. For a born-and-bred Australian like her, Christmas was all about the long, hot sticky days of summer. Cicadas chirruping in the warm air as the family walked to a midnight church service. Lunch outdoors, preferably around a pool or at the beach. Then it struck her—Dominic had a distinct trace of an English accent. That might explain his aversion to festivities Down Under style. But something still didn't seem quite right. His words sounded…too practised, as if he'd recited them a hundred times before.

He continued, warming to his point as she wondered

about the subtext to his spiel. 'Then there's the fact that the whole thing is over-commercialised to the point of being ludicrous. I saw Christmas stuff festooning the shops in September.'

She almost expected him to snarl a Scrooge-like *Bah! Humbug!* but he obviously restrained himself.

'You have a point,' she said. 'And carols piped through shopping malls in October? So annoying.'

'Quite right,' he said. 'This whole obsession with extended Christmas celebrations, it…it…makes people who don't celebrate it—for one reason or another—feel…feel excluded.'

His words faltered and he looked away in the direction of the pool but not before she'd seen the bleakness in his eyes. She realised those last words hadn't been rehearsed. That he might be regretting them. Again she had that inane urge to comfort him—without knowing why he needed comforting.

She knew she had to take this carefully. 'Yes,' she said slowly. 'I know what you mean.' That first Christmas without Anthony had been the bleakest imaginable. And each year after she had thought about him and the emptiness in her heart he had left behind him. But she would not share that with this man; it was far too personal. And nothing to do with the general discussion about Christmas.

His mouth twisted. 'Do you?'

She forced her voice to sound cheerful and impersonal. Her ongoing sadness over Anthony was deeply private. 'Not me personally. I love Christmas. I'm lucky enough to come from a big family—one of five kids. I have two older brothers and a sister and a younger sister. Christmas with our extended family was always—still is—a special time of the year. But my parents knew that wasn't the case for everyone. Every year we shared our celebration with children who weren't as fortunate as we were.'

'Charity cases, you mean,' he said, his voice hard-edged with something she couldn't identify.

'In the truest sense of the word,' she said. 'We didn't query them being there. It meant more kids to play with on Christmas Day. It didn't even enter our heads that there would be fewer presents for us so they could have presents too. Two of them moved in with us as long-term foster kids. When I say I'm from five, I really mean from seven. Only that's too confusing to explain.'

He gave a sound that seemed a cross between a grunt and a cynical snort.

She shrugged, inexplicably hurt by his reaction. 'You might think it goody-two-shoes-ish but that's the way my family are, and I love them for it,' she said, her voice stiff and more than a touch defensive.

'Not at all,' he said. 'I think it…it sounds wonderful. You were very lucky to grow up in a family like that.' With the implication being he hadn't?

'I know, and I'm thankful. And my parents' strong sense of community didn't do us any harm. In fact those Christmas Days my family shared with others got me thinking. It was what kept me up last night. I had an idea.'

'Fire away,' he said.

She channelled all her optimism and enthusiasm to make her voice sound convincing to Sydney's most notorious Scrooge. 'Wouldn't it be wonderful if you opened this beautiful home on Christmas Day for a big lunch party for children and families who do it hard on Christmas Day? Not as a gimmick. Not as a stunt. As a genuine act of hospitality and sharing the true spirit of Christmas.'

CHAPTER FOUR

DOMINIC STARED AT Andie in disbelief. Hadn't she heard a word he'd said about his views on Christmas? She looked up at him, her eyes bright with enthusiasm but backlit by wariness. 'Please, just consider my proposal,' she said. 'That's all I ask.' He could easily fire her for straying so far from the brief and she must know it—yet that didn't stop her. Her tenacity was to be admired.

Maybe she had a point. No matter what she or anyone else thought, he was not a Scrooge or a hypocrite. To make a holiday that could never be happy for him happy for others had genuine appeal. He was aware Christmas *was* a special time for a huge percentage of the population. It was just too painful for him to want to do anything but lock himself away with a bottle of bourbon from Christmas Eve to Boxing Day.

Deep from within, he dredged memories of his first Christmas away from home. Aged seventeen, he'd been living in an underground car park beneath an abandoned shopping centre project. His companions had been a ragtag collection of other runaways, addicts, criminals and people who'd lost all hope of a better life. Someone had stolen a branch of a pine tree from somewhere and decorated it with scavenged scraps of glittery paper. They'd all stood around it and sung carols with varying degrees of sobriety. Only he had stood aloof.

Now, he reached out to where Andie was twisting her

necklace so tightly it was in danger of snapping. Gently, he disengaged her hand and freed the string of beads. Fought the temptation to hold her hand for any longer than was necessary—slender and warm in his own much bigger hand. Today her nails were painted turquoise. And, as he'd noticed the day before, her fingers were free of any rings.

'Your idea could have merit,' he said, stepping back from her. Back from her beautiful interesting face, her intelligent eyes, the subtle spicy-sweet scent of her. 'Come and sit outside by the pool and we can talk it over.'

Her face flushed with relief at his response and he realised again what spunk it had taken for her to propose something so radical. He was grateful to whoever had sent Party Planner Number Four his way. Andie was gorgeous, smart and not the slightest in awe of him and his money, which was refreshing. His only regret was that he could not both employ her and date her.

He hadn't told the complete truth about why he'd been unable to sleep the night before. Thoughts of her had been churning through his head as much as concerns about the party. He had never felt so instantly attracted to a woman. Ever. If they had met under other circumstances he would have asked her out by now.

'I really think it could work,' she said as she walked with him through the doors and out to the pool area.

For a heart-halting second he thought Andie had tuned into his private thoughts—that she thought dating her could work. *Never.* He'd met his ex-wife, Tara, when she'd worked for his company, with disastrous consequences. The whole marriage had, in fact, been disastrous—based on lies and deception. He wouldn't make that mistake again—even for this intriguing woman.

But of course Andie was talking about her party proposal in businesslike tones. 'You could generate the right kind of publicity—both for your potential business partner and in general,' she said as he settled her into one of the white outdoor armchairs that had cost a small fortune because of its vintage styling.

'While at the same time directly benefiting people who do it tough on the so-called Big Day,' he said as he took the chair next to her.

'Exactly,' she said with her wide, generous smile. When she smiled like that it made him want to make her do it again, just for the pleasure of seeing her face light up. *Not a good idea.*

Her chair was in the shade of one of the mature palm trees he'd had helicoptered in for the landscaping but the sun was dancing off the aqua surface of the pool. He was disappointed when she reached into her satchel, pulled out a pair of tortoiseshell-rimmed sunglasses and donned them against the glare. They looked 'vintage' too. In fact, in her white clothes and turquoise necklace, she looked as if she belonged here.

'In principal, I don't mind your idea,' he said. 'In fact I find it more acceptable than the other.'

Her smile was edged with relief. 'I can't tell you how pleased that makes me.'

'Would the lunch have to be on actual Christmas Day?' he said.

'You could hold it on Christmas Eve or the week leading up to Christmas. In terms of organisation, that would be easier. But none of those peripheral days is as lonely and miserable as Christmas Day can be if you're one…one of the excluded ones,' she said. 'My foster sister told me that.'

The way she was looking at him, even with those too-perceptive green eyes shaded from his view, made him think she was beginning to suspect he had a deeply personal reason for his anti-Christmas stance.

He'd only ever shared that reason with one woman—Melody, the girl who'd first captivated, then shredded, his teenage heart back in that car park squat. By the time Christmas had loomed in the first year of his marriage to Tara, he'd known he'd never be sharing secrets with her. But there was something disarming about Andie that seemed to invite confidences—something he had to stand guard against. She might not be what she seemed—and he had learned the painful lesson not to trust his first impressions when it came to beautiful women.

'I guess any other day doesn't have the same impact,' he reluctantly agreed, not sure he would be able to face the festivities. Did he actually have to be present on the day? Might it not be enough to provide the house and the meal? No. To achieve his goal, he knew his presence would be necessary. Much as he would hate every minute of it.

'Maybe your marketing people will have other ideas,' she said. 'But I think opening your home on the actual December twenty-five to give people who really need it a slap-up feast would be a marvellous antidote to your Scrooge…sorry, *miser*…I mean *cheap* reputation.' She pulled a face. 'Sorry. I didn't actually mean any of those things.'

Why did it sting so much more coming from her? 'Of course you did. So does everyone else. People who have no idea of what and where I might give without wanting any fanfare.' The main reason he wanted to secure the joint venture was to ensure his big project in Brisbane would continue to be funded long after his lifetime.

She looked shamefaced. 'I'm sorry.'

He hated that people like Andie thought he was stingy. Any remaining reservations he might hold about the party had to go. He needed to take action before this unfair reputation become so deeply entrenched he'd never free himself from it. 'Let's hope the seasonal name-calling eases if I go ahead with the lunch.'

She held up a finger in warning. 'It wouldn't appease everyone. Those cynical journalists might not be easily swayed.'

He scowled. 'I can't please everyone.' But he found himself, irrationally, wanting to please *her*.

'It might help if you followed through with a visible, ongoing relationship with a charity. If the media could see…could see…'

Her eyes narrowed in concentration. He waited for the end of her sentence but it wasn't forthcoming. 'See what?'

'Sorry,' she said, shaking her head as if bringing herself back to earth. 'My thoughts tend to run faster than my words sometimes when I'm deep in the creative zone.'

'I get it,' he said, though he wasn't sure what the hell being in the creative zone meant.

'I meant your critics might relent if they could see your gesture was genuine.'

He scowled. 'But it *will* be genuine.'

'You know it and I know it but they might see it as just another publicity gimmick.' Her eyes narrowed again and he gave her time to think. 'What if you didn't actually seek publicity for this day? You know—no invitations or press releases. Let the details leak. Tantalise the media.'

'For a designer, you seem to know a lot about publicity,' he said.

She shrugged. 'When you work in magazines you pick up a lot about both seeking and giving publicity. But your marketing people would have their own ideas, I'm sure.'

'I should talk it over with them,' he said.

'As it's only six weeks until Christmas, and this would be a big event to pull together, may I suggest there's not a lot of discussion time left?'

'You're right. I know. But it's a big deal.' So much bigger for him personally than she realised.

'You're seriously considering going ahead with it?'

He so much preferred it to the Z-list celebrity party. 'Yes. Let's do it.'

She clapped her hands together. 'I'm so glad. We can make it a real dream-come-true for your guests.'

'What about you and your business partners? You'd have to work on Christmas Day.'

'Speaking for me, I'd be fine with working. True spirit of Christmas and all that. I'll have to speak to Gemma and Eliza, but I think they'd be behind it too.' Securing Dominic Hunt's business for Party Queens was too important for them to refuse.

'What about caterers and so on?' he asked.

'The hospitality industry works three hundred and sixty-five days a year. It shouldn't be a problem. There are also people who don't celebrate Christmas as part of their culture who are very happy to work—especially for holiday pay rates. You don't have to worry about all that—that's our job.'

'And the guests? How would we recruit them?' He was about to say he could talk to people in Brisbane, where he was heavily involved in a homeless charity, but stopped himself. That was too connected to the secret part of his life he had no desire to share.

'I know the perfect person to help—my older sister, Hannah, is a social worker. She would know exactly which charities to liaise with. I think she would be excited to be involved.'

It was her. *Andie.* He would not be considering this direction if it wasn't for her. The big glitzy party had seemed so wrong. She made him see what could be right.

'Could we set up a meeting with your sister?' he asked.

'I can do better than that,' she said with a triumphant toss of her head that set her oversized earrings swaying. 'Every Wednesday night is open house dinner at my parents' house. Whoever of my siblings can make it comes.

Sometimes grandparents and cousins too. I know Hannah will be there tonight and I'm planning to go too. Why don't you come along?'

'To your family dinner?' His first thought was to say no. Nothing much intimidated him—but meeting people's families was near the top of the list.

'Family is an elastic term for the Newmans. Friends, waifs and strays are always welcome at the table.'

What category would he be placed under? His memory of being a real-life stray made him wince. Friend? Strictly speaking, if circumstances were different, he'd want to be more than friends with Andie. Would connecting with her family create an intimacy he might later come to regret?

He looked down at his watch. Thought about his plan to return to the office.

'We need to get things moving,' she prompted.

'I would like to meet your sister tonight.'

Her wide smile lit her eyes. 'I have a really good feeling about this.'

'Do you always go on your feelings?' he asked.

She took off her sunglasses so he was treated to the directness of her gaze. 'All the time. Don't you?'

If he acted on his feelings he would be insisting they go to dinner, just the two of them. He would be taking her in his arms. Tasting her lovely mouth. Touching. Exploring. *But that wouldn't happen.*

He trusted his instincts when it came to business. But trusting his feelings when it came to women had only led to bitterness, betrayal and the kind of pain he never wanted to expose himself to again.

No to feeling. *Yes* to pleasant relationships that mutually fulfilled desires and were efficiently terminated before emotions ever became part of it. And with none of the complications that came with still having to work with that person. Besides, he suspected the short-term liaison that was all he had to offer would not be acceptable to Andie. She had *for ever* written all over her.

Now it was her turn to look at her watch. 'I'll call my mother to confirm you'll be joining us for dinner. How about I swing by and pick you up at around six?'

He thought about his four o'clock meeting. 'That's early for dinner.'

'Not when there are kids involved.'

'Kids?'

'I have a niece and two nephews. One of the nephews belongs to Hannah. He will almost certainly be there, along with his cousins.'

Dominic wasn't sure exactly what he was letting himself in for. One thing was for certain—he couldn't have seen himself going to a family dinner with any of Party Planners Numbers One to Three. And he suspected he might be in for more than one surprise from gorgeous Party Planner Number Four.

Andie got up from the chair. Smoothed down her white trousers. They were nothing as revealing as her flyaway skirt but made no secret of her slender shape.

'By the way, I'm apologising in advance for my car.'

He frowned. 'Why apologise?'

'I glimpsed your awesome sports car in the garage as I came in yesterday. You might find my hand-me-down hatchback a bit of a comedown.'

He frowned. 'I didn't come into this world behind the wheel of an expensive European sports car. I'm sure your hatchback will be perfectly fine.'

Just how did she see him? His public image—Scrooge, miser, rich guy—was so at odds with the person he knew himself to be. That he wanted her to know. But he could not reveal himself to her without uncovering secrets he would rather leave buried deep in his past.

CHAPTER FIVE

DOMINIC HAD FACED down some fears in his time. But the prospect of being paraded before Andie's large family ranked as one of the most fearsome. As Andie pulled up her hatchback—old but in good condition and nothing to be ashamed of—in front of her parents' home in the northern suburb of Willoughby, sweat prickled on his forehead and his hands felt clammy. How the hell had he got himself into this?

She turned off the engine, took out the keys, unclipped her seat belt and smoothed down the legs of her sleek, very sexy leather trousers. But she made no effort to get out of the car. She turned her head towards him. 'Before we go inside to meet my family I… I need to tell you something first. Something…something about me.'

Why did she look so serious, sombre even? 'Sure, fire away,' he said.

'I've told them you're a client. That there is absolutely nothing personal between us.'

'Of course,' he said.

Strange how at the same time he could be relieved and yet offended by her categorical denial that there ever could be anything *personal* between them.

Now a hint of a smile crept to the corners of her mouth. 'The thing is…they won't believe me. You're good-looking, you're smart and you're personable.'

'That's nice of you to say that,' he said. He noticed she hadn't added that he was rich to his list of attributes.

'You know it's true,' she said. 'My family are determined I should have a man in my life and have become the most inveterate of matchmakers. I expect they'll pounce on you. It could get embarrassing.'

'You're single?' He welcomed the excuse to ask.

'Yes. I…I've been single for a long time. Oh, I date. But I haven't found anyone special since…since…' She twisted right around in the car seat to fully face him. She clasped her hands together on her lap, then started to twist them without seeming to realise she was doing it. 'You need to know this before we go inside.' The hint of a smile had completely dissipated.

'If you think so,' he said. She was twenty-eight and single. What was the big deal here?

'I met Anthony on my first day of university. We were inseparable from the word go. There was no doubt we would spend our lives together.'

Dominic braced himself for the story of a nasty break-up. Infidelity? Betrayal? A jerk in disguise as a nice guy? He was prepared to make polite noises in response. He knew all about betrayal. But a *quid pro quo* exchange over relationships gone wrong was not something he ever wanted to waste time on with Andie or anyone else.

'It ended?' he said, making a terse contribution only because it was expected.

'He died.'

Two words stated so baldly but with such a wealth of pain behind them. Dominic felt as if he'd been punched in the chest. Nothing he said could be an adequate response. 'Andie, I'm sorry,' was all he could manage.

'It was five years ago. He was twenty-three. He…he went out for an early-morning surf and didn't come back.' He could hear the effort it took for her to keep her tone even.

He knew about people who didn't come back. Goodbyes left unsaid. Personal tragedy. That particular kind of pain. 'Did he…? Did you—?'

'He…he washed up two days later.' She closed her eyes as if against an unbearable image.

'What happened?' He didn't want her to think he was interrogating her on something so sensitive, but he wanted to find out.

'Head injury. An accident. The doctors couldn't be sure exactly how it happened. A rock? His board? A sandbank? We'll never know.'

'Thank you for telling me.' He felt unable to say anything else.

'Better for you to know than not to know when you're about to meet the family. Just in case someone says something that might put you on the spot.'

She heaved a sigh that seemed to signal she had said what she felt she had to say and that there would be no further confidences. Why should there be? *He was just a client.* Something prompted him to want to ask—was she over the loss? Had she moved on? But it was not his place. Client and contractor—that was all they could be to each other. Besides, could anyone *ever* get over loss like that?

'You needed to be in the picture.' She went to open her door. 'Now, let's go in—Hannah is looking forward to meeting you. As I predicted, she's very excited about getting involved.'

Her family's home was a comfortable older-style house set in a chaotic garden in a suburb where values had rocketed in recent years. In the car on the way over, Andie had told him she had lived in this house since she was a baby. All her siblings had. He envied her that certainty, that security.

'Helloo!' she called ahead of her. 'We're here.'

He followed her down a wide hallway, the walls crammed with framed photographs. They ranged from old-fashioned sepia wedding photos, dating from pre-Second World War, to posed studio shots of cherubic babies. Again he found himself envying her—he had only a handful of family photos to cherish.

At a quick glance he found two of Andie—one in a green checked school uniform with her hair in plaits and that familiar grin showing off a gap in her front teeth; another as a teenager in a flowing pink formal dress. A third caught his eye—an older Andie in a bikini, arm in arm with a tall blond guy in board shorts who was looking down at her with open adoration. The same guy was with her in the next photo, only this time they were playing guitars and singing together. Dominic couldn't bear to do more than glance at them, aware of the tragedy that had followed.

Just before they reached the end of the corridor, Andie stopped and took a step towards him. She stood so close he breathed in her scent—something vaguely oriental, warm and sensual. She leaned up to whisper into his ear and her hair tickled his neck. He had to close his eyes to force himself from reacting to her closeness.

'The clan can be a bit overwhelming *en masse*,' she said. 'I won't introduce you to everyone by name; it would be unfair to expect you to remember all of them. My mother is Jennifer, my father is Ray. Hannah's husband is Paul.'

'I appreciate that,' he said, tugging at his collar that suddenly seemed too tight. As an only child, he'd always found meeting other people's families intimidating.

Andie gave him a reassuring smile. 'With the Newman family, what you see is what you get. They're all good people who will take you as they find you. We might even get some volunteers to help on Christmas Day out of this.'

The corridor opened out into a spacious open-plan family room. At some time in the last twenty years the parents had obviously added a new extension. It looked dated now but solid—warm and comfortable and welcoming. Delicious aromas emanated from the farmhouse-style kitchen in the northern corner. He sniffed and Andie smiled. 'My mother's lasagne—wait until you taste it.'

She announced him with an encompassing wave of her arm. 'Everyone, this is Dominic. He's a very important new client so please make him welcome. And yes, I know he's gorgeous but it's strictly business between us.'

That was met with laughter and a chorus of 'Hi, Dominic!' and 'Welcome!' Andie then briefly explained to them about the party and Hannah's likely role in it.

There were so many of them. Andie's introduction had guaranteed all eyes were on him. About ten people, including kids, were ranged around the room, sitting in comfortable -looking sofas or around a large trestle table.

Each face came into focus as the adults greeted him with warm smiles. It wasn't difficult to tell who was related—Andie's smile was a strong family marker that originated with her father, a tall, thin man with a vigorous handshake. Her mother's smile was different but equally welcoming as she headed his way from the kitchen, wiping her hands on her apron before she greeted him. Three young children playing on the floor looked up, then kept on playing with their toys. A big black dog with a greying muzzle, lying stretched out near the kids, lifted his head, then thumped his tail in greeting.

Andie's sister Hannah and her husband, Paul, paused in their job of setting the large trestle table to say hello. His experience with social workers in his past had been good—a social worker had pretty much saved his life—and he was not disappointed by Hannah's kind eyes in a gentle face.

'I straight away know of several families who are facing a very grim Christmas indeed,' she said. 'Your generous gesture would make an immense difference to them.'

Andie caught his eye and smiled. Instinctively, he knew she had steered him in the right direction towards her sister. If all Andie's ideas for his party were as good as this one, he could face the Christmas Day he dreaded with more confidence than he might have expected.

Andie's policy of glaring down any family member who dared to even hint at dating possibilities with Dominic was working. Except for her younger sister, Bea, who could not resist hissing, 'He's hot,' at any opportunity, from passing the salad to refilling her water glass. Then, when Andie didn't bite, Bea added, 'If you don't want him, hand him over to me.' Thankfully, Dominic remained oblivious to the whispered exchanges.

Her family had, unwittingly or not, sat Dominic in the same place at the table where Anthony had sat at these gatherings. *Andie and Ant—always together.* She doubted it was on purpose. Dominic needed to sit between Hannah and her and so it had just happened.

In the years since he'd died, no man had come anywhere near to replacing Anthony in her heart. How could they? Anthony and she had been two halves of the same soul, she sometimes thought. Maybe she would never be able to love anyone else. *But she was lonely.* The kind of loneliness that work, friends, family could not displace.

In the months after Anthony's death her parents had left Anthony's customary seat empty out of respect. Unable to bear the emptiness that emphasised his absence, she had stopped coming to the family dinners until her mother had realised the pain it was causing. From then on, one of her brothers always occupied Anthony's chair.

Now she told herself she was okay with Dominic sitting there. He was only a client, with no claim to any place in her heart. Bringing him along tonight had worked out well—one of those spur-of-the-moment decisions she mightn't have made if she'd given it more thought.

Dominic and Hannah had spent a lot of time talking—but he'd managed to chat with everyone else there too. They were obviously charmed by him. That was okay too. *She* was charmed by him. Tonight she was seeing a side of him, as he interacted with her family, that she might never have seen in everyday business dealings.

Her sister was right. *Dominic was hot.* And Andie was only too aware of it. She was surprised at the fierce urge of possessiveness that swept over her at the thought of 'handing over' Dominic to anyone else. Her sister could find her own hot guy.

Even at the dinner table, when her back was angled away from him to talk to her brother on her other side, she was aware of Dominic. His scent had already become familiar—citrus-sharp yet warm and very masculine. Her ears were tuned into the sound of his voice—no matter where he was in the room. Her body was on constant alert to that attraction, which had been instant and only continued to grow with further contact. On their way in, in the corridor, when she'd drawn close to whisper so her family would not overhear, she'd felt light-headed from the proximity to him.

It had been five years now since Anthony had gone—the same length of time they'd been together. She would never forget him but that terrible grief and anguish she had felt at first had eventually mellowed to a grudging acceptance. She realised she had stopped dreaming about him.

People talked about once-in-a-lifetime love. She'd thought she'd found it at the age of eighteen—and a cruel fate had snatched him away from her. Was there to be only one great love for her?

Deep in her heart, she didn't want to believe that. Surely there would be someone for her again? She didn't want to be alone. One day she wanted marriage, a family. She'd been looking for someone like Anthony—and had been constantly disappointed in the men she'd gone out with. But was it a mistake to keep on looking for a man like her teenage soulmate?

Thoughts of Dominic were constantly invading her mind. He was so different from Anthony there could be no comparison. Anthony had been blond and lean, laidback and funny, always quick with a joke, creative and musical. From what she knew of Dominic, he was quite the opposite. She'd dismissed him as not for her. But her body's reaction kept contradicting her mind's stonewalling. How could she be so certain he was Mr Wrong?

Dessert was being served—spring berries and homemade vanilla bean ice cream—and she turned to Dominic at the precise moment he turned to her. Their eyes connected and held and she knew without the need for words that he was happy with her decision to bring him here.

'Your family is wonderful,' he said in a low undertone.

'I think so,' she said, pleased. 'What about you? Do you come from a large family?'

A shadow darkened his eyes. He shook his head. 'Only child.'

She smiled. 'We must seem overwhelming.'

'In a good way,' he said. 'You're very lucky.'

'I know.' Of course she and her siblings had had the usual squabbles and disagreements throughout their childhood and adolescence. She, as number four, had had to fight for her place. But as adults they all got on as friends as well as brothers and sisters. She couldn't have got through the loss of Anthony without her family's support.

'The kids are cute,' he said. 'So well behaved.'

Her nephews, Timothy and Will, and her niece, Caitlin,

were together down the other end of the table under the watchful eye of their grandmother. 'They're really good kids,' she agreed. 'I adore them.'

'Little Timothy seems quite…delicate,' Dominic said, obviously choosing his words carefully. 'But I notice his older cousin looks after him.'

A wave of sadness for Hannah and Paul's little son overwhelmed her. 'They're actually the same age,' she said. 'Both five years old. Timothy just looks as though he's three.'

'I guess I don't know much about kids,' Dominic said, shifting uncomfortably in his chair.

She lowered her voice. 'Sadly, little Timothy has some kind of rare growth disorder, an endocrine imbalance. That's why he's so small.'

Dominic answered in a lowered voice. 'Can it be treated?'

'Only with a new treatment that isn't yet subsidised by the public health system. Even for private treatment, he's on a waiting list.' It was the reason why she drove an old car, why Bea had moved back home to save on rent, why the whole family was pulling together to raise the exorbitant amount of money required for tiny Timothy's private treatment.

But she would not tell Dominic that. While she might be wildly attracted to him, she still had no reason to think he was other than the Scrooge of his reputation. A man who had to be forced into a public display of charity to broker a multi-million-dollar business deal. Not for one moment did she want him to think she might be angling for financial help for Timothy.

'It's all under control,' she said as she passed him a bowl of raspberries.

'I'm glad to hear that,' he said, helping himself to the berries and then the ice cream. 'Thank you for inviting me tonight and for introducing me to Hannah. The next step is for you and your business partners to come in to my headquarters for a meeting with my marketing people. Can the three of you make it on Friday?'

CHAPTER SIX

ANDIE AND HER two business partners, Gemma and Eliza, settled themselves in a small waiting room off the main reception area of Dominic's very plush offices in Circular Quay. She and her fellow Party Queens had just come out of the Friday meeting with Dominic, his marketing people and senior executives in the boardroom and were waiting for Dominic to hear his feedback.

Situated on Sydney Cove, at the northern end of the CBD, the area was not just one of the most popular harbourside tourist precincts in Sydney—it was also home to the most prestigious office buildings. Even in this small room, floor-to-ceiling glass walls gave a magnificent close view of the Sydney Harbour Bridge and a luxury cruise liner in dock.

Andie couldn't help thinking the office was an ideal habitat for a billionaire Scrooge. Then she backtracked on the thought. That might not be fair. He hated the term and she felt vaguely disloyal even thinking it. Dominic was now totally committed to the Christmas Day feast for underprivileged families and had just approved a more than generous budget. She was beginning to wonder if his protestation that he was *not* a Scrooge had some truth in it. And then there was his gift to her mother to consider.

As she pondered the significance of that, she realised her thoughts had been filled with nothing much but Dominic since the day she'd met him. Last night he had even invaded her dreams—in a very passionate encounter that made her blush at the hazy dream memory of it. *Did he kiss like that in real life?*

It was with an effort that she forced her thoughts back to business.

'How do you guys think it went?' she asked the other two. 'My vote is for really well.' She felt jubilant and buoyant—Dominic's team had embraced her idea with more enthusiasm than she could ever have anticipated.

'Considering the meeting was meant to go from ten to eleven and here it is, nearly midday, yes, I think you could say that,' said Eliza with a big smile splitting her face.

'Of course that could have had something to do with Gemma's superb macadamia shortbread and those delectable fruit mince pies,' said Andie.

'Yes,' said Gemma with a pleased smile. 'I thought I could describe until I was blue in the face what I wanted to serve for the lunch, but they'd only know by tasting it.'

Party Queens' foodie partner had not only come up with a detailed menu for Dominic's Christmas Day lunch, but she'd also brought along freshly baked samples of items from her proposed menus. At the end of the meeting only a few crumbs had remained on the boardroom's fine china plates. Andie had caught Dominic's eye as he finished his second pastry and knew it had been an inspired idea. The Christmas star shaped serviettes she had brought along had also worked to keep the meeting focused on the theme of traditional with a twist.

'I think they were all-round impressed,' said Eliza. 'We three worked our collective socks off to get our presentations so detailed and professional in such a short time. Andie, all the images and samples you prepared to show the decorations and table settings looked amazing—I got excited at how fabulous it's going to look.'

'I loved the idea of the goody bags for all the guests too,' said Gemma. 'You really thought of everything.'

'While we're doing some mutual backslapping I'm giving yours a hearty slap, Eliza,' said Andie. 'Their finance guy couldn't fault your detailed costings and timelines.'

Eliza rubbed her hands together in exaggerated glee. 'And I'm sure we're going to get more party bookings from them. One of the senior marketing people mentioned her daughter was getting married next year and asked me did we do weddings.'

'Well done, Party Queens,' said Andie. 'Now that the contract is signed and the basic plan approved I feel I can relax.' Her partners had no idea of how tight it had been to get Dominic across the line for the change from glitz and glamour to more humble with heart.

She and her two friends discreetly high-fived each other. The room was somewhat of a goldfish bowl and none of them wanted to look less than professional to any of Dominic's staff who might be walking by.

Eliza leaned in to within whispering distance of Andie and Gemma. 'Dominic Hunt was a surprise,' she said in an undertone. 'I thought he'd be arrogant and overbearing. Instead, I found myself actually liking him.'

'Me too,' said Gemma. 'Not to mention he's so handsome. I could hardly keep my eyes off him. And that voice.' She mimed a shiver of delight.

'But *he* couldn't keep his eyes off Andie,' said Eliza. 'You'd be wasting your time there, Gemma.'

Had he? Been unable to keep his eyes off her? Andie's Dominic radar had been on full alert all through the meeting. Again she'd that uncanny experience of knowing exactly where he was in the room even when her back was turned. Of hearing his voice through the chatter of others. She'd caught his eye one too many times to feel comfortable. Especially with the remnants of that dream lingering in her mind. She'd had to force herself not to let her gaze linger on his mouth.

'Really, Andie?' said Gemma. 'Has he asked you out?'

'Nothing like that,' Andie said.

Eliza nodded thoughtfully. 'But you like him. Not in the way I liked him. I mean you *really* like him.'

Andie had no intention of admitting anything to anyone. She forced her voice to sound cool, impartial—though she doubted she would fool shrewd Eliza. 'Like you, I was surprised at how easy he is to get on with and how professional he is—even earlier this week when I switched the whole concept of his party into something he had never envisaged.' That overwhelming attraction was just physical—nothing more.

'And you totally didn't get how hot he was?' said Gemma. 'Don't expect me to believe that for one moment.'

Eliza rolled her eyes at Andie. 'I know what's coming next. *He's not your type*. How many times have I heard you say that when you either refuse a date or dump a guy before you've even had a chance to get to know him?'

Andie paused. 'Maybe that's true. Maybe that's why I'm still single. I'm beginning to wonder if I really know what *is* my type now.'

Her friendships with Gemma and Eliza dated from after she'd lost Anthony. They'd been sympathetic, but never really got why she had been so determined to try and find another man cast in the same mould as her first love. That her first love had been so perfect she'd felt her best chance of happiness would be with someone like Anthony.

Trouble was, they'd broken the mould when they'd made Anthony. Maybe she just hadn't been ready. Maybe she'd been subconsciously avoiding any man who might challenge her. Or might force her to look at why she'd put her heart on hold for so long. *Dominic would be a challenge in every way.* The thought both excited and scared her.

Eliza shook her head. 'It's irrelevant anyway,' she said. 'It would be most unwise for you to start anything with Dominic Hunt. His party is a big, important job for us and we don't have much time to organise it. It could get very messy if you started dating the client. Especially when I've never known you to stay with anyone for more than two weeks.'

'In my eagerness to get you fixed up with a handsome rich guy, I hadn't thought of that,' said Gemma. 'Imagine if you broke up with the billionaire client right in the middle of the countdown to the event. Could get awkward.'

'It's not going to happen, girls,' Andie said. 'I won't lie and say I don't think he's really attractive. But that's as far as it goes.' Thinking of last night's very intimate dream, she crossed her fingers behind her back.

'This is a huge party for us to pull together so quickly. We've got other jobs to get sorted as well. I can't afford to get…distracted.' How she actually stopped herself from getting distracted by Dominic was another matter altogether.

'I agree,' said Eliza. 'Eyes off the client. Okay?'

Andie smiled. 'I'll try,' she said. 'Seriously, though, it's really important for Dominic that this party works. He's got a lot riding on it. And it's really important for us. As you say, Eliza, more work could come from this. Not just weddings and private parties. But why not his company's business functions too? We have to think big.'

Gemma giggled. 'Big? Mr Hunt is way too big for me anyway. He's so tall. And all those muscles. His face is handsome but kind of tough too, don't you think?'

'Shh,' hissed Eliza, putting her finger to her lips. 'He's coming.'

Andie screwed up her eyes for a moment. How mortifying if he'd caught them gossiping about him. She'd been just about to say he wasn't too big for her to handle.

Along with the other two, she looked up and straightened her shoulders as Dominic strode towards them. In his dark charcoal suit he looked every inch the billionaire businessman. And, yes, very big.

She caught her breath at how handsome he looked. At the same time she caught his eye. And got the distinct impression that, of the three women in the room, she was the only one he really saw.

Did Andie get more and more beautiful every time he saw her? Dominic wondered. Or was it just the more he got to know her, the more he liked and admired her?

He had been impressed by her engaging and professional manner in the boardroom—the more so because he was aware she'd had such a short time to prepare her presentation. Her two business partners had been impressive too. It took a lot to win over his hard-nosed marketing people but, as a team, Party Queens had bowled them over.

The three women got up from their seats as he approached. Andie, tall and elegant in a deceptively simple caramel-coloured short dress—businesslike but with a snug fit that showed off her curves. Her sensational legs seemed to go on for ever to end in sky-high leopard-skin-print stilettos. He got it. She wanted to look businesslike but also let it be known who was the creative mind behind Party Queens. It worked.

Gemma—shorter, curvier, with auburn hair—and sophisticated, dark-haired Eliza were strikingly attractive too. They had a glint in their eyes and humour in their smiles that made him believe they could enjoy a party as well as plan them. But, in his eyes, Andie outshone them. Would any other woman ever be able to beat her? It was disturbing that a woman who he had known for such a short time could have made such an impression on him.

He addressed all three, while being hyper aware of

Andie as he did so. Her hair pulled back in a loose knot that fell in soft tendrils around her face, her mouth slicked with coral gloss, those remarkable green eyes. 'As I'm sure you're aware,' he began, 'my marketing team is delighted at both the concept for the party and the way you plan to implement the concept to the timeline. They're confident the event will meet and exceed the target we've set for reputation management and positive media engagement.'

It sounded like jargon and he knew it. But how else could he translate the only real aim of the party: to make him look less the penny-pincher and more the philanthropist?

'We're very pleased to be working with such a professional team,' said Eliza, the business brains of the partnership. But all three were business savvy in their own way, he'd realised through the meeting.

'Thank you,' he said. He glanced at his watch. 'The meeting ran so late it's almost lunchtime. I'm extending an invitation to lunch for all of you,' he said. 'Not that restaurants around here, excellent as they are, could match the standard of your cooking, Gemma.'

'Thank you,' said Gemma, looking pleased. 'But I'm afraid I have an appointment elsewhere.'

'Me too, and I'm running late,' said Eliza. 'But we couldn't possibly let you lunch alone, Mr Hunt, could we, Andie?'

Andie flushed high on those elegant cheekbones. 'Of course not. I'd be delighted to join Dominic for lunch.'

Her chin tilted upwards and he imagined her friends might later be berated for landing her in this on her own. Not that he minded. The other women were delightful, but lunch one-on-one with Andie was his preferred option.

'There are a few details of the plan I need to finalise with Dominic anyway,' she said to her friends.

Dominic shook hands with Gemma and Eliza and they

headed towards the elevators. He turned to Andie. 'Thank you for coming to lunch with me,' he said.

She smiled. 'Be warned, I'm starving. I was up at the crack of dawn finalising those mood boards for the presentation.'

'They were brilliant. There's only one thing I'd like to see changed. I didn't want to mention it in the meeting as it's my personal opinion and I didn't want to have to debate it.'

She frowned, puzzled rather than worried, he thought. 'Yes?'

He put his full authority behind his voice—he would not explain his reasons. Ever. 'The Christmas tree. The big one you have planned for next to the staircase. I don't want it.'

'Sure,' she said, obviously still puzzled. 'I thought it would be wonderful to have the tree where it's the first thing the guests see, but I totally understand if you don't want it there. We can put the Christmas tree elsewhere. The living room. Even in the area near where we'll be eating. Wherever you suggest.'

He hadn't expected this to be easy—he knew everyone would expect to see a decorated tree on Christmas Day. 'You misunderstood me. I mean I don't want a Christmas tree anywhere. No tree at all in my house.'

She paused. He could almost see her internal debate reflected in the slight crease between her eyebrows, the barely visible pursing of her lips. But then she obviously thought it was not worth the battle. 'Okay,' she said with a shrug of her slender shoulders. 'No tree.'

'Thank you,' he said, relieved he wasn't going to have to further assert his authority. At this time of year, Christmas trees were appearing all over the place. He avoided them when he could. But he would never have a tree in his home—a constant reminder of the pain and loss and guilt associated with the festive season.

They walked together to the elevator. When it arrived, there were two other people in it. They got out two floors below. Then Dominic was alone in the confined space of the elevator, aware of Andie's closeness, her warm scent. What was it? Sandalwood? Something exotic and sensual. He had the craziest impulse to hold her closer so he could nuzzle into the softness of her throat, the better to breathe it in.

He clenched his fists beside him and moved as far as he could away from her so his shoulder hit the wall of the elevator. That would be insanity. And probably not the best timing when he'd just quashed her Christmas tree display.

But she wouldn't be Andie if she didn't persevere. 'Not even miniature trees on the lunch table?' she asked.

'No trees,' he said.

She sighed. 'Okay, the client has spoken. No Christmas tree.'

The elevator came to the ground floor. He lightly placed his hand at the small of her back to steer her in the direction of the best exit for the restaurant. Bad idea. Touching Andie even in this casual manner just made him want to touch her more.

'But you're happy with the rest of the plan?' she said as they walked side by side towards the restaurant, dodging the busy Sydney lunchtime crush as they did.

'Very happy. Except you can totally discard the marketing director's suggestion I dress up as Santa Claus.'

She laughed. 'Did you notice I wrote it down but didn't take the suggestion any further?' Her eyes narrowed as she looked him up and down in mock inspection. 'Though it's actually a nice idea. If you change your mind—'

'No,' he said.

'That's what I thought,' she said, that delightful smile dancing around the corners of her mouth.

'You know it's been a stretch for me to agree to a Christmas party at all. You won't ever see me as Santa.'

'What if the marketing director himself could be convinced to play Santa Claus?' she said thoughtfully. 'He volunteered to help out on the day.'

'This whole party thing was Rob Cratchit's idea so that might be most appropriate. Take it as an order from his boss.'

'I'll send him an email and say it's your suggestion,' she said with a wicked grin. 'He's quite well padded and would make a wonderful Santa—no pillow down the front of his jacket required.'

'Don't mention that in the email or all hell will break loose,' he said.

'Don't worry; I can be subtle when I want to,' she said, that grin still dancing in her eyes as they neared the restaurant.

In Dominic's experience, some restaurants were sited well and had a good fit-out; others had excellent food. In this case, his favourite place to eat near the office had both—a spectacular site on the top of a heritage listed building right near the water and a superlative menu.

There had been no need to book—a table was always there for him when he wanted one, no matter how long the waiting list for bookings.

An attentive waiter settled Andie into a seat facing the view of Sydney Harbour. 'I've always wanted to eat at this restaurant,' she said, looking around her.

'Maybe we should have our meetings here in future?'

'Good idea,' she said. 'Though I'll have to do a detailed site inspection of your house very soon. We could fit in a meeting then, perhaps?'

'I might not be able to be there,' he said. 'I have a series of appointments in other states over the next two weeks. Any meetings with you might have to be via the Internet.'

Was that disappointment he saw cloud her eyes. 'That's a shame. I—'

'My assistant will help you with access and the security code,' he said. He wished he could cancel some of the meetings, but that was not possible. Perhaps it was for the best. The more time he spent with Andie, the more he wanted to break his rules and ask her on a date. But those rules were there for good reason.

'As you know, we have a tight timeline to work to,' she said. 'The more we get done early the better, to allow for the inevitable last-minute dramas.'

'I have every confidence in you that it will go to plan.'

'Me too,' she said with another of those endearing grins. 'I've organised so many Christmas room sets and table settings for magazine and advertising clients. You have to get creative to come up with something different each year. This is easier in a way.'

'But surely there must be a continuity?' he asked, curious even though Christmas was his least favourite topic of conversation.

'Some people don't want to go past traditional red and green and that's okay,' she said. 'I've done an entire room themed purple and the client was delighted. Silver and gold is always popular in Australia, when Christmas is likely to be sweltering—it seems to feel cooler somehow. But—'

The waiter came to take their orders. They'd been too busy talking to look at the menu. Quickly they discussed their favourites before they ordered: barramundi with prawns and asparagus for him; tandoori roasted ocean trout with cucumber salsa for her and an heirloom tomato salad to share. They each passed on wine and chose mineral water. 'Because it's a working day,' they both said at the exact time and laughed. *It felt like a date.* He could not let his thoughts stray that way. Because he liked the idea too much.

'You haven't explained the continuity of Christmas,' he said, bringing the conversation back to the party.

'It's nothing to do with the baubles and the tinsel and everything to do with the feeling,' she said with obvious enthusiasm. 'Anticipation, delight, joy. For some it's about religious observance, spirituality and new life; others about sharing and generosity. If you can get people feeling the emotion, then it doesn't really matter if the tree is decorated in pink and purple or red and green.'

How about misery and fear and pain? Those were his memories of Christmas. 'I see your point,' he said.

'I intend to make sure your party is richly imbued with that kind of Christmas spirit. Hannah told me some of the kids who will be coming would be unlikely to have a celebration meal or a present and certainly not both if it wasn't for your generosity.'

'I met with Hannah yesterday; she mentioned how important it will be for the families we're inviting. She seems to think the party will do a powerful lot of good. Your sister told me how special Christmas is in your family.' It was an effort for him to speak about Christmas in a normal tone of voice. But he seemed to be succeeding.

'Oh, yes,' said Andie. 'Heaven help anyone who might want to celebrate it with their in-laws or anywhere else but my parents' house.'

'Your mother's a marvellous cook.'

'True, but Christmas is well and truly my dad's day. My mother is allowed to do the baking and she does that months in advance. On the day, he cooks a traditional meal—turkey, ham, roast beef, the lot. He's got favourite recipes he's refined over the years and no one would dare suggest anything different.'

Did she realise how lucky she was? How envious he felt when he thought about how empty his life had been of the kind of family love she'd been gifted with. He'd used to think he could start his own family, his own traditions, but his ex-wife had disabused him of that particular dream. It involved trust and trust was not a thing that came easily to him. Not when it came to women. 'I can't imagine you would want to change a tradition.'

'If truth be told, we'd be furious if he wanted to change one little thing,' she said, her voice warm with affection for her father. *She knew.*

He could see where she got her confidence from—that rock-solid security of a loving, supportive family. But now he knew she'd been tempered by tragedy too. He wanted to know more about how she had dealt with the loss of her boyfriend. But not until it was appropriate to ask.

'What about you, Dominic—did you celebrate Christmas with your family?' she asked.

This never got easier—which was why he chose not to revisit it too often. 'My parents died when I was eleven,' he said.

'Oh, I'm so sorry,' she said with warm compassion in her eyes. 'What a tragedy.' She paused. 'You were so young, an only child…who looked after you?'

'We lived in England, in a village in Norfolk. My father was English, my mother Australian. My mother's sister was staying with us at the time my parents died. She took me straight back with her to Australia.' It was difficult to keep his voice matter of fact, not to betray the pain the memories evoked, even after all this time.

'What? Just wrenched you away from your home?' She paused. 'I'm sorry. That wasn't my call to say that. You were lucky you had family. Did your aunt have children?'

'No, it was just the two of us,' he said and left it at that. There was so much more he could say about the toxic relationship with his aunt but that was part of his past he'd rather was left buried.

Wrenched. That was how it had been. Away from everything familiar. Away from his grandparents, whom he didn't see again until he had the wherewithal to get himself back to the UK as an adult. Away from the dog he'd adored. Desperately lonely and not allowed to grieve, thrust back down in Brisbane, in the intense heat, straight into the strategic battleground that was high school in a foreign country. To a woman who had no idea how to love a child, though she had tried in her own warped way.

'I'd prefer not to talk about it,' he said. 'I'm all grown up now and don't angst about the past.' Except when it was dark and lonely and he couldn't sleep and he wondered if he was fated to live alone without love.

'I understand,' she said. But how could she?

She paused to leave a silence he did not feel able to fill.

'Talking about my family,' she finally said, 'you're my mother's new number one favourite person.'

Touched by not only her words but her effort to draw him in some way into her family circle, he smiled. 'And why is that?'

'Seriously, she really liked you at dinner on Wednesday night. But then, when you had flowers delivered the next day, she was over the moon. Especially at the note that said she cooked the best lasagne you'd ever tasted.'

'I'm glad she liked them. And it was true about the lasagne.' Home-made anything was rarely on the menu for him so he had appreciated it.

'How did you know pink was her favourite colour in flowers?'

'I noticed the flowers she'd planted in her garden.'

'But you only saw the garden so briefly.'

'I'm observant,' he said.

'But the icing on the cake was the voucher for dinner for two at their local bistro.'

'She mentioned she liked their food when we were talking,' he said.

'You're a thoughtful guy, aren't you?' she said, tilting her head to the side.

'Some don't think so,' he said, unable to keep the bitterness from his voice.

She lowered her voice to barely a whisper so he had to lean across the table to hear her, so close their heads were touching. Anyone who was watching would think they *were* on a date.

She placed her hand on his arm in a gesture of comfort which touched him. 'Don't worry. The party should change all that. I really liked Rob's idea that no media would be invited to the party. That journalists would have to volunteer to help on the day if they wanted to see what it was all about.'

'And no photographers allowed, to preserve our guests' privacy. I liked that too.'

'I really have a good feeling about it,' she said. She lifted her hand off his arm and he felt bereft of her touch.

He nodded. If it were up to him, if he didn't *have* to go ahead with the party, he'd cancel it at a moment's notice. Maybe there was a touch of Scrooge in him after all.

But he didn't want Andie to think that of him. Not for a moment.

He hadn't proved to be a good judge of women. His errors in judgement went right back to his aunt—he'd loved her when she was his fun auntie from Australia. She'd turned out to be a very different person. Then there'd been Melody—sweet, doomed Melody. At seventeen he'd been a man in body but a boy still in heart. He'd been gutted at her betrayal, too damn wet behind the ears to realise a teenage boy's love could never be enough for an addict. Then how could he have been sucked in by Tara? His ex-wife was a redhead like Melody, tiny and delicate. But her frail exterior hid an avaricious, dishonest heart and she had lied to him about something so fundamental to their marriage that he could never forgive her.

Now there was Andie. He didn't trust his feelings when he'd made such disastrous calls before. *'What you see is what you get,'* she'd said about her family.

Could he trust himself to judge that Andie was what she appeared to be?

He reined in his errant thoughts—he only needed to trust Andie to deliver him the party he needed to improve his public image. Anything personal was not going to happen.

CHAPTER SEVEN

'ANDIE, I NEED to see you.' Dominic's voice on her smartphone was harsh in its urgency. It was eight a.m. and Andie had not been expecting a call from him. He'd been away more than a week on business and she'd mainly communicated with him by text and email—and only then if it was something that needed his approval for the party. The last time she'd seen him was the Friday they'd had lunch together. The strictly business lunch that had somehow felt more like a date. But she couldn't let herself think like that.

'Sure,' she said. 'I just have to—'

'Now. Please. Where do you live?'

Startled at his tone, she gave him the address of the apartment in a converted warehouse in the inner western suburb of Newtown she shared with two old schoolfriends. Her friends had both already left for work. Andie had planned on a day finalising prop hire and purchase for Dominic's party before she started work for a tuxedo-and-tiara-themed twenty-first birthday party.

She quickly changed into skinny denim jeans and a simple loose-knit cream top that laced with leather ties at the neckline. Decided on her favourite leopard-print stilettos over flats. And make-up. And her favourite sandalwood and jasmine perfume. What the heck—her heart was racing at the thought of seeing him. She didn't want to seem as though she were trying too hard—but then again she didn't want to be caught out in sweats.

When Dominic arrived she was shocked to see he didn't look *his* sartorial best. In fact he looked downright dishevelled. His black hair seemed as if he'd used his fingers for a comb and his dark stubble was one step away from a beard. He was wearing black jeans, a dark grey T-shirt and had a black leather jacket slung over his shoulders. Immediately he owned the high-ceilinged room, a space that overwhelmed men of lesser stature, with the casual athleticism of his stance, the power of his body with its air of tightly coiled energy.

'Are you alone?' he asked.

'Yes,' she said. *Yes!*

Her first thought was that he looked hotter than ever—so hot she had to catch her breath. This Dominic set her pulse racing even more than executive Dominic in his made-to-measure Italian suits.

Her second thought was that he seemed stressed—his mouth set in a grim line, his eyes red-rimmed and darkly shadowed. 'Are you okay?' she asked.

'I've come straight from the airport. I just flew in from Perth.' Perth was on the other side of Australia—a six-hour flight. 'I cut short my trip.'

'But are you okay?' She forced her voice to sound calm and measured, not wanting him to realise how she was reacting to his untamed good looks. Her heart thudded with awareness that they were alone in the apartment.

With the kind of friendly working relationship they had now established, it would be quite in order to greet him with a light kiss on his beard-roughened cheek. But she wouldn't dare. She might not be able to resist sliding her mouth across his cheek to his mouth and turning it into a very different kind of kiss. And that wouldn't do.

'I'm fine. I've just…been presented with…with a dilemma,' Dominic said.

'Coffee might help,' she said.

'Please.'

'Breakfast? I have—'

'Just coffee.'

But Andie knew that sometimes men who said they didn't want anything to eat needed food. And that their mood could improve immeasurably when they ate something. Not that she'd been in the habit of sharing breakfast with a man. Not since… She forced her mind back to the present and away from memories of breakfasts with Anthony on a sun-soaked veranda. Her memories of him were lit with sunshine and happiness.

Dominic dragged out a chair and slumped down at her kitchen table while she prepared him coffee. *Why was he here?* She turned to see him with his elbows on the tabletop, resting his head on his hands. Tired? Defeated? Something seemed to have put a massive dent in his usual self-assured confidence.

She slid a mug of coffee in front of him. 'I assumed black but here's frothed milk and sugar if you want.'

'Black is what I need,' he said. He put both hands around the mug and took it to his mouth.

Without a word, she put a thick chunk of fresh fruit bread, studded with figs and apricots, from her favourite baker in King Street in front of him. Then a dish of cream cheese and a knife. 'Food might help,' she said.

He put down his coffee, gave her a weary imitation of his usual glower and went to pick up the bread. 'Let me,' she said and spread it with cream cheese.

What was it about this man that made her want to comfort and care for him? He was a thirty-two-year-old billionaire, for heaven's sake. Tough, self-sufficient. Wealthier than she could even begin to imagine. And yet she sometimes detected an air of vulnerability about him that wrenched at her. A sense of something broken. But it was not up to her to try and fix him. He ate the fruit bread in two bites. 'More?' she asked.

He nodded. 'It's good,' he said.

Andie had to be honest with herself. She wanted to comfort him, yes. She enjoyed his company. But it was more than that. She couldn't deny that compelling physical attraction. He sat at her kitchen table, his leather jacket slung on the back of the chair. His tanned arms were sculpted with muscle, his T-shirt moulded ripped pecs and abs. With his rough-hewn face, he looked so utterly *male*.

Desire, so long unfamiliar, thrilled through her. She wanted to kiss him and feel those strong arms around her, his hands on her body. *She wanted more than kisses.* What was it about this not-my-type man who had aroused her interest from the moment she'd first met him?

When he'd eaten two more slices of fruit bread, he pushed his plate away and leaned back in his seat. His sigh was weary and heartfelt. 'Thank you,' he said. 'I didn't realise I was hungry.'

She slipped into the chair opposite him and nursed her own cooling cup of coffee to stop the impulse to reach over and take his hand. 'Are you able to tell me about your dilemma?' she asked, genuinely concerned.

He raked his hands through his hair. 'My ex-wife is causing trouble. Again.'

In her research into Dominic, Andie had seen photos of Tara Hunt—she still went by his name—a petite, pale-skinned redhead in designer clothes and an over-abundance of jewellery.

'I'm sorry,' she said, deciding on caution in her reaction. 'Do you want to tell me about it?' Was that why he wanted to see her? To cry on her shoulder about his ex-wife? Dominic didn't seem like a crying-on-shoulders kind of guy.

He went to drink more coffee, to find his mug was

nearly empty. He drained the last drops. 'You make good coffee,' he said appreciatively.

'I worked as a barista when I was a student,' she said.

She and Anthony had both worked in hospitality, saving for vacation backpacker trips to Indonesia and Thailand. It seemed so long ago now, those days when she took it for granted they had a long, happy future stretched out ahead of them. They'd been saving for a trip to Eastern Europe when he'd died.

She took Dominic's mug from him, got up, refilled it, brought it back to the table and sat down again. He drank from it and put it down.

Dominic leaned across the table to bring him closer to her. 'Can I trust you, Andie?' he asked in that deep, resonant voice. His intense grey gaze met hers and held it.

'Of course,' she said without hesitation.

He sat back in his chair. 'I know you're friends with journalists, so I have to be sure what I might talk to you about today won't go any further.' The way he said it didn't sound offensive; in fact it made her feel privileged that he would consider her trustworthy. Not to mention curious about what he might reveal.

'I assure you, you can trust me,' she said.

'Thank you,' he said. 'Tara found out about my impending deal with Walter Burton and is doing her best to derail it.'

Andie frowned. 'How can she do that?'

'Before I married Tara, she worked for my company in the accounts department. She made it her business to find out everything she could about the way I ran things. I didn't know, but once I started dating her she used that knowledge to make trouble, hiding behind the shield of our relationship. None of my staff dared tell me.'

'Not good,' Andie said, wanting to express in no uncertain terms what she thought of his ex, yet not wanting to get into a bitching session about her.

'You're right about that,' he said. 'It's why I now never date employees.'

His gaze met hers again and held it for a long moment. Was there a message in there for her? If she wasn't a contractor, would he ask her out? If she hadn't promised her partners to stay away from him, would she suggest a date?

'That policy makes…sense,' she said. What about after Christmas, when she and Dominic would no longer be connected by business? Could they date then? A sudden yearning for that to happen surprised her with its intensity. *She wanted him.*

'It gets worse,' he continued. 'A former employee started his own business in competition with me—' Andie went to protest but Dominic put up his hand. 'It happens; that's legit,' he said. 'But what happened afterwards wasn't. After our marriage broke up, Tara used her knowledge of how my company worked to help him.'

Andie couldn't help her gasp of outrage. 'Did her…her betrayal work?'

'She gave him the information. That didn't mean he knew how to use it. But now I've just discovered she's working with him in a last-minute rival bid for the joint venture with Walter Burton.'

Andie shook her head in disbelief. 'Why?' Her research had shown her Tara Hunt had ended up with a massive divorce settlement from Dominic. Per day of their short marriage, she had walked away with an incredible number of dollars.

Dominic shrugged. 'Revenge. Spite. Who knows what else?'

'Surely Walter Burton won't be swayed by that kind of underhand behaviour?'

'Traditional values are important to Walter Burton. We

know that. That's why we're holding the party to negate the popular opinion of me as a Scrooge.'

'So what does your ex-wife have to do with the deal?'

Dominic sighed, a great weary sigh that made Andie want to put comforting arms around him. She'd sensed from the get-go he was a private person. He obviously hated talking about this. Once more, she wondered why he had chosen to.

He drew those dark brows together in a scowl. 'Again she's raked over the coals of our disastrous marriage and talked to her media buddies. Now she's claiming I was unfaithful—which is a big fat lie. According to her, I'm a womaniser, a player and a complete and utter bastard. She dragged out my old quote that I will never marry again and claims it's because I'm incapable of settling with one woman. It's on one of the big Internet gossip sites and will be all over the weekend newspapers.' He cursed under his breath.

Andie could see the shadow of old hurts on his face. He had once loved his ex enough to marry her. A betrayal like this must be painful, no matter how much time had elapsed. She had no such angst behind her. She knew Anthony had been loyal to her, as she had been to him. *First love.* Sometimes she wondered if they might have grown apart if he'd lived. Some of their friends who had dated as teenagers had split when they got older. But she dismissed those thoughts as disloyal to his memory.

Andie shook her head at Dominic's revelations about his ex—it got worse and worse. 'That's horrible—but can't you just ignore it?'

'I would ignore it, but she's made sure Walter Burton has seen all her spurious allegations set out as truth.'

Andie frowned. 'Surely your personal life is none of Mr Burton's business? Especially when it's not true.' She believed Dominic implicitly—why, she wasn't completely sure. Trust went both ways.

'He might think it's true. The *"bed-hopping billionaire"*,' the article calls me.' Dominic growled with wounded outrage. 'That might be enough for Burton to reconsider doing business with me.'

Andie had to put her hand over her mouth to hide her smile at the description.

But Dominic noticed and scowled. 'I know it sounds ludicrous, but to a moralistic family man like Walter Burton it makes me sound immoral and not the kind of guy he wants to do business with.'

'Why do you care so much about the deal with Mr Burton? If you have to pretend to be someone you're not, how can it be worth it?'

'You mean I should pretend *not* to be a bed-hopping billionaire?'

'You must admit the headline has a certain ring to it,' Andie said, losing her battle to keep a straight face.

That forced a reluctant grin from him. 'A tag like that might be very difficult to live down.'

'Is…is it true? Are you a bed-hopping guy?' She held her breath for his reply.

'No. Of course I've had girlfriends since my divorce. Serial monogamy, I think they call it. But nothing like what this scurrilous interview with my ex claims.'

Andie let out her breath on a sigh of relief. 'But do you actually need to pursue this deal if it's becoming so difficult? You're already very wealthy.'

Dominic's mouth set in a grim line. 'I'm not going to bore you with my personal history. But home life with my aunt was less than ideal. I finished high school and got out. I'd tried to run away before and she'd dragged me back. This time she let me go. I ended up homeless, living in a squat. At seventeen I saw inexplicably awful things a boy that age should never see. I never again want to be without money and have nowhere to live. That's all I intend to say about that.' He nodded to her. 'And I trust you not to repeat it.'

'Of course,' she said, rocked by his revelations, aching to know more. *Dominic Hunt was a street kid?* Not boring. There was so much more about his life than he was saying. She thought again about his scarred knuckles and broken nose. There had been nothing about his past in her online trawling. She hoped he might tell her more. It seemed he was far more complex than he appeared. Which only made him more attractive.

'My best friend and first business partner, Jake Marlow, is also in with me on this,' he said. 'He wants it as much as I do, for his own reasons I'm not at liberty to share.'

'Okay,' she said slowly. 'So we're working on the party to negate the Scr…uh…the other reputation, to get Mr Burton on board. What do you intend to do about the bed-hopper one?'

'When Burton contacted me I told him that it was all scuttlebutt and I was engaged to be married.'

She couldn't help a gasp. 'You're engaged?' She felt suddenly stricken. 'Engaged to who?'

'I'm not engaged. I'm not even dating anyone.'

'Then why…?' she said.

He groaned. 'Panic. Fear. Survival. A gut reaction like I used to have back in that squat. When you woke up, terrified, in your cardboard box to find some older guy burrowing through your backpack and you told him you had nothing worth stealing even though there was five dollars folded tiny between your toes in your sock. If that money was stolen, you didn't eat.'

'So you lied to Mr Burton?'

'As I said, a panic reaction. But it gets worse.' Again he raked his fingers through his hair. 'Burton said he was flying in to Sydney in two weeks' time to meet with both me and the other guy. He wants to be introduced to my fiancée.'

Andie paused, stunned at what Dominic had done, appalled that he had lied. 'What will you do?'

Again he leaned towards her over the table. 'I want you to be my fiancée, Andie.'

CHAPTER EIGHT

DOMINIC WATCHED ANDIE'S reactions flit across her face—shock and indignation followed by disappointment. In him? He braced himself—certain she was going to say *no*.

'Are you serious?' she finally said, her hands flat down on the table in front of her.

'Very,' he said, gritting his teeth. He'd been an idiot to get himself into a mess like this. *Panic.* He shouldn't have given in to panic in that phone call with Walter Burton. He hadn't let panic or fear rule him for a long time.

Andie tilted her head to one side and frowned. 'You want me to *marry* you? We hardly know each other.'

Marriage? Who was talking about marriage? 'No. Just to *pretend*—' Whatever he said wasn't going to sound good. 'Pretend to be my fiancée. Until after the Christmas party.'

Andie shook her head in disbelief. 'To pretend to be engaged to you? To lie? No! I can't believe you asked me to…to even think of such a thing. I'm a party planner, not a…a…the type of person who would agree to that.'

She looked at him as though she'd never seen him before. And that maybe she didn't like what she saw. Dominic swallowed hard—he didn't like the feeling her expression gave him. She pushed herself up from the chair and walked away from the table, her body rigid with disapproval. He was very aware she wanted to distance herself from him. He didn't like that either. It had seemed so intimate, drinking coffee and eating breakfast at her table. And he *had* liked that.

He swivelled in his chair to face her. 'It was a stupid thing to do, I know that,' he said. He had spent the entire flight back from Perth regretting his impulsive action. 'But it's done.'

She turned around, glared at him. 'Then I suggest you undo it.'

'By admitting I lied?'

She shrugged. 'Tell Mr Burton your fiancée dumped you.'

'As if that would fly.'

'You think it's beyond belief that a woman would ever dump you?'

'I didn't say that.' Though it was true. Since it had ended with Melody, he had always been the one to end a relationship. 'It would seem too…sudden.'

'Just like the sudden engagement?'

'It wouldn't denote…stability.'

'You're right about that.' She crossed her arms in front of her chest—totally unaware that the action pushed up her breasts into an enticing cleavage in the V-necked top she wore. 'It's a crazy idea.'

'I'm not denying that,' he growled. He didn't need to have his mistake pointed out to him. 'But I'm asking you to help me out.'

'Why me? Find someone else. I'm sure there would be no shortage of candidates.'

'But it makes sense for my fiancée to be you.' He could be doggedly persistent when he wanted to be.

He unfolded himself from the too-small chair at the kitchen table. Most chairs were too small for him. He took a step towards her, only for her to take a step back from him. 'Andie. Please.'

Her hair had fallen across her face and she tossed it back. 'Why? We're just client and contractor.'

'Is that all it is between us?'

'Of course it is.' But she wouldn't meet his gaze and he felt triumphant. *So she felt it too.* That attraction that had flashed between them from the get-go.

'When I opened the door to the beautiful woman with the misbehaving skirt—' that got a grudging smile from her '—I thought it could be more than just a business arrangement. But you know now why I don't date anyone hired by the company.'

'And Party Queens has a policy of not mixing business with…with pleasure.' Her voice got huskier on the last words.

He looked her direct in the face, pinning her with his gaze. 'If it ever happened, it would be pleasure all the way, Andie, I think we both know that.' She hadn't quite cleared her face of a wisp of flyaway hair. He reached down and gently smoothed it back behind her ear.

She trembled under his touch. A blush travelled up her throat to stain her cheeks. 'I've never even thought about it, the…the *pleasure,* I mean,' she said.

She wouldn't blush like that if she hadn't. Or flutter her hands to the leather laces of her neckline. *Now who was lying?*

She took a deep breath and he tried to keep his gaze from the resulting further exposure of her cleavage. 'I don't want to be involved in this mad scheme in any way,' she said. 'Except to add your pretend fiancée—when you find one—to the Christmas party guest list.'

'I'm afraid you're already involved.'

She frowned. 'What do you mean?'

Dominic took the few steps necessary back to his chair and took out his smartphone from the inside pocket of his leather jacket. He scrolled through, then handed it to Andie.

She stared at the screen. 'But this is me. *Us*.'

The photo she was staring at was of him and her at a restaurant table. They were leaning towards each other, looking into each other's faces, Andie's hand on his arm.

'At the restaurant in Circular Quay, the day of the Friday meeting,' she said.

'Yes,' he said. The business lunch that had felt like a date. In this photo, it *looked* like a date.

She shook her head, bewildered. 'Who took it?'

'Some opportunistic person with a smartphone, I expect. Maybe a trouble-making friend of Tara's. Who knows?'

She looked back down at the screen, did some scrolling of her own. He waited for her to notice the words that accompanied the image on the gossip site.

Her eyes widened in horror. 'Did you see this?' She read out the heading. *'"Is This the Bed-Hopping Billionaire's New Conquest?"'* She swore under her breath—the first time he had heard her do so.

'I'm sorry. Of course I had no idea this was happening. But, in light of it, you can see why it makes sense that my fake fiancée should be you.'

She shook her head. 'No. It doesn't make any sense. That was a business lunch. Not the…the romantic rendezvous it appears to be in the picture.'

'You know that. I know that. But the way they've cropped the photo, that's exactly what it seems. Announce an engagement and suddenly the picture would make a whole lot of sense. Good sense.'

Her green eyes narrowed. 'This photo doesn't bother me. It will blow over. We're both single. Who even cares?'

He'd been stunned to see the expression in his eyes as he'd looked into her face in the photo. It had looked as if he wanted to have her for dessert. Had she noticed? No wonder the gossip site had drawn a conclusion of romantic intrigue.

'If you're so indifferent, why not help me out?' he said. 'Be my fake fiancée, just until after Christmas.'

'Christmas is nearly a month away. Twenty-five days, to be precise. For twenty-five days I'd have to pretend to be your fiancée?'

'So you're considering it? Because we've already been "outed", so to speak, it wouldn't come out of the blue. It would be believable.'

'Huh! We've only known each other for two weeks. Who would believe it?'

'People get married on less acquaintance,' he said.

'Not people like me,' she said.

'You don't think anyone would believe you could be smitten by me in that time? I think I'm offended.'

'Of course not,' she said. 'I…I believe many women would be smitten by you. You're handsome, intelligent—'

'And personable, yes, you said. Though I bet you don't think I'm so personable right now.'

She glared at him, though there was a lilt to the corners of her mouth that made it seem like she might want to smile. 'You could be right about that.'

'Now to you—gorgeous, sexy, smart Andie Newman.' Her blush deepened as he sounded each adjective. 'People would certainly believe I could be instantly smitten with such a woman,' he said. 'In fact they'd think I was clever getting a ring on your finger so quickly.'

That flustered her. 'Th…thank you. I…I'm flattered. But it wouldn't seem authentic. We'd have to pretend so much. It would be such deception.'

With any other woman, he'd be waiting for her to ask: *What's in it for me?* Not Andie. He doubted the thought of a reward for her participation had even entered her head. He would have to entice her with an offer she couldn't refuse. And save the big gun to sway her from her final refusal.

'So you're going to say "yes"?'

She shook her head vehemently. 'No. I'm not. It wouldn't be right.'

'What's the harm? You'd be helping me out.'

She spun on her heel away from him and he faced her back view, her tensely hunched shoulders, for a long moment before she turned back to confront him. 'Can't you see it makes a mockery of…of a man and a woman committing to each other? To spending their lives together in a loving union? That's what getting engaged is all about. Not sealing a business deal.'

He closed his eyes at the emotion in her voice, the blurring of her words with choking pain. Under his breath he cursed fluently. Because, from any moral point of view, she was absolutely right.

'Were you engaged to…to Anthony?' he asked.

Her eyes when she lifted them to him glistened with the sheen of unshed tears. 'Not officially. But we had our future planned, even the names of our kids chosen. That's why I know promising to marry someone isn't something you do lightly. And not…not for a scam. Do you understand?'

Of course he did. He'd once been idealistic about love and marriage and sharing his life with that one special woman. But he couldn't admit it. Or that he'd become cynical that that kind of love would ever exist for him. Too much rode on this deal. Including his integrity.

'But this isn't really getting engaged,' he said. 'It's just …a limited agreement.'

Slowly she shook her head. 'I can't help you,' she said. 'Sorry.'

Dominic braced himself. He'd had to be ruthless at times to get where he'd got. To overcome the disadvantages of his youth. *To win.*

'What if by agreeing to be my fake fiancée you were helping someone else?' he said.

She frowned. 'Like who? Helping Walter Burton to make even more billions? I honestly can't say I like the sound of that guy, linking business to people's private lives. He sounds like a hypocrite, for one thing—you know, rich men and eyes of needles and all that. I'm not lying for him.'

'Not Walter Burton. I mean your nephew Timothy.' The little boy was his big gun.

'What do you mean, Timothy?'

Dominic fired his shot. 'Agree to be my fake fiancée and I will pay for all of Timothy's medical treatment—both immediate and ongoing. No limits. Hannah tells me there's a clinic in the United States that's at the forefront of research into treatment for his condition.'

Andie stared at him. 'You've spoken to Hannah? You've told Hannah about this? That you'll pay for Timothy if I agree to—'

He put up his hand. 'Not true.'

'But you—'

'I met with Hannah the day after the dinner with your family to talk about her helping me recruit the families for the party. At that meeting—out of interest—I asked her to tell me more about Timothy. She told me about the American treatment. I offered *then* to pay all the treatment—airfares and accommodation included.'

The colour rushed back into Andie's cheeks. 'That... that was extraordinarily generous of you. What did Hannah say?'

'She refused.'

'Of course she would. She hardly knows you. A Newman wouldn't accept charity. Although I might have tried to convince her.'

'Maybe you could convince her now. If Hannah thought

I was going to be part of the family—her brother-in-law, in fact—she could hardly refuse to accept, could she? And isn't it the sooner the better for Timothy's treatment?'

Andie stared at Dominic for a very long moment, too shocked to speak. 'Th…that's coercion. Coercion of the most insidious kind,' she finally managed to choke out.

A whole lot more words she couldn't express also tumbled around in her brain. Ruthless. Conniving. Heartless. And yet…he'd offered to help Timothy well before the fake fiancée thing. *Not a Scrooge after all.* She'd thought she'd been getting to know him—but Dominic Hunt was more of a mystery to her than ever.

He drew his dark brows together. 'Coercion? I wouldn't go that far. But I did offer to help Timothy without any strings attached. Hannah refused. This way, she might accept. And your nephew will get the help he needs. I see it as a win-win scenario.'

Andie realised she was twisting the leather thronging that laced together the front of her top and stopped it. Nothing in her life had equipped her to make this kind of decision. 'You're really putting me on the spot here. Asking me to lie and be someone I'm not—'

'Someone you're not? How does that work? You'd still be Andie.'

She found it difficult to meet his direct, confronting gaze. Those observant grey eyes seemed to see more than she wanted him to. 'You're asking me to pretend to be… to pretend to be a woman in love. When…when I'm not.' She'd only ever been in love once—and she didn't want to trawl back in her memories to try and relive that feeling—love lost hurt way too much. She did have feelings for Dominic beyond the employer/contractor relationship—but they were more of the other 'l' word—lust rather than love.

His eyes seemed to darken. 'I suppose I am.'

'And you too,' she said. 'You would have to pretend to be in love with…with me. And it would have to look darn authentic to be convincing.'

This was why she was prevaricating. As soon as he'd mentioned Timothy, she knew she would have little choice but to agree. If it had been any other blackmailing billionaire she would probably have said "yes" straight away—living a lie for a month would be worth it for Timothy to get the treatment her family's combined resources couldn't afford.

But not *this* man. How could she blithely *pretend* to be in love with a man she wanted as much as she wanted him? It would be some kind of torture.

'I see,' he said. Had he seriously not thought this through?

'We would be playing with big emotions, here, Dominic. And other people would be affected too. My family thinks you hung the moon. They'd be delighted if we dated—a sudden engagement would both shock and worry them. At some stage I would have to introduce you to Anthony's parents—they would be happy for me and want to meet you.'

'I see where you're going,' he said, raking his hand through his hair once more in a gesture that was becoming familiar.

She narrowed her eyes. 'And yet…would it all be worth it for Hannah to accept your help for Timothy?' She put up her hand to stop him from replying. 'I'm thinking out loud here.'

'And helping me achieve something I really want.'

There must be something more behind his drive to get this American deal. She hoped she'd discover it one day, sooner rather than later. It might help her understand him.

'You've backed me into a corner here, Dominic, and I can't say I appreciate it. How can I say "no" to such an incredible opportunity for Timothy?'

'Does that mean your answer is "yes"?'

She tilted her chin upwards—determined not to capitulate too readily to something about which she still had serious doubts. 'That's an unusual way to put it, Dominic—rather like you've made me a genuine proposal.'

Dominic pulled a face but it didn't dull the glint of triumph in his eyes. He thought he'd won. But she was determined to get something out of this deal for herself too.

Andie had no doubt if she asked for recompense—money, gifts—he'd give it to her. Dominic was getting what he wanted. Timothy would be getting what he so desperately needed. But what about *her*?

She wasn't interested in jewellery or fancy shopping. What she wanted was *him.* She wanted to kiss him, she wanted to hold him and she very much wanted to make love with him. Not for fake—for real.

There was a very good chance this arrangement would end in tears—her tears. But if she agreed to a fake engagement with this man, who attracted her like no other, she wanted what a fiancée might be expected to have—*him.* She thought, with a little shiver of desire, about what he'd said: *pleasure all the way.* She would be fine with that.

'Would it help if I made it sound like a genuine proposal?' he said, obviously bemused.

That hurt. Because the way he spoke made it sound as if there was no way he would ever make a genuine proposal to her. Not that she wanted that—heck, she hardly knew the guy. But it put her on warning. *Let's be honest,* she thought. She wanted him in her bed. But she also wanted to make darn sure she didn't get hurt. This was just a business deal to him—nothing personal involved.

'Do it,' she said, pointing to the floor. 'The full down-on-bended-knee thing.'

'Seriously?' he said, dark brows raised.

'Yes,' she said imperiously.

He grinned. ‘Okay.’

The tall, black denim-clad hunk obediently knelt down on one knee, took her left hand in both of his and looked up into her face. ‘Andie, will you do me the honour of becoming my fake fiancée?’ he intoned in that deep, so-sexy voice.

Looking down at his roughly handsome face, Andie didn’t know whether to laugh or cry. ‘Yes, I accept your proposal,’ she said in a voice that wasn’t quite steady.

Dominic squeezed her hand hard as relief flooded his face. He got up from bended knee and for a moment she thought he might kiss her.

‘But there are conditions,’ she said, pulling away and letting go of his hand.

CHAPTER NINE

ANDIE ALMOST LAUGHED out loud at Dominic's perplexed expression. He was most likely used to calling the shots—in both business and his relationships. 'Conditions?' he asked.

'Yes, conditions,' she said firmly. 'Come on over to the sofa and I'll run through the list with you. I need to sit down; these heels aren't good for pacing in.' The polished concrete floor was all about looks rather than comfort.

'Do I have any choice about these "conditions"?' he grumbled.

'I think you'll see the sense in them,' she said. This was not going to go all his way. There was danger in this game she'd been coerced into playing and she wanted to make sure she and her loved ones were not going to get hurt by it.

She led him over to the red leather modular sofa in the living area. The apartment in an old converted factory warehouse was owned by one of her roommates and had been furnished stylishly with Andie's help. She flopped down on the sofa, kicked off the leopard stilettos that landed in an animal print clash on the zebra-patterned floor rug, and patted the seat next to her.

As Dominic sat down, his muscular thighs brushed against hers and she caught her breath until he settled at a not-quite-touching distance from her, his arm resting on the back of the sofa behind her. She had to close her eyes momentarily to deal with the rush of awareness from his already familiar scent, the sheer maleness of him in such close proximity.

'I'm interested to hear what you say,' he said, angling his powerful body towards her. He must work out a lot to have a chest like that. She couldn't help but wonder what it would feel like to splay her hands against those hard muscles, to press her body against his.

But it appeared he was having no such sensual thoughts about *her.* She noticed he gave a surreptitious glance to his watch.

'Hey, no continually checking on the clock,' she said. 'You have to give time to an engagement. Especially a make-believe one, if we're to make it believable. Not to mention your fake fiancée just might feel a tad insulted.'

She made her voice light but she meant every word of it. She had agreed to play her role in this charade and was now committed to making it work.

'Fair enough,' he said with a lazy half-smile. 'Is that one of your conditions?'

'Not one on its own as such, but it will fit into the others.'

'Okay, hit me with the conditions.' He feinted a boxer's defence that made her smile.

'Condition Number One,' she said, holding up the index finger of her left hand. 'Hannah never knows the truth—not now, not ever—that our engagement is a sham,' she said. 'In fact, none of my family is *ever* to know the truth.'

'Good strategy,' said Dominic. 'In fact, I'd extend that. *No one* should ever know. Both business partners and friends.'

'Agreed,' she said. It would be difficult to go through with this without confiding in a friend but it had to be that way. *No one must know how deeply attracted she was to him.* She didn't want anyone's pity when she and Dominic went their separate ways.

'Otherwise, the fallout from people discovering they'd been deceived could be considerable,' he said. 'What's next?'

She held up her middle finger. 'Condition Number Two—a plausible story. We need to explain why we got engaged so quickly. So start thinking…'

'Couldn't we just have fallen for each other straight away?'

Andie was taken aback. She hadn't expected anything that romantic from Dominic Hunt. 'You mean like "love at first sight"?'

'Exactly.'

'Would that be believable?'

He shook his head in mock indignation. 'Again you continue to insult me…'

'I didn't mean…' She'd certainly felt *something* for him at first sight. Sitting next to him on this sofa, she was feeling it all over again. But it wasn't *love*—she knew only too well what it was like to love. To love and to lose the man she loved in such a cruel way. Truth be told, she wasn't sure she wanted to love again. It hurt too much to lose that love.

'I don't like the lying aspect of this any more than you do,' he said. He removed his arm from the back of the sofa so he could lean closer to her, both hands resting on his knees. 'Why not stick to the truth as much as possible? You came to organise my party. I was instantly smitten, wooed you and won you.'

'And I was a complete walkover,' she said dryly.

'So we change it—you made me work very hard to win you.'

'In two weeks—and you away for one of them?' she said. 'Good in principle. But we might have to fudge the timeline a little.'

'It can happen,' he said. 'Love at first sight, I mean. My

parents…apparently they fell for each other on day one and were married within mere months of meeting. Or so my aunt told me.'

His eyes darkened and she remembered he'd only been eleven years old when left an orphan. If she'd lost her parents at that age, her world would have collapsed around her—as no doubt his had. But he was obviously trying to revive a happy memory of his parents.

'How lovely—a real-life romance. Did they meet in Australia or England?'

'London. They were both schoolteachers; my mother was living in England. She came to his school as a temporary mathematics teacher; he taught chemistry.'

Andie decided not to risk a feeble joke about their meeting being explosive. Not when the parents' love story had ended in tragedy. 'No wonder you're clever then, with such smart parents.'

'Yes,' he said, making the word sound like an end-of-story punctuation mark. She knew only too well what it was like not to want to pursue a conversation about a lost loved one.

'So we have a precedent for love at first sight in your family,' she said. 'I…I fell for Anthony straight away too. So for both of us an…an instant attraction—if not *love*—could be feasible.' Instant and ongoing for her—but he was not to know that.

That Dominic had talked about his parents surprised her. For her, thinking about Anthony—as always—brought a tug of pain to her heart but this time also a reminder of the insincerity of this venture with Dominic. She knew what real commitment should feel like. But for Timothy to get that vital treatment she was prepared to compromise on her principles.

'Love at first sight it is,' he said.

'*Attraction* at first sight,' she corrected him.

'Surely it would had to have led to love for us to get engaged,' he said.

'True,' she conceded. He tossed around concepts of love and commitment as if they were concepts with which to barter, not deep, abiding emotions between two people who cared enough about each other to pledge a lifetime together. *Till death us do part.* She could never think of that part of a marriage ceremony without breaking down. She shouldn't be thinking of it now.

'Next condition?' he said.

She skipped her ring finger, which she had trouble keeping upright, and went straight for her pinkie. 'Condition Number Three: no dating other people—for the duration of the engagement, that is.'

'I'm on board with that one,' he said without hesitation.

'Me too,' she said. She hadn't even thought about any man but Dominic since the moment she'd met him, so that was not likely to be a hardship.

He sat here next to her in jeans and T-shirt like a regular thirty-two-year-old guy—not a secretive billionaire who had involved her in a scheme to deceive family and friends to help him make even more money. If he were just your everyday handsome hunk she would make her interest in him known. But her attraction went beyond his good looks and muscles to the complex man she sensed below his confident exterior. She had seen only intriguing hints of those hidden depths—she wanted to discover more.

Andie's thumb went up next. 'Resolution Number Four: I dump you, not the other way around. When this comes to an end, that is.'

'Agreed—and I'll be a gentleman about it. But I ask you not to sell your story. I don't want to wake up one morning to the headline *"My Six Weeks with Scrooge"*.'

He could actually *joke* about being a Scrooge—Dominic had come a long way.

'Of course,' she said. 'I promise not to say *"I Hopped Out of the Billionaire's Bed"* either. Seriously, I would never talk to the media. You can be reassured of that.'

'No tacky headlines, just a simple civilised break-up to be handled by you,' he said.

They both fell silent for a moment. Did he feel stricken by the same melancholy she did at the thought of the imagined break-up of a fake engagement? And she couldn't help thinking she'd like a chance to hop *into* his bed before she hopped *out* of it.

'On to Condition Number Five,' she said, holding up all five fingers as she could not make her ring finger stand on its own. 'We have to get to know each other. So we don't get caught out on stuff we would be expected to know about each other if we were truly…committing to a life together.'

How different this fake relationship would be to a real relationship—getting to know each other over shared experiences, shared laughter, shared tears, long lazy mornings in bed…

Dominic sank down further into the sofa, his broad shoulders hunched inward. 'Yup.' It was more a grunt than a word.

'You don't sound keen to converse?'

'What sort of things?' he said with obvious reluctance. Not for the first time, she had a sense of secrets deeply held.

'For one thing, I need to know more about your marriage and how it ended.' And more about his time on the streets. And about that broken nose and scarred knuckles. And why he had let people believe he was a Scrooge when he so obviously wasn't. Strictly speaking, she probably didn't *need* to know all that about him for a fake engagement. Fact was, she *wanted* to know it.

'I guess I can talk to you about my marriage,' he said,

still not sounding convinced. 'But there are things about my life that I would rather remain private.'

What things? 'Just so long as I'm not made a fool of at some stage down the track by not knowing something a real fiancée would have known.'

'Fine,' he grunted in a response that didn't give her much confidence. She ached to know more about him. And yet there was that shadow she sensed. She wouldn't push for simple curiosity's sake.

'As far as I'm concerned, my life's pretty much an open book,' she said, in an effort to encourage him to open up about his life—or past, to be more specific. 'Just ask what you need to know about me and I'll do my best to answer honestly.'

Was any person's life truly an open book? Like anyone else, she had doubts and anxieties and dumb things she'd done that she'd regretted, but nothing lurked that she thought could hinder an engagement. No one would criticise her for finding love again after five years. In truth, she knew they would be glad for her. So would Anthony.

She remembered one day, lying together on the beach. *'I would die if I lost you,'* she'd said to Anthony.

'Don't say that,' he'd said. *'If anything happened to me, I'd want you to find another guy. But why are we talking like this? We're both going to live until we're a hundred.'*

'Why not schedule in a question-and-answer session?' Dominic said.

She pulled her thoughts back to the present. 'Good idea,' she said. 'Excellent idea, in fact.'

Dominic rolled his eyes in response.

'Oh,' she said. 'You weren't serious. I…I was.'

'No, you're right. I guess there's no room for spontaneity in a fake engagement.' It was a wonder he could get the words out when his tongue was so firmly in his cheek. 'A question-and-answer session it is. At a time to be determined.'

'Good idea,' she said, feeling disconcerted. Was all this just a game to him?

'Are there any more conditions to come?' he asked. 'You're all out of fingers on one hand, by the way.'

'There is one more very important condition to come—and may I remind you I do have ten fingers—but first I want to hear if there's anything you want to add.'

She actually had two more conditions, but the final condition she could not share with him: *that she could not fall for him*. She couldn't deal with the fallout in terms of pain if she were foolish enough to let down the guard on her heart.

Andie's beautiful green eyes had sparkled with good humour in spite of the awkward position he had put her into. *Coerced* her into. But now her eyes seemed to dim and Dominic wondered if she was being completely honest about being an 'open book'.

Ironically, he already knew more about Andie, the fake fiancée, than he'd known about Tara when he'd got engaged to her for real. His ex-wife had kept her true nature under wraps until well after she'd got the wedding band on her finger. *What you see is what you get.* He so wanted to believe that about Andie.

'My condition? You have to wear a ring,' he said. 'I want to get you an engagement ring straight away. Today. Once Tara sees that she'll know it's serious. And the press will too. Not to mention a symbol for when we meet with Walter Burton.'

She shrugged. 'Okay, you get me a ring.'

'You don't want to choose it yourself?' He was taken aback. Tara had been so avaricious about jewellery.

'No. I would find it…sad. Distressing. The day I choose

my engagement ring is the day I get engaged for real. To me, the ring should be a symbol of a true commitment, not a…a prop for a charade. But I agree—I should wear one as a visible sign of commitment.'

'I'll organise it then,' he said. He had no idea why he should be disappointed at her lack of enthusiasm. She was absolutely right—the ring would be a prop. But it would also play a role in keeping it believable. 'What size ring do you wear?'

'I haven't a clue,' she said. She held up her right hand to show the collection of tiny fine silver rings on her slender fingers. Her nails were painted cream today. 'I bought these at a market and just tried them on until I found rings that fitted.' She slid off the ring from the third finger of her right hand. 'This should do the trick.' She handed it to him. It was still warm with her body heat and he held it on his palm for a moment before pocketing it.

'What style of engagement ring would you like?' he asked.

Again she shrugged. 'You choose. It's honestly not important to me.'

A hefty carat solitaire diamond would be appropriate—one that would give her a good resale value when she went to sell it after this was all over.

'Did you choose your ex-wife's engagement ring?' Andie asked.

He scowled at the reminder that he had once got engaged for real.

Andie pulled one of her endearing faces. 'Sorry. I guess that's a sensitive issue. I know we'll come to all that in our question-and-answer session. I'm just curious.'

'She chose it herself. All I had to do was pay for it.' That alone should have alerted him to what the marriage was all about—giving her access to his money and the lifestyle it bought.

'That wasn't very...romantic,' Andie said.

'There was nothing romantic about my marriage. Shall I tell you about it now and get all that out of the way?'

'If you feel comfortable with it,' she said.

'Comfortable is never a word I would relate to that time of my life,' he said. 'It was a series of mistakes.'

'If you're ready to tell me, I'm ready to listen.' He thought about how Andie had read his mood so accurately earlier this morning—giving him breakfast when he hadn't even been aware himself that he was hungry. She was thoughtful. And kind. Kindness wasn't an attribute he had much encountered in the women he had met.

'The first mistake I made with Tara was that she reminded me of someone else—a girl I'd met when I was living in the squat. Someone frail and sweet with similar colouring—someone I'd wanted to care for and look after.' It still hurt to think of Melody. Andie didn't need to know about her.

'And the second mistake?' Andie asked, seeming to understand he didn't want to speak further about Melody. She leaned forward as if she didn't want to miss a word.

'I believed her when she said she wanted children.'

'You wanted children?'

'As soon as possible. Tara said she did too.'

Andie frowned. 'But she didn't?'

Even now, bitterness rose in his throat. 'After we'd been married a year and nothing had happened, I suggested we see a doctor. Tara put it off and put it off. I thought it was because she didn't want to admit to failure. It was quite by accident that I discovered all the time I thought we'd been trying to conceive, she'd been on the contraceptive pill.'

Andie screwed up her face in an expression of disbelief and distaste. 'That's unbelievable.'

'When I confronted her, she laughed.' He relived the horror of discovering his ex-wife's treachery and the realisation she didn't have it in her to love. Not him. Certainly not a child. Fortunately, she hadn't been clever enough to understand the sub-clauses in the pre-nuptial agreement and divorce had been relatively straightforward.

'You had a lucky escape,' Andie said.

'That's why I never want to marry again. How could I ever trust another woman after that?'

'I understand you would feel that way,' she said. 'But not every woman would be like her. Me…my sisters, my friends. I don't know anyone who would behave with such dishonesty. Don't write off all women because of one.'

Trouble was, his wealth attracted women like Tara.

He was about to try and explain that to Andie when her phone started to sound out a bar of classical music.

She got up from the sofa and headed for the kitchen countertop to pick it up. 'Gemma,' she mouthed to him. 'I'd better take it.'

He nodded, grateful for the reprieve. Tara's treachery had got him into this fake engagement scenario with Andie, who was being such a good sport about the whole thing. He did not want to waste another word, or indeed thought, on his ex. Again, he thanked whatever providence had sent Andie into his life—Andie who was the opposite of Tara in every way.

He couldn't help but overhear Andie as she chatted to Gemma. 'Yes, yes, I saw it. We were having lunch after the meeting that Friday. Yes, it does look romantic. No, I didn't know anyone took a photo.'

Andie waved him over to her. 'Shall I tell her?' she mouthed.

He gave her the thumbs-up. 'Yes,' he mouthed back as he got up. There was no intention of keeping this 'engagement' secret. He walked over closer to Andie, who was standing there in bare feet, looking more beautiful in jeans than any other woman would look in a ball gown.

'Actually, Gemma, I…haven't been completely honest with you. I…uh…we…well, Dominic and I hit it off from the moment we first saw each other.'

Andie looked to Dominic and he nodded—she was doing well.

She listened to Gemma, then spoke again. 'Yes. We are…romantically involved. In fact…well…we're engaged.' She held the phone out from her ear and even Dominic could hear the excited squeals coming from Gemma.

When the squeals had subsided, Andie spoke again. 'Yes. It is sudden. I know that. But…well…you see I've learned that you have to grab your chance at happiness when you can. I…I've had it snatched away from me before.' She paused as she listened. 'Yes, that's it. I didn't want to wait. Neither did he. Gemma, I'd appreciate it if you didn't tell anyone just yet. Eliza? Well, okay, you can tell Eliza. I'd just like to tell my family first. What was that? Yes, I'll tell him.' She shut down her phone.

'So it's out,' he said.

'Yes,' she said. 'No denying it now.'

'What did Gemma ask you to tell me?'

She looked up at him. 'That she hoped you knew what a lucky guy you are to…to catch me.'

He looked down at her. 'I know very well how lucky I am. You're wonderful in every way and I appreciate what you're doing to help me.'

For a long moment he looked down into her face—still, serious, even sombre without her usual animated expression. Her eyes were full of something he couldn't put a name to. But not, he hoped, regret.

'Thank you, Andie.'

He stepped closer. For a long moment her gaze met his and held it. He saw wariness but he also saw the stirrings of what he could only read as invitation. To kiss his pretend fiancée would probably be a mistake. But it was a mistake he badly wanted to make.

He lifted his hand to her face, brushed first the smooth skin of her cheek and then the warm softness of her lips with the back of his knuckles. She stilled. Her lips parted under his touch and he could feel the tremor that ran through her body. He dropped his hand to her shoulder, then dipped his head and claimed her mouth in a firm gentle kiss. She murmured her surprise and pleasure as she kissed him back.

CHAPTER TEN

DOMINIC WAS KISSING her and it was more wonderful than Andie ever could have imagined. His firm, sensuous mouth was sure and certain on hers and she welcomed the intimate caress, the nudging of his tongue against the seam of her lips as she opened her mouth to his. His beard growth scratched her face but it was a pleasurable kind of pain. *The man knew how to kiss.*

But as he kissed her and she kissed him back she was shocked by the sudden explosion of chemistry between them that turned something gentle into something urgent and demanding. She wound her arms around his neck to bring him closer in a wild tangle of tongues and lips as she pressed herself against his hard muscular chest. He tasted of coffee and hot male and desire. Passion this instant, this insistent was a surprise.

But it was too soon.

She knew she wanted him. But she hadn't realised until now just how *much* she wanted him. And how careful she would have to be to guard her heart. Because these thrilling kisses told her that intimate contact with Dominic Hunt might just become an addiction she would find very difficult to live without. To him, this pretend engagement was a business ploy that might also develop into an entertaining game on the side. *She did not want to be a fake fiancée with benefits.*

When it came down to it, while she had dated over the

last few years, her only serious relationship had been with a boy who had adored her, and whom she had loved with all her heart. Not a man like Dominic, who had sworn off marriage and viewed commitment so lightly he could pretend to be engaged. Her common sense urged her to stop but her body wanted more, more, more of him.

With a great effort she broke away from the kiss. Her heart was pounding in triple time, her breath coming in painful gasps. She took a deep steadying breath. And then another.

'That…that was a great start on Condition Number Six,' she managed to choke out.

Dominic towered over her; his breath came in ragged gasps. He looked so darkly sensual, her heart seemed to flip right over in her chest. 'What?' he demanded. 'Stopping when we'd just started?'

'No. I…I mean the actual kiss.'

He put his hand on her shoulder, lightly stroking her in a caress that ignited shivers of delight all through her.

'So tell me about your sixth condition,' he said, his deep voice with a broken edge to it as he struggled to control his breathing.

'Condition Number Six is that we…we have to look the part.'

He frowned. 'And that means…?'

'I mean we have to act like a genuine couple. To seem to other people as if we're…we're crazy about each other. Because it would have to be…something very powerful between us for us to get engaged so quickly. In…real life, I mean.'

She found it difficult to meet his eyes. 'I was going to say we needed to get physical. And we just did…get physical. So we…uh…know that there's chemistry between us. And that…that it works.'

He dropped his hand from her shoulder to tilt her chin

upwards with his finger so she was forced to meet his gaze. 'There was never any doubt about that.'

His words thrummed through her body. That sexual attraction had been there for her the first time she'd met him. *Had he felt it too?*

'So the sixth condition is somewhat superfluous,' she said, her voice racing as she tried to ignore the hunger for him his kiss had ignited. 'I think we might be okay, there. You know, holding hands, arms around each other. Appropriate Public Displays of Affection.' It was an effort to force herself to sound matter of fact.

'This just got to be my favourite of all your conditions,' he said slowly, his eyes narrowing in a way she found incredibly sexy. 'Shall we practise some more?'

Her traitorous body wrestled down her hopelessly outmatched common sense. 'Why not?' she murmured, desperate to be in his arms again. He pulled her close and their body contact made her aware he wanted her as much as she wanted him. She sighed as she pressed her mouth to his.

Then her phone sang out its ringtone of a piano sonata.

'Leave it,' growled Dominic.

She ignored the musical tone until it stopped. But it had brought her back to reality. There was nothing she wanted more than to take Dominic by the hand and lead him up the stairs to her bedroom. She intended to have him before this contract between them came to an end.

But that intuition she usually trusted screamed at her that to make love with him on the first day of their fake engagement would be a mistake. It would change the dynamic of their relationship to something she did not feel confident of being able to handle.

No sooner had the ringtone stopped than it started again.

Andie untangled herself from Dominic's embrace and

stepped right back from him, back from the seductive reach of his muscular arms.

'I…I have to take this,' she said.

She answered the phone but had to rest against the kitchen countertop to support knees that had gone shaky and weak. Dominic leaned back against the wall opposite her and crossed his arms against his powerful chest. His muscles flexed as he did so and she had to force herself to concentrate on the phone call.

'Yes, Eliza, it's true. I know—it must have been a surprise to you. A party?' Andie looked up to Dominic and shook her head. He nodded. She spoke to Eliza. 'No. We don't want an engagement party. Yes, I know we're party queens and it's what we do.' She rolled her eyes at Dominic and, to her relief, he smiled. 'The Christmas party is more than enough to handle at the moment,' she said to Eliza.

We. She and Dominic were a couple now. A fake couple. It would take some getting used to. So would handling the physical attraction between them.

'The wedding?' Eliza's question about the timing of the wedding flustered her. 'We…we…uh…next year some time. Yes, I know next year is only next month. The wedding won't be next month, that's for sure.' *The* wedding—wouldn't a loved-up fiancée have said *our* wedding?

She finished the call to Eliza and realised her hands were clammy. 'This is not going to be easy,' she said to Dominic.

'I never thought it would be,' he said. Was there a double meaning there?

'I have no experience in this kind of deception. The first thing Eliza asked me was when are we getting married. She put me on the spot. I…I struggled to find an answer.'

He nodded slowly. 'I suggest we say we've decided on a long engagement. That we're committed but want to use the engagement time to get to know each other better.'

'That sounds good,' she said.

The deceptive words came so easily to him while she was so flustered she could scarcely think. She realised how hopelessly mismatched they were: he was more experienced, wealthier, from a completely different background. And so willing to lie.

And yet... That kiss had only confirmed how much she wanted him.

Her phone rang out again. 'Why do I get the feeling this phone will go all day long?' she said, a note of irritation underscoring her voice. She looked on the caller ID. 'It's my fashion editor friend, Karen. I knew Gemma wouldn't be able to stop at Eliza,' she told Dominic as she answered it.

The first part of the conversation was pretty much a repeat of the conversation she'd had with Gemma. But then Karen asked should she start scouting around for her wedding dress. Karen hunted down bargain-priced clothes for her; of course she'd want to help her with a wedding. 'My wedding dress? We…uh…haven't set a date for the wedding yet. Yes, I suppose it's never too early to think about the dress. Simple? Vintage inspired? Gorgeous shoes?' She laughed and hoped Karen didn't pick up on the shrill edge to her laughter. 'You know my taste only too well, Karen. A veil? A modest lace veil? Okay. Yes. I'll leave it to you. Thank you.'

'Your friends move fast,' Dominic said when she'd disconnected the call.

'They're so thrilled for me. After…after…well, you know. My past.' Her past of genuine love, unsullied by lies and deception.

'Of course,' he said.

She couldn't bring herself to say anything about the kisses they'd shared. It wasn't the kind of thing she found easy to talk about. Neither, it appeared, did he.

He glanced down at his watch. The action drew her attention to his hands. She noticed again how attractive they were, with long strong fingers. And thought how she would like to feel them on her body. Stroking. Caressing. Exploring. *She had to stop this.*

'I know I'm breaking the terms of one of your conditions,' he said. 'But I do have to get to the office. There are cancelled meetings in other states to reschedule and staff who need to talk to me.'

'And I've got to finalise the furniture hire for the Christmas party. With two hundred people for lunch, we need more tables and chairs. It's sobering, to have all those families in need on Christmas Day.'

'Hannah assures me it's the tip of a tragic iceberg,' said Dominic.

They both paused for a long moment before she spoke. 'I also have to work on a tiaras-and-tuxedos-themed twenty-first party. Ironic, isn't it, after what we've just been saying?' But organising parties was her job and brought not only employment to her and her partners but also the caterers, the waiting staff and everyone else involved.

'I didn't think twenty-first parties were important any more, with eighteen the legal age of adulthood,' Dominic said.

'They're still very popular. This lovely girl turning twenty-one still lives at home with her parents and has three more years of university still ahead of her to become a veterinarian. I have to organise tiaras for her dogs.'

'Wh...what?' he spluttered. 'Did you say you're putting a tiara on a *dog*?'

'Her dogs are very important to her; they'll be honoured guests at the party.'

He scowled. 'I like dogs but that's ridiculous.'

'We're getting more and more bookings for dog parties.

A doggy birthday boy or girl invites their doggy friends. They're quite a thing. And getting as competitive as the kids' parties. Of course it's a learning curve for a party planner—considering doggy bathroom habits, for one thing.'

'That is the stupidest—'

Andie put up her hand. 'Don't be too quick to judge. The doggy parties are really about making the humans happy—I doubt the dogs could care less. Frivolity can be fun. Eliza and I have laid bets on how many boys will arrive wearing tiaras to the vet student's twenty-first.'

She had to smile at his bah-humbug expression.

'By the time I was twenty-one, I had established a career in real estate and had my first million in sight.'

That interested her. 'I'd love to know about—'

He cut her off. 'Let's save that for the question-and-answer session, shall we?'

'Which will start…?'

'This afternoon. Can you come to my place?'

'Sure. It doesn't hurt to visit the party site as many times as I can.'

'Only this time you'll be coming to collect your engagement ring.'

'Of…of course.' She had forgotten about that. In a way, she dreaded it. 'And to find out more about you, fake fiancé. We have to be really well briefed to face my family tomorrow evening.'

She and Anthony had joked that by the time they'd paid off their student loans all they'd be able to afford for an engagement ring would be a ring pull from a can of soft drink. The ring pull would have had so much more meaning than this cynical exercise.

She felt suddenly subdued at the thought of deceiving her family. Her friends were used to the ups and downs of dating. A few weeks down the track, they'd take a broken engagement in their stride. If those kisses were anything to go by, she might be more than a tad upset when her time with Dominic came to an end. She pummelled back down to somewhere deep inside her the shred of hope that perhaps something real could happen between them after the engagement charade was done.

'When will you tell your parents?' Dominic asked.

'Today. They'd be hurt beyond belief if they found out from someone else.'

'And you'll talk to Hannah about Timothy?'

'At the family dinner. We should speak to her and Paul together.'

'I hope she won't be too difficult to convince. I really want to help that little boy.'

'I know,' she said, thinking of how grateful her family would be to him. How glad she was she'd agreed to all this for her tiny nephew's sake. But what about Dominic's family? This shouldn't be all about hers. 'What about your aunt? Do we need to tell her?'

The shutters came slamming down. 'No. She's out of the picture.'

The way he said it let her know not to ask more. Not now anyway.

Dominic shrugged on his leather jacket in preparation to go. She stared, dumbstruck, feasting her eyes on him. *He was so hot.* She still felt awkward after their passionate kissing session. Should she reach up and kiss him on the cheek?

While she was making up her mind, he pulled her close for a brief, exciting kiss on her mouth. She doubted there could be any other type of kiss but exciting from Dominic. 'Happy to fulfil Condition Number Six at any time,' he said, very seriously.

She smiled, the tension between them immediately dissipated. But she wasn't ready to say goodbye just yet.

'Before you go…' She picked up her smartphone again. 'The first thing my friends who don't know you will want to see is a photo of my surprise new fiancé.'

He ran his hand over his unshaven chin. 'Like this? Can't it wait?'

'I like your face like that. It's hot. No need to shave on my behalf.' Without thinking, she put her fingers up to her cheek, where there was probably stubble rash. *His kiss had felt so good.*

'If you say so,' he said, looking pleased.

'Just lean against the door there,' she said. 'Look cool.'

He slouched against the door and sent her a smouldering look. The wave of want that crashed through her made her nearly drop the phone. 'Do I look *cool*?' he said in a self-mocking tone. 'I thought you liked *hot*?'

'You know exactly what I mean.' She was discovering a light-hearted side to Dominic she liked very much.

Their gazes met and they both burst into laughter. He looked even more gorgeous when he laughed, perfect teeth white in his tanned face, and she immediately captured a few more images of him. Who would recognise this good-humoured hunk in jeans and leather jacket as the billionaire Scrooge of legend?

'What about a selfie of us together?' she asked. 'In the interests of authenticity,' she hastily added.

Bad idea. She stood next to him, aware of every centimetre of body contact, and held her phone out in front of them. She felt more self-conscious than she could ever remember feeling. He pulled her in so their faces were close together. She smiled and clicked, and as she clicked again he kissed her on the cheek.

'That will be cute,' she said.

'Another?' he asked. This time he kissed her on the mouth. *Click. Click. Click.* And then she forgot to click.

After he had left, Andie spent more minutes than she should scrolling through the photos on her phone. *No one would know they were faking it.*

CHAPTER ELEVEN

DOMINIC NOW KNEW more about diamond engagement rings than even a guy who was genuinely engaged to be married needed to know. He'd thought he could just march into Sydney's most exclusive jewellery store and hand over an investment-sized price for a big chunk of diamond. Not so.

The sales guy—rather, *executive consultant*—who had greeted him and ushered him into a private room had taken the purchase very seriously. He'd hit Dominic with a barrage of questions. It was unfortunate that the lady was unable to be there because it was very important the ring would suit her personality. What were the lady's favourite colours? What style of clothes did she favour? Her colouring?

'Were you able to answer the questions?' Andie asked, her lips curving into her delightful smile.

She had just arrived at his house. After she'd taken some measurements in the old ballroom, he had taken her out to sit in the white Hollywood-style chairs by the pool. Again, she looked as if she belonged. She wore a natural-coloured linen dress with her hair piled up and a scarf twisted and tied right from the base of her neck to the top of her head. It could have looked drab and old-fashioned but, on her, with her vintage sunglasses and orange lipstick, it looked just right.

Last time she'd been there he'd been so caught up with her he hadn't thought to ask her would she like a drink.

He didn't want a live-in housekeeper—he valued his privacy too much—but his daily housekeeper had been this morning and the refrigerator was well stocked. He'd carried a selection of cool drinks out to the poolside table between their two chairs.

'You're finding this story amusing, aren't you?' he said, picking up his iced tea.

She took off her sunglasses. 'Absolutely. I had no idea the rigmarole involved in buying an engagement ring.'

'Me neither. I thought I'd just march in, point out a diamond ring and pay for it.' This was a first for him.

'Me too,' said Andie. 'I thought that's what guys did when they bought a ring.'

'Oh, no. First of all, I'd done completely the wrong thing in not having you with me. He was too discreet to ask where you were, so I didn't have to come up with a creative story to explain your absence.'

'One less lie required anyway,' she said with a twist of her lovely mouth. 'Go on with the story—I'm fascinated.'

'Apparently, the done thing is to have a bespoke ring—like the business suits I have made to measure.'

'A bespoke ring? Who knew?' she said, her eyes dancing.

'Instead, I had to choose from their ready-to-wear couture pieces.'

'I had no idea such a thing existed,' she said with obvious delight. *Her smile*. It made him feel what he'd thought he'd never feel again, made him want what he'd thought he'd never want.

'You should have been there,' he said. 'You would have had fun.' He'd spent the entire time in the jewellery store wishing she'd been by his side. He could imagine her suppressing giggles as the consultant had run through his over-the-top sales pitch.

'Perhaps,' she said, but her eyes dimmed. 'You know

my reasons for not wanting to get involved in the purchase. Anyway, what did you tell them about my—' she made quote marks in the air with her fingers '—"personal style"? That must have put you on the spot?'

'I told the consultant about your misbehaving skirt—only I didn't call it that, of course. I told him about your shoes that laced up your calves. I told him about your turquoise necklace and your outsized earrings. I told him about your leopard-print shoes and your white trousers.'

Andie's eyes widened. 'You remember all that about what I wear?'

'I did say I was observant,' he said.

Ask him to remember what Party Planners Numbers One to Three had been wearing for their interviews and he would scarcely recall it. But he remembered every detail about her since that errant breeze at his front door had blown Andie into his life.

At the jewellery store, once he'd relaxed into the conversation with the consultant, Dominic had also told him how Andie was smart and creative and a touch unconventional and had the most beautiful smile and a husky, engaging laugh. 'This is a lucky lady,' the guy had said. 'You must love her very much.'

That had thrown Dominic. 'Yes,' he'd muttered. *Love* could not enter into this. He did not want Andie to get hurt. And hurt wasn't on his personal agenda either. He didn't think he had it in him to love. To give love you had to be loved—and genuine love was not something that had been part of his life.

'So… I'm curious,' said Andie. What kind of ring did you—did I—end up with?'

'Not the classic solitaire I would have chosen. The guy said you'd find it boring.'

'Of course I wouldn't have found it boring,' she said not very convincingly.

'Why do I not believe you?' he said.

'Stop teasing me and show me the darn ring,' she said.

Dominic took out the small, leather, case from his inside suit jacket pocket. 'I hope you like it,' he said. *He wanted her to like it.* He didn't know why it was suddenly so important that she did.

He opened the case and held it out for Andie to see. Her eyes widened and she caught her breath. 'It…it's exquisite,' she said.

'Is it something you think you could wear?' he asked.

'Oh, yes,' she said. 'I love it.'

'It's called a halo set ring,' he said. 'The ring of little diamonds that surround the big central diamond is the halo. And the very narrow split band—again set with small diamonds—is apparently very fashionable.'

'That diamond is enormous,' she said, drawing back. 'I'd be nervous to wear it.'

'I got it well insured,' he said.

'Good,' she said. 'If I lost it, I'd be paying you back for the rest of my life and probably still be in debt.'

'The ring is yours, Andie.'

'I know, for the duration,' she said. 'I promise to look after it.' She crossed her heart.

'You misunderstand. The ring is yours to keep after… after all this has come to an end.'

She frowned and shook her head vehemently. 'No. That wasn't part of the deal. Timothy's treatment was the deal. I give this ring back to you when…when I dump you.'

'We'll see about that,' he said, not wanting to get into an argument with her. As far as he was concerned, this ring was *hers*. She could keep it or sell it or give it away—he never wanted it back. 'Now, shouldn't I be getting that diamond on your finger?'

He was surprised to find his hand wasn't steady as he took the ring out of its hinged case. It glittered and sparkled as the afternoon sunlight danced off the multi-cut facets of the diamonds. 'Hold out your hand,' he said.

'No', she said, again shaking her head. 'Give it to me and I'll put it on myself. This isn't a real engagement and I don't want to jinx myself. When I get engaged for real, my real fiancé will put my ring on my wedding finger.'

Again, Dominic felt disappointed. Against all reason. He wanted to put the ring on her finger. But he understood why he shouldn't. He felt a pang of regret that he most likely would never again be anyone's 'real fiancé'—and a pang of what he recognised as envy for the man who would win Andie's heart for real.

He put the ring back in its case. 'You do want to get married one day?'

He wasn't sure if she was still in love with the memory of her first boyfriend—and that no man would be able to live up to that frozen-in-time ideal. Melody had been his first love—but he certainly held no romanticised memories of her.

'Of course I do. I want to get married and have a family. I…I… It took me a long time to get over the loss of my dreams of a life with Anthony. I couldn't see myself with anyone but him. But that was five years ago. Now… I think I'm ready to move on.'

Dominic had to clear his throat to speak. 'Okay, I see your point. Better put on the ring yourself,' he said.

Tentatively, she lifted the ring from where it nestled in the velvet lining of its case. 'I'm terrified I'll drop it and it will fall into the pool.' She laughed nervously as she slid it on to the third finger of her left hand. 'There—it's on.' She held out her hand, fingers splayed to better display the ring. 'It's a perfect fit,' she said. 'You did well.'

'It looks good on you,' he said.

'That sales guy knew his stuff,' she said. 'I can't stop looking at it. It's the most beautiful ring I've ever seen.'

She looked up at him. 'I still have my doubts about the wisdom of this charade. But I will enjoy wearing this magnificent piece of jewellery. Thank you for choosing something so perfect.'

'Thank you for helping me out with this crazy scheme,' he said. The scheme that had seemed crazy the moment he'd proposed it and which got crazier and crazier as it went along. But it was important he sealed that deal with Walter Burton. And was it such a bad thing to have to spend so much time with Andie?

Andie took a deep breath to try and clear her head of the conflicting emotions aroused by wearing the exquisite ring that sat so perfectly on her finger. *The ring pull would have been so much more valuable.* This enormous diamond with its many surrounding tiny diamonds symbolised not love and commitment but the you-scratch-my-back-and-I'll-scratch-yours deal between her and Dominic.

Still, she couldn't help wondering how he could have chosen a ring so absolutely *her.*

'I've been thinking about our getting-to-know-each-other session,' she said. 'Why don't we each ask the other three questions?'

'Short and to the point,' he said with obvious relief.

'Or longer, as needs might be. I want to be the best fake fiancée I can. No way do I want to be caught out on something important I should know about you. I didn't like the feeling this morning when I froze as Karen questioned me about our wedding plans.'

Dominic drank from his iced tea. To give himself time to think? Or plan evasive action? 'I see where you're going. Let's see if we can make it work.'

Andie settled back in the chair. She didn't know whether to be disappointed or relieved there was a small table between her and Dominic. She would not be averse to his thigh nudged against hers—at the same time, it would undoubtedly be distracting. 'Okay. I'll start. My Question Number One is: How did you get from street kid to billionaire?'

Dominic took his time to put his glass back down on the table. 'Before I reply, let's get one thing straight.' His gaze was direct. 'My answers are for you and you alone. What I tell you is to go no further.'

'Agreed,' she said, meeting his gaze full-on. 'Can we get another thing straight? You can trust me.'

'Just so long as we know where we stand.'

'I'm surprised you're not making me sign a contract.' She said the words half in jest but the expression that flashed across his face in response made her pause. She sat forward in her seat. 'You thought about a contract, didn't you?'

With Dominic back in his immaculate dark business suit, clean-shaven, hair perfectly groomed, she didn't feel as confident with him as she had this morning.

'I did think of a contract and quickly dismissed it,' he said. 'I do trust you, Andie.'

Surely he must be aware that she would not jeopardise Timothy's treatment in any way? 'I'm glad to hear that, Dominic, because this won't work if we don't trust each other—it goes both ways. Let's start. C'mon—answer my question.'

He still didn't answer. She waited, aware of the palm leaves above rustling in the same slight breeze that ruffled the aquamarine surface of the pool, the distant barking of a neighbour's dog.

'You know I hate this?' he said finally.

'I kind of get that,' she said. 'But I couldn't "marry" a man whose past remained a dark secret to me.'

Even after the question-and-answer session, she suspected big chunks of his past might remain a secret from her. Maybe from anyone.

He dragged in a deep breath as if to prepare himself for something unpleasant. 'As I have already mentioned, at age seventeen, I was homeless. I was living in an underground car park on the site of an abandoned shopping centre project in one of the roughest areas of Brisbane. The buildings had only got to the foundation stage. The car park was…well, you can imagine what an underground car park that had never been completed was like. It was a labyrinth of unfinished service areas and elevator shafts. No lights, pools of water whenever it rained, riddled with rats and cockroaches.'

'And human vermin too, I'll bet.' Andie shuddered. 'What a scary place for a teenager to be living—and dangerous.'

He had come from such a dark place. She could gush with sympathy and pity. But she knew instinctively that was not what he wanted to hear. Show how deeply moved she was at the thought of seventeen-year-old Dominic living such a perilous life and he would clam up. And she wanted to hear more.

Dominic's eyes assumed a dark, faraway look as though he was going back somewhere in his mind he had no desire to revisit. 'It was dangerous and smelly and seemed like hell. But it was also somewhere safer to sleep than on the actual streets. Darkness meant shadows you could hide in, and feel safe even if it was only an illusion of safety.'

She reached out and took the glass from his hand; he seemed unaware he was gripping it so tightly he might break it. 'Your home life must have been kind of hellish too for you to have preferred that over living with your aunt.'

'Hell? You could say that.' The grim set of his mouth let her know that no more would be forthcoming on that subject.

'Your life on the streets must have been…terrifying.'

'I toughened up pretty quick. One thing I had in my favour was I was big—the same height I am now and strong from playing football at school. It was a rough-around-the-edges kind of school, and I'd had my share of sorting out bullies there.' He raised his fists into a fighting position in a gesture she thought was unconscious.

So scratch the elite private school. She realised now that Dominic was a self-made man. And his story of triumph over adversity fascinated her. 'So you could defend yourself against thugs and…and predators.'

Her heart went out to him. At seventeen she'd had all the security of a loving family and comfortable home. But she knew first-hand from her foster sisters that not all young people were that fortunate. It seemed that the young Dominic had started off with loving parents and a secure life but had spiralled downwards from then on. What the heck was wrong with the aunt to have let that happen?

She reached over the table and trailed her fingers across his scarred knuckles. 'That's how you got these?' It was amazing the familiarity a fake engagement allowed.

'I got in a lot of fights,' he said.

'And this?' She traced the fine scar at the side of his mouth.

'Another fight,' he said.

She dropped her hands to her sides, again overwhelmed by that urge to comfort him. 'You were angry and frightened.'

He shifted uncomfortably in his seat. 'All that.'

'But then you ended up with this.' She waved her hand to encompass the immaculate art deco pool, the expensively landscaped gardens, the superb house. It was an oasis of beauty and luxury.

'My fighting brought me to the attention of the police. I was charged with assault,' he said bluntly.

She'd thought his tough exterior was for real—had sensed the undercurrents of suppressed rage.

'Believe me, the other guy deserved it,' he said with an expression of grim satisfaction. 'He was drug-dealing scum.'

'What happened? With the police, I mean.' He'd been seventeen—still a kid. All she'd been fighting at that age was schoolgirl drama.

'I got lucky. The first piece of luck was that I was under eighteen and not charged as an adult. The second piece of luck was I was referred to a government social worker—Jim, his name was. Poor man, having to deal with the sullen, unhappy kid I was then couldn't have been easy. Jim was truly one of the good guys—still is. He won my confidence and got me away from that squat, to the guidance of another social worker friend of his down the Queensland Gold Coast.'

'Sun, surf and sand,' she said. She knew it sounded flippant but Dominic would not want her to pity his young self.

'And a booming real estate market. The social worker down there was a good guy too. He got me a job as a gofer in a real estate agency. I was paid a pittance but it was a start and I liked it there. To cut a long story short, I was soon promoted to the sales team. I discovered I was good at selling the lifestyle dream, not just the number of bedrooms and bathrooms. I became adept at gauging what was important to the client.'

'Because you were observant,' she said. And tough and resilient and utterly admirable.

'That's important. Especially when I realised the role the woman played in a residential sale. Win her over and you more than likely closed the sale.'

Andie could see how those good looks, along with intuition and charm and the toughness to back it up, could have accelerated him ahead. 'Fascinating. And incredible how you've kept all the details away from the public. Surely people must have tried to research you, would have wanted to know your story?'

'As a juvenile, my record is sealed. I've never spoken about it. It's a time of my life I want well behind me. Without Jim the social worker, I might have gone the other way.'

'You mean you could have ended up as a violent thug or a drug dealer? I don't believe that for a second.'

He shrugged those broad street-fighter shoulders. 'I appreciate your faith in me. But, like so many of my fellow runaways, I could so easily have ended up…broken.'

Andie struggled to find an answer to that. 'It…it's a testament to your strength of character that you didn't.'

'If you say,' he said. But he looked pleased. 'Once I'd made enough money to have my own place and a car—nowhere as good as your hatchback, I might add—I started university part-time. I got lucky again.'

'You passed with honours?' She hadn't seen a university degree anywhere in her research on him but there was no harm in asking.

'No. I soon realised I knew more about making money and how business operated than some of the teachers in my commerce degree. I dropped out after eighteen months. But in a statistics class I met Jake Marlow. He was a brilliant, misunderstood geek. Socially, I still considered myself an outcast. We became friends.'

'And business partners, you said.' He was four years older than she was, and yet had lived a lifetime more. And had overcome terrible odds to get where he had.

'He was playing with the concept of ground-breaking online business software tools but no bank would loan him the money to develop them. I was riding high on commissions. We set up a partnership. I put in the money he needed. I could smell my first million.'

'Let me guess—it was an amazing success?'

'That software is used by thousands of businesses around the world to manage their digital workflow. We made a lot of money very quickly. Jake is still developing successful new software.' His obvious pride in his friend warmed his words.

'And you're still business partners.'

He nodded. 'The success of our venture gave me the investment dollars I needed to also spin off into my own separate business developing undervalued homemaker centres. We call them bulky goods centres—furnishing, white goods, electricals.'

'I guess the Gold Coast got too small for you.' That part she'd been able to research.

'I moved to Sydney. You know the rest.'

In silence she drank her mineral water with lime, he finished his iced tea. He'd given her a lot to think about. Was that anger that had driven him resolved? Or could it still be bubbling under the surface, ready to erupt?

He angled himself to look more directly at her. 'Now it's your turn to answer my question, Andie,' he said. 'How did you get over the death of your…of Anthony?'

She hadn't been expecting that and it hit her hard. But he'd dug deep. She had to too. 'I… I don't know that I will ever be able to forget the shock of it. One minute he was there, the next minute gone. I… I was as good as a widow, before I'd had the chance to be a bride.'

Dominic nodded, as if he understood. Of course he'd lost his parents.

'We were staying the weekend at his parents' beach house at Whale Beach. Ant got up very early, left a note to say he'd gone surfing, kissed me—I was asleep but awake enough to know he was going out—and then he was gone. Of course I blamed myself for not going with him. Then I was angry he'd gone out by himself.'

'Understandably,' he said and she thought again how he

seemed to see more than other people. She had no deep, dark secrets. But, if she did, she felt he'd burrow down to them without her even realising it.

'After Anthony died, I became terrified of the sea. I hated the waves—blamed them for taking him from me, which I know was all kinds of irrational. Then one day I went to the beach by myself and sat on the sand. I remember hugging my knees as I watched a teenage boy, tall and blond like Anthony, ride a wave all the way into the shore, saw the exultation on his face, the sheer joy he felt at being one with the wave.'

'If this is bringing back hurtful memories, you don't have to go any further.'

'I'm okay… When someone close dies, you look for a sign from them—I learned I wasn't alone in that when I had counselling. That boy on his board was like a message from Anthony. He died doing something he truly loved. I ran into the surf and felt somehow connected to him. It was a healing experience, a turning point in my recovery from grief.'

'That's a powerful story,' Dominic said.

'The point of it is, it's five years since he died and of course I've moved on. Anyone who might wonder if my past could affect our fake future can be assured of that. Anthony was part of my youth; we grew up together. In some ways I'm the person I am because of those happy years behind me. But I want happy years ahead of me too. I've dated. I just haven't met the right person.'

For the first time she wondered if she could feel more for Dominic than physical attraction. For a boy who had been through what he had and yet come through as the kind of man who offered to pay for a little boy's medical treatment? Who was more willing to open his house to disadvantaged people than celebrities? There was so much more to Dominic than she ever could have imagined—and the more she found out about him the more she liked about him.

And then there were those kisses she had not been able to stop thinking about—and yearning for more.

'I appreciate you telling me,' he said.

She poured herself another long, cool mineral water. Offered to pour one for Dominic, but he declined.

'On to my next question,' she said. 'It's about your family. Do you have family other than your aunt? My mother will certainly want to know because she's already writing the guest list for the wedding.'

'You told your mother about the engagement?'

'She couldn't be more delighted. In fact…well…she got quite tearful.' Andie had never felt more hypocritical than the moment she realised her mother was crying tears of joy for her.

'That's a relief,' he said.

'You could put it that way. I didn't realise quite how concerned they were about me being…lonely. Not that I am lonely, by the way—I have really good friends.' But it was not the same as having a special someone.

'I'm beginning to see that,' he said. 'I'm surprised we've been able to have this long a conversation without your phone going off.'

'That's because I switched it off,' she said. 'There'll probably be a million messages when I switch it back on.'

'So your mother didn't question our…haste?'

'No. And any guilt I felt about pulling the wool over her eyes I forced firmly to the back of my mind. Timothy getting the treatment he needs is way more important to my family than me finding a man.' She looked at him. 'So now—the guest list, your family?'

'My aunt and my mother were the only family each other had. So there is no Australian family.'

'Your aunt has…has passed away?' There was something awkward here that she didn't feel comfortable probing. But they were—supposedly—planning to get married. It made sense for her to know something of his family.

'She's in the best of residential care, paid for by me. That's all I want to say about her.'

'Okay,' she said, shaken by the closed look on his face.

'I have family in the UK but no one close since my grandparents died.'

'So no guests from your side of the family for our imaginary wedding?'

'That's right. And I consider the subject closed. In fact, I've had a gutful of talking about this stuff.'

'Me too,' she said. Hearing about his difficult youth, remembering her early loss was making her feel down. 'I reckon we know enough about each other now to be able to field any questions that are thrown at us. After all, we're not pretending to have known each other for long.'

She got up from her chair, walked to the edge of the pool, knelt at the edge and swished her hand through the water. 'This is such a nice pool. Do you use it much?'

'Most days I swim,' he said, standing behind her. 'There's a gym at the back of the cabana too.'

She imagined him working out in his gym, then plunging into the pool, muscles pumped, spearing through the water in not many clothes, maybe in *no* clothes.

Stop it!

She got up, wishing she could dive in right now to cool herself down. 'Do you like my idea to hire some lifeguards so the guests can swim on Christmas Day?'

'It's a good one.'

'And you're okay with putting a new swimsuit and towel in each of the children's goody bags? Hannah pointed out that some of the kids might not have a swimsuit.'

'I meant to talk to you about that,' he said. Surely he wasn't going to query the cost of the kids' gifts? She would be intensely disappointed if he did. 'I want to buy each of the adults a new swimsuit too; they might not have one either,' he said. 'I don't want anyone feeling excluded for any reason we can avoid.'

She looked up at him. 'You're not really a Scrooge, are you?'

'No,' he said.

'I don't think people are going to be calling you that for much longer. Certainly not if I've got anything to do with it.'

'But not a word about my past.'

'That's understood,' she said, making a my-lips-are-sealed zipping motion over her mouth. 'Though I think you might find people would admire you for having overcome it.'

The alarm on her watch buzzed. 'I'm running late,' she said. 'I didn't realise we'd been talking for so long.'

'You have an appointment? I was going to suggest dinner.'

'No can do, I'm afraid.' Her first impulse was to cancel her plans, to jump at the opportunity to be with Dominic. But she would not put her life on hold for the fake engagement.

'I have a hot date with a group of girlfriends. It's our first Tuesday of the month movie club. We see a movie and then go to dinner. We're supposed to discuss the movie but we mainly catch up on the gossip.' She held out her hand, where the diamond flashed on the third finger of her left hand. 'I suspect this baby is going to be the main topic of conversation.'

She made to go but, before she could, Dominic had pulled her close for a kiss that left not a scrap of lipstick on her mouth and her hair falling out of its knot.

It was the kind of kiss she could get used to.

CHAPTER TWELVE

ANDIE SAT AT her desk in the Party Queens' headquarters. 'Headquarters' was rather a grand term for their premises. It comprised an industrial kitchen where Gemma could do her thing; a workroom used for making props; a storage area; and an area loosely termed an office, where she and her two partners squeezed in their desks.

To say they were frantically busy would be an understatement. The weeks leading up to Christmas and New Year were the busiest time of the year for established party planners. For a new company like Party Queens to be so busy was gratifying. But it was the months after the end of the long Aussie summer vacation they had to worry about for advance bookings. Business brain, Eliza, was very good at reminding them of that.

Andie's top priority was Dominic's Christmas party. Actually, it was no longer just his party. As his fiancée, she had officially become co-host. But that didn't mean she wasn't flat-out with other bookings, including a Christmas Eve party for the parents of their first eighteenth party girl. Andie wanted to pull out all the stops for the people who'd given Party Queens their very first job. And then there was the business of being Dominic's fake fiancée—almost a job on its own.

Andie had been 'engaged' to Dominic for ten days and so far so good. She'd been amazed that no one had seriously queried the speed at which she had met, fallen in love with and agreed to marry a man she had known for less than a month.

The swooning sighs of 'love at first sight' and 'how romantic' from her girlfriends she understood, not so much the delight from her pragmatic father and the tears of joy from her mother. She hardly knew Dominic and yet they were prepared to believe she would commit her life to him?

Of course it was because her family and friends had been worried about her, wanted her to be happy, had been concerned she had grieved for Anthony for too long.

'Your dad and I are pleased for you, sweetheart, we really are,' her mother had said. 'We were worried you were so fearful about loving someone again in case you lost them, that you wouldn't let yourself fall in love again,' she'd continued. 'But Dominic is so strong, so right for you; I guess he just broke through those barriers you'd spent so long putting up. And I understand you didn't want to waste time when you knew what it was like to have a future snatched away from you.'

Really? She'd put up *barriers*? She'd just been trying to find someone worthy of stepping into Anthony's shoes. Now she'd found a man who had big boots of his own and would never walk in another man's shadow. *But he wasn't really hers.*

'You put us off the scent by telling us Dominic wasn't your type,' Gemma had said accusingly. Gemma, who was already showing her ideas for a fabulous wedding cake she planned to bake and decorate for her when the time came. Andie felt bad going through images of multi-tiered pastel creations with Gemma, knowing the cake was never going to happen.

Condition Number One, that she and Dominic didn't *ever* tell *anyone* about the deception, seemed now like a very good idea. To hear that their engagement had been a cold-blooded business arrangement was never going to go down well with all these people wishing them well.

At last Wednesday's family dinner, Dominic had been joyfully welcomed into the Newman family. 'I'm glad you saw sense about how hot he was,' her sister Bea had said, hugging her. 'And as for that amazing rock on your finger… Does Dominic have a brother? No? Well, can you find me someone just like him, please?'

But every bit of deception was all worth it for Timothy. After the family dinner, Andie and Dominic had drawn Hannah and Paul aside. Now that Dominic was to be part of the family—or so they thought—her sister and her husband didn't take much convincing to accept Dominic's offer of paying all Timothy's medical expenses.

Dominic's only condition was that they kept him posted on their tiny son's progress. 'Of course we will,' Hannah had said, 'but Andie will keep you updated and you'll see Timothy at family functions. You'll always be an important part of his life.' And the little boy had more chance of a better life, thanks to Dominic's generosity.

Later, Hannah had hugged her sister tight. 'You've got yourself a good man, Andie, a very, very good man.'

'I know,' said Andie, choked up and cringing inside. She was going to have to come up with an excellent reason to explain why she 'dumped' Dominic when his need for the fake engagement was over.

There had only been one awkward moment at the dinner. Her parents wanted to put an announcement of the engagement in the newspaper. 'Old-fashioned, I know, but it's the right thing to do,' her mother had said.

She'd then wanted to know what Dominic's middle name was for the announcement. Apparently full names were required, Andrea Jane Newman was engaged to Dominic *who*?

She had looked at Dominic, eyes widened by panic.

She should have known that detail about the man she was supposedly going to marry.

Dominic had quickly stepped in. 'I've kept quiet about my middle name because I don't like it very much,' he'd said. 'It's Hugo. Dominic Hugo Hunt.'

Of course everyone had greeted that announcement with cries of how much they loved the name Hugo. 'You could call your first son Hugo,' Bea had suggested.

That was when Andie had decided it was time to go home. She felt so low at deceiving everyone, she felt she could slink out of the house at ankle level. If it wasn't for Timothy, she would slide that outsize diamond off her finger and put an end to this whole deception.

Dominic had laughed the baby comment off—and made no further mention of it. He'd wanted a baby with his first wife—how did he feel about children now?

Her family was now expecting babies from her and Dominic. She had not anticipated having to handle that expectation. But of course, since then, the image of a dear little boy with black spiky hair and grey eyes kept popping into her mind. A little boy who would be fiercely loved and never have to face the hardships his father had endured.

She banished the bordering on insane thoughts to the area of her brain reserved for impossible dreams. Instead, she concentrated on confirming the delivery date of two hundred and ten—the ten for contingencies—small red-and-white-striped hand-knitted Christmas stockings for Dominic's party. They would sit in the centre of each place setting and contain all the cutlery required by that person for the meal.

She had decided on a simple red-and-white theme, aimed squarely at pleasing children as well as the inner child of the adults. Tables would be set up in the ballroom for a sit-down meal served from a buffet. She wanted it to be as magical and memorable as a Christmas lunch in the home of a billionaire should be—but without being intimidating.

Gemma had planned fabulous cakes, shaped and frosted like an outsize white candle and actually containing a tea light, to be the centrepiece of each table. Whimsical Santa-themed cupcakes would sit at each place with the name of the guest piped on the top. There would be glass bowls of candy canes and masses of Australian Christmas bush with its tiny red flowers as well as bowls of fat red cherries.

Andie would have loved to handle all the decorations herself but it was too big a job. She'd hired one of her favourite stylists to coordinate all the decorations. Jeremy was highly creative and she trusted his skills implicitly. And, importantly, he'd been happy to work on Christmas Day.

She'd been careful not to discuss anything too 'Christmassy' with Dominic, aware of his feelings about the festive season. He still hadn't shared with her just why he hated it so much; she wondered if he ever would. There was some deep pain there, going right back to his childhood, she suspected.

The alarm on her computer flashed a warning at her the same time the alarm on her watch buzzed. Not that she needed any prompts to alert her that she was seeing Dominic this evening.

He had been in meetings with Walter Burton all afternoon. Andie was to join them for dinner. At her suggestion, the meal was to be at Dominic's house. Andie felt that a man like Walter might prefer to experience home-style hospitality; he must be sick of hotels and restaurants. Not that Dominic's house was exactly the epitome of cosy, but it was elegant and beautiful and completely lacking in any brash, vulgar display of wealth.

A table set on the terrace at the front of the house facing the harbour. A chef to prepare the meal. A skilled waiter to serve them. All organised by Party Queens with a menu devised by Gemma. Eliza had, as a matter of course, checked with Walter's personal assistant as to the tycoon's personal dietary requirements.

Then there would be Andie, on her best fiancée behaviour. After all, Mr Burton's preference for doing business with a married man was the reason behind the fake engagement.

Not that she had any problem pretending to be an attentive fiancée. That part of the role came only too easily. Her heartbeat accelerated just at the thought of seeing Dominic this evening. He'd been away in different states on business and she'd only seen him a few times since the family dinner. She checked her watch again. There was plenty of time to get home to Newtown and then over to Vaucluse before the guest of honour arrived.

Dominic had been in Queensland on business and only flown back into Sydney last night. He'd met Walter Burton from a very early flight from the US this morning. After an afternoon of satisfactory meetings, Dominic had taken him back to his hotel. The American businessman would then make his own way to Vaucluse for the crucial dinner with Dominic and Andie.

As soon as he let himself in through the front door of the house Dominic sensed a difference. There was a subtle air of expectation, of warmth. The chef and his assistant were in the kitchen and, if enticing aromas had anything to do with it, dinner was under way. Arrangements of exotic orchids were discreetly arranged throughout the house. That was thanks to Andie.

It was all thanks to Andie. He would have felt uncomfortable hosting Walter Burton in his house if it weren't for her. He would have taken him to an upscale restaurant, which would have been nice but not the same. The older man had been very pleased at the thought of being invited to Dominic's home.

And now here she was, heading towards him from the terrace at the eastern end of the house where they would dine. He caught his breath at how beautiful she looked in a body-hugging cream top and matching long skirt that wrapped across the front and revealed, as she walked, tantalising glimpses of long slender legs and high heeled ankle-strap sandals. Her hair was up, but tousled strands fell around her face. Her only jewellery was her engagement ring. With her simple elegance, again she looked as if she belonged in this house.

'You're home,' she said in that husky voice, already so familiar.

Home. That was the difference in his house this evening. *Andie's presence made it a home.* And he had not felt he'd had a real home for a long time.

But Andie and her team were temporary hired help—she the lead actress in a play put on for the benefit of a visiting businessman. *This was all just for show.*

Because of Walter Burton, because there were strangers in the house, they had to play their roles—he the doting fiancé and she his betrothed.

Andie came close, smiling, raised her face for his kiss. Was that too for show? Or because she was genuinely glad to see him? At the touch of her lips, hunger for her instantly ignited. He closed his eyes as he breathed in her sweet, spicy scent, not wanting to let her go.

A waiter passed by on his way to the outdoor terrace, with a tray of wine glasses.

'I've missed you,' Andie murmured. For the waiter's benefit or for Dominic's? She sounded convincing but he couldn't be sure.

'Me too—missed you, I mean,' he said stiffly, self-consciously.

That was the trouble with this deception he had initiated. It was only too easy to get caught between a false intimacy and an intimacy that could possibly be real. Or could it? He broke away from her, stepped back.

'Is this another misbehaving skirt?' he asked.

He resisted the urge to run his hand over the curve of her hip. It would be an appropriate action for a fiancé but stepping over the boundaries of his agreement with Andie. Kisses were okay—their public displays of affection had to look authentic. Caresses of a more intimate nature, on the other hand, were *not* okay.

She laughed. 'No breeze tonight so we'll never know.' She lowered her voice. 'Is there anything else you need to brief me about before Mr Burton arrives? I've read through the background information you gave me. I think I'm up to speed on what a fiancée interested in her future husband's work would most likely know.'

'Good,' he said. 'I have every faith you won't let me down. If you're not sure of anything, just keep quiet and I'll cover for you. Not that I think I'll have to do that.'

'Fingers crossed I do you proud,' she said.

Walter Burton arrived punctually—Dominic would have been surprised if he hadn't. The more time he spent with his prospective joint venture partner, the more impressed he was by his acumen and professionalism. *He really wanted this deal.*

Andie greeted the older man with warmth and charm. Straight away he could see Walter was impressed.

She led him to the front terrace where the elegantly set round table—the right size for a friendly yet business orientated meal—had been placed against a backdrop of Sydney Harbour, sparkling blue in the light of the long summer evening. As they edged towards the longest day on December the twenty-second, it did not get dark until after nine p.m.

Christmas should be cold and dark and frosty. He pushed the painful thought away. Dwelling on the past was not appropriate here, not when an important deal hung in the balance.

Andie was immediately taken with Walter Burton. In his mid-sixties and of chunky build, his silver hair and close-trimmed silver beard gave him an avuncular appearance. His pale blue eyes actually sparkled and she had to keep reminding herself that he could not be as genial as he appeared and be such a successful tycoon.

But his attitude to philanthropy was the reason she was here, organising the party, pretending to be Dominic's betrothed. He espoused the view that making as much money as you could was a fine aim—so long as you remembered to share it with those who had less. 'It's a social responsibility,' he said.

Dominic had done nothing but agree with him. There was not a trace of Scrooge in anything he said. Andie had begun to believe the tag was purely a media invention.

Walter—he insisted she drop the 'Mr Burton'—seemed genuinely keen to hear all the details of the Christmas party. He was particularly interested when she told him Dominic had actively sought to dampen press interest. That had, as intended, flamed media interest. They already had two journalists volunteer to help out on that day—quite an achievement considering most people wanted to spend it with their families or close friends.

Several times during the meal, Andie squeezed Dominic's hand under the table—as a private signal that she thought the evening was going well. His smile in return let her know he thought so too. The fiancée fraud appeared to be doing the trick.

The waiter had just cleared the main course when Walter sat back in his chair, relaxed, well fed and praising the excellent food. Andie felt she and Dominic could also finally relax from the knife-edge of tension required to impress the American without revealing the truth of their relationship.

So Walter's next conversational gambit seemed to come from out of the blue. 'Of course you understand the plight of your Christmas Day guests, Dominic, as you've come from Struggle Street yourself,' he said. 'Yet you do your utmost to hide it.'

Dominic seemed shocked into silence. Andie watched in alarm as he blanched under his tan and gripped the edge of the table so his knuckles showed white. 'I'm not sure what you mean,' he said at last.

Walter's shrewd eyes narrowed. 'You've covered your tracks well, but I have a policy of never doing business with someone I haven't fully researched. I know about young Nick Hunt and the trouble he got into.'

Dominic seemed to go even paler. 'You mean the assault charge? Even though it never went to court. Even though I was a juvenile and there should be no record of it. How did you—?'

'Never mind how I found out. But I also discovered how much Dominic Hunt has given back to the world in which he had to fight to survive.' Walter looked to Andie. 'I guess you don't know about this, my dear.'

'Dominic has told me about his past,' she said cautiously. She sat at the edge of her seat, feeling trapped by uncertainty, terrified of saying the wrong thing, not wanting to reveal her ignorance of anything important. 'I also know how very generous he is.'

'Generous to the point that he funds a centre to help troubled young people in Brisbane.' Andie couldn't help a gasp of surprise that revealed her total lack of knowledge. 'He hasn't told you about his Underground Help Centre?' Walter didn't wait for her to answer. 'It provides safe emergency accommodation, health care, counselling, rehab—all funded by your fiancé. Altogether a most admirable venture.'

Why had Dominic let everyone think he was a Scrooge?

'You've done your research well, Walter,' Dominic said. 'Yes, I haven't yet told Andie about the centre. I wanted to take her to Brisbane and show her the work we do there.'

'I'll look forward to that, darling,' she said, not having to fake her admiration for him.

Dominic addressed both her and Walter. 'When I started to make serious money, I bought the abandoned shopping centre site where I'd sought refuge as a troubled runaway and redeveloped it. But part of the site was always going to be for the Underground Help Centre that I founded. I recruited Jim, the social worker who had helped me, to head it up for me.'

Andie felt she would burst with pride in him. Pride and something even more heartfelt. He must hate having to reveal himself like this.

Walter leaned towards Dominic. 'You're a self-made man and I admire that,' he said. 'You're sharing the wealth you acquired by your own hard work and initiative and I admire that too. What I don't understand, Dominic, is why you keep all this such a big secret. There's nothing to be ashamed of in having pulled yourself up by your bootstraps.'

'I'm not ashamed of anything I've done,' Dominic said. 'But I didn't want my past to affect my future success. Especially, I didn't want it to rub off on my business partner, Jake Marlow.'

Andie felt as if she was floundering. Dominic had briefed her on business aspects she might be expected to know about tonight, but nothing about this. She could only do what she felt was right. Without hesitation, she reached out and took his hand so they stood united.

'People can be very judgemental,' she said to Walter. 'And the media seem to be particularly unfair to Dominic. I'm incredibly proud of him and support his reasons for wanting to keep what he does in Brisbane private. To talk about that terrible time is to relive it, over and over again. From what Dominic has told me, living it once would be more than enough for anyone.'

Dominic squeezed her hand back, hard, and his eyes were warm with gratitude. Gratitude and perhaps—just perhaps—something more? 'I can't stop the nightmares of being back there,' he said. 'But I can avoid talking about it and bringing those times back to life.'

Andie angled herself to face Walter full-on. She was finding it difficult to keep her voice steady. 'If people knew about the centre they'd find out about his living rough and the assault charge. People who don't know him might judge him unfairly. At the same time, I'd love more people to know how generous and kind he actually is and—' She'd probably said enough.

Walter chuckled. 'Another thing he's done right is his choice of fiancée.'

Dominic reached over to kiss her lightly on the lips. 'I concur, Walter,' he said. Was it part of the act or did he really mean it?

'Th...thank you,' stuttered Andie. She added Walter to the list of people who would be disappointed when she dumped Dominic.

'I'm afraid I can't say the same for your choice of first wife,' Walter said.

Dominic visibly tensed. 'What do you mean?'

'I met with her and your former employee this morning. He's an impressive guy, though not someone I feel I want to do business with. But your ex-wife made it clear she would do anything—and I stress *anything*—to seal the deal. She suggested that to me—happily married for more than forty years and who has never even looked at another woman.'

Dominic made a sound of utter disgust but nothing more. Andie thought more of him that he didn't say anything to disparage Tara, appalling though her behaviour had been. Dominic had more dignity.

'The upshot of this is, Dominic, that you are exactly the kind of guy I want to do business with. You and your delightful wife-to-be. You make a great team.'

Dominic reached over to take Andie's hand again. 'Thank you, Walter. Thank you from us both.'

Andie smiled with lips that were aching from all her false smiles and nodded her thanks. The fake engagement had done exactly what it was intended to. She should be jubilant for Dominic's sake. But that also meant there would soon be no need to carry on with it. And that made her feel miserable. *She wasn't doing a very good job of guarding her heart.*

When Andie said goodnight to Dominic, she clung to him for a moment longer than was necessary. Playing wife-to-be for the evening had made her start to wish a real relationship with Dominic could perhaps one day be on the cards.

Perhaps it was a good thing she wouldn't see Dominic again until Christmas Eve. He had to fly out to Minneapolis to finalise details with Walter, leaving her to handle the countdown to the Christmas party. And trying not to think too much about what had to happen after Christmas, when her 'engagement' would come to an end.

CHAPTER THIRTEEN

IT WAS MIDDAY on Christmas Eve and as Andie pushed open the door into Dominic's house she felt as if she was stepping into a nightmare. The staircase railings were decorated as elegantly as she'd hoped, with tiny lights and white silk cord. The wreath on the door was superb. But dominating the marble entrance hall was an enormous Christmas tree, beautifully decorated with baubles and ornaments and winking with tiny lights. She stared at it in shocked disbelief. *What the heck was that doing there?*

When she said it out loud she didn't say *heck* and she didn't say it quietly.

Her stylist Jeremy's assistant had been rearranging baubles on the lower branches of the tree. She jumped at Andie's outburst and a silver bauble smashed on to the marble floor. Calmly, very calmly, Andie asked the girl where Jeremy was. The girl scuttled out to get him.

Throughout all the Christmas party arrangements, through all the fake fiancée dramas, Andie had kept her cool. Now she was in serious danger of losing it. She had planned this party in meticulous detail. Of all the things that could go wrong, it would have to be this—Dominic would think she had deliberately defied his specific demand. And she didn't want him thinking badly of her.

Jeremy came into the room with a swathe of wide red ribbons draped over his outstretched arm. Andie recognised them as the ones to be looped and tied into extravagant bows on the back of the two hundred chairs in the ballroom.

She had to grit her teeth to stop herself from exploding. 'Why is there a Christmas tree in here?' Her heart was racing with such panic she had to put her hand on her chest to try and slow it.

'Because this entrance space cried out for one. How can you have a Christmas party without a tree?' Jeremy said. 'I thought you'd made a mistake and left it off the brief. Doesn't it look fabulous?'

'It does indeed look fabulous. Except the client specifically said *no tree*.' She could hear her voice rising and took a deep breath to calm herself.

How had she let this happen? Maybe she should have written *NO CHRISTMAS TREE* in bold capitals on every page of the briefing document. She'd arrived here very early this morning to let the decorating crew in and to receive final deliveries of the extra furniture. Jeremy had assured her that all was on track. And it was—except for this darn tree.

'But why?' asked Jeremy. 'It seems crazy not to have a tree.'

Crazy? Maybe. She had no idea why—because Dominic, for all his talk with Walter Burton over dinner that night that had seemed so genuine, still refused to let her in on the events in his past he held so tightly to himself. He'd drip-fed some of the details but she felt there was something major linked to Christmas he would not share. It made her feel excluded—put firmly in her place as no one important in his life. And she wanted to be important to him. She swallowed hard. *Had she really just admitted that to herself?*

'The client actually has a thing against Christmas trees,' she said. 'You might even call it a phobia. For heaven's sake, Jeremy, why didn't you call me before you put this up?' Her mouth was dry and her hands felt clammy at the thought of Dominic's reaction if he saw the tree.

'I'm sorry,' said Jeremy, crestfallen. 'You didn't specify not to include a tree in the decorations. I was just using my initiative.'

On other jobs she'd worked with Jeremy she'd told him to think for himself and not bother her with constant calls, so she couldn't be *too* cranky with him. Creative people could be tricky to manage—and Jeremy's work was superb. The tree was, in fact, perfect for the spot where he'd placed it.

She took a step back to fully appraise its impact. The tree looked spectacular, dressed in silver with highlights of red, in keeping with her overall colour scheme. She sighed her pleasure at its magnificence. This perfect tree would make a breathtaking first impression for the guests tomorrow. To the children it would seem to be the entrance to a magical world. It spoke of tradition, of hope, of generosity. Everything they were trying to achieve with this party. It would make Dominic look good.

The beautiful tree was beginning to work its magic on her. Surely it would on Dominic too? He'd come such a long way since that first day, when he'd been so vehemently anti everything Christmas. *Christmas was not Christmas without a tree.*

She took a series of deep, calming breaths. Dominic should at least have the chance to see the tree in place. To see how wonderful it looked there. Maybe the sight of this tree would go some way towards healing those hidden deep wounds he refused to acknowledge.

She turned to Jeremy, the decision firm in her mind. 'We'll leave it. You've done such a good job on the tree, it would be a real shame to have to take it down.'

'What about the client?'

'He's a client but he's also my fiancé.' The lie threatened to choke her but she was getting more adept at spinning falsehoods. 'Leave him to me. In the meantime, let me give you a hand with placing the final few ornaments on the lower branches,' she said. She was wearing work clothes—jeans, sneakers and a loose white shirt. She rolled up her sleeves and picked up an exquisite glass angel. Her hand wasn't quite steady—if only she was as confident as she had tried to appear.

Dominic was due back in to Sydney early this evening. *What if he hated the tree?* Surely he wouldn't. He seemed so happy with everything else she'd done for the party; surely he would fall in love with the tree.

But it would take a Christmas miracle for him to fall in love with *her*.

She longed for that miracle. Because she couldn't deny it to herself any longer—she had developed feelings for him.

Dominic had managed to get an earlier flight out of Minneapolis to connect with a non-stop flight to Sydney from Los Angeles. Nonetheless, it was a total flight of more than twenty hours. Despite the comfort of first class, he was tired and anxious to get away from the snow and ice of Minnesota and home to sunny Sydney. A bitterly cold Christmas wasn't quite as he'd remembered it to be.

Overriding everything else, he wanted to get home to Andie. He had thought about her non-stop the whole trip, wished she'd been with him. Next time, he'd promised Walter, he'd bring Andie with him.

As the car he'd taken from the airport pulled up in front of his house, his spirits lifted at the thought of seeing her. He hadn't been able to get through to her phone, so he'd called Party Queens. Eliza had told him she was actually at his house in Vaucluse, working on the decorations for the party.

On the spur of the moment, he'd decided not to let her know he'd got in early. It might be better to surprise her. He reckoned if she didn't know he was coming, she wouldn't have time to put on her fake fiancée front. Her first reaction to him would give him more of a clue of her real feelings towards him.

Because while he was away he had missed her so intensely, he'd been forced to face *his* real feelings towards *her*. He was falling in love with her. Not only was he falling in love with her; he realised he had never had feelings of such intensity about a woman.

Melody had been his first love—and sweet, damaged Melody had loved him back to the extent she was capable of love. But it hadn't been enough. That assault charge had happened because he had been protecting her. Protecting her from a guy assaulting her in an alley not far from the takeaway food shop where he'd worked in the kitchen in return for food and a few dollars cash in hand.

But the guy had been her dealer—and possibly her pimp. Melody had squealed at Dominic to leave the guy alone. She'd shrieked at him that she knew what she was doing; she didn't need protecting. Dominic had ignored her, had pulled the creep off her, smashed his fist into the guy's face. Then the dealer's mates had shown up and Dominic had copped a beating too. But, although younger than the low-lifes, he'd been bigger, stronger and inflicted more damage. The cops had taken him in, while the others had disappeared into the dark corners that were their natural habitat. And Melody had gone with them without a backward glance, leaving him with a shattered heart as well as a broken nose. He'd never seen her again.

Of course Melody hadn't been her real name. He'd been too naïve to realise that at the time. Later, when he'd set up the Underground Help Centre, he'd tried to find her but without any luck. He liked to think she was living a safe happy life somewhere but the reality was likely to be less cosy than that.

Then there'd been Tara—the next woman to have betrayed him. The least thought he gave to his ex-wife the better.

But Andie. Andie was different. He felt his heart, frosted over for so long, warm when he thought about her. *What you saw was what you got.* Not only smart and beautiful, but loyal and loving. He'd told her more about his past than he'd ever told anyone. He could be himself with her, not have to pretend, be Nick as well as Dominic. Be not the billionaire but the man. Their relationship could be real. *He could spend his life with Andie.*

And he wanted to tell her just that.

The scent of pine needles assaulted his senses even before he put his key in his front door. The sharp resin smell instantly revived memories of that Christmas Eve when he'd been eleven years old and the happy part of his childhood had come to its terrible end. Christmas trees were the thing he most hated about Christmas.

The smell made him nauseous, started a headache throbbing in his temples. Andie must be using pine in some of the decorations. It would have to go. He couldn't have it in the house.

He pushed the door silently open—only to recoil at what he saw.

There was a Christmas tree in his house. A whopping great Christmas tree, taking up half his entrance hallway and rising high above the banisters of the staircase.

What the hell? He had told Andie in no uncertain terms there was to be no Christmas tree—anywhere. He gritted his teeth and fisted his hands by his sides. *How could she be so insensitive?*

There was a team of people working on the tree and its myriad glitzy ornaments. Including Andie. He'd never thought she could be complicit in this defiance of his wishes. He felt let down. *Betrayed.*

She turned. Froze. Her eyes widened with shock and alarm when she saw him. A glass ornament slid from her hands and smashed on the floor but she scarcely seemed to notice.

'What part of "no Christmas tree" did you not get, Andie?'

She got up from her kneeling position and took a step towards him, put up her hands as if to ward off his anger. The people she was with scuttled out of the room, leaving them alone. But he bet they were eavesdropping somewhere nearby. The thought made him even more livid.

'Dominic, I'm sorry. I know you said no tree.'

'You're damn right I did.'

'It was a mistake. The tree was never meant to be here. There were some…some crossed lines. I wasn't expecting it either. But then I saw it and it's so beautiful and looks so right here. I thought you might…appreciate it, might see how right it is and want to keep it.'

He could feel the veins standing out on his neck, his hands clenched so tight they hurt. 'I don't see it as beautiful.'

Her face flushed. She would read that as an insult to her skills. He was beyond caring. 'Why? Why do you hate Christmas trees?' she said. 'Why this…this irrational dislike of Christmas?'

Irrational? He gritted his teeth. 'That's none of your concern.'

'But I want it to be. I thought I could help you. I—'

'You thought wrong.'

Now her hands were clenched and she was glaring at him. 'Why won't you share it with me—what makes you hurt so much at this time of year? Why do I have to guess? Why do I have to tiptoe around you?' Her voice rose with each question as it seemed her every frustration and doubt rushed to the surface.

Dominic was furious. How dared she put him through this…this humiliation?

'Don't forget your place,' he said coldly. 'I employ you.' With each word he made a stabbing motion with his finger to emphasise the words. 'Get rid of the tree. Now.'

He hated the stricken look on Andie's face, knowing he had put it there. But if she cared about him at all she never would have allowed that tree to enter his house. He could barely stand to look at her.

For a long moment she didn't say anything. 'Yes,' she said finally, her voice a dull echo of its usual husky charm. 'Yes, sir,' she added.

In a way he appreciated the defiance of the hissed 'sir'. But he was tired and jet-lagged and grumpy and burning with all the pain and loss he associated with Christmas—and Christmas trees in particular. Above all, he was disappointed in her that she thought so little of his wishes that she would defy him.

His house was festooned with festive paraphernalia. Everywhere he looked, it glittered and shone, mocking him. He'd been talked into this damn party against his wishes. *He hated Christmas.* He uttered a long string of curses worthy of Scrooge.

'I'm going upstairs. Make sure this tree is gone when I come back down. And all your people as well.' He glared in the general direction of the door through which her team had fled.

She met his glare, chin tilted upwards. 'It will take some time to dismantle the tree,' she said. 'But I assure you I will get rid of every last stray needle so you will never know it was there.' She sounded as though she spoke through gritted teeth. 'However, I will need all my crew to help me. We have to be here for at least a few more hours. We still have to finish filling the goody bags and setting the tables.' She glared at him. 'This is *your* party. And you know as well as I do that it must go on. To prove you're not the Scrooge people think you are.'

Some part of him wanted to cross the expanse of floor between them and hug her close. To tell her that of course he understood. That he found it almost impossible to talk about the damage of his childhood. To knuckle down and help her adorn his house for the party tomorrow. But the habits of Christmases past were hard to break.

So was the habit of closing himself off from love. Letting himself love Andie would only end in disappointment and pain, like it had with every other relationship. For her as well as himself. *It seemed he was incapable of love.*

'Text me when you're done,' he said.

He stomped up the stairs to his study. And the bottle of bourbon that waited there.

Andie felt humiliated, angry and upset. How dared Dominic speak to her like that? *'Don't forget your place.'* His harsh words had stabbed into her heart.

Jeremy poked his head around the door that connected through to the living room. She beckoned him to come in. She forced her voice to sound businesslike, refused to let even a hint of a tear burr her tone. 'I told you he wouldn't be happy with the tree.' Her effort at a joke fell very flat.

'Don't worry about it,' Jeremy said, putting a comforting hand on her shoulder. 'We'll get rid of this tree quick-smart. No matter your man is in a mood. The show has to go on. You've got two hundred people here for lunch tomorrow.'

'Thanks, Jeremy,' she said. 'Dominic has just got off a long flight. He's not himself.' But her excuses for him sounded lame even to her own ears.

Was that angry man glaring at her with his fists clenched at his sides the true Dominic? She'd known the anger was there bubbling below the surface, was beginning to understand the reasons for it. But she'd thought that anger that had driven him to violence was in his past. How could she possibly have thought she'd fallen in love with him? She didn't even know the man.

'What do you suggest we do with the tree?' Jeremy asked. 'There are no returns on cut trees.'

Andie's thoughts raced. 'We've got a Christmas Eve party happening elsewhere tonight. The clients have put up a scrappy old artificial tree that looks dreadful. We'll get this delivered to them with the compliments of Party Queens. Keep whatever ornaments you can use here; the rest we'll send with the tree. Let's call a courier truck now.'

Seething, she set to work dismantling the beautiful tree. As she did so, she felt as if she were dismantling all her hopes and dreams for love with Dominic. The diamond ring felt like a heavy burden on her finger, weighted by its duplicity and hypocrisy. While he'd stood there insulting her, she'd felt like taking the ring off and hurling it at him. If it had hit him and drawn blood she would have been glad. His words had been so harsh they felt like they'd drawn blood from her heart.

But of course she couldn't have thrown her ring at him while there were other people in the house. She would be professional right to the end. After all, wasn't she known for her skill at dealing with difficult people?

In spite of that, she'd had her fill of this particular difficult man. He'd got what he wanted from her in terms of his American deal. She'd got what her family needed for Timothy. Both sides of the bargain fulfilled. He'd been her employer, her fake fiancé—she'd liked to think they'd become friends of a sort. She'd wanted more—but that was obviously not to be. She'd stick it out for the Christmas lunch. Then she'd be out of here and out of his life.

The crew worked efficiently and well. When they were done and the tree was gone she waved them goodbye and wished them a Merry Christmas. But not before asking them to please not repeat what they might have heard today. Talk of Dominic's outburst could do serious damage to the rehabilitation of his Scrooge image.

By the time they had all gone it was early evening. She stood and massaged the small of her back where it ached. She would let Dominic know she was done and going home. But she had no intention of texting him as he'd asked. Not asked. *Demanded.* She had things to say that had to be said in person.

CHAPTER FOURTEEN

WITH A HEAVY HEART—wounded hearts *hurt*—Andie made her way up the stylishly decorated staircase, its tiny lights discreetly winking. She hadn't been up here before, as this part of the house was off-limits for the party. When she thought of it, she actually had no idea where Dominic could be.

The first two doors opened to two fashionably furnished empty bedrooms. The third bedroom was obviously his—a vast bed with immaculate stone-coloured linens, arched windows that opened to a sweeping view of the harbour. But he wasn't there.

Then she noticed a door ajar to what seemed like a study.

There was no response to her knock, so she pushed it open. The blinds were drawn. Dominic lay sprawled asleep on a large chesterfield sofa. The dull light of a tall, arching floor lamp pooled on him and seemed to put him in the spotlight.

His black lace-up business shoes lay haphazardly at the end of the sofa. He had taken off his jacket and removed his tie. The top buttons of his shirt were undone to reveal an expanse of bare, well-muscled chest her traitorous libido could not help but appreciate as it rose and fell in his sleep.

His right arm fell to the floor near a bottle of bourbon. Andie picked it up. The bottle was nearly full, with probably no more than a glassful gone. Not enough for him to be drunk—more likely collapsed into the sleep of utter exhaustion. She put the bottle on the desk.

There was a swivel-footed captain's chair near the sofa with a padded leather seat. She sat on the edge of it and watched Dominic as he slept. Darn it, but that wounded heart of hers beat faster as she feasted her eyes on his face, which had become so familiar. So…so—she nearly let herself think *so beloved.* But that couldn't be.

She swallowed hard at the lump that rose in her throat. Why on earth had she let herself fall for a man who was so difficult, so damaged, so completely opposite to the man who had made her so happy in the past?

Dominic's hair stood up in spikes. He obviously hadn't shaved since he'd left Minneapolis and his beard was in that stubble stage she found so incredibly sexy. She hadn't realised how long and thick his eyelashes were. His mouth was slightly parted. She longed to lean over and kiss it. She sighed. There would be no more kissing of this man.

He moaned in his sleep and she could see rapid eye movement behind his lids as if he were being tortured by bad dreams. She could not help but reach out to stroke his furrowed forehead. He returned to more restful sleep. Then his eyes flickered open. Suddenly he sat up, startling her. He looked around, disorientated, eyes glazed with sleep. He focused on her.

'Andie,' he breathed. 'You're here.' He gave a huge sigh, took her hand and kissed it. 'I didn't think I'd ever see you again.'

He didn't deserve to, she thought. But her resolve was weakening.

'Are you okay?' she said, trying to ignore the shivers of pleasure that ran up her arm from his kiss. He had been rude and hurtful to her.

'I've just had a horrible dream,' he said.

'What kind of dream?'

'A nightmare. I was in a cemetery and saw my own headstone.'

She shook her head. 'No, Dominic—I don't want to hear this.' The day of Anthony's funeral had been the worst day of her life. When she'd had to accept she'd never see him again. She couldn't bear to think of Dominic buried under a headstone.

But he continued in a dramatic tone she didn't think was appropriate for such a gruesome topic. 'It said: 'Here lies Dominic—they called him Scrooge'. And I think it was Christmas Day.'

Not so gruesome after all. She couldn't help a smile.

'You think my nightmare was funny?' he said, affronted.

'I'm sure it was scary at the time. But you'll never be called Scrooge again. Not after tomorrow. I…I'm sorry about what I said earlier. About your…your Scroogeness, I mean.'

He slammed the hand that wasn't holding hers against his forehead. 'The Christmas tree. I'm sorry, Andie. That was unforgivable. Pay your crew a bonus to make up for it, will you, and bill it to me.'

Did he think everything could be solved by throwing money at it?

'I'm also sorry about the tree, Dominic. It was an honest mistake. It's all gone now.'

Maybe she'd been in the wrong too, to imagine he might like the tree when he'd been so vehement about not having one in the house. But she hadn't been wrong about expecting better behaviour from him.

He shuddered. 'It was a shock. The smell of it. The sight of it. Brought back bad memories.'

She shifted in her seat but did not let go of his hand. 'Do you think it might be time to tell me why Christmas trees upset you so much? Because I didn't like seeing that anger. Especially not directed at me. How can I understand you when I don't know what I'm dealing with?'

He grimaced as if stabbed by an unpleasant memory. 'I suppose I have to tell you if I want you to ever talk to me again.'

'I'm talking to you now.'

She remembered what she'd said about recalling unpleasant memories being like reliving them. But this had to come out—one way or another. Better it was with words than fists.

'Christmas Eve is the anniversary of my parents' deaths.'

She squeezed his hand. 'Dominic, I'm so sorry.' That explained a lot. 'Why didn't you say so before?'

'I…I didn't want people feeling sorry for me,' he said gruffly.

'People wouldn't have… Yes, they would have felt sorry for you. But in a good way.' Could all this Scrooge business have been solved by him simply explaining that? 'Can you tell me about it now?'

'There…there's more. It was cold and frosty. My parents went out to pick up the Christmas tree. A deer crossed the road and they braked to avoid it. The road was icy and the car swerved out of control and crashed into a barrier. That's how they died. Getting the damn Christmas tree.'

She couldn't find the words to say anything other than she was sorry again.

'It was…it was my fault they died.'

Andie frowned. 'How could it be your fault? You were eleven years old.'

'My aunt told me repeatedly for the next six years it was my fault.'

'I think you'd better tell me some more about this aunt.'

'The thing is, it really *was* my fault. I'd begged my parents for a real tree. We had a plastic one. My best friend had a real one; I wanted a real one. If they hadn't gone out to get the tree I wanted they wouldn't have died.'

'You've been blaming yourself all these years? It was an accident. How any competent adult could let you blame yourself, I can't imagine.'

'Competent adult and my aunt aren't compatible terms,' he said, the bitterness underlying his words shocking her.

'I keep asking you about her; it's time you gave me some answers.' Though she was beginning to dread what she might hear.

'She used alcohol and prescription meds to mask her serious psychological problems. I know that now as an adult. As a kid, I lived with a bitter woman who swung between abuse and smothering affection.'

'And, as a kid, you put up with a lot in the hope of love,' Andie said softly, not sure if Dominic actually heard her. She could see the vulnerability in that strong-jawed handsome face, wondered how many people he had ever let be aware of it. She thought again of that little boy with the dark hair. Her vision of Dominic's son merged with that of the young, grieving, abused Dominic. And her heart went out to him.

The words spilled out of him now, words that expressed emotions dammed for years. 'She was particularly bad at Christmas because that's when she'd lost her sister—which was, in her eyes, my fault. When she got fed up with me, she locked me in a cupboard. The physical abuse stopped when I got bigger than her. The mental abuse went on until the day I ran away. Yet all that time she held down a job and presented a reasonable face to the world. I talked to a teacher at school and he didn't believe me. Told me to man up.'

'I honestly don't know what to say…' But she hated his aunt, even though she was aware she'd been a deeply troubled person. No child should be treated like that.

'Say nothing. I don't want to talk about it any more. I'm thirty-two years old. That was all a long time ago.'

'But, deep down, you're still hurting,' she whispered. 'Dominic, I'm so sorry you had to go through all that. And I admire you so much for what you became after such a difficult start.'

Words could only communicate so much. Again, she felt that urge to comfort him. This time, she acted on it. She leaned over to him and kissed him, tasted bourbon on his lips, welcomed the scrape of his stubble on her skin. Immediately, he took the kiss deeper.

The kiss went on and on, passion building, thrilling her. But it was more than sensual pleasure; it was a new sense of connection, of shared emotion as well as sensation.

He broke the kiss to pull her shirt up and over her head. His shirt was already half unbuttoned. It didn't take much to have it completely undone and to slide it off his broad shoulders and muscular arms. She caught her breath in awe at the male perfection of his body.

She wanted him. Dominic had got what he wanted from Walter. Timothy was booked for the treatment he needed. She had promised herself to go after what she wanted—him—and now was her time. It might never be more than this. She knew it and was prepared to take that risk. But she hoped for so much more.

She hadn't known him for long but she had the same kind of certainty—that it could be for ever—as she'd felt for Anthony. A certainty she'd thought she'd never feel again. *For ever love.* Had she been given a chance for that special connection again? She thought *yes*, but could she convince Dominic she could bring him the kind of happiness that had seemed to evade him—that he deserved?

He threw his head back and moaned his pleasure as she planted urgent kisses down the firm column of his throat, then back up to claim his mouth again. He tasted so good, felt so good.

He caught her hands. 'Andie, is this what you want? Because we have to stop it now if you don't,' he said, his voice husky with need.

'Don't you dare stop,' she murmured.

He smiled a slow, seductive smile that sent her heart rate rocketing. 'In that case…' He unfastened the catch on her jeans. 'Let's see if we can get these jeans to misbehave…'

Satisfied, replete, her body aching in the most pleasurable of ways, Andie drowsed in his arms as Dominic slept. But she couldn't let herself sleep.

If she'd been a different kind of person she would have stayed there. Perhaps convinced Dominic to shower with her when they woke. She would enjoy soaping down that powerful body. Heaven knew what kind of fun they could have with the powerful jets of water in his spacious double shower. Then they could retire to spend the rest of the evening in that enormous bed of his.

But Andie was not that person. There was the Christmas Eve party she had committed to this evening. As the party planner, she was obliged to call in to see all was well. She also had to check the big tree had made its way there safely—though the eighteen-year-old daughter had texted Andie to thank her, thrilled with the 'real tree'.

There was nothing like the smell of pine resin and the beauty of a natural tree. As eleven-year-old Dominic had known. Her heart went out to that little boy who lived in the damaged soul of the big male, sleeping naked next to her, his arm thrown possessively over her. She was also naked, except for her engagement ring, shining with false promise under the lamplight.

She had agreed to see her family tonight. Tomorrow, Christmas Day, would be the first Christmas lunch she had not spent with them. She was surprised her father had taken it so lightly. 'You have to stand by Dominic, love. That party is not just a job for you now. You're his future wife.'

If only.

Reluctantly, she slid away from Dominic, then quietly got dressed. She would see him in the morning. Tomorrow was Christmas Day, a holiday she loved and he hated. Now she could see why. She ached to turn things around for him—if he would let her.

She looked at his face, more relaxed than she had seen it, and smiled a smile that was bittersweet. They had made love and it had been magnificent. But nothing had changed between them. Tomorrow she was facing the biggest party of her career so far. She would be by the side of the man she had fallen in love with, not knowing for how much longer he would be a part of her life.

When the truth was, she wanted Dominic for Christmas. Not just his body—his heart as well.

Somehow, tomorrow she would have to confess to Dominic the truth of how she felt about him. That she wanted to try a relationship for real. She hoped he felt the same. If so, this would be the best Christmas she had ever had. If not… Well, she couldn't bear to think about *if not.*

CHAPTER FIFTEEN

DOMINIC AWOKE ON Christmas morning as he was accustomed to waking on December the twenty-fifth—alone. It was very early, pale sunlight filtering through the blinds. He reached out his hand to the sofa beside him in the vain hope that Andie might still be there, only to find the leather on that side disappointingly cool to the touch. He closed his eyes again and breathed in the scent of her that lingered in the room, on his skin. Then was overtaken by an anguished rush of longing for her that made him double over with gut-wrenching pain.

He remembered her leaving his side, her quiet footsteps around the room, the rustling as she slid on her clothes. Then her leaning towards him, murmuring that she had to go. She had duties, obligations. He'd pulled her back close to him, tried to convince her with his hands, with his mouth why she should stay. But she'd murmured her regret, kissed him with a quick fierce passion, told him he had jet lag to get over. Then she'd gone.

All he'd wanted to say to her still remained unsaid.

Of course she'd gone to the other people in her life who needed her and loved her. The only commitment she'd made to him was based on the falsehoods he'd engendered and coerced her into. She'd played her role to perfection. So well he was uncertain what might be fact and what might be fiction. But surely making love to him with such passion and tenderness had not been play-acting?

He noticed the bourbon bottle on the desk, lid on, barely touched. This would be the first Christmas he could remember that he hadn't tried to obliterate. The first Christmas that he woke to the knowledge that while Andie might not be here now, she soon would be. And that his perfect, empty house would be filled with people. People who had known hardship like he had and whom he was in the position to help by making their Christmas Day memorable.

Not for the first time, he thought of the possibility of opening a branch of the Underground Help Centre here in Sydney, where it was so obviously needed. Profits from the joint venture with Walter could help fund it. He had much to learn from Walter—he could see it was going to end up a friendship as well as a business partnership.

For the first Christmas in a long time he had something to look forward to—and it was all thanks to Andie.

He hauled himself off the sofa and stretched out the cricks in his back. The sofa was not the best place to sleep—though it had proved perfectly fine for energetic lovemaking. He paused, overwhelmed by memories of the night before. *Andie.* Hunger for her threatened to overwhelm him again—and not just for her beautiful, generous body. He prayed to whatever power that had brought her to him to let him keep her in his life. He hoped she would forgive the way he'd behaved—understand why. And know that it would never happen again.

He headed down the stairs and stood in the entrance hall. Not a trace of the tree remained, thank heaven. He breathed in. And none of that awful smell. Andie had been well meaning but misguided about the tree—now she understood.

The ballroom was all set up, with tables and chairs adorned in various combinations of red and white. A large buffet table area stretched along the wall closest to the kitchen. He'd approved the menu with Gemma and knew within hours it would be groaning with a lavish festive feast. The dishes had been chosen with the diverse backgrounds of the guests in mind—some were refugees experiencing their first Christmas in Australia.

He still couldn't have tolerated a tree in the house but he had to admit to a stirring of interest in the celebrations—more interest than he'd had in Christmas since he'd been a child. Andie was clever—children would love all this and adults should also respond to the nostalgia and hope it evoked. Hadn't she said Christmas was about evoking emotion?

Thanks to the tragedy on Christmas Eve all those years ago, thanks to the way his aunt had treated him in the years that followed, the emotions the season had evoked for him had been unhappy in the extreme. Was there a chance now for him to forge new, happy memories with a kind, loving woman who seemed to understand his struggles?

Andie had said he could trust her, but after his display of anger over the Christmas tree last night would she let herself trust *him*?

There was a large Santa Claus figurine in the corner with rows of canvas, sunshine-themed goody bags stacked around it. Of course it should have been a tree—but the Santa worked okay too as a compromise. The sturdy bags could double as beach bags, the ever-practical Andie had pointed out to him. She had thought of everything. There were gifts there for the volunteers too.

The house seemed to hum with a quiet anticipation and he could feel his spirits rise. Christmas Day with Andie in his house must surely be a step up on the ones he'd been forced to endure up until now.

He swung open the doors and headed to his gym for a workout.

* * *

An hour later Andie arrived with the chef and his crew. Dominic had long given her a pass code to get in and out of fortress Vaucluse.

She was wearing working gear of shorts, T-shirt and sneakers. Later she would change into her beautiful new red lace dress and gorgeous shoes—strappy and red with tassels—in time to greet their guests. She took her dress on its hanger and her bag into the downstairs bathroom. As she did, she noticed the doors to the garden were open and someone was in the pool. She went out to investigate.

Of course it was Dominic, his powerful body spearing through the water. No wonder he had such well-developed muscles with vigorous swimming like this. She watched, mesmerised at his rhythmic strokes, the force of his arms and powerful kick propelling him with athletic grace.

She didn't say anything but maybe her shadow cast on the water alerted him to her presence. Maybe he caught sight of her when he turned his head to breathe. He swam to the edge of the pool and effortlessly pulled himself out of the water, muscles rippling. He wasn't even out of breath.

She almost swooned at the sight of him—could a man be more handsome? Memories of the ecstasy they had given each other the night before flashed through her, tightening her nipples and flooding her body with desire.

His wet hair was slick to his head, the morning sunlight refracted off droplets of water that clung to his powerfully developed shoulders and cut chest, his veins stood out on his biceps, pumped from exertion. And then there were the classic six-pack, the long, strong legs. He didn't have a lot of body hair for such a dark man, but what there was seemed to flag his outrageous masculinity.

She wanted him more than ever. Not just for a night. For many nights. Maybe every night for the rest of her life. There was so much she wanted to say to him but, for all the connection and closeness and *certainty* she had felt last night, she didn't know how to say it.

Her engagement ring glinted on her left hand. The deal with Walter was done. Dominic's Scrooge reputation was likely to be squashed after the party today. How much longer would this ring stay on her finger? What, if anything, would be her role in Dominic's life? She wanted to say something about last night, bring up the subject of the future, but she just couldn't. 'Happy Christmas,' she said instead, forcing every bit of enthusiasm she could muster into her voice.

He grabbed a towel from the back of the chair and slung it around his shoulders, towelling off the excess water. 'H… Happy Christmas to you too,' he said, his voice rusty in the way of someone unused to uttering those particular words. She wondered how long since he had actually wished anyone the Season's greetings.

He looked down into her face and she realised by the expression in his eyes that he might be as uncertain as she was.

Hope flared in her heart. 'Dominic, I—'

'Andie, I—'

They both spoke at the same time. They laughed. Tried again.

'About last night,' he said.

'Yes?' she said.

'I wanted to—'

But she didn't hear what he had to say, didn't get a chance to answer because at that moment the chef called from the doors that opened from the ballroom that Gemma and Eliza were there and needed to be buzzed in.

Dominic groaned his frustration at the terminated conversation. Andie echoed his groan.

'Later,' she said as she turned away, knowing that it

would be highly unlikely for them to get another private moment together for the next few hours.

Dominic found the amount of noise two hundred people could generate—especially when so many of them were children—quite astounding. He stood on the edge of the party, still at the meet-and-greet stage, with appetisers and drinks being passed around by waiters dressed as Christmas elves.

Santa Claus, otherwise known as Rob Cratchit, his Director of Marketing, sidled up next to him. 'It's going even better than I expected,' he said through his fake white beard. 'See that woman over there wiping tomato sauce off the little boy's shirt? She's a journalist, volunteering for the day, and one of your most strident Scrooge critics. She actually called you a multi-million-dollar miser. But I think she's already convinced that today is not some kind of cynical publicity stunt.'

'Good,' said Dominic. Strange that the original aim of this party—to curry favour with Walter Burton—seemed to have become lost. Now it was all about giving people who had it tough a heart-warming experience and a good meal. And enjoying it with Andie by his side.

'Good on you for dressing up as Santa Claus,' he said to Rob. Andie had been right—Rob made the perfect Santa and he had the outgoing personality to carry it off.

'Actually, *you're* the Santa Claus. I talked to one nice lady, a single mum, who said her kids would not have got Christmas lunch or a Christmas present this year, unless a charity had helped out. She said this was so much better than charity. You should mingle—a lot of people want to thank you.'

'I'm not the mingling type,' Dominic said. 'I don't need to be thanked. I just signed the cheques. It should be Andie they're thanking; this was all her idea.'

‘She’s brilliant,’ said Rob. ‘Smart of you to snap her up so quickly. You’re a lucky man.’

‘Yes,’ said Dominic, not encouraging further conversation. He’d never been happy discussing his personal life with anyone. The thought that—unless he said something to her—this might be the last day he had with Andie in his life was enough to sink him into a decidedly unfestive gloom.

He hadn’t been able to keep his eyes off Andie as she flitted around the room, looking her most beautiful in a very stylish dress of form-fitting lace in a dusky shade of Christmas red. It was modest but hugged every curve and showed off her long, gorgeous legs. He tried not to think of how it had felt to have those legs wrapped around him last night…

‘Well, mustn’t linger,’ said Rob. ‘I have to be off and do the *ho-ho-ho* thing.’

As Rob made his way back into the throng, Andie rang a bell for attention and asked everyone to move towards the entrance hall. ‘Some of the children and their parents are singing carols for us today.’ She’d told Dominic a few of the adults were involved in street choirs and had been happy to run through the carols with the kids.

There was a collective gasp from the ‘audience’ as they saw the children lined up on the stairs, starting from the tiniest to the teenagers with the adults behind. Again Andie had been right—the stairs made the most amazing showcase for a choir. Each of the choir members wore a plain red T-shirt with the word *‘choir’* printed in white lowercase letters. It was perfect, gave them an identity without being ostentatious.

Andie met his gaze from across the room and she smiled. He gave her a discreet thumbs-up. Professional pride? Or something more personal?

The choir started off with the Australian Christmas

carol 'Six White Boomers' where Santa's reindeer were replaced by big white kangaroos for the Australian toy delivery. It was a good icebreaker, and had everyone laughing and clapping and singing along with the chorus.

As Dominic watched, he was surprised to see Andie playing guitar up on the balcony with two other guitarists. She was singing too, in a lovely warm soprano. He remembered that photo of her playing guitar in the hallway of her parents' home and realised how much there was he still didn't know about her—and how much he wanted to know.

When the choir switched to classics like 'Silent Night' and 'Away in a Manger', Dominic found himself transported back to the happy last Christmas when his parents were alive and they'd gone carol singing in their village. *How could he have forgotten?*

The music and the pure young voices resonated and seemed to unlock a well of feeling he'd suppressed—unable perhaps to deal with the pain of it during those years of abuse by his aunt. He'd thought himself incapable of love—because he had been without love. But he *had* been loved back then, by his parents and his grandparents—loved deeply and unconditionally.

He'd yearned for that love again but had never found it. His aunt had done her best to destroy him emotionally but the love that had nurtured him as a young child must have protected him. The realisation struck him—he had loved women incapable of loving him back, and all this time had thought the fault was his when those relationships had failed.

Andie's voice soared above the rest of the choir. Andie, who he sensed had a vast reserve of love locked away since she'd lost her boyfriend. He wanted that love for himself and he wanted to give her the love she needed. How could he tell her that?

He tried to join in with the words of the carol but his throat closed over. He pretended to cough. Before he made an idiot of himself by breaking down, he pushed his way politely through the crowd and made his way out to the cabana, the only place where he could be alone and gather his thoughts.

But he wasn't alone for long. Andie, her eyes warm with concern, was soon with him. 'Dominic, are you okay?' she said, her hand on his arm. 'I know how you feel about Christmas and I was worried—'

'I'm absolutely fine—better than I've been for a long time,' he said.

He picked up her left hand. 'Take off your ring and give it to me, please.'

Andie froze. She stared at him for a long moment, trying to conceal the pain from the shaft of hurt that had stabbed her heart. So it had come to this so soon. Her use was over. Fake fiancée no longer required. Party planner no longer required. Friend, lover, confidante and whatever else she'd been to him no longer required. *She was surplus to requirements.*

Dominic had proved himself to be generous and thoughtful way beyond her initial expectations of Scrooge. But she must not forget the cold, hard fact—people who got to be billionaires in their twenties must have a ruthless streak. And he'd reneged on his offer that she could keep the ring—not that she'd had any intention of doing so. To say she was disappointed would be the world's biggest understatement.

She felt as though all the energy and joy was flowing out of her to leave just a husk. The colour drained from her face—she must look like a ghost.

With trembling fingers, she slid off the magnificent ring and gave it back to him, pressing it firmly into the palm of his hand. Her finger felt immediately empty, her hand unbalanced.

'It's yours,' she said and turned on her heel, trying not to stagger. She would not cry. She would not say anything snarky to him. She would just walk out of here with dignity. *This was her worst Christmas Day ever.*

'Wait! Andie! Where are you going?'

She turned back to see Dominic with a look of bewilderment on his handsome, tough face. 'You're not going to leave me here with your ring?'

Now it was her turn to feel bewildered. '*My* ring? Then why—?' she managed to choke out.

He took her hand again and held it in a tight grip. 'I'm not doing a good job of this, am I?'

He drew her closer, cleared his throat. 'Andie, I… I love you, and I'm attempting to ask you to marry me. I'm hoping you'll say "yes", so I can put your ring back on your wedding finger where it belongs, as your *real* fiancé, as a *real* engagement ring. Just like you told me you wanted.'

She was stunned speechless. The colour rushed back into her face.

'Well?' he prompted. 'Andrea Jane Newman, will you do me the honour of becoming my wife?'

Finally she found her words. Although she only needed the one. 'Yes,' she said. 'I say "yes".'

With no further ado, he slid the beautiful ring back into its rightful place. To her happy eyes it seemed to flash even more brilliantly.

'Dominic, I love you too. I think maybe it *was* love at first sight the day I met you. I never really had to lie about that.'

She wound her arms around his neck and kissed him. They kissed for a long time. Until they were interrupted by a loud knock on the door of the pool house. Gemma.

'Hey, you two, I don't know what's going on in there

and I don't particularly want to know, but we're about to serve lunch and your presence is required.'

'Oh, yes, of course—we're coming straight away,' Andie called, flustered.

Dominic held her by the arm. 'Not so fast. There's something else I want to ask you. What would you like for Christmas?'

His question threw her. She had to think very hard. But then it came to her. 'All I want for Christmas is for us to get married as soon as possible. I… I don't want to wait. You…you know why.'

Anthony would have wanted this for her—to grab her second chance of happiness. She knew that as certainly as if he'd been there to give her his blessing.

'That suits me fine,' Dominic said. 'The sooner you're my wife the better.'

'Of course it takes a while to organise a wedding. Next month. The month after. I don't want anything too fussy anyway, just simple and private.'

'We'll have to talk to the Party Queens,' he said.

She laughed. 'Great idea. I have a feeling we'll be the best people for the job.'

She could hardly believe this was true, but the look in his eyes told her she could believe it. She wound her arms around his neck again. 'Dominic Hugo Hunt, you've just made this the very best Christmas of my life.'

He heaved a great sigh and she could see it was as if the weight of all those miserable Christmases he'd endured in the past had been thrown off. 'Me too,' he said. 'And all because of you, my wonderful wife-to-be.'

CHAPTER SIXTEEN

ANDIE FOUND HERSELF singing 'Rudolph the Red-Nosed Reindeer' as she drove to Dominic's house five days later. She couldn't remember when she'd last sung in the car—and certainly not such a cheesy carol as 'Rudolph'. No, wait. 'Six White Boomers' was even cheesier. But the choir had been so wonderful at Dominic's Christmas party she'd felt it had become the heart of the very successful party. The carols had stayed in her head.

It had only been significant to her, but it was the first time she'd played her guitar and sung in public since Anthony had died. She'd healed in every way from the trauma of his loss, although she would never forget him. Her future was with Dominic. How could she ever have thought he was not her type?

She didn't think Dominic would be burdened with the Scrooge label for too much longer. One of his most relentless critics had served as a volunteer at the party—and had completely changed her tune. Andie had committed to heart the journalist's article in one of the major newspapers.

Dominic Hunt appears more Santa Claus than Scrooge, having hosted a lavish Christmas party, not for celebrities and wealthy silvertails but for ordinary folk down on their luck. A publicity stunt? No way.

She suspected Dominic's other private philanthropic work would eventually be discovered—probably by the digging of this same journalist. But, with the support of her love and the encouragement of Walter Burton, she thought he was in a better place to handle the revelations of his past if and when they came to light.

Dominic had invited her for a special dinner at his house this evening, though they'd had dinner together every evening since Christmas—and breakfast. She hadn't been here for the last few days; rather, he'd stayed at her place. She didn't want to move in with him until they were married.

But he'd said they had to do something special this evening as they wouldn't be able to spend New Year's Eve together—December the thirty-first would be the Party Queens' busiest night yet.

She was looking forward to dinner together, just the two of them. It was a warm evening and she wore a simple aqua dress that was both cool and elegant. Even though they were now engaged for real, they were still getting to know each other—there was a new discovery each time they got the chance to truly talk.

As she climbed the stairs to his house, she heard the sounds of a classical string quartet playing through the sound system he had piped through the house. Dominic had good taste in music, thank heaven. But when she pushed open the door, she was astounded to see a live quartet playing in the same space where the ill-fated Christmas tree had stood. She smiled her delight. It took some getting used to the extravagant gestures of a billionaire.

Dominic was there to greet her, looking darkly handsome in a tuxedo. She looked down at her simple dress in dismay. 'I didn't realise it was such an occasion or I would have worn something dressier,' she said.

Dominic smiled. 'You look absolutely beautiful. Anyway, if all goes well, you'll be changing into something quite different.'

She tilted her head to the side. 'This is all very intriguing,' she said. 'I'm not quite sure where you're going with it.'

'First of all, I want to say that everything can be cancelled if you don't want to go ahead with it. No pressure.'

For the first time she saw Dominic look like he must have looked as a little boy. He seethed with suppressed excitement and the agony of holding on to a secret he was desperate to share.

'Do tell,' she said, tucking her arm through the crook of his elbow, loving him more in that moment than she had ever loved him.

A big grin split his face. 'I'm going to put my hands over your eyes and lead you into the ballroom.'

'Okay,' she said, bemused. Then she guessed it. The family had been determined to give her an engagement party. Now that she and Dominic actually were genuinely engaged she would happily go along with it. She would act suitably surprised. And be very happy. Getting engaged to this wonderful man was worth celebrating.

She could tell she was at the entrance to the ballroom. 'You can open your eyes now,' said Dominic, removing his hands.

There was a huge cry of 'Surprise!' Andie was astounded to see the happy, smiling faces of all her family and friends as well as a bunch of people she didn't recognise but who were also smiling.

What was more, the ballroom had been transformed. It was exquisitely decorated in shades of white with hints of pale blue. Round tables were set up, dressed with white ruffled cloths and the backs of the chairs looped with antique lace and white roses. It was as if she'd walked into a dream. She blinked. But it was all still there when she opened her eyes.

Dominic held her close. 'We—your family, your friends, me—have organised a surprise wedding for you.'

Andie had to put her hand to her heart to stop it from pounding out of her chest. 'A wedding!'

She looked further through the open glass doors to see a bridal arch draped with filmy white fabric and white flowers set up among the rows of blue agapanthus blooming in the garden. Again she blinked. Again it was still there when she opened her eyes.

'Your wedding,' said Dominic. '*Our* wedding. You asked to be married as soon as possible. I organised it. With some help from the Party Queens. Actually, a *lot* of help from the Party Queens. Jake Marlow and some other friends of mine are also here.'

'It…it's unbelievable.'

'Only if it's what you want, Andie,' Dominic said, turning to her so just she could hear. 'If it's too much, if you'd rather organise your own wedding in your own time, this can just turn into a celebration of our engagement.'

'No! I want it. It's perfect.' She turned to the expectant people who seemed to have all held their breath in anticipation of her response and gone silent. 'Thank you. I say I do—well, I'm *soon* going to say I do!'

There was an eruption of cheers and happy relieved laughter. 'Here comes the bride,' called out one of her brothers.

Andie felt a swell of joy and happy disbelief. It was usually her organising all the surprise parties. To have Dominic do this for her—well, she felt as if she was falling in love with him all over again.

But the party planner in her couldn't resist checking on the details. 'The rings?' she asked Dominic. He patted his breast pocket. 'Both ready-to-wear couture pieces,' he said.

'And this is all legal?'

'Strictly speaking, you need a month's notice of intent to be married—and we filled out our form less than a month ago. But I got a magistrate to approve a shorter notice period. It's legal all right.'

Her eyes smarted with tears of joy. This was really happening. She was getting married today to the man she adored and in front of the people she loved most in the world.

Her fashion editor friend, Karen, dashed out from the guests and took her by the arm. 'Hey! No tears. I've got my favourite hair and make-up artist on hand and we don't want red eyes and blotchy cheeks. Let's get your make-up done. She's already done your bridesmaids.'

'My bridesmaids?'

'Your sisters, Hannah and Bea, Gemma, Eliza and your little niece, Caitlin. The little nephews are ring-bearers.'

'You guys have thought of everything.'

Turning around to survey the room again, she noticed a fabulous four-tiered wedding cake, covered in creamy frosting and blue sugar forget-me-nots. It was exactly the cake she'd talked about with Gemma. She'd bet it was chocolate cake on the bottom layers and vanilla on the top—Gemma knew she disliked the heavy fruitcake of traditional wedding cakes.

'Wait until you see your wedding dresses,' said Karen.

'Dresses?'

'I've got you a choice of three. You'll love them all but there's one I think you'll choose. It's heavy ivory lace over silk, vintage inspired, covered at the front but swooping to the back.'

'And a veil? I always wanted to wear a veil on my wedding day.' This all felt surreal.

'I've got the most beautiful wisp of silk tulle edged with antique lace. You attach it at the back of a simple halo band twisted with lace and trimmed with pearls. A touch vintage, a touch boho—very Andie. Oh, and your mother's pearl necklace for your "something borrowed".'

'It sounds divine.' She hugged Karen and thanked her. 'I think you know my taste better than I do myself.'

It *was* divine. The dress, the veil, the silk-covered shoes that tied with ribbons around her ankles, the posy of white old-fashioned roses tied with mingled white and blue ribbon. The bridesmaids in their pale blue vintage style dresses with white rosebuds twisted through their hair. The little boys in adorable mini white tuxedos.

As she walked down the magnificent staircase on her father's arm, Andie didn't need the guests' *oohs* and *aahs* to know she looked her best and the bridal party was breathtaking. She felt surrounded by the people she cared for most—and who cared for her. She wouldn't wish anything to be different.

Dominic was waiting for her at the wedding arch, flanked by his best man, Jake Marlow—tall, broad-shouldered, blond and not at all the geek she'd imagined him to be—with her brothers and Rob Cratchit as groomsmen.

She knew she had to walk a stately, graceful bride's walk towards her husband-to-be. But she had to resist the temptation to pick up her skirts and run to him and the start of their new life as husband and wife.

Dominic knew the bridesmaids looked lovely and the little attendants adorable. But he only had eyes for Andie as she walked towards him, her love for him shining from her eyes.

As she neared where he waited for her with the celebrant, a stray breeze picked up the fine layers of her gown's skirts and whirled them up and over her knees. She laughed and made no attempt to pin them down.

As her skirts settled back into place, their glances met

and her lips curved in an intimate exchange of a private joke that had meaning only for two. It was just one of many private connections he knew they would share, bonding and strengthening their life as partners in the years of happy marriage that stretched out ahead of them.

Finally she reached him and looked up to him with her dazzling smile. He enfolded her hand in his as he waited with her by his side to give his wholehearted assent to the celebrant's question. 'Do you, Dominic Hugo Hunt, take this woman, Andrea Jane Newman, to be your lawful wedded wife?'

CHAPTER SEVENTEEN

Christmas Day the following year.

ANDIE STOOD WITHIN the protective curve of her husband's arm as she admired the fabulous Christmas tree that stood in the entrance of their Vaucluse home. It soared almost to the ceiling and was covered in exquisite ornaments that were set to be the start of their family collection, to be brought out year after year. Brightly wrapped gifts were piled around its base.

Christmas lunch was again being held here today, but this time it was a party for just Andie's family and a few other waifs and strays who appreciated being invited to share their family's celebration.

The big Scrooge-busting party had been such a success that Dominic had committed to holding it every year. But not here this time. This year he'd hired a bigger house with a bigger pool and invited more people. He'd be calling in to greet his guests later in the day.

Andie hadn't had to do a thing for either party. She'd had her input—how could a Party Queen not? But for this private party the decorating, table settings and gift-wrapping had all been done by Dominic and her family.

After much cajoling, Andie had convinced her father to transfer his centre of cooking operations to Dominic's gourmet kitchen—just for this year. Although Dad had grumbled and complained about being away from familiar territory, Andie knew he was secretly delighted at the top-of-the-range equipment in the kitchen. The aromas that were wafting to her from the kitchen certainly smelled like the familiar traditional family favourites her father cooked each year. She couldn't imagine they would taste any less delicious than they would cooked in her parents' kitchen.

It was people who made the joy of Christmas and all the people she cherished the most were here to celebrate with her.

And one more.

The reason for all the disruption lay cradled in her arms. Hugo Andrew Hunt had been born in the early hours of Christmas Eve.

The birth had been straightforward and he was a healthy, strong baby. Andie had insisted on leaving the hospital today to be home for Christmas. Dominic had driven her and Hugo home so slowly and carefully they'd had a line of impatient cars honking their horns behind them by the time they'd got back to Vaucluse. He was over the moon about becoming a father. This was going to be one very loved little boy.

'Weren't you clever, to have our son born on Christmas Eve?' he said.

'I'm good at planning, but not *that* good,' she said. 'He came when he was ready. Maybe…maybe your parents sent him.' She turned her head so she could look up into Dominic's eyes. 'Now Christmas Eve will be a cause for celebration, not mourning, for you.'

'Yes,' he said. 'It will—because of you.'

Andie looked down at the perfect little face of her slumbering son and felt again the rush of fierce love for this precious being she'd felt when the midwife had first laid him on her tummy. He had his father's black hair but it was too soon to tell what colour his eyes would be.

Her husband, he-who-would-never-be-called-Scrooge-again, gently traced the line of little Hugo's cheek with his finger. 'Do you remember how I said last year was the very best Christmas of my life? Scratch that. This one is even better.'

'And they will get better and better,' she promised, turning her head for his kiss.

As they kissed, she heard footsteps on the marble floor and then an excited cry from her sister Bea. 'They're home! Andie, Dominic and baby Hugo are home!'

* * * * *

COMING SOON!

We really hope you enjoyed reading this book.
If you're looking for more romance
be sure to head to the shops when
new books are available on

Thursday 20th November

To see which titles are coming soon, please visit

millsandboon.co.uk/nextmonth